C. M. Newcomb

Sept. 1949

The Wrath and the Wind

THE WRATH
and
THE WIND

A NOVEL BY
ALEXANDER KEY

THE BOBBS-MERRILL COMPANY • INC.
Indianapolis   *Publishers*   New York

*To Cobb and Noble, who taught me
to believe in miracles, and to
Uncle Steve, who took a chance*

The Wrath and the Wind

Prologue

HE COULD not remember it all, and that was well.

But sometimes when the long winds came, when they came with their slow grinding monotony out of the southeast, a restlessness beyond all control would seize upon him and drive him forth to pace the limits of the town. He hated the wind. It tore the flesh from his nerves and for a while destroyed him with the knowledge that all is futile and transitory, and at these times he lived again in moments when the world had come to an end. . . . And yet the wind was not so bad as the still nights. On the very still moonlit nights he would awaken suddenly and find himself listening to the sea and the voices of it. Always he seemed to hear a crying in the sound of it, a wailing of the lost ones in torment; and, far out where the surf drummed upon the island beaches, there would be the great undertone, the black and terrible threat of doom.

He would cry out against it and sit up cursing it until she drew him gently back beside her and held him close like a child. "It is all past and gone," she would whisper. "None of it matters now. . . ."

"Ah—" slowly comprehending, relaxing under the comforting awareness of her, for she had become his refuge at these times "we are together, at home. We are back in Sodom."

But it was no longer Sodom, as he used to think of it. As they grew older together, he came to see it for what it was: a dying place at the river's end, forlorn and asleep and forgotten. Yet there would always be moments when, with a startling clarity, he would look out upon the empty harbor and see it forested with masts, or stare at the crumbling warehouses and see the baled cotton overflowing and piled high for blocks down the

9

street. But these visions were seldom unsettling; the present was more peaceful and therefore preferable. It was the apothecary's shop that troubled him.

He avoided it when he thought of it in time, but his feet sometimes found it of their own volition when he was thirsty. It was very small and weathered; great green and gray lichens dappled its sides; and its roof, shaded by an orange tree, was a mass of ferns. It was not old, but it looked ancient, and it was partly this outer corrosion that shocked him. It symbolized something in the country, something insidious, a subtle poison that crept into everything and slowly destroyed it. The shop always seemed to him, and rightfully, like a beggar inhabiting the tattered finery of his betters, for it crouched upon a corner of a great foundation of masonry that covered most of the block, all of which was now overgrown with palms and oleanders and rare shrubs from what had formerly been a garden.

On occasion he failed to see the shop altogether, for, almost at the exact spot where it now stood, another door had opened, and here the taproom of the Mansion House had once dispensed the best vintages ever seen in the Floridas. And this was greatly troubling, for then he would discover that he had actually entered the shop and called for his accustomed three fingers of *Habana* rum. But the apothecary, always understanding and with never a flicker of a smile upon his wizened face, would reach behind the counter and pour the correct amount from a demijohn he kept on hand for the purpose.

To the apothecary and a few who remembered, he was a hero. The rest accepted him as they accepted her: as a curious but familiar fixture. They lived quietly, undisturbed save for the few trusting patients who came somewhat furtively to his tiny office at the side of the house. Except for his lapses, their lives flowed in a tranquil infinity of days in which time was hardly reckoned. They were happy in each other, and, because time had little meaning for them, it only lightly touched them. And so, in their unworldly way, perhaps they were singularly blessed.

Chapter One

I

It was a year of heat, and many storms, and great disaster. The first heavy gale of the season of 1841 evolved like most southeasters and began as a slow grinding wind, warm and heavy with tropic moisture, and faintly spiced with a vernal fragrance where it slanted off the green morass of lower Florida. Later, swelling to its roaring fullness, it drove two brigs and a fine new bark upon the reefs above Key West, and for three days pounded the beaches of the Upper Gulf with a great booming that could be heard for miles inland. In the new wilderness port of St. Joseph—"wickedest city in the South"—it flattened the tent where, nightly, the gaunt apostle Ledbetter had been shouting his predictions of fire and doom; and on the adjacent bay at Apalachicola—Sodom to the former port's Gomorrah—it wrecked a number of small craft and ravaged the fleet of cotton barges that had been servicing the vessels in the outer anchorage.

Somewhere offshore from the latter port a Salem barkentine, listing and minus her mizzen topmast, lay hove to while most of the thirty-odd souls aboard her waited anxiously for dawn and a pilot; and a few miles to windward of her the armed brig *Peregrine,* on patrol for a schooner believed to be smuggling blacks from Cuba, was just beginning to ride comfortably after one of the worst thrashings of her life. The schooner under suspicion was even then passing within gunshot of the *Peregrine,* but in the night's blackness no one aboard either vessel, save the schooner's mate perhaps, was aware of the other's proximity.

The schooner, a small shoal topsail craft that had been built expressly for the island run, had come through with very little damage except to her cargo. After sounding the pumps and checking the gear forward, young Finch, the mate, together with the Bruin boy, had removed the battens and tarpaulin from the main hatch and pried off one of the covers. It was the first time in nearly four days that it had been safe to do this, and the action was more from the mate's curiosity than because of any concern for the suffocating wretches below. Now the two were crouched over the coaming, their mutual animosity momentarily forgotten while they listened. The hold was an inky pit and no sound that came from it could be distinguished as human.

The Bruin boy said, "Christ, how them bastards stink!"

"Sure they stink," Finch told him. "If'n you was down there, by God, you'd be stinkin' too."

"Not like that, I wouldn't. I ain't no damn black bastard."

"Nobody said you was. But you'd be dead, an' you'd stink."

"I ain't a-arguin' with ye. Let's git a light an' look at 'em."

"No," said Finch. "We ain't a-showin' no light to nobody. We're fetchin' in close an' there's folks around."

"Huh? How ye figger that?"

There were factors involved in Finch's figuring that he could not have explained even to himself, nor was he inclined to discuss the secret and mysterious workings of his mind with what he considered a mere foremast hand, even though Bat Bruin was the son of old Mace Bruin who owned the barracoon up at

Whisky George landing. "Stop askin' questions," he ordered, "an' git for'rard an' take a soundin'."

With a surly and reluctant "Aye," the Bruin boy started away, and then half-turned and spoke over his shoulder: "Er ... *he's* up. A-takin' a *shave!*"

"Dammit," Finch snarled at him. "If'n Cap'n Maury aims to take him a shave any hour day or night, an' he has to stand on his head to do it, that's his own goddamn business. Now git your lazy ass for'rard an' start that lead a-goin' before I batten your big ears down."

Finch, unaccountably irritated, watched the loose amorphous shadow of the Bruin boy slide away into the starboard gloom, and reflected that trouble was already overdue from that quarter. It was about time he gave Bat a good working over.

He spat and started aft, absently fingering the fine down on his jaw. He was a tow-headed Biloxi youth, hardly twenty, and his inability to raise anything resembling a beard had long been a touchy subject with him. Only the Bruin boy seemed aware of this weakness. The others, and Bat to some extent, were cowed; they endured him with considerable respect for his artistry with knife and knuckles as well as for his several other accomplishments, none of which, however, had to do with reading or writing or even handling a sextant. Finch, like his forebears, negotiated the Gulf with a combination of compass, lead line and instinct, and he could guess his position almost within a cable's length by a sounding and the feel of the wind on his ear.

At the after house he paused, fascinated and greenly envious of what he could make out through the partially open slide.

In the feeble glow of the cabin lamp the captain, a sinewy man of thirty with a curling black mane of hair, was delicately balancing himself while he removed the storm's accumulation of whiskers. The act required some juggling ability as well as the muscular co-ordination of a cat; he was bare to the waist and every movement sent a smooth feline ripple up his back and across his rather wide golden-brown shoulders. To Finch the razor's work was stark desecration, and if it had to be done at all—which seemed a damn nuisance as well as a waste—it could easily have awaited a more favorable hour ashore. Yet he knew well enough that the captain would have performed the rite even earlier had the weather permitted. This scrupulous attention to his person, however, was only a minor manifestation of Captain Maury's strangeness; in two years of close association with him Finch was as far from complete understanding as he had been at the beginning. He knew only that Maury St. John, with his black moods and perversities and sudden fits of temper and ebullience, was a product of a far different world from his own. Once Captain Maury glanced up, and though it would have been impossible to see out into the night, the heavy black slanting brows that shadowed the long narrowed eyes gave him such a look of intense piercing concentration that Finch, always uneasy under that glance, had the uncomfortable feeling of having been observed.

Finch turned guiltily away and tried to give his attention to the ship. He was tired, and his thoughts wandered.

He coulda taken twice as many o' them bucks aboard, he thought. But no! *Fifty-nine's enough,* he says. *I'll not stack 'em in like cordwood—not on this trip.* Hell! Them fellers is jest varmints, an' that's how ye gotta handle 'em. But half the time he pets 'em.

Finch spat again. His restless gaze drifted down-wind across a portion of the night, centered on an invisible point and involuntarily hung there. His mind still dwelt on the captain. But he knows how to pick 'em. Lordy, I never seen such bucks! They can't all be dead. You couldn't kill them bastards. . . .

With his eyes still unconsciously searching, he listened to the Bruin boy call out the soundings, and by some mental legerdemain that he himself did not understand, computed that with a little luck with the tide, late evening should see them tied up at Mace Bruin's place in the swamps. The sudden vision of the swamps renewed an old tingling in him. In fact, memory of what he had lately encountered in Bruin's compound had spoiled his nights ashore in Matanzas. She must live up there with Johnny Coot's people beyond the big cypress, he told himself. If'n she's one of 'em I gotta be careful, but I bet I kin find 'er. I'll rig up one o' Bruin's bateaux an' let on I'm goin' huntin' for a spell.

The swamp vision vanished and he was all at once alert as his mind registered the patch of dark that had caught his eye. "Hey, Bat," he called. "Kin ye make out anything to loo'ard? A green light, mebbe?"

"I can't see nothin'."

"Then skin yo' eyes an' keep a-lookin'." And silently he added, An' damn ye, ye sonofabitch, I seen ye a-follerin' 'er all around like a dirty dawg that mornin'. If'n I ketch ye goin' after her . . .

II

Below, the captain very carefully wiped his razor and opened a kit that contained, among other things, an assortment of fine surgical instruments and a small store of pharmaceuticals. He dropped the razor into the kit and started to close it, then pulled the kit open again and prodded the case containing the instruments with a long wiry forefinger. "Damn!" he said, and closed the kit quickly and threw it over on his bunk. He found a clean linen shirt in his locker, buttoned it on and got into a neat gray jacket that seemed oddly out of place on such a vessel. It was made of fine Scotch twill and he had had it tailored by Livesey in London. He fingered it a moment and frowned and thought of the brown moors and the mists and the black hedgerows out of London; and in the same instant he smelled again the reek of formaldehyde and alcohol and death in the anatomy classes—they always smelled the same, those anatomy classes, even in Paris—and he heard Dr. Mason-Henry saying,

"Those bloody Parisians! What do they know but pills and art? They'll teach you nothing." And probably because of that, for he was getting fed up with the stubborn British, he'd gone on anyway to Paris. Pills and art! Suddenly he swore with feeling and blew out the cabin lamp and swung bareheaded up the companion ladder.

By his reckoning it was almost dawn, but when he pushed open the slide and stood on deck there was only a dull and barely perceptible flush overhead, nor was there any glimmer of a star. The east astern was still a questionable void, a liquid blackness that almost instantly erased the schooner's pale phosphorescent wake. But the wind had gone down, and the sound and the fury of it were gone. The seas were still running high, only now they were long tired seas and the *Salvador* with her scrap of a foresail was sliding down them easily, rolling a bit but taking it like a lady and not even wetting her decks. It seemed startlingly quiet after so much sound.

The little Cuban hunchback at the wheel spoke softly in greeting; glancing up from the binnacle, he added, "She steady wes' nor'wes'."

"H'm. Everything all right, Esteban?"

"Dem black fella, I t'ink dey all dead."

"Christ! They'd better not be! Where's Finch?"

" 'E jus' go for'rard. I t'ink 'e mebbe see somet'ings."

No, the captain thought, they couldn't be dead. A few, maybe, but not all of them. They mustn't be dead. He couldn't have them die! . . .

He moved swiftly along the lee rail, feeling his way rather than seeing. His eyes were not yet accustomed to the dark.

Amidships he stopped abruptly, almost nauseated by the smell coming from the opened hatch. Some of them were dead. He knew the smell of death. That smell had been creeping through the bulkheads for days, but it had been faint and subtly filling the vessel and he had been living with it and not realizing; now the full power of it poured upon him. He clutched the rail with both hands and held on tightly and shook his head, then he let go of the rail and slid over to the weather side of the hatch and braced himself against the bulwarks. He felt very tired and old and the taste in his mouth was the taste of failure.

It had been a hell of a week. All the crew had been sick and the blacks had been sick, and there'd been times when there were only Finch and himself to work ship; times when they'd had to crawl on deck, too wretchedly sick and weak to stand. And it had started off bad in the Stream the first morning out. Six hours out and they'd been chased—by an American, he'd thought at first. But it had turned out to be a Britisher. Damn the bastards! What right had they to send a patrol craft to the Gulf? Did they think they owned all the seas? The damn unctuous British who'd made millions at the trade they were now trying to stop! But for them he could have beaten the weather. He could have come up coastwise and made an easy trip of it in the lee of the land and kept the blacks on deck, and everything would have been all right. But instead he'd had to batten them below and run off soundings; then the weather had caught him.

It had been a hell of a week, but this was the worst of it.

He got down on his knees and peered over into the blackness of the hatch. Nothing stirred. He called to them, but he might have called to the dead.

He got up and leaned against the bulwarks again and pressed the palms of his hands against his eyes and wished the dawn would hurry. He wanted suddenly to be ashore, to be done with the whole wretched business.

At last he turned forward and sought Finch on the forecastle head.

The mate and the Bruin boy were clinging to a lifeline and staring fixedly into the northwest.

"What the devil is it, Finch?"

"Dunno, suh." The mate fished a piece of tobacco from his

hip pocket, bit off a piece and began working it with exasperating slowness in his jaws. "I keep a-seein' things. First 'twas somethin' off to loo'ard yonder. But I reckon we're past it. Mighta been a vessel. Now hit's something else—more to the west'ard. Thought 'twas a light, but hit mighta been a porpoise. Them porpoises, they're all around us tonight, jumpin'. The mackerel must be runnin'."

"Perhaps we'd better ease up a trifle."

"I done eased up a couple times to git around things. Every time I do hit I see somethin' else. Hit's one o' them nights."

It was one of those ghostly nights in which not even tangible things like the spars and rigging seemed to have substance. It was the way everything must look, he thought, to the eyes of the dead. Each time the bow rose he strained to see over the crest of the swell ahead, but there was only the nothingness into which the swells seemed to float away and vanish. But overhead the flush was brightening. It gave him the strange feeling of sailing at the bottom of a vast abyss.

Uneasiness was creeping through his weariness. "What's the lead say, Finch?"

"Sand at six, suh, an' lumpy."

"We're getting close in."

"Aye, suh. A couple hours off the Pass."

"We're off Dog Island? You're sure?"

"Ain't no mistakin' them lumps."

"Then we'd better shake out more canvas as soon as it brightens. We don't want to be caught up here under short sail. The *Peregrine's* up here."

"Aye, suh. I was thinkin' o' that. But that *Peregrine*, she don't worry me none."

"She'd better worry you. She saw us go out, and she'll be watching for us to come back, sure as billy hell."

"Them Yankees." Finch sent a stream of spittle over the knighthead. "They don't know this water. Let 'em take after us in that ole bucket. I'll lead 'em over some spots that'll knock 'er bottom out."

"That's not the idea. We can't waste any more time fooling around. We've got to get in."

A long following swell overtook them; the stern rose and the schooner yawed a little under the thrust and raced downhill. Then she answered her helm and swung, a bit too sharply, and for a moment the stench of the open hatch drifted across the forecastle head. The smell hit Maury like an accusing conscience. The Bruin boy made a gurgling noise. "Cap'n Maury," he began presently, "don't ye reckon we'd . . . better close that there hatch?"

"You was raised with niggers," Finch answered. "Don't ye like the smell of 'em?"

"I don't like 'em dead no more'n you do."

"If'n they're dead," Finch said practically, "we might as well leave hit open. We gotta heave 'em out when it gits light. Ye reckon they're dead, Cap'n Maury?"

"There're some dead ones. But they're not all dead."

"We couldn't hear no sound down there."

"They're dazed—in a sort of stupor, I think."

That was it, he told himself unreasonably: A few were dead, but the rest were just stupefied. They could get air through the forward bulkhead—not enough to clear the foulness, but enough, surely, to keep life in them. They'd had a tin of biscuit, and there'd been a scuttlebutt of water lashed to a stanchion. He hoped it hadn't broken loose.

"Can you see anything out yonder now?" he asked.

"Nary thing, suh. Hit's comin' up a damn fog."

He could make out the fog, little vague streamers of it. The night was purpling. The flush overhead was widening and spreading westward. He snapped his fingers in irritation at his own uneasiness and moved aft, waiting for the dawn. His, he told himself, was not the temperament for this sort of thing. One should be colder, more like Two-Jack, who handled matters ashore. Only, Two-Jack would have been quite out of place at sea. It was impossible to associate that suave and softbodied and Napoleonesque little man with the more active part of such an enterprise as this. Suddenly he hated Two-Jack intensely.

The sky flamed with golden banners. Finch routed out the remaining hands, a very dirty and sleepy trio of teen-age flotsam; the helm was put down, the big mainsail sweated up and a jib broken out. By the time they were on their course again it was pearly dawn and foggy, and the wind had become no more than a soft morning breeze. The seas were going down rapidly.

Finch hunched over the hatch coaming. "There's a heap o' dead uns down there," he announced sourly. He stood up, swearing softly. "We—we got to git rid of 'em, suh. I reckon the sooner we git started, the quicker we'll be done with it."

"Wait a minute, Finch."

Maury glanced down into the hatch and then went over to the rail. He had no legitimate excuse for delaying what had to be done, but he hated this final admission of failure. He rubbed his eyes wearily and peered about. They were on the edge of a thinning fog bank, with little veils and spearheads of fog creeping ahead, low-lying and opalescent. The sea was purple in the open lanes, and over it the fog shimmered fantastically in a hundred colors as the sun tried to break through. He cursed it for the beauty he could not feel. It seemed only ghastly and unreal. And worse, it was impossible to see more than a hundred yards ahead.

"Did you hear something just then?" he asked suddenly, sharply uneasy.

"I didn't hear nothin'. Only them gulls. They're all around."

"I thought I——"

Somewhere a bell rang. It was sweet and clear, and it might have been directly overhead. A ship's bell.

"Jesusgod!" Finch bleated, and Maury saw the mate stand rigid beside him for an instant, then whirl and go scrambling into the starboard rigging.

The captain ran aft, wondering if it was the *Peregrine's* bell he had heard. "All hands stand by," he called quietly. "Sharp, now!"

Like an echo, softer, the bell rang again. In the fog there was no telling its direction.

Abruptly Finch, swinging into the foretop, bawled loudly, "Sail ho! Dead ahead! *Har-r-r-d a—wea-a-a-ther!*"

"Start fore and main sheets! Lively!"

The wheel spun and blocks creaked, and Maury heard the helmsman's fervent "*Madre!*"

He called to Finch, "What the devil is she?"

"A brig—— No, a big barkentine—an' she's in trouble!"

She materialized as suddenly as a thunderclap in the gold dawn mist, too suddenly for him to relish the relief that she was not the *Peregrine* after all. There was a moment when she was a great gray-winged ghost ahead, and almost in the same instant the veil separating them vanished, and for a little while the red morning sun burned bright on her. She was so close by the time he eased the helm that he could clearly see the faces of those on deck.

Under shortened sail she was riding sluggishly, barely under way; she had a sharp list to larboard and from her mizzen dangled a mass of cordage that had not yet been cleared. All her pumps were being manned, and water gushed steadily from her scuppers and ran in white streams over her sleek black topsides. For an instant before the mist obscured her stern, he thought he saw three figures on her quarter-deck, but when it came into view again he could see only two.

He was at once interested and highly curious, for he was sure he had seen a woman there, a tall young blonde woman dressed in green. He ordered the helm down; the schooner nosed about, swung past the vessel's high gilded stern and came up under her quarter, gradually losing way. Now he could read the name, *Catherine Delafield, Salem,* on the transom. The name caught his fancy. He had heard it before, somewhere. He sought it in his memory and was hardly aware that Finch had come aft and was standing beside him, scowling nervously.

The two men he had noticed on the barkentine's quarter-deck were leaning over the taffrail. One, black-bearded and broad as a dory and with a brass trumpet under his arm, cupped a hand to his mouth. "Ahoy!" he bellowed hoarsely. "We need a pilot! Are you a pilot boat?"

"Where do you want to go?"

"To the nearest port! We're making water!"

Maury's eyes swung past them, unconsciously searching for the woman in green; there was no sign of her and he decided that she had been only an illusion of the sunlight and fog. In the sea's lonesomeness a woman is always in a man's thoughts. He shook his head and, looking at Finch, read sudden consternation and worry in the mate's face; then he glanced over at the hatch and thought of Bruin and Two-Jack, who would be waiting up in the swamps, and it occurred to him that this was a most inopportune moment for any shifting of responsibilities. Finch wasn't liking the idea a particle, and Two-Jack would be furious.

He shrugged. "Very well," he called. "I'll take care of you."

He had a premonitory feeling that he was making a mistake, but the thought was not troublesome. He had made many mistakes. Anyway, Finch was quite capable of taking over at this point and going on to Bruin's place.

He hurried below for his kit and bag, and it was only when he was throwing things into his bag that he noticed Finch had followed.

The mate gulped. "Er . . . Cap'n Maury, don't ye reckon we'd better . . ."

"Eh? Someone has to take 'em in, Finch."

"Yessuh, but——"

"No buts." He knew what Finch was thinking. It was the cold logic that, in their own precarious position, the other vessel should be ignored entirely. But a man could not always be governed by logic. "It's either you or me, Finch. That vessel

draws a lot of water. West Pass is the only place she can get in
—and you know what the Pass is like. D'you think you could
handle her?"

"I . . . I dunno, suh. I never tried nothin' that size."

"That settles it then. You're staying here and taking over."

"Aye, suh. But you . . . this fog . . ."

"It'll burn off in an hour, and then I'll be all right. Now, as
soon as you're clear, check over those poor devils and get rid
of the stiff ones."

"Aye, suh."

"Don't touch the limp ones—just the stiff ones. Understand?"

"Aye, suh."

"Turn the rest over to Bruin and tell him to doctor 'em till
I get there. There'll be some broken bones, so be careful. And
when they're unloaded, have the hold cleaned and limed. I'll
meet you at Bruin's place tomorrow, as soon as I can get there.
Now, put the boat over and have Bruin's boy ready at the oars."

"Aye, suh."

Finch swung on deck, scowling. With slow smoldering pro-
fanity he ordered the boat unlashed and put over the side.
Reaching the open hatch amidships he stopped short, and then
stooped and swiftly heaved the cover back in place. Finally,
with a long curious look at the barkentine, he reached for his
tobacco and decided that he might as well have held his peace.

Chapter Two

I

F OG ALMOST obscured the schooner as her boat slid across
the smooth channel in the barkentine's lee. Maury tossed
his bag aboard and stood poised a moment in the stern
sheets with his kit in one hand. When a swell lifted him high
enough he swung lightly into the chains and over the rail. He
picked up his bag, turned to survey the storm's damage and the
haggard faces at the pumps, then made his way up the ladder
to the quarter-deck.

The bearded captain and the other man were still at the taffrail, peering out at the vanishing schooner. As Maury came
up and dropped his gear beside the binnacle, they both turned
and stared at him silently, the one cholerically, the second grimly
and with what seemed to be cold accusal in his sunken eyes.
Maury looked from one to the other, instantly aware of the
discord between them and making a guess that the pale gaunt
elderly passenger with the gray bushing hair and uncompromis-
ing eyes was, in all probability, the vessel's owner. In the so-
bering presence of these two his temporary feeling of well-being

24

suddenly deserted him, and he wondered why he had ever been fool enough to come aboard.

"I'm Maury St. John of Apalachicola," he began, speaking to the captain. "I'm on my way home, and I'll be very happy to assist you in."

"And we're damn glad to have your assistance, sir," the captain replied in a voice hoarse with fatigue. "I'm Captain Adams," he added, offering his hand. "This gentleman is Mr. Delafield, of Delafield and Company, Salem. We're seventeen days out of Salem, bound for St. Joseph." He sighed, tugged irritably at his beard as if to waken himself, then rubbed his bloodshot eyes. "Now, sir, are we anywhere near our destination?"

"About twelve hours running, but with the tide against you you'd have to stand off till morning to get in. How long can you keep afloat?"

"We're keeping the water down, but the men are tiring. Now, this other place——"

"Just a moment, Eben," Delafield interrupted testily. "We'd better clear up a few points before going farther. Young man, about that schooner. Just what is your connection with her?"

"She's my vessel."

"I see. And are you a licensed bar pilot?"

"Why, no, but——"

"Devil take it, Aaron," the captain broke in. "We've been all over that. What difference does it make who or what he is as long as he knows the coast and can get us in?" He turned to Maury. "I take it you know what you're about, sir, or you wouldn't have come aboard."

Maury raised a slanting eyebrow. "I hold master's papers, if that will help your peace of mind. I also know the passes thoroughly."

"That isn't the point," said Delafield. His voice was asthmatic, with a rasp that grated unpleasantly on the ear. "The point is, Eben, that if he isn't a licensed pilot, we're under no obligation to him for boarding us. No great obligation. And I'll have you know that I have certain ingrained convictions on the matter of slavery. Furthermore, I know a slave ship when I smell one! The schooner was carrying Negroes! And by the living God, I'll have no dealings whatever with anyone engaged in that abominable traffic!"

"Now listen to me, Aaron——"

"I've listened to you enough, Eben! We've shifted a bit of ballast and had a beating, but our predicament is in no wise as bad as you imagine it. I suggest that you settle with this man and dispense with him as quickly as possible. We can pick up a legitimate pilot later."

Maury turned quickly to the rail and searched the fog. There was no sign of the *Salvador*. He turned back and thrust his hands into the pockets of his jacket and looked with cold anger at the gaunt Delafield. "I'm afraid, sir, that you'll have to put up with my abominable presence. My vessel has gone. And since you've presumed so much about me, I'll not bother to explain—except to say that I was rather putting myself out to help you people. I thought you were in serious trouble. You said you wanted to be taken to the nearest port—which happens to be Apalachicola where I was bound. It was only an act of common courtesy to help you. But if you don't care for my help, you can damn well go to hell!"

"By God," Adams exploded, "this is no time for nonsense! Mister, you have my apologies. And you, Aaron, for once you're going to listen to me!"

"You've had my opinion," snapped the other, unbending. "If you don't care to act upon it, Eben, that's your affair. I wash my hands of it entirely." He brushed his thin bony hands together, turned stiffly away and, wheezing a little, went with much dignity down the ladder.

Adams glared after him balefully, then permitted himself an interval of relieved blasphemy before bellowing for the mate and ordering the bosun to rout out the forecastle. Finally he

shook his head and rubbed his bloodshot eyes again. "I'm
sorry about all this, mister," he said wearily. "I just hope you'll
overlook it. I've had it for seventeen days myself, so I trust
you can bear a short spell of it. Mr. Delafield is a fine man
really. A mighty fine man. I've known 'im all my life. He's
got his faults like any of us, and he gets in your craw sometimes, but he can't help it. He's ill. He's a very ill man, and it
makes him difficult."

"So I've perceived," Maury said dryly.

"Well, don't let 'im worry you. As for me, I don't give a
damn whether you had niggers or nanny goats aboard. I've done
a bit of blackbirding myself when I was younger. Here's Mr.
Johnson. Now let's settle this business about where we are
and where we're going."

The mate, a lean horse-faced man, came up the ladder, acknowledged Maury with a grunt and spread a limp chart near
the wheel. "Water's gaining for'rard," he muttered. "We got
to git in somewhere pretty soon. But this goddamn fog——"

"Forget the fog," Maury told him. "Shake out your reefs
and get under way, due west, and give me soundings every
quarter-hour. This fog should burn off in time for us to pick
up St. George light."

"Ye're takin' us in at West Pass?"

"West Pass it is, and there'll be just tide enough at noon to
get you through. Then I'll have to ground you in the lee of the
island. In the morning the lighters can come out from town
and unload you."

"So it's Apalachicola," the mate commented. "Well, well!
There'll be folks aboard won't be liking that." He gave a sour
chuckle, then descended hurriedly to the spar deck to rouse the
hands sleepwalking from the forecastle. Presently his strident
voice could be heard the length of the ship. "Blast ye, this is
no funeral yet! Shake the lead out o' your feet an' put your
backs into it! Ye want to go ashore tonight? Then look alive!"

Sail fluttered aloft, snapped taut, and the barkentine came

clumsily to life. She paid off slowly, and the sharp cant of her
decks lessened a trifle as she began her uneasy run to the west.

Maury, listening to the leadsman sing out the soundings, felt
a peculiar disembodiment as if the past half hour had been a
ridiculous fragment out of time, a tragicomedy without beginning or end that he had merely witnessed from afar. Suddenly
he was very much concerned over leaving Finch, as well as
mildly amazed at his own temerity in changing decks. But this
was like everything else in his life. He had always been changing decks, so to speak, and sailing off on a tangent. It seemed
impossible to order one's life, to plan and follow through on a
course of reason. Something always happened. Something un-
accountable, some sudden decision or act of the moment.

It was like that affair in Paris. If he had stayed in London,
none of it would have happened. But he had gone to Paris, and
there was Hélène. And in a stupid minute he had tossed away
his good name and his future, everything of accepted value, in
fact, but his neck. He had saved his precious neck by running
away to sea.

But all that was years ago. None of it seemed to matter now,
not even the shooting of Hélène's husband. He had thought once
that he could never live without Hélène; at the moment he had
difficulty in even recalling her features. A hundred times sharper
in his mind was the vision he had had of the woman in green.
He could see her clearly again in that instant of the bright burning sunrise. A tall young woman, a girl really. Her hair had
been like a golden turban edged with fire. Had he only imagined
her? It still seemed a little odd.

His reflections were interrupted by Mr. Johnson coming aft
to see to the clearing of the mizzen. The fog was lifting a trifle
and now Captain Adams, after hearing the mate's report of conditions forward, gave orders to be called when the Pass was
abeam and went unsteadily below.

"Asleep on his feet," the mate commented, and scowled aloft

at the hands struggling with the dangling cordage. "We lost our gaff, but we'll bend on a tris'l soon's that mess is out o' the way. She'll handle with that." He rubbed his long horse face and grumbled in a lower tone, "It's been a hell of a v'yage."

"So I've gathered."

"Too goddamn many opinions, what with the Old Man orderin' this, an' the owner that, an' Miss Catherine . . ." This last seemed quite beyond his capabilities, so he changed the subject. "I near forgot. Would ye like a bit o' breakfast, sir?"

"I could do with some. You . . . er . . . mentioned a lady being aboard?"

"Aye." The mate blinked solemnly and looked away. "She's aboard, mister. Ye can't miss 'er. The very vessel's named for 'er."

In his mind he saw again the vision of the blonde Diana in the sea-green dress, but he was disappointed when he went below and entered the small salon. There was a lady present, but she was an elderly one of about sixty, a gray, mousy little person in a dark challis dress. He stood with head bowed for nearly a minute while Delafield, at the head of the table, finished prayer; he then took his seat at the farther end near two of the ship's officers who mumblingly introduced themselves as the purser and the junior mate. Neither man presumed to bridge that portion of the table between passengers and crew by any further introductions; in fact, they might have been breakfasting at different tables. Delafield ignored him entirely, but once the woman glanced up and nodded with a sweet smile as if he were a familiar member of the ship's company whom she had been seeing every morning. There was an odd vagueness about her that gave him the impression she was existing only in some remote ephemeral world of her own. He wondered if she could possibly be the Miss Catherine the mate had mentioned.

The meal consisted of coffee, fried ham and stacks of thin, pale pancakes, which he disliked but ate of heartily. It was the first hot food he had had in days. No one spoke except the gangling cabin boy who hurried with a repressed cheeriness to replenish the cakes and coffee.

The woman finished first, murmured something indistinguishable to Delafield and drifted out like a shadow without substance. The purser and the junior mate soon followed. Maury felt himself being regarded with judicial disapproval from the other end of the table.

"I did not get your name," said Delafield in his grating voice.

"Nor did I get yours," Maury replied indifferently, glancing up. He thought, You cantankerous Yankee bastard, you're not speaking to a poor clerk in your office.

A glint came in the pale sunken eyes and a faint flush brightened the gaunt sagging cheeks. "My name is Delafield!" the grating voice snapped. "Aaron Delafield, and don't you forget it, sir!"

"Delighted," said Maury, inclining his head. "Mine is St. John. Maury St. John, sir. And if you can remember mine, I'll do my utmost to remember yours."

The long straight line of a mouth thinned, then pursed a little. "I trust Captain Adams made satisfactory arrangements with you?"

"Arrangements? If you mean recompense for a favor, why, certainly not. Or do gentlemen charge for favors in your part of the world?"

"Mr. St. John," the other rasped peremptorily, "I am only trying to do the right thing. You must not think me ungrateful for your assistance. If I have been hasty in my judgment of you, it is only because I am a God-fearing man, and I find it impossible to reconcile myself to those degrading precepts which allow the keeping of fellow humans in bondage. I abhor slavery."

"So do many of us in the South, Mr. Delafield. But the economy of the country is based on it—so there is little we can do about it except tolerate it and make the best of it."

"My point is that one does not have to tolerate it."

"You are an Abolitionist, Mr. Delafield?"

"Not actively, but I thoroughly sympathize with the movement, sir. And you cannot deny that you had slaves aboard. I smelled them."

"Nauseating, wasn't it?"

"This is hardly a subject for levity, sir. You had slaves aboard, and by the odor they must have been there for some time."

"Not so long. But we were caught in the weather, and there was nothing I could do but batten 'em below for their own safety. It was unpleasant, but——" Maury shrugged. He was becoming tired of this discussion and the man's irritating personality. "Since you are so interested in my private affairs, I may as well tell you that I bought the blacks farther along the coast, and I'm transporting them up to my own plantation above Apalachicola."

"I would hardly have taken you for a plantation owner, Mr. St. John. However, in my own mind I make little distinction between the man who smuggles slaves into the country and the man who buys them ashore and profits from their toil. The law will hang one and call the other an honorable citizen, but to me they are equally guilty. If you will permit me to say so— and, understand, I'm being entirely impersonal—I find that the attitude of the average person of your class toward the poor African is hypocritical and detestable. Only the gravest consequences can result from it."

"Perhaps. Slavery is an old evil. I'll not waste breath defending it. But while those of us who profit from it directly may be guilty, at least our hypocrisy can hardly match that of you gentlemen who condemn it and yet indirectly subscribe to it."

"Eh? How do you mean, sir?"

Maury stood up and pointed casually to the cone of sugar on the table. "Take that. I noticed you used a bit of it in your coffee. Without slave labor you wouldn't have it. And the shirt you are wearing. An excellent shirt, sir, made of the very finest long staple. But it was grown by slave labor, and no doubt woven by Northern weavers who are no better off than slaves and probably get less to eat. And if you are engaged in shipping, Mr. Delafield, I am sure you have profited a great deal in the transportation of baled cotton and other freight that was produced and even loaded on your ships by the lowly African. Oh, it's a foul state of affairs, sir, and slavery is detestable, but where would you be without it?"

Smiling thinly, he turned away from the other's angry glare and made his way to the quarter-deck.

During the interval of breakfast something about the ship had changed. He felt this instantly as he went up the ladder. A fresh vigor livened the men at the pumps; Mr. Johnson appeared to be everywhere at once, and even the vessel seemed to have picked up speed.

Then, as he came up by the helmsman, he stopped suddenly, finding himself staring at a young woman in a sea-green dress. She was standing at the curve of the taffrail where he had first seen her, peering out curiously at the thinning fog. He shook his head, half expecting her to vanish again, but she did not.

II

Captain Adams removed his shoes and jacket and, as was his habit before retiring, took his private log from the safety of his desk and opened it to his last entry. After methodically sharpening a goose quill, he began with heavy jabbings: "April 7, 1841 . . ." And then, overcome by the sudden inertia of fatigue and relief, he dropped the quill and sat staring dully at the date while he rumbled small obscenities into the voluminous darkness of his beard. Long strain had almost robbed him of the desire for sleep.

From the spar deck he could hear the slow rhythmic clatter

as the tired watch labored at the pumps. At the moment it would have given him little concern if he had been forced to order the boats over the side and consign the vessel to hell and Neptune. An unworthy attitude, perhaps, for one in his position, but he had never held a command that had aroused in him so little love and so much ire. Some ships, he thought, are born for disaster, and the sooner they are given up to the sea, the better for those who follow it.

He thumbed clumsily through the log to the aphoristic entries of the preceding weeks and suddenly came to the conclusion that he had been a fool for ignoring his presentiments and that it was time he retired.

"I have long been of the Considerate Opinion," he had written early in March, "that only Ill can be expected of a vessel that gives Trouble at her Launching. And it is my Conviction, after forty years of Tribulations upon the Deep, that blessed little Good can come of having the Owner and his Family aboard on a Maiden Voyage. And what have I done? In a moment of Weak Mindedness and Sentiment I have allowed myself to be prevailed upon to sign as Master of the *Catherine Delafield,* and to take her and her Owner to the Floridas . . . and well knowing that during the Launching Ceremony she jammed fast upon the Ways and that it took all Hell and half of Salem to pry her free."

He would feel no surprise, he told himself, if some sudden and final calamity overtook the vessel before she docked, for she had been in trouble almost from the moment of her conception. She had caught fire in the yard, and after her inauspicious launching and numerous accidents during the rigging she had been laid up all winter for repairs. One fool thing after another. And after long delays she had headed out in March to get caught in one of the worst sleet storms in a decade. Off Hatteras some of the brick ballast had started to shift. The brick had been well stowed and dunnaged, and even Hatteras should never have shifted it; but it had broken loose and they were listing and making a little water even before they rounded into the Gulf and the real nightmare began.

From some far pinnacle to which his mind, in lieu of sleep, had momentarily retreated, he cast about for a cause, for some explanation of the vessel's predilection for misfortune. And almost immediately the answer, like a lamprey in a virid pool, curved poisonously into his realm of logic. It was her name. She was bewitched by her name, and by the unholy presence of her namesake. Had Aaron christened his new vessel after his dead wife Lucia—an estimable woman in spite of her many peculiarities—then surely everything would have been different. But no, the name chosen was the daughter's. And Catherine herself was aboard, not merely as a passenger but as a reigning personality. The ship seemed possessed with her.

For the first time in years he thought abstractly of Catherine and found himself, as usual, at a complete loss to understand her. Even as a child she had been a stranger to him. It seemed incredible that Aaron had sired her, and that she was a product of the ordered scheme of New England living. There was something in her, some force, some uncommon vitality, that set her entirely apart from her background. It couldn't have come down to her from Aaron's side. She must have got it from her mother. She was, in fact, almost the image of her mother.

Lucia had been a Creole. But not dark like most of the French. Very blonde was Lucia, and she came of a high and wealthy family, although he had almost never heard her mention her people. She was a strange one, a cool quiet woman who fitted herself so well into the New England way that you hardly thought of her as a foreigner of sorts—and yet you always had the feeling that she was hiding the greater part of herself. Aye, but a fine enough woman was Lucia, and no blame to her if Catherine was Catherine. You could take two perfectly good ingredients at times, stir them up and turn out a brew that the devil wouldn't have in his kitchen.

Captain Adams reached for his quill again. He made an

effort to record the incidents of the past twenty-four hours, but, finding the written thought momentarily beyond him, sighed and thrust the journal back into his desk and then stretched gratefully on his bunk.

He wondered how matters would have been if Lucia had lived. In spite of Aaron's health this business of uprooting everything and coming to the Floridas was all Catherine's doing. He could feel it in his bones.

Chapter Three

SHE WAS in her early twenties, Maury saw, a tall, straight girl with a flawless white skin and a handsome body, her hair coiled in a rich turban of finely sculptured gold. She turned her head and coolly swept him with her eyes, and he automatically bowed, hiding a sudden confusion that he had not felt since an early and unexpected meeting with a princess royal. To his relief Mr. Johnson came up the ladder behind him, and at the mate's fawning embarrassment in her presence some of his composure returned.

"Miss Delafield, ma'am," the mate began awkwardly, "this gentleman's Mr. . . . er . . . ah——"

"St. John," said Maury, bowing again. "Maury St. John. Your servant, ma'am."

She acknowledged him with a faint and almost queenly nod, and the mate added, "He's takin' us in."

"That's very kind of him," she said, and the mate, suddenly at a loss, retreated to the weather side and gave his attention to the ship.

Her eyes, Maury noted, were very long and sage-green, and her voice, instead of having the sharp Yankee ring he had expected, was a soft contralto. It was very disconcerting. No woman with such a body had a right to eyes and a voice like hers. At the moment he could not have defined her beauty, for he was struck by something magnetic and compelling in her physically that he found a little overwhelming. It seemed inconceivable that she could be old Delafield's daughter.

"You're taking us to St. Joseph?" she asked.

"No, ma'am. To Apalachicola."

She caught her breath in dismay. "But we're bound for St. Joseph! Isn't it possible for us to go on there instead of to this other place?"

"I'm very sorry, but it's almost out of the question. The two cities are fairly close by land, but by water it's another matter. With tide and wind as they are, it means a difference of at least a day."

"Oh, dear. I'd so hoped . . ."

An immense, yellow tortoise-shell cat had appeared on the quarter-deck and now it came over and began rubbing sinuously against the skirt of her green twill dress. She stooped and lifted it in her arms with a little laugh, cooing as she tickled its chin. "Tawny, you silly old yellow devil, you! Are you getting tired of the sea? But you'll soon be home. . . ." She stroked it absently and then set it back on deck and seemed to forget it entirely and to be oblivious of everything around her, her lips faintly smiling with some mental projection while she stared off through the thinning fog.

Maury studied her covertly while he listened with half an ear to the leadsman. She was a big, vital girl almost as tall as he, with nice hands and smooth, rounded arms and a fine column of a neck that might have been carved from marble. Not really beautiful, perhaps, but she seemed so with her regal body and her almost classic cast of features. Her mouth was full and wide and sensual, except for the clean sharp chiseling of the lips. In an older person those lips would have been cruel.

His mind roved around her, trying to probe the woman of her. At first she had seemed mature and worldly, even arrogant.

Now he realized it was her magnetic vitality, coupled with a deep reserve that seemed to hold her apart from reality. An uncommonly fine bit of flesh, he thought. Yet there was something about her . . .

Forcibly he tore his mind from her and gave his attention to the leeward distance.

The mist was burning away and there was bright blue water ahead. As the sun grew hot on his back he began to worry a little about Finch. By now Finch should be running in through the upper Pass. And if his own calculations were correct, it was time the lookout saw the dunes on the island.

He was relieved when presently the lookout cried, "Land ho! Broad on the starb'd beam!"

The news momentarily stopped the pumps and the men crowded gawking to the lee rail. Mr. Johnson immediately put a damper on their spirits by pointing out that there was much nearer soil at six fathoms, straight down, and that it was coming closer by inches; then he stepped to the rail and examined the horizon with his glass.

Finishing his inspection, he was about to hand the glass to Maury when Catherine turned to him eagerly. "Oh, may I, please?"

The mate, who always seemed to be struck with a spastic affliction whenever she looked at him, fumbled the glass and nearly dropped it; but she took it quickly, heedless of him, her attention immediately centering on an almost invisible triangle of white in the distance. Her face was bright with excitement. "What is it? A dune?"

Maury nodded. "The Devil's Punchbowl, on St. George Island."

She studied it quietly for nearly a quarter of an hour, then suddenly gave a little bubbling laugh of delight. "Oh, there they are! Palms! The sun is just coming out on them."

"You've never seen palms before?"

"Only in drawings. I've always ached for the sight of them, all my life. . . ."

She held the glass a long time while the island crept closer. In the receding mist it began to loom like an enchanted place, then it became a reality with the bright sun picking out the tumbled line of palmetto-covered dunes and the long, gleaming beach curving off over the rim of the sea. Behind the dunes rose the tall, dark ranks of pines, and spacing them in the lower areas, cool and secretive in the sun's glare, were the little close groves of palms. There was color everywhere, color undreamed. She had never seen water so blue and so green and purple. It was purple under the cloud shadows, and near the island there were long streaks as bright as an emerald.

Suddenly it seemed impossible to her that there had ever been a storm, for when the mists burned away it was as if by some witchery she had passed through a curtain from one world to another—from the darkness of winter to a strange bright tropic world that had only half existed in her imagination. It had been gray winter when she left Salem; and, though the air had turned steadily warmer after rounding the Virginia capes, the vessel had run into rain and overcast and the impression of winter had lingered. Nor had her first sight of the Gulf Stream dispelled it. They had entered that magic current on a night, and by the following dawn a heavy sea was crashing over the weather bow and the sun was only a pale disk behind low-flying scud. It had stormed ever since, and she had continued on in grayness until this morning, until this sudden passing through the curtain.

She had not minded the storm. Even during the worst of it she had felt neither fear nor illness; some heritage in her had responded to it and she had reveled in its fury, almost loving it. But with the passing of the wildness something in her had quieted, and now she was eager for the land and for the new home that lay not very far beyond the curve of the island.

Salem. Gray Salem. The gray of time and prayer and order and sameness; the reserved, tranquil gray of life on Chestnut Street with its nice propriety and wealth. You lived with virtue and God on Chestnut Street, and only the young men ever escaped the pattern. They went to sea. God in heaven, how she hated it! She had always hated it, and ever since her mother's death she had schemed to get away from it. Her father of course was Salem, and from him perhaps had stemmed much of the grayness of it; but her feeling was inextricably associated with her mother and with her mother's odd coldness and restrictions. It was as if her mother had forever tried to force her into ways that were the antithesis of every secret yearning. And yet she was certain that her mother, too, had hated Salem and all New England.

Deep in her, hidden, she had felt a queer surge of gladness when her mother died. It was like the unlocking of a door that had always been closed, a strange, bright secret door leading into an exotic garden. She had been nearly seventeen when that happened, and for more than four years now the door had been open, the garden waiting.

She had known her father would be difficult, but the knowledge had in no way troubled her. She had seen how her mother, hiding an adamantine self under a calm quiet submissive surface, had always had her way. It had been easy enough to take her mother's place, but it had required time and care to uproot a tree that had been so long a-growing.

Fortunately her father had his ailments. From the beginning she had kept him constantly aware of them, driving him to bed with every mild attack and conspiring with the family doctor to suggest a milder climate. At first she did not care where they went. She would have compromised for the Hebrides if the move would have placed Chestnut Street forever behind her. But a letter from her godfather, Rodman Carey, pointed the way. Carey, himself an invalid and a former associate of Delafield and Company, had settled in St. Joseph. "This is without doubt the brightest and most promising place in the South," he wrote. "It is growing like a mushroom, and a few thinking gentlemen have pooled their resources to build a rail-

road that will bring us most of the vast cotton traffic of Georgia
and Alabama that now pours down the Chattahoochee River.
Our rival town of Apalachicola, at the mouth of the river, has
but an indifferent harbor and is doomed to die because of it.
But this little city has a wonderful bay, wide and deep, and
even now the shipping going out of it is beginning to put Mobile
and Charleston in the shade. From the money here one would
never suspect that other parts of the country have been suffering such great distress financially. . . ."

Aaron, who had had his fill of the depression, was much interested in the letter. But he had a hundred objections to moving south, and slavery was the hub of them. The South was
an unhallowed land of feudalism and he wanted none of it.

But never for an instant did Catherine relent. She worried
over him, made him see that the raw New England winters
would soon be the death of him, and daily became more affectionate and solicitous while she undermined his will and de-
votedly preyed upon his constitution. A tougher oak than
Aaron would have weakened under these ministrations. And
now Carey, who had always been her ally, was easily stimu-
lated into further expansiveness along the proper channels:
" . . . As for the climate, it is like the best to be found along
the Mediterranean; I never wear a greatcoat here, and often
in January I am quite comfortable out of doors in the lightest
clothing. And there are sulphur spring waters here, Aaron,
that will be of great benefit to your ailments. I have been in
every port east and south, and while each has its appeal, I have
found in no other spot the idyllic charm of this little corner of
Paradise. Fortunately the better people are all from New
England. As I was remarking only last evening to Mrs. Call,
the governor's lady—they spent their summers here, and the
governor . . . "

St. Joseph. Gay, bright, tropical St. Joseph. The Carey letters gave it substance, and subtly clothed it in an aura that
Catherine herself found irresistibly fascinating. It became her

garden, and all her unfathomed longing centered on it. But at the last, as she had planned, it was Aaron who proposed leaving Salem and going there.

Catherine lowered the glass and was suddenly aware that the man from the schooner had become acquainted with her cat and was actually holding it in his arms. This was an incredible step for Tawny, for never before had the big cat permitted such familiarity from any stranger, particularly a man.

"Why, Tawny," she exclaimed, "what in the world's come over you?"

She saw Maury look up with a quick smile that showed his strong, white, even teeth. And then she felt the stab of his eyes; they were dark and flecked under the black arching brows, and something about them, something that was at once caressing and sharply penetrating, sent a tingling up her back. He had seemed shy at first, but now she was conscious of an easy worldliness in him that had been lacking in the young men she had known. He's like a sword, she thought, if a sword could be handsome.

"Anything wrong, ma'am?" he asked.

"It . . . it's my cat. I don't know what you've done to him, but he won't let even my father touch him. You're the first person . . ."

"That's simple. He's just recognized me for a spiritual brother. He's quite a beast." He set the big cat down, caressed its back a moment and straightened. "I can't get over the fact that you're real flesh and blood," he added, smiling again. "I saw you for a moment just before I hove to in the fog, and then you vanished. I decided you were only an illusion."

She laughed. "You'll have me pinching myself in a minute. All this is so unreal to me that I'm not quite sure I'm actually here. I mean . . . well, it's like coming out of a long dreary night into something you've only imagined. It's so strange. Anyway, I went below just before you came aboard. Father and

Captain Adams were . . . were having an argument, and I didn't want to get mixed up in it."

"I see. The mate told me there was a lady aboard, but when I saw only an elderly one at breakfast I didn't know what to make of it."

"Oh, that's Cousin Etta—Miss Etta Lamb. She's a sort of distant connection; she's been our housekeeper for years. I . . . I hope you'll not feel too offended over Father's attitude. He isn't well, and he's had a very bad time of it."

He shrugged and said nothing, and she was silent for a moment. Then she gave him a sidelong glance with her long eyes. "Just what were you really doing out here with a boatload of black people?"

"That's what your father wanted to know. What do you think?"

"I think," she said archly, "that hidden under the gentleman there's a great deal of the rascal."

He chuckled, suddenly sure of his ground. "Faith, I knew you had the devil in you! I'll have to be careful. New England, bah! Cold stone and ice. They never bred you."

"I was born in Salem," she told him coolly.

"Then you're a changeling. The witches played a trick on your father."

"I'd say the trick was played on me. They could have left me in a better place. I mean, a more interesting place."

"Well, St. Joseph ought to suit you. Are you going to live there?"

"We certainly are. We already have a house there."

"Lucky person. It's hard to get a house in St. Joseph."

"Oh, ours was designed and cut out in Boston and shipped down last fall to be put together. It seems such a funny way to build a house, but when we wrote Uncle Rod he said it was the only thing to do."

"He was quite right. Half the places down here were cut out in the North and shipped down. It saves time. This is new country and it's hard to get materials. Possibly I know your uncle. I'm well acquainted in St. Joseph, and the name Delafield sounds so familiar. I've been trying to place it."

"But he isn't actually my uncle. He's my godfather, and his name isn't Delafield. It's Carey."

"Eh? Rodman Carey?"

"Why, yes. Do you really know him?"

He grinned. "No one really knows him, but I suppose I do know him better than most. He's my best friend. Lord, what an idiot I've been! Rod told me a long time ago about you folks coming down, and I forgot all about it. But then I haven't seen him lately. I don't get over to St. Joseph very often. Only thing was, Rod didn't tell me much about you. Guess he was saving you as a big surprise."

Color brightened her cheeks, and then all at once the last of her reserve vanished and she turned to him with eager questions. How was Uncle Rod Carey? And the house—had he seen it? How did it look? And St. Joseph—she must know all about St. Joseph.

He remembered the house. It had not been finished at the time Carey had taken him through it, but even then it was becoming one of the most imposing places on the beach, where all the finer homes were. Though it had been originally designed as a large but simple Georgian affair, Carey had insisted on adding double verandas. They gave it a strong New Orleans flavor. "Really dresses up the old box," Carey had said. "Makes a mansion of it. Gad, imagine a house down here without verandas! Aaron won't care for it at first—he's plain as a dried herring. But Kitty will love it."

Kitty. He recalled now that Carey had always spoken of her as Kitty, as if she were still a young girl.

"Surely," he said, "Rod's told you all about himself and what he's done down here. He's one of the patron Saints. He and the Forbes bunch——"

"Saints? Forbes?"

He chuckled. "Everyone calls the St. Joseph people Saints. It has nothing to do with their moral state. In fact you might say that a moral state doesn't exist down here—except on the surface, in our politer circles. Anyway, there was a lot of trouble on the coast a few years ago, and Rod was back of it. He started St. Joseph."

"No! I can't believe it! Why, he's never mentioned——"

"Rod's a big man down here. He may be a cripple, but it's never kept him from getting around and stirring up things. He's got a finger in everything that goes on. You've heard of the Forbes Grant, of course?"

"That Spanish grant that there's been so much talk about?"

He nodded and pointed to the island, and his hand swept eastward. "That's part of it, and the whole coast as far as you can see, and on up to the border. Millions of acres, a big slice of West Florida. A Scotch trading outfit, the Forbes Company, got it from Spain. It included all the land on which the city of Apalachicola was built. Well, no one in the place ever questioned the Forbes title—until cotton began pouring down the river from all those new plantation lands up in Georgia. Then suddenly the place was booming—and everybody woke up to the fact that a bunch of speculators had acquired part of the Forbes tract and were claiming everything in the city. Lord, what a racket that started! They took the matter to Washington, and the Supreme Court decided in favor of the speculators."

"But that was awful! What did the people do? What happened?"

"Plenty happened. I wasn't here then, but Rod was. He'd just arrived. He thought it would be a good joke on the speculators to move everybody out of Apalachicola and start a new city. And that's just what he did. He——"

"You . . . you mean there wasn't any St. Joseph? Nothing?"

"Nothing but pines and an empty bay, thirty miles farther up the coast. Rod got everybody together who hated the speculators, and they went over to the other bay and built a new port. They did it practically overnight. I've never heard of anything like it, but that's what they did. They built St. Joseph, and to look at it now you'd think it had been there always. There must be eight or ten thousand people there now."

"Good heavens, what a story! And to think that Uncle Rod . . ."

She shook her head and peered over at the island, silent for a while. Then she turned to him again. "But Apalachicola— what of it?"

"Well, the migration didn't really hurt it. For every man that left, two more came to take his place. So now it's booming too. Jammed with people. Cotton is pouring down the river, more of it than ever—more than enough for both places. They built the biggest hostelry on the coast, the Mansion House; any night there you can see men cutting the deck for a thousand."

Her sage-green eyes were bright. "Tell me more."

"You'd have to see it for yourself—see the background of it. This isn't the South. It's . . . well, it's another world. It's a tropic wilderness, most of it under water. In all this stretch of country there are only these two ports—and no other habitation, except some hidden Indian villages back in the swamps. And it's all swamp when you get away from the beach. Swamps and more swamps. Thousands of square miles of 'em, black as Africa. Black and deadly, and yet very beautiful. . . ."

She listened, absorbed, while he talked on in snatches, and for the first time she began to realize there was far more to this new land than the small idyllic picture Carey had painted. Swamps. Vast, incredible swamps. Trackless save for the great sprawling red octopus of a river with its many arms, its maze of twisting water lanes; " . . . *There are bayous that stretch all the way from the back door of St. Joseph, so that river steamers can run through the swamps between it and*

Apalachicola. . . . At high water you can paddle anywhere in a bateau, paddle for a week and hardly ever see the light of day. But God help you if you get lost. . . ."

Black and deadly. Renegades and river pirates and Indians. The country was still at war with the Seminole. And down through all this darkness swept the highway of the river. A red river, bringing wealth from the plantation lands to the north. Men fought and bled and died for the wealth it brought and tossed it away on the turn of a card. A red river, red with more than the bright clay of Georgia. . . .

A cruising pilot schooner overtook them and dogged their wake awhile, questing for business. A lighthouse pricked the island's distant curve, grew tall and white, and beyond it, startling as spilled paint, a stream of red cut sharply into the sea's blue.

The Pass. Even here, miles from its mouth, the river showed its might. *" . . . I've seen that red water fifty miles down the coast."*

The bay, when they crept into it from the narrow Pass at noon, was a huge sheet of glittering bronze. Deer watched them from the beach of the leeward island, small gray deer that stood motionless for minutes and then suddenly erupted into darting shadows that went bounding over the dunes to vanish in the green jungle. A flock of roseate spoonbills crossed their bow. Fish hawks and pelicans were everywhere, wheeling, hovering, plummeting suddenly for mullet. And all around them little egrets, as airy and light as fairy things, were drifting like wind-borne thistledown.

Several miles ahead lay the main anchorage, scattered with vessels riding like toys in the distance. To larboard, as they came about, stretched the dark line of the coast. A somber coast, brooding and mysterious. Only a faraway plume of smoke from an invisible cotton steamer marked the port at the river's mouth—but the glass revealed a point of land with white houses peeping from the shadows of palm and live oak, and beyond it the river's mouth became a vast sweep of minor bays and islands and greening marshes where many rivers seemed to open to the sea.

Marsh and jungle and red water and illimitable distance. Wild, wild . . . and lonesome and brooding and remote.

Nothing in the Carey letters had given her even a hint of this. She clung tightly to the rail, searching the dark horizon for something that would identify it with things familiar. Except for the toy ships and that one vague spot of habitation, there was nothing. She felt suddenly lost. She had dreamed of coming into a dock, of seeing life and color and movement. But instead the vessel was nosing in close to the lonely island, sliding now through mud, coming to rest in a cradle of mud.

And this, then, was to be her land.

Already she could feel the shadow on it. It had crept into her mind, to hover always in the background of her thoughts and never to dissolve.

Chapter Four

I

THE SHIP'S boat, manned by Mr. Johnson and six men and crowded with baggage, tacked interminably through the long hot afternoon; finally the wind died at sundown, and the last two painful miles to the mainland were negotiated under oars. Since it was impossible to pull against the strong ebb from the river that swept past the main docks, a landing had to be made at one of the small piers on the shallow bay front.

It was twilight when Catherine stepped ashore. The earth seemed to heave and roll with the sea's motion as she went slowly across the sand. She stopped beside a beached cotton barge and looked wearily around, then drew a deep breath and straightened. Ahead a boardwalk stretched along a lush and overgrown shore where palm tangles and flowering shrubs nearly hid the picket fences. Beyond them in the shadowed houses tapers and sperm-oil lamps were beginning to glow. The air was sweet with strange blossoms, and alive and throbbing with the singing of insects and the mad jingling of frogs. Some-

where a spinet tinkled and a woman sang. Under the unexpected headiness of it she felt a sudden lifting of spirits that the
afternoon had denied. Thinking of Salem, cold and bleak as
death, she gave a low bubbling laugh of release and took her
father's arm.

"Isn't this exciting, darling? How do you like it, Cousin
Etta?"

Aaron grunted and, glancing at Etta, pinched and vague beyond her usual level of remoteness, remarked irritably that both
he and Etta had had a day of it and that they were more concerned about the town's accommodations than its climate.
"This Mansion House you've mentioned," he said to Maury,
"is it far from here?"

"Just a short walk, sir."

"And is it a thoroughly respectable hostelry?"

"I think you'll find it quite satisfactory, Mr. Delafield."

Maury was about to add that he maintained a suite of rooms
there, but decided that the fact would hardly be accepted as a
recommendation. "We can leave all the baggage here with one
of the men," he suggested. "I'll send some colored boys down
for it later."

He led them up the boardwalk and around the curving bay
front to the main part of town near the river.

It was very old, this place. He could feel its age in the
crushed shell under his feet, the ancient shell of centuries of
mollusk-eating races. It paved the streets and lay solidly
under everything, a reminder that man had always lived here.
Probably this spot, this remote jutting of shell and sand and
alluvium and hoary trees where river and sea met, had seen
continuous habitation for a thousand years. And it seemed to
resent newness, for it quickly cast its cloak of age on every recent thing. It somehow gave to the present town—this young
city with its sprawling new houses and lighted streets that ran
down to the main square and the market place along the river—
a look of lazy and sedate dignity as if it had been here always.

Then suddenly, as he led his party into the crowded main square—crowded with its nightly pageantry of silk and buckskin and crinoline and calico and homespun, and jammed on either side with baled cotton from the overflowing warehouses—it became apparent that this was only an island in the wilderness, a frontier. Rich, tough, bawdy, fun-loving and noisy. Sailors sang, drank, fought; sailors of all nations staggered arm in arm with girls of all colors. Gamblers and sly traders and trappers in greasy leggings rubbed elbows with prosperous gentlemen in frock coats; a squaw trundled a cart of fat pine kindling tied in neat bundles, and a sleek black houseboy in a white jacket dodged past with a bucket of precious ice that had come down as ballast from the North. Upon a torchlighted platform in the center of the square a bellowing auctioneer was disposing of a group of half-naked slaves chained to the railing; and coming up the walk from the Georgia steamer, lately docked, were a florid upcountry planter with his family and retinue of servants, several young men in the smart blue uniform of the Franklin Guards, escorting the giggling members of a theatrical troupe, and a procession of ragged black boys struggling with leather trunks and carpetbags. Behind them strode the dapper French consul and a lean and meticulously groomed man in pale gray, a politician named Bishop, whose duels had become the talk of the Territory.

The French consul spoke politely to Maury and went on, but Bishop stopped and, with a nod in the direction of the auctioneer, said with lazy insolence, "Some o' your blacks, St. John?" As he spoke his cold eyes went to Catherine and seemed to devour her in a long, hungry glance.

Aaron came up before Maury could reply and rasped indignantly, "What's going on over yonder? Is that a slave auction?"

"It is," Maury bit out, suddenly furious as Bishop moved off, grinning, through the crowd. "Would you care to go over and watch it, sir?"

Aaron glared at him. "I prefer to get away from the degrading spectacle as quickly as possible. What's happened to that fool Johnson?"

"You might ask him in the morning. They've all left us."

"Humph! Which way is the Mansion House?"

"Across the street."

Aaron turned and was struck to silence by the sight of the opulent, three-storied and many-columned structure that was beginning to cast its nightly glitter over the town. It looked down on the square, ignoring it, an immense Mount Vernon whose magnificence quite belied the primitive darkness that stretched almost from its back door. It made the best in Boston seem a little drab.

Opulence encompassed them as they crossed the great veranda. Always at this hour there was an air of subdued festivity about the place: house slaves in scarlet jackets were gliding through the halls with tapers and trays of drinks, dinner couples were drifting in from the carriages drawing up outside, the strains of the newest Viennese waltz were floating softly from the ballroom. Catherine's eyes began to sparkle. She glanced at her father and knew, by the slight pursing of his lips, that he was both impressed and disapproving. All this, the slaves and the glitter and the flow of easy wealth, would be a bit too much for him. But he would have to get used to it. She would see to that. Her own mouth tightened a little, and then a sudden ripple of laughter drew her attention to the huge stairway where a half-dozen young girls were hurrying down, twittering like sparrows. They were wearing Paris creations, the very latest.

Her quick envy died as she realized that every male eye in the place was turned on her approvingly. Then in dismay her hand darted up to smooth her hair, and she was acutely conscious of her sunburn and the fact that an afternoon in an open boat had played havoc with her dress.

"Who is that red-haired man in gray?" she asked Maury. "The one who spoke to you outside."

"Hugh Bishop. He's from Tallahassee."

"He seems to think very well of himself."

Maury's nose wrinkled in distaste. "He'd like to be governor, but he'll never make it."

"Why not?"

"His kind die early down here."

The major-domo, a fat black old Negro in livery with tufts of gray wool at his temples, hurried up to them, his grin of welcome showing a double keyboard of flawless ivory. The expected silver changed hands.

"My rooms ready, Nolly?"

"Yassuh! Dey's *always* ready."

"Nolly, I've brought some friends. Mr. Delafield and his family. I trust you can manage well for them."

Nolly looked sad. He spread his hands. "Marse Maury, dis place is *full*! Dey's gentlemens a-sleepin' two to a bed, jes' like a plain ordinary. Honest, we ain't got nothin' fittin' ——"

"Oh, that's all right. Just give them my place. There's plenty of room for them there, and they should be very comfortable. And remember, Nolly, they are my guests. See that they have every courtesy of the house. Oh, yes—send some boys down to the little pier at the Galt place to pick up our bags."

He looked sidelong at Aaron and was rewarded by the other's extreme discomfiture.

Aaron demurred, protested, but found himself forced to accept this final act of courtesy. He would have preferred a slap in the face.

"I've friends all over town," Maury assured him. "I'll be well taken care of. If you'll pardon me, I'll run up and get an article or two, and . . . er . . . when everyone is ready, perhaps you and your family will do me the honor of joining me at dinner."

Aaron could not refuse.

II

Knowing that he must rise before dawn to get to Bruin's place, he excused himself early. A restlessness was on him so he went into the taproom and ordered a rum and casually inquired about Two-Jack. The gambler had not been around all day. Maury finished his rum and went on through into the gaming rooms and searched the tables. Not seeing Two-Jack, he started to leave, but one of the players, a great flabby Nero of a man named Munn, insisted that he draw up a chair and buy a hand.

"Thanks, Flavy," he mumbled. "Too damn tired. Just got back from New Orleans."

Munn, who headed the powerful land company that had taken over the Forbes interests, was playing a threesome with one of the local cotton factors and Crom Davies, a St. Joseph banker. There was something revolting about Flavy Munn that good tailoring only seemed to accentuate. He looked like a man who had always done everything to excess: His red swollen face was blotched with purple; his great jowls puffed out over the white scarf that he habitually wore to hide his scrofulous neck; he had horribly protruding eyes, and his lump of a body filled his chair like a bloated spider.

"New Orleans?" he wheezed hoarsely, slyly. "You all been to New Orleans again? Aw now, Maury, you're always goin' there."

"Guess it's time to change my routine," Maury told him and added with smiling malice, "I'm surprised you aren't over at St. Joseph, spending the week end with Josie Bangs. What's the matter, Flavy? Don't her girls like you any more?" He loathed Flavy, whose manipulations had caused the rebellion

that had built St. Joseph. And yet, because the man was long
overdue for the grave, Maury was mildly amazed and secretly
curious every time he saw Munn alive.

"Phah! Them bitches." Flavy was not offended. "I wish
Josie'd git some new ones. Come on, Crom, what's a-holdin'
you up?"

Maury left. For a moment he wondered about Crom Davies,
thin and gray, sitting there so silently. It was rather unusual
to see him here in company with Flavy, since the two represented interests that had long been at war. Could anything
be wrong in St. Joseph? Then he decided that it was only a
routine matter that had forced the banker over here to spend
an uncomfortable evening with the opposition.

He entered the main hall, looking for Nolly, and suddenly
found himself face to face with Hugh Bishop, the dueling politician from Tallahassee.

"Not playin' tonight?" Bishop drawled.

"Not tonight, Hugh."

"That's too damn bad. Kinda hoped I'd have a chance to
recover a few coppers."

The two stood silently regarding each other, like flint and
steel wary of meeting. Bishop was taller and a few years older,
with a shock of wiry red hair that was beginning to turn a little
sandy at the temples. Always impeccable in appearance and
stiffly correct—this probably to cover up a background that
had not included too many of the niceties—he managed to
make an impressive figure before a crowd, but at close range his
features were too blunt to be distinguished. They were cold
and calculating. He came of a newly rich family of plantation
owners who were becoming politically powerful in the Territory.

"The luck o' some people," he said presently, condescend-
ingly. "How'd you manage it?"

"Manage what?"

"Meeting her. You picked a beauty. She'll be the talk o'
the coast."

"Your approval is so flattering, Hugh. I regret that I can't oblige you with an introduction."

"Wouldn't trouble you for one. I'd kinda like my introduction from another quarter." Bishop smiled faintly, quite pleased with himself, and strode on into the taproom.

The bastard, Maury thought. The ornery, stiff-assed bastard.

Grimly he tracked down Nolly in the pantry. "Did Two-Jack leave any message for me?"

"Nawsuh."

"My boy Cricket been around?"

"Ain't seen 'im since you left, suh."

"H'm. Well, send my bags over to Dr. Garver's house."

He went outside, preoccupied, followed by a black boy carrying his things. Cricket, of course, was still up at Whisky George, waiting. And undoubtedly Two-Jack was there by now and had seen the worst.

He cursed softly.

The Garver place was two blocks over, on one of the cross streets coming up from the bay. It was a small plain cottage in need of paint, surrounded by a picket fence in need of repair. The windows were dark, but he opened the gate and went up on the little porch. The boy placed his bags by the door, caught the copper he tossed and left. He tapped on the door and then opened it—it was never locked—and thrust his head inside and called. A warm odor of cabbage and chemicals and baby clothes filled the hall. The dim interior seemed to be in its usual state of disorder. Probably Juan and May were over at one of the neighbors for the evening.

Though he knew he was always welcome to enter, a natural reticence forbade him to cross the threshold. He closed the door, feeling a little lost, and went out through the gate and sauntered slowly along the dim street in the direction of the bay. There were other places he could have gone; but, in spite of May's frightful housekeeping, he preferred to walk off his restlessness and return there later. The Garvers were a queer couple, yet he always felt at home with them.

At the bay front he hesitated and then turned west on the boardwalk. Ahead the walk ran irregularly along a low sand-and-shell bluff above the beach. The more imposing homes were farther back in town or out on the river highland. Here the houses were less pretentious, but in the lush seclusion of the bay front they seemed infinitely more charming. A sickle moon was rising over the sea and the night air was pleasantly cool.

He reached in time a long fence smothered in honeysuckle and trumpet vine. The yard it enclosed was more generous than the others, and the small quaint cottage had a captain's walk on the roof. It was a mansion in miniature, with a row of small columns across the front and curved windows that showed the fine hand of the shipwright who had built it. Looking at it now he felt a moment's pride of ownership and a sudden regret and longing. Unlike many of his possessions, which he had won at cards, he had planned this place himself and had it built. But, thanks to Tulita, he had never lived in it. She had been hinting for a long time that he serve notice to the tenants and give up his rooms. It would have been a more convenient arrangement; only, a very little of Tulita went a long way.

Frowning, he continued along the walk, and almost before he realized it he was standing by her gate. There was a lighted ship's lantern in the corner window—a sign that old José, her father, was out on the bay fishing.

He had hardly thought of Tulita for days, and now it gave him a sudden feeling of guilt to know that she was waiting for him, expecting him. His hand hesitated on the gate. In the next moment he was visioning her, feeling the need for her; his nostrils dilated and the blood throbbed to his temples with a slow heavy pounding. He thrust the gate open and went up the narrow shell-bordered walk and tapped lightly on the door.

There were rapid footsteps, and the door was thrown open. Tulita squealed, and her entwining arms drew him quickly inside. In the next instant she was all over him, kissing him with a mad exuberance. "Mother of God—you are back! You are back!"

He petted her and absently wiped his mouth with the back of his hand. She reminded him sometimes of an eager spaniel hungering for affection. She was a slim, dark, avid girl with quick black eyes and thin nervous fingers that were always plucking at him. Tonight she was wearing a black silk dressing gown, and it made her seem ever so much thinner and darker. Latins, he thought, should never wear black.

She kissed him again, running her hands through his hair and rumpling his collar and pulling at his buttons. Suddenly her hands were still and she drew back, looking at him intently.

"Are you seeck? Are you tired? You are so . . . so——What is the matter?"

"Nothing's the matter. I'm a little tired. It was a hell of a trip."

She pouted, pecked at him once more experimentally and froze in his arms. "*Que va,* tonight you are not right. Do you not love me?"

He grinned and patted her behind. "Why, of course! I——"

"Phah! You do not say eet right!"

"How do you want me to say it?"

Abruptly she twisted out of his arms, and he could see the storm brewing.

"You are tired of me, no?"

"Don't be foolish. I got back only a little while ago. I brought in another vessel that was in trouble. I'm tired, and I've got troubles myself. I've got to get up to Bruin's place."

"*Por dios!* 'E is tired and 'e had troubles and 'e must go up into the swamps to see thees goddamn Bruin—tonight?"

"As soon as I can get there," he growled.

She eyed him intently. "Somewhere," she said flatly, "you have met somebody."

"I'm always meeting people. I meet a lot of people."

"You have met somebody," she repeated accusingly, her voice rising.

"For Christ's sake, I come out here specially to——"

"You have met a woman! Your eyes are full of her! Do you t'ink I do not know how a man acts when 'e has met a woman that blinds 'im? You stand there looking at me and you do not see me! Am I not beautiful? 'Ave you not eyes in your head? 'Ave I ever denied you anything? *Mil diablos!* You are like all men! You——"

"Tulita——"

"Cabrón!"

"Listen, Tulita——"

"God damn you, go away! Go back to 'er!" She snatched up a copper bowl and hurled it at him, and suddenly she was screaming and throwing everything within reach.

He ducked and ran.

Her screaming suddenly stopped, and as he went out through the gate he heard her call his name, urgently at first, and then despairingly. He strode swiftly away, afraid she might come running after him, but the only part of her that followed was the anguish of her sobbing. It clung to him, poisoning his self-esteem and filling him with a baffled dissatisfaction with the way life had handled him.

He wandered around the edge of town for an hour, plagued by the thought that he had managed his thirty years very badly.

When he returned to the Garver place he was relieved to see a light in the window.

Chapter Five

I

THE RIVER, nearing its long journey's end, spreads out like a mighty clutching hand with a dozen writhing, greedy fingers reaching for the sea. But the sea is loath to feel the muddy touch of it, and for time beyond time has been casting barriers of sand in the river's face; and always the river has overwhelmed the barriers, filling the spaces in between with alluvium and secretly hiding its work with the darkness and the silence of gum trees and tupelo and cypress. And in the ceaseless battle the river's fingers have grown ever longer and more crooked, and the black reaches of the swamps so vast that no one man is ever likely to see the whole of them.

In his day Mace Bruin had covered as much of that shrouded silence as anyone, but now at seventy, though he would still occasionally vanish in his bateau for a week or more, he spent most of his time at his small kingdom on Whisky George. The spot was in reality an island, one of the many formed by the tangles of the river's eastern fingers. Its location was ideal for the questionable commerce that had been flowing through there long before the time when old "Whisky George" Bruin, Mace's father, had built the "nigger pen" on a bit of higher ground beyond his house. A schooner, coming up one of the shadowy channels with the tide, could moor at Mace's door and unload directly on the bank. Later, any freight consigned for points inland could be taken by bateau through the upper swamp and deposited at a cordwood landing on the main river, there to wait some lesser cotton steamer bound for Georgia. A three-hour sail across the upper bay in his sloop would take Mace to Apalachicola; St. Joseph was also accessible to him had he ever desired to go there, for a great bloated thumb of the river juts many miles westward before it is lost in the jungles, and one of the many bayous opening from it had become the back-door approach to the new port. It was by this latter route that small coffles of blacks sometimes reached Jug Slatter's establishment on the outskirts of St. Joseph.

But Mace hated the noise and confusion of many people; and though he was widely known (if seldom seen) and was astonishingly well-informed on local matters, he had not set foot in either town for more than three years. There was little need, in fact, for him to stir from his high-perched veranda to learn anything, for news came to him deviously on many silent paddles and it was said that with his one good eye he could discern more in a moment than all his bastard offspring could in an hour with their combined vision. He was a tall, grim, rawboned man with coal-black lusterless hair which he kept pulled back smooth and plaited in a whiplike queue at the nape of his neck. Except for a few straggling chin whiskers like a thin mandarin's beard, his face was almost hairless—a peculiarity probably inherited from his mother, a half-breed Muskogee woman from up the river. This aboriginal strain was further evident in his high cheek ridges and the suggestion of gold under his skin. But his most notable feature was his eye.

Concerning this, Two-Jack had once remarked to Maury that the thing made him uncomfortable just to be near it.

"That damn eye of his, *mon ami*—the good one I mean—she is as sharp as a lizard's and as cold as a rattler's. I would not want such an eye squinting at me over that rifle he always carries."

"Then don't play any tricks on him."

"You do me a great injustice, *mon ami*. I do not play tricks on people." The two were always watchfully polite with each other.

"Don't misunderstand me. I was speaking figuratively. Mace doesn't go hunting for trouble. I'll grant you he's a malignant-looking creature, but it's mainly the way his left eyelid droops while the other remains wide open. It gives him that damn calculating stare. You don't realize at first that the droopy eye is blind."

"Most true. But he is malignant."

"Like the swamps. The evil in him is the evil of the swamps. Basically he's honest."

"Your statement she is two-headed," said Two-Jack. "My business with him I keep on a cash basis and both derringers primed when I go near him."

Old Mace, on his own part, accepted Two-Jack only tentatively and with considerable penetration recognized him as an individual whose weaknesses made him far more dangerous than would the natural cupidity of his kind. He rather hoped Maury realized this also, but he said nothing. It was not his policy to activate himself in matters that did not concern him or to offer unsolicited advice even to a man he liked. So he watched the partnership of the two with interest, privately predicting trouble. Trouble between others always amused him. He accepted it as a natural thing, enjoying it as a spectator but never interfering unless he were asked or unless it conflicted with his own way of life and became an annoyance. Then, implacably and coldly, he would settle it as he saw fit. When two of his mulatto offspring got into a bitter feud over the attentions of some of the visiting traders, Mace summarily sold

them to Jug Slatter who resold them up the river. Mace was
not avaricious and the money meant little to him; the disposal
to Slatter was merely a quick and convenient method of ridding
himself of an irritation. To the obstreperous who crossed his
path he would say only, "Git a-goin'—an' keep shy o' me."
Only a fool was slow to obey that order, or got in his way there-
after. Mace had killed many men. Throughout the swamps
he was unloved but considerably respected, and in any matter
of arbitration his word was final. On Whisky George he was
absolute monarch.

On the morning after the storm Two-Jack, reasoning that if
the *Salvador* survived she would soon make her appearance,
went aboard a Georgia packet with his bateau and Negro. Two
hours upstream the packet slowed and the bateau was put over
the side. Two-Jack and the Negro crawled into it, and with a
few strokes of the Negro's paddle they were swallowed in the
swamp's blackness.

A Creole, he was known only by the water-front Anglicizing
of his real name, which was Jules Tujaques. In his broad hat,
black frock coat, pale trousers and polished black boots he was
a Napoleonesque figure, soft-bodied and complacent and outrageously out of place in these surroundings.

With the river at flood stage, the only dry land for many
miles, save a few scattered ridges, was Bruin's place on Whisky
George. Toward this the Negro laid a straight course, paddling
steadily without sound. Two-Jack sat stiffly in the bow, holding a short pole in front of him to break the spider webs and
flay the coiled dangers that he imagined lurked in every shadow.
He had unbuttoned his coat so that he might instantly reach
the derringers thrust in the pockets of his scarlet waistcoat.

He hated the swamps. The silence, the eternal twilight, the
writhing shapes of the great trees that rose demoniacally in the
gloom, the crawling vines like nightmarish serpents, the long
hoary beards of moss trailing in the turgid water—all these filled

him with a loathing, an excessive dread. He was deathly
afraid of snakes, and he had a cold horror of the immense
glittering-eyed spiders that spread their ten-foot webs between
the trees. At any gaming table Two-Jack, in luck or out of it,
could be the embodiment of cool insolence; but in these vast
and imponderable depths he was quickly cowed to an acute
consciousness of his own insignificance.

It was with relief, tinged with uneasiness of a different order,
that he reached Whisky George that afternoon. He was never
quite sure how Mace would receive him, and he rather suspected
that he was tolerated mainly because of Maury. But chiefly
his concern lay in the business aspects of the *Salvador's* safe
arrival. It was of more importance than he cared to admit. In
the past these ventures had been merely a pleasant source of
additional revenue. But now he was involved in other matters,
and he had been very unlucky.

It was appalling, this lack of luck. "Eight times I cut the
deck," he muttered, "and eight times I lose. *Sacré bleu*—and
it was my own deck! A child could have picked those cards.
Have I lost my touch?" He had lost much money, that was certain, and now he dare not look at another card until the spell
was broken.

His mind suffered a momentary storm as the bateau slid
across an open channel to the landing, and by the time he
stepped ashore it had come to him that what he really needed
was a new woman. Not just another woman, but a young and
interesting and very different one. For a new woman, carefully
chosen, was a fresh chapter in life. It was a change that always
brought him luck. Ah-yah, that was the answer. He must sell
Maria and Sarah both and buy himself a new one.

He stood uncertainly at the dark landing, knowing well
enough that his coming had been noted by one of Bruin's
watchers. The cool air was sweet with the mixed fragrance of
swamp blooms and wood smoke, but he found this distasteful
and took out his green silk handkerchief, heavily scented with

a new French cologne, and sniffed it while he searched the openings of several dim water lanes for sign of the *Salvador*. He could see only the squat shape of Bruin's old sloop filling the entrance of the nearest one. A small flatboat and a covey of bateaux and dugouts were tied up in the shadows on his left. Directly in front of him, dominating the landing, the approaches and even the open compound stretching back on the higher ground, was Bruin's big log house set high on stilts. It was a curious place with narrow windows like a blockhouse and a long flight of steps leading up to the veranda. At the rear, opening on the compound, was another section built at a different level, where Bruin did his trading.

Seeing no one on the veranda, he started up the moss-hung path to the compound. Here some of Bruin's numerous progeny, all ages and colors, were broiling bits of venison at a communal fire while several older women scraped deer hides strung between poles. Their happy chatter ceased as he approached, but no one looked at him or spoke. On his right a half-dozen small log huts on stilts peeped from a tight growth of Spanish oranges. Rising on the other side were the tall palings of the "nigger pen." The narrow gate of it was open and Bruin, dressed as usual in his leather breeches and gray linen shirt and carrying his rifle under his arm, was coming out. With Bruin was young Finch.

Two-Jack masked his sudden surprise and hurried forward. "My frien'," he said, in reply to Bruin's silent nod and brief raised palm. And to Finch: "So you have come back. Ah-yah, that is good. But the schooner I do not see."

"She's downstream about a mile," said Finch. "The tide run out on me."

"You have a rough trip, no?"

"We had a little trouble," Finch answered noncommittally. He had never liked Two-Jack.

"Ah-yah. She storm very bad. You are lucky to be in now. You did not lose any men, no?"

"We lost all but fourteen," Finch told him with relish. "An' half o' them is busted to hell."

Two-Jack chilled inside. He ran the edge of his tongue over suddenly dry lips while he struggled for composure. Finally he achieved a shrug. "Where is M'sieu Maury?"

"In town I reckon. We come acrost a big vessel a-leakin' bad an' hard up fer a pilot. He took 'er in."

"*Sacré bleu,* no!"

Old Mace, watching sardonically, grunted and motioned toward the house. "Come," he ordered. "I'll git ye a drink."

II

Maury, using the same means and route that Two-Jack had taken, but paddling alone, reached Whisky George the following afternoon. He was humming to himself with a momentary peace of mind that sprang almost wholly from his surroundings; he loved the swamps as much as Two-Jack hated them and within them he nearly always experienced a feeling of release. The episode with Tulita no longer troubled him. The affair was finished, and that was a good thing. As for the *Salvador,* he had already counted off the trip as a complete loss. It was too bad, but it was over now and it belonged to the past. There was no use letting it spoil the day. The day was like wine and the swamps were beautiful. Little pools of sunlight dappled the open stretches, gleaming on the yellow of jessamine and the cascading purple of wild wisteria. Owls looked down like curious gnomes and turned their heads all the way around to watch him as he passed, and flocks of little green parakeets flashed in the cypress tops. Aye, the swamps were glorious, and in the peace of them one could be grateful just for life itself.

Then peace departed as the bateau finally slid across the channel to Bruin's landing and his nostrils caught the reek of the *Salvador.*

The schooner was tied up in a creek opening farther downstream and he could hear Finch cursing the black boys who were cleaning out the hold. Cricket, his diminutive manservant, was waiting for him at the landing. The Negro rolled his eyes up at the log house and he saw Bruin sitting on the steps, smoking, and Two-Jack pacing the narrow veranda.

He went slowly up the steps. Bruin got up and shook hands, a rare courtesy extended to only a few, and Two-Jack stopped pacing and eyed him without expression, the thumbs of his small round womanish hands hooked in the pockets of his glaring waistcoat.

"Well?" said Maury, and Two-Jack announced softly, "Finch came in with fourteen live ones."

"Fourteen!"

"Ah-yah. Fourteen out of fifty-nine. The news makes you happy?"

"I'm happy that any of them are alive. Thank God for it! I was afraid they were all dead."

Two-Jack said, "All of them might as well be dead. I cannot sell broken bones. Where are you going?"

"To have a look at 'em, of course. Those poor damn devils . . ."

"You should have looked after them earlier," Two-Jack snapped. "Sit down. I want to hear about the trip."

"Get it from Finch."

"I've heard it from Finch. Now I want it from you."

"Well, goddammit, you can wait!"

Swearing inaudibly he hurried down the steps and around to the pen where the surviving Negroes had been laid out on pallets in one of the huts.

The first sight of them wrung him to pity and self-condemnation. Some were delirious. Others rolled their great white eyes at him, mutely pleading. Fourteen—but the unseen dead were there too, silently accusing. He tried to tell himself that he was not at fault, that had the trip gone well everyone of them would have been much better off in the Floridas than in Cuba. Much better off. The fault lay with the English for interfering. And with this small sop to his conscience he summed up their injuries, got his Negro and three of Bruin's people to help and then stripped down to his waist and went furiously to work. Some of them had little wrong, but others were in critical shape and taxed his skill. Presently he forgot himself utterly, and for hours was lost in the absorbing problems of setting and splinting complicated fractures and trying to save an arm where splintered bone had slashed through skin.

It was nearly dark when he finished. Tired to exhaustion, he went down to the landing and plunged into the cold water; finally he dressed and went up and stretched out in one of Bruin's net hammocks. Relaxing, he had a pleasant feeling of accomplishment. He had done a good job on those fellows. Of the fourteen he would possibly lose two; but they had a chance, and he would watch them through the night.

And so, in a small measure, he justified his existence.

Two-Jack came out of the door and sat down stiffly on the steps, and Bruin's big yellow woman brought them rum. Two-Jack sniffed the drink, frowned, tossed it down quickly and wiped his mouth with his silk handkerchief. "Phah!" he spat. "That stuff she is rotten!"

Maury watched him, tolerant now and amused. He sipped slowly, relishing the flavor. "It's very good, I'll have you know. I brought it up myself. Got it from Delarobia in Matanzas."

"All rum is bad."

They were silent, and a limpkin cried off in the swamp. Two-Jack flinched. "Damn things. They sound like ghosts." He turned half about, scowling. "Now you tell me what happened."

"Why recriminate? You've had it all from Finch."

"Ah-yah, but I want it from you. From the beginning."

"Oh, hell, all right. The damn English tricked me, and I ran into weather getting away from them."

"Tell me, about the English."

"They were flying American colors and had their guns hid-

den. I knew it wasn't the *Peregrine* or any of our Revenue
Marine, and I didn't believe a Britisher would be on patrol in
our own waters—although a slaver's fair game for any gunboat. Anyway I ran up British colors—and they switched colors
in a hurry and came after me. So I bent on everything I had
but the cook's apron and ran for it. I had to run away off
soundings, and then the weather caught me." He sighed.
"That's all there was to it."

"No," said Two-Jack, "that was not all. There was this
barkentine."

"Well, what of her?"

"You shouldn't have taken her in."

"Somebody had to do it. She was in trouble."

"You didn't have to do it."

"Well, I did it anyway."

"And this woman on board—she was pretty, no?"

"What woman?"

"Always there is a woman. There was one aboard."

"There were two aboard, since you consider it so important."

"Ah-yah, women are always important. You should have
stayed with the *Salvador*."

"Devil take it, what difference does it make?" Maury sat up.
"The dead were dead. I'm not God. I couldn't have put life
back in 'em!"

"You might have saved a few more. You should have stayed
aboard and looked after them until you got in. You had no
business running off and leaving everything to Finch."

"Must we go all over that again?"

"I am telling you what I think. This is a matter of business.
I put money into this. Much money. But do I make money?
No. I cannot afford to lose money—not now."

"Stop growling. I lost too."

"Not what I did, for you owe me money. When you lose, I
lose double, for then you are slow to repay me. I do not like
that."

"Very well. You do not like it. What are you going to do about it?"

"You will have to repay me some way. And very quickly. I must have money."

They were silent for a while.

Maury finished his drink and started to pour himself another, then decided he did not want to drink any more. At least not with Two-Jack. You drank only with friends. Not, of course, that Two-Jack had ever been his friend. What they'd had was merely a loose partnership; and, because each had supplied what the other lacked, the arrangement had been mutually profitable for a time.

But now, in the silence, the partnership was being dissolved.

Maury set his noggin on the floor. "How much do you figure I owe you?"

"Five thousand dollars," Two-Jack replied instantly.

"Really?" Maury raised an eyebrow. "I think you must be wrong."

"I am never wrong about figures. You borrow, and you forget. You play the cards with me and lose—and forget."

"Like hell! According to you I owed you about three thousand before I went down to Matanzas. I can't make five out of it."

"The other two thousand, it is for dead men that I cannot sell."

"Oh, no! We share and share alike. That was our agreement. I find the Negroes, run the risk and bring them in. You pay the costs and arrange the distribution. Mace and Slatter get their share, and we split the rest. We've made money in the past. You shouldn't complain if we lose a little now."

"I am not complaining," Two-Jack rapped out angrily. "I am talking business! With money and women you are a child. Worse, a fool. I give you ten thousand dollars to buy a hundred black men. You buy fifty-nine. You——"

"They were less than two hundred apiece—a bargain for those fellows."

"Bah! You do not bring in fifty-nine. You bring in fourteen. Those fourteen, they are not worth a York shilling now. Maybe someday they will bring five, six thousand dollars—but none of that will be profit. So I say that you owe me at least two thousand for your foolishness."

"I don't owe you a damn thing for this trip. And I have only your word for it that I owe you three thousand for past foolishness."

"You doubt my word?"

"Don't press me about either my doubts or my debts. I'll pay you—but not till I'm damn good and ready." He had never played cards with Two-Jack except when he was too drunk to know better.

"You have nothing more to say?"

"I've said it."

Again they were silent. Out in the near-dark the limpkins resumed their eerie crying. Two-Jack, a square hard shadow on the steps, twitched his head around, listening, and then he stood up slowly. For a minute he seemed to study the swamps, irresolute, and then suddenly he straightened and called for his Negro. While he waited he took out his handkerchief and wiped the palms of his hands. It was a gesture Maury had seen him make many times, always at the conclusion of an evening's play. The act had a certain significance now. Two-Jack was through; the dissolution of the partnership was complete.

And since they had never been friends, their status henceforth would have to be that of enemies.

The Negro came with a lantern, stood blinking a moment at the blackness across the channel and at a sharp word from his master reluctantly untied the bateau and bailed it out. Two-Jack went over to the landing and wedged himself aboard. At that minute old Bruin, having finished a small exchange of hides and rum in the storehouse, came down the walk.

"Ye hain't a-stayin' fer supper?" he coyly asked.

"I have business at home. Thank you for your hospitality, M'sieu Bruin."

"Hit's a long piece to town. The night air, hit's mighty on-healthy sometimes." There was almost a threat in the way Bruin said it, though Maury recognized it for sheer drollery.

Two-Jack muttered an obscenity and growled at the Negro. The bateau slid across the channel. For a few seconds the lantern winked through the trees, then it disappeared.

Bruin stood fingering his pointed mandarin's beard. "The bastard's riled," he commented. "Fust time he ever went home in the dark."

Maury followed him up the steps. Bruin set his rifle carefully against the railing, poured rum and stretched out in a hammock to wait for supper. "Ye had it out with 'im?" he asked sociably.

"Yeah."

"Ye shoulda shot the sonofabitch right here. Then ye wouldn't have it to do later."

"He's not worth the bother."

"H'm. Ever kilt a man?"

"One. I've always regretted it."

" 'Tain't nothin' to regret—less'n 'twas an accident."

"It was in a way. I lost my temper. I—— Oh, hell! It was one of those things. It just happened."

"Shouldn't be that way. Feller ought to make up his mind to it, know what he's about."

"We're not all built alike, Mace."

"Sho. But killin's natural. An' when yo' mind's made up to it, ye got the upper hand right away when ye run foul some bastard that's killin'-bad."

Bruin seldom talked, but there were times when he could be expansive. "All men are dogs," he went on. "Black uns an' white uns—they're all the same. Jes' dogs." He spoke profanely and at length upon the subject, then finished his rum and sighed peacefully. "Course," he went on, "there's good dogs an' bad uns. Take Slatter. He's a sly dog, full o' tricks, but he ain't bad. Leastways, not killin'-bad. Now Two-Jack, he's sly an' he's ornery. In 'is own way he's as ornery as McSwade o' Roatán. Them two varmints is killin'-bad."

All this was a word of caution, Maury saw. To be the recipient of it showed that Mace must like him more than he had realized.

"Have you seen McSwade lately?" he asked.

"No, I told the bastard to keep shut o' me. But I hear he sailed into St. Joseph recent."

"He's got nerve. Did he bring in any blacks?"

"Dunno, but Slatter kin tell ye. H'm . . . that reminds me— Slatter sent word he'd like to see ye."

"He didn't say why?"

"No, but likely McSwade figgers in it. I reckon McSwade landed something."

The two fell silent, waiting for supper. The smell of frying ham was strong in the air. There would be yams to go with it, Maury knew, dark-red and sweet, and squash and early peas from the communal garden beyond the compound. And at this same hour, miles away at the Mansion House, Catherine would be in the great dining room, with a half-dozen liveried waiters at her elbow, trying to make up her mind how many of the forty-odd meat courses she wanted to try. He smiled suddenly, remembering last evening. She had eaten like a famished woodsman: shrimp, wood duck, scallops and oysters and more oysters. Where the hell had she put it?

She had been in the back of his mind all day. He thought of her mouth, with its fullness and its sharp and almost cruel chiseling; and then of her body, rich and lithe and vital with suppressed power. A tigress. A young tigress. She belonged to the Carnivora—and maybe to the devil.

An interesting bit of flesh, aye—but it had been silly of Tulita to jump on him with all her accusations. They were entirely unfounded. He had no time for anyone like Catherine, and it would make no difference to him if he never saw her again.

He was wondering what Jug Slatter wanted when the yellow woman announced supper. He rose lazily. "What's happened to Finch?" he asked.

"Nothin' yet," came Bruin's laconic answer.

"Eh? Is anything likely to happen?"

"Mebbe. Him an' that ugly Bat o' mine, they're goin' huntin' —so they let on."

"Not together!"

Bruin chuckled. "Naw. Them two, they been a-sneakin' around all afternoon gittin' ready to go someplace, each tryin' to keep t'other from knowin'."

"What are they up to?"

"Oh, there's a li'l yeller girl—a *hokte*—lives up yonder near the Tuskenegge's country. She come down to trade a spell back, an' them two was a-follerin' her around the hull damn day."

"So that's it. Well, they'll get into trouble if they go up there."

"Apt to. The Tuskenegge, he don't come down no more. When he wants something, he sends him a *hokte* here to trade. 'Tain't nothin' to me, but folks goin' alone upcountry, they better be careful. The Tuskenegge, he's talked the Apalachee into goin' in with the Seminole. They kilt a couple travelers over on the Marianna Road t'other day."

"Good Lord, won't we ever settle our troubles with the Seminole?"

"Not less'n we learn to leave 'em alone."

After supper he returned to the stockade. Some of the Negroes were in great pain, which he eased by giving them bits of gum opium. There was no change in the condition of the two most seriously hurt. He left them finally and went back to Bruin's house. He poured himself a noggin of rum and sat down and tried to drink it. But a restlessness drove him to his feet and he wandered down to the landing and back and then began pacing the veranda.

"Ye need a woman," Bruin said at last. " 'Tain't good fer a man to be too long without a woman."

Maury said nothing, and Bruin went on: "Got several smart lookers, e'en if I am they pappy. Bonnie, she's the purtiest an' she kinda hankers after ye. Ye kin have her."

Maury shook his head. "I don't want a woman," he mumbled.

Then he gripped the railing with both hands, hard, while he stared unseeingly at the fireflies making a fantasy of the night. He did want a woman, but only a certain one. Odd that the wanting of that one should have robbed him of all desire for any other. The fact of it struck him all at once, poured over him like a wave, staggered and engulfed him. He wanted Catherine. He wanted her more than he had ever believed it possible to want any woman.

Oh, Christ, he thought, what's happened to me?

Just before dark, at the edge of a small slough opening beyond the compound, Finch stowed a jug of water and a compass among the other things in his bateau. He was about ready to leave, and he stood checking the various items in his mind and wondering whether he should start out immediately or wait until morning. He had not seen Bat since noon, and Bat was still an uncertain factor in his plans. He was quite sure, however, that his preparations had escaped the other's notice.

It was something of a shock, therefore, when he turned and discovered Bruin's son watching him from the edge of the palmetto tangle bordering the slough. In the dusk Bat's broad, dark and slightly pockmarked face with its little feral eyes was indistinguishable; but the flat protruding head and long, loose outline of him were unmistakable.

Finch was unpleasantly conscious of a prickling up his back. He had not heard the least sound, and yet here was Bat.

"What the hell d'ye want?" he snapped.

The palmettos rustled and Bat took a step into the open. Here on his own home soil this misanthropic and only white offspring of Bruin seemed a different person. The dusk lent him the malignant cloak of his father.

"Folks——" Bat spoke slowly—"said ye was aimin' to go huntin'."

"Well, what of it? I heard the same o' you."

Bat came a little closer. "Where're ye goin'?"

"None o' your goddamn business."

"We ain't out to sea now. Ye can't talk to me that-a-way."

"I'm a-talkin' to ye that-a-way. An' what's more, if I catch any sonofabitch a-tryin' to foller me, I'll damn sure fix 'im good!"

"Now lissen here——"

"Ye heard me!"

Bat took a bold step forward. "Talk mighty big fer a li'l pissant what can't e'en grow whiskers. I got a good mind to cut ye loose."

Finch planned his attack and acted on the instant. He gave a sudden twist of his mouth and spat, sending a stream of tobacco juice at Bat's face. Almost at the same moment he lashed out with his left fist and then with his right. In the gloom his spittle missed its exact mark and, instead of blinding Bat, merely sprayed his forehead. But the fists struck hard and Bat stumbled back into the palmettos. Finch dived after him.

They rolled in the palmettos and then back into the open, kicking, clawing, thrashing, biting when they could, each trying to gouge, throttle, twist or pound the other into insensibility, and each succeeding only in keeping the other too occupied to draw his knife. Their breath came in hot rasping gasps of hatred.

Finally with a heave of his long, loose frame Bat tore away and got his hand on the hilt of his knife. But as the blade was freed, Finch's knee caught him hard in the groin. Bat shrieked and collapsed. The knife slid away from his numbed fingers. Finch hit him again, clamped his fingers around Bat's throat and banged his head on the ground. Bat lay still.

Finch saw the knife, grabbed it, hesitated, then cursed and threw it away. He had never killed, and he was unable to bring himself to it now. Bat was badly beaten, and that was enough.

It was almost dark, but Finch saw no reason for delaying now. In an hour or so he could reach one of the dry ridges near the big cypress and so be well on his way by morning. He peered down at Bat, heard him groan, then grinned suddenly and crawled into the bateau and pushed off.

As he paddled away he was whistling softly in anticipation, unmindful of the crying of the limpkins.

Chapter Six

MAURY RETURNED to the Garvers' the following evening, bringing a leg of venison from Mace and a cask of rum from the *Salvador*. The rum was for May. Not many women cared for it, but she was inordinately fond of it and, like him, loved to sip it slowly, enjoying the heady flavor and the scent of cane. May could consume great quantities of it. She immediately had her maid Celeste pour a goblet full and, nonchalantly holding the nursing baby to her breast with one arm, stood drinking and gossiping in the doorway of the bedroom while he washed and changed his clothes. Nothing ever bothered May, not even the detail of a child that had appeared some months prior to wedlock. She was a big, dark, boisterous beetle-browed woman, so mannishly like Juan in appearance that, biologically, their union seemed a bit outrageous.

"Lord love us!" she said, pleasurably smacking her lips, "this tastes like some of that good Matanzas stuff! You didn't get it in New Orleans."

"Why not?"

"Humph! You were down *south* again. I know. You'd better be careful. I hope that Tulita doesn't know too much about your goings and comings. She'll get you in trouble one of these days."

"I saw her the other evening. For the last time."

"So I guessed. You didn't act like yourself when you came in. Hey, Juan!" she bellowed suddenly. "That damn chemical is driving us out of the house! That man!" she went on. "He'll blow us to bits with his awful experiments one of these days. What a doctor! But he's made snow. Real snow. I scraped some off that crazy machine yesterday. Imagine!"

"Really?" Maury had stripped down to his skin and was sponging himself off at the commode. He would have considered it an indecency if any other woman had stood here watching him, but May was different. Only in a place like this, he thought, where almost anything was accepted and half the people did about as they chose, could she have found life tolerable. And Juan was content to neglect his medical practice while he experimented with his "cold machine." If it could actually be made to chill off a room, as Juan hoped, it would be a great boon to fever patients. They did suffer terribly here in the summer. . . .

"So it really works?" Maury asked.

"No," said Juan, suddenly thrusting his head through the doorway. "The damn thing's as temperamental as a woman. Sometimes I think I ought to throw it away and start all over again." He was a big, quiet heavy-boned man, swarthier even than May. He looked Spanish, and there was a sort of Iberian poise about him that contrasted oddly with May's boisterousness, but he was a foundling and knew nothing of his forebears.

"My dear," he said gently, "can't you allow a gentleman a little privacy during his toilet?"

"Oh, hell," laughed May, "he's used to women—and I won't eat him up. Will you look at those shoulders! He's like Perseus. If you were built like that——"

"If I were a jealous man I'd have throttled you long ago."

"Oh, shut up and pour me some more rum. Lordy, that's good stuff!"

"You'll be flowing rum instead of milk if you keep on."

"Well, that would be a saving. Maury, you're staying for supper, of course?"

"Thank you, but I have a . . . a sort of engagement."

May looked at him shrewdly. "With those Yankees you told me about? The Delafields?"

"Er . . . yes. It wasn't definite. I mean, they'd planned to be here a few days until they could have their furniture and things taken off the ship. And I'd mentioned, if I returned in time ———"

"I saw them yesterday. They were on their way to St. Joseph with Clifford Saxon. I understand he's invited them to stay at his house until their own place is ready."

"No!"

"Yes, indeed. They're gone. So I guess you'll have venison with us tonight, my lad." She dallied with her glass, then erupted with honest envy, "Lordy me, she's beautiful! She's got the most superb figure I've ever laid eyes on. Everybody in town is talking about her."

Maury said nothing. He scowled into the mirror and re-signedly pulled on a pair of fawn-colored trousers.

"But she's not for you," May added.

He turned and looked at her, and Juan spoke quickly. "Goodness, May, you're taking a lot for granted. And anyhow, what's wrong with Maury?"

"There's nothing wrong with him. Except that down here nobody's quite what he was born or used to be. He's just what he is now. And what's Maury now?"

"A good surgeon gone to hell," said Juan judiciously. "But he's still a good surgeon. And few medical men have anywhere near his perception ———"

"Oh, twaddle! You miss the point. What if he were a practicing medical man running around giving pills for the ague and

dosing old women? I ask you, what of it? What are you? Just
because you've spent nine years learning how to cheat the
grave, does that make you any better than old Billy Peters the
butcher? The world doesn't think so. But if you'd dabble a
bit in cotton and make twenty thousand dollars that you didn't
earn, why, you'd begin to be important. What's a doctor? Why,
a doctor's any ignorant fool with leeches and a rusty lancet.
Maybe, once in a while, he knows something like Maury—but
do they ever call on him to deliver a child? Horrors, no! To
bring a child into the world you've got to be a gabbling old
crone with dirty hands and a bag of——"

"Aw, shut up!" grumbled Juan. "You're a gabbling old
crone yourself."

"No," said Maury, "she's an unnerving philosopher. In her
gentle way she's merely reminding us that the medical profession has never achieved either social or financial recognition.
Which is why, no doubt, you've occasionally run for public office and served as mayor. And maybe it explains why I've
strayed some myself from the thorny path. A man hates to feel
unimportant." He shrugged. "I'm not hungry. I think I'll go
over to my rooms and get some sleep."

He walked disconsolately over to the Mansion House, his
manservant Cricket following with his bags.

His rooms were in a corner of the third floor, looking out over
the bay. They were distinctive and individual and hardly
seemed like a lone man's abode. Most of the furnishings were
his own. The immense ebony four-poster that jammed the
bedroom and some of the other heavier pieces were salvage from
a Spanish ship; these were lightened by many little objects he
had found in the islands and in La Guira, Colón and Vera
Cruz: delicate glass and gay bric-a-brac and rugs and bright
pottery and some fine baroque Spanish silver. The place, if
a little overcrowded, was sumptuously comfortable, and in the
past it had always been pleasant to return to it from the sea.

This evening it seemed stuffy and somehow lacking in privacy. The hotel was full and he could feel the encroaching presence of many people about him. Damn them, he thought, and wondered why he had ever managed to live here so long. Suddenly he felt a sharp dissatisfaction with his whole way of life.

He dismissed Cricket and walked over to the south window of the study and peered out at the bay. He had had no intention of remaining here after building the cottage. But there were the Gradys. They'd come along, badly needing a place, and at the time it had seemed expedient to rent it to them. And the Gradys were such nice people that he'd never had the heart to serve notice to them. And so there they were.

He picked up a spyglass and idly studied the island. From this elevation, even in the waning light, the far-off Delafield barkentine was clearly visible. A schooner and a barge were tied up on opposite sides of her, and a black gang was still hard at the business of removing her cargo. He thought he could see Captain Adams on the poop.

He set the glass down and began pacing the room. Disappointment sharpened his dissatisfaction. All the way back from Whisky George he had been anticipating the moment of seeing Catherine again. It had never occurred to him that she might be gone.

And she was staying with the Saxons. Well, that was only natural, for the Saxon place was on the beach, adjoining the new Delafield mansion. Good, God-fearing conservatives, the Saxons—or at least they had prayers every night, believed in the Whig party and the greater destiny of St. Joseph and the Saxons and never served anything stronger than vaguely sherried punch at their balls. Catherine, probably, wouldn't be overjoyed with the pompous Maude and her simpering Patty. But old Clifford and Aaron ought to get along fairly well together.

As he thought of the Saxons and Catherine staying with them, the acid of May Garver's wisdom began eating deeper. Down here he was little except the questionable entity he had made of himself. For a few years he had enjoyed the picaresque and anonymous cloak under which he had hidden all that he supposed himself to be—but now there no longer seemed to be anything under the cloak. May was horribly right.

Darkly he sought the rum bottle in the liquor cabinet and poured himself a drink. He downed it almost in a gulp and poured another. Then he turned and looked at Kul, the stone image he had found in the ruins on Cozumel. Kul, enthroned now on the liquor cabinet between silver candlelabra, leered back, hideous and evil and wise and imponderable.

"Tell me, Illustrious Kul—what am I now?"

And the voice of Kul, stony-deep and cold and ghostly from the pit of time, seemed to reply: "Nothing. Nothing at all."

"That's rather unsettling."

"It is the truth."

"You needn't be so impersonal about it."

"Truth is impersonal. Take stock of yourself, St. John. Just what do you think you are?"

"Well, to begin with, I'm a man. A fair example of God's noblest——"

"Man! Bah! In one day I have been offered the hearts of a thousand men. And where are they now? I have watched ten times ten thousand of them die. Does it matter now? They built cities and called them great—but what of them now? Has the earth changed its course because of them, or gained an ounce in weight? Is the soil any richer from their rot? I could show you deserts that were gardens before man came. Man! Destroyer of his fellows! A scourge and a plague and a thing of filth that makes a blight on the earth! Bah! Man is a disease."

"I won't argue the matter. But I'm still a man, so let's get down to earth and consider me. As a member of the human race I have my points."

"Name them."

"I am a good surgeon."

"Oh, you can set a fracture and repair a knife wound—as men have been doing for forty centuries. But your victims still scream in agony and die of countless ills that a knife could cure. You are endowed with the ability to uncover new facts in both surgery and medicine—but are you seeking this knowledge? No. You turn your back on it because it does not happen to flatter your pride and purse."

"I'm not a crusader. I want my privacy."

"You do not have to crusade to be a seeker of knowledge. But you do not seek. You waste yourself. So one point must be charged against you."

"But I don't waste myself entirely! The water front comes to me—surreptitiously, of course—but I help them. I always help them. And I never charge."

"True. That makes a point in your favor. However, the net result is zero. What else have you to say for yourself?"

"I have money in the bank."

"Money, bah! But I'll not digress on that topic, St. John. The fact is, you owe as many dollars as you own. A point against you."

"But I own land, two houses."

"You have never made a home of either house. And, to be delicate, all you have ever done was to dally a bit in one of them. As for the land, that plantation I've heard you speak about so glibly, that stretch of swamp you won at cards, I could charge many points against you. You could, perhaps, have improved it and done something with it, for much of it is good land, high and dry. But all you've ever used it for was as a training station for raw Africans."

"You're too damn clever at making nothing out of me. There's the *Salvador*. A good, tight little schooner. She can show her heels to anything afloat."

"She smells, St. John. And all the paint and cleaning in the world can never hide the fact that she is a magdalen among her kind. Forty-five black men smothered to death aboard her. That should be forty-five points against you, but since I cannot hold even black men in high regard, I will be charitable and chalk them up as one. Perhaps, if you scrape some, you may uncover a few minor matters in your favor—but the net result would still be zero. So you see, you are nothing. Possibly a bit less than nothing, for in the eyes of man you are neither solvent nor respectable."

"Oh, a pox on you, you devilish idol!"

Maury resumed his drinking.

Suddenly he glared at Kul again. "You've seen too much. You are old and evil. And you are not helping me by telling me what I already know. I'm adrift and I've lost my course, —I need help. And there is a woman. . . ."

The laughter of Kul was a deep unpleasantness. "I have been waiting for you to ask about the woman. I have gazed upon her nakedness. She is beautiful. You lust for her. It is a bad thing."

"Perhaps I love her. I don't know. Anyway, why should it be a bad thing?"

"You could never truly love her. She is narcissistic and selfish, and there are other things about her we need not discuss—unless you wish to face them."

"Open my eyes. Let me see her clearly."

"Very well. She——"

"No—no! Forget it. It doesn't matter. It would change nothing. Oh, hell and heaven, why should I want her? Why did this have to happen to me?"

"You are a fool, St. John. And you are getting drunk."

"You stone bastard." He dashed a spray of rum in Kul's face. "Stone. That's all you are. Cold stone. What could you know of life and warmth and love?"

From the bowels of Kul came a sigh, like the faint movement of dead air long imprisoned in a cavern. "I have seen more life, St. John, than any living thing will ever see. In my time I was

great among the gods. Many men have worshiped me. I have
been feared and hated too. I have known warmth. And once,
yes, I knew love. A child loved me. She came and played with
me, not thinking me ugly or evil or mighty and untouchable.
She kissed me and placed a flower in my lap. For this sacrilege
she was killed."

A drop of rum, which might have been a tear, coursed down
the pitted cheek of Kul. "It is a strange thing, love. All men
seek it in one way or another, but few find it because they do
not know it. At least, St. John, you are fortunate in knowing
it, so you should not be confused. I speak of Adrienne."

"We can leave her out of this."

"How can we? Has anyone ever loved you more?"

He looked uncomfortably at Kul, then turned away, troubled.
No one had ever meant so much to him as his sister Adrienne.
But of course what he had felt for her had nothing to do with
man's regard for woman. It was something quite different. Or
was all love, in its purity, the same? He pondered the point
and then lost it in the sudden haunting memory of Adrienne.
They had always been so close, for there had been only the two
of them against their father and stepmother and all the stiff-
necked in-laws of the tribe. Damn the lot of them! If he'd
only kept her from marrying that Henri Guidry, she would
probably be alive now. He should have come back and taken her
away from Henri, instead of going on to Paris on Henri's money
she'd sent him. Damn Henri and his money, and damn Paris!
Maybe she hadn't lived to hear about what happened there. He
hoped not. It would have broken her heart. Poor little
Adrienne.

His bottle was empty and he needed another drink. There
was no rum left in the cabinet, but he remembered he had placed
a demijohn of it in the big chest in the bedroom. He went into
the bedroom and was immediately conscious of a faint and half-
familiar odor that he could not identify. It was so faint that
few men in his condition would have been aware of it, but his

nostrils unconsciously dilated, questing, and then he remembered. It was something Catherine had worn the other night at dinner. A sort of deep-forest scent that reminded him of wild blossoms.

Wild blossoms. That was like her. It was a ghost of a fragrance and he stood awhile sniffing it before he sought the demijohn, sharply aware that Catherine had been here, had used his things, had slept in his bed and had left part of herself behind. A woman always left something of herself in every room she occupied.

Etta Lamb had been here too, and Aaron had used the study, but Catherine had almost effaced them both. She might have stayed here alone. His eyes went to the bed, visioning her in it, and then he saw the small white square of the note. It was lying in the center of the coverlet. A sealed note.

He held it a moment, savoring what it might contain, and then he broke the seal and stared at the bold and yet rounded and feminine handwriting.

"Please forgive me," it began without address, "for leaving so quickly before I could thank you for everything you have done for us. We are riding over with our neighbor Mr. Saxon, who has invited us to stay with him until our house is habitable. You must stop in and see us when you are in St. Joseph." It was signed almost impersonally with her full name, but as an afterthought she had added, "What a marvelous bed! But your idol is hideous. It seems almost alive. Wherever did you find so many odd things?"

He read it over several times and then, with a full glass in his hand, went back and, reeling a little, showed his teeth at Kul. He cursed Kul and drank and suddenly smashed the glass hard in Kul's face and turned away, feeling violently, irrepressibly alive, his dissatisfaction with life having risen to a vast and insatiable hungering for it.

Chapter Seven

I

IN THREE days of steady searching Finch had penetrated the drowned area beyond the lower swamp, and, although he had found some habitable ground and one small deserted village, he had seen no one.

He laid his paddle across a thwart, and the bateau drifted into an open pondlike area ringed with old dead cypresses. The gaunt tops of some of the larger trees supported huge eyries where generations of eagles had nested. They seemed abandoned now, and from the rim of one of them a lone fish crow, like an evil jester in a haunted land, flew up with a hollow derisive cawing and flapped away through the swamp. In the late afternoon stillness the place seemed inexpressively lonesome and remote.

He was uneasy without being afraid. Uneasiness had wakened him at dawn and stayed with him through the day, yet he had no thought of turning back. Even without the vision of the yellow girl, sheer curiosity would have driven him on.

He glanced at the box compass between his feet and then to his left where the sun was hidden behind the mystery of black-etched cypress tops. Only once today had he glimpsed the sun, and that was around noon when he had crossed another stretch of open water. He had been working north, but in the dark, sinuous maze of water lanes he had lost all sense of approximate location.

As his restless eyes probed the dark edges of the pond, some impulse made him turn and glance back. He was in time to glimpse a movement through the drowned trees behind him.

A heron maybe, or a snakebird? Or was it a bateau?

He hung on the paddle, staring intently for nearly a minute but seeing nothing. Probably a large bird of some kind, he thought. No one could be following him. Surely not Bat. Then in an instant he forgot Bat altogether, for he could smell, faintly, wood smoke and what seemed to be fish cooking.

Curious, a little apprehensive, he held the bateau motionless until he had determined the direction of the fire. Cautiously he resumed paddling.

The pond dwindled into a long, curving run. He felt warmth on his shoulders and looked around and blinked at a ripe orange sun winking at him through a break in the trees. The sudden brilliance of it blinded him. He did not see Bat Bruin fifty yards away. Nor, when he turned to search for the hidden fire, did he notice the shadowed pilings of the cabin set back in the tangle.

The Bruin boy stopped paddling and slid behind the bole of a big cypress. He had never been to this place, but he knew he was near the Tuskenegge's country if not actually in it. Various people lived in the area: Besides the Apalachees there were runaway Negroes, half-breeds and families of renegades and mixed bloods existing in almost total seclusion from others of their kind. Some of these last, though they traded with his father, were more to be feared than the Indians.

Bat had lost all interest in the yellow girl. His groin still ached from the thrust of Finch's knee. The aching came in waves that rose through him and turned into hate, building a mountain of hate.

Knowing his enemy's approximate destination had made the finding of him not too difficult, for one must inevitably cross certain stretches of open water before reaching the upper swamp. He had finally sighted Finch at noon, but it had been from a distance, and he had followed doggedly ever since, trying to anticipate the other's changes of course and so maneuver himself into a position for an unobstructed shot.

Here at last was Finch in the open, an easy target. Only, there was the hidden cabin over at the end of the run.

Bat raised his rifle, then lowered it, scowling. He waited. In a moment Finch would see the cabin and turn back.

But no, Finch was going on, blindly on.

"God damn ye!" Bat muttered. "Can't ye see nothin'?"

In sudden fury and frustration he swung the bateau into the open, quickly caught up the rifle and lined the sights on Finch's back.

The swamp echoed and re-echoed the whipping crash of the shot.

He saw Finch spring up and spin half about, clawing, and fall across a thwart with one hand trailing in the water. The bateau rocked dangerously but did not go over.

Forgetting caution, Bat thrust the rifle aside and seized the paddle. Perhaps Finch was not yet dead. He must see his face, see him die, see the agony of death.

The swamp denied him this final satisfaction. A puff of powder smoke blossomed near the cabin, and a musket ball skipped over the water and cut a splinter from his paddle blade. With the sudden shock of it he nearly dropped the paddle, then he swung about in a frenzy for the cover of the timber. He glanced back once before heading reluctantly for Whisky George, and saw Finch lying motionless where he had fallen.

Slowly Finch's bateau drifted down the run. It nosed into a vine tangle and stopped. Presently a dugout containing an Indian girl slid from the darkness near the cabin. With a timid glance around, she paddled quickly over to Finch and began towing his bateau into the shadows of her landing.

II

In the mail that Cricket brought up with his morning coffee Maury found, among sundry bills and an emotional note from Tulita, a letter from Rodman Carey. Carey begged him to come over for a visit.

His first thought was to pack his bags and send Cricket out to hire a carriage. Then he noticed that the letter was dated a week ago, before Catherine's arrival. Suddenly angry at his eagerness to see her again, he tossed the letter aside, telling himself that he had no business in St. Joseph, and that he would be a fool to go running after a woman who, in all probability, would give him nothing but trouble.

And so, like a man struggling to delay the taking of a dangerous but irresistible drug, he began the torture of seeing how long he could remain away.

He helped Juan with his cold machine. He lost money at cards, went to the theater, drank, lost more money at cards and drank again. He did not see Two-Jack, but he heard of Two-Jack's odd run of luck. Everyone had heard about it.

Flavy Munn, the head of the big land company at Apalachicola, said, "It was funny as hell. There was a bunch of us here, an' we all took a turn cuttin' the deck with 'im. He lost every time. Lost thutty thousand dollars. The bastud ain't been in here since."

"Well, you won't see him till he's found himself a new fancy girl."

"What's that got to do with it?"

"Changes his luck," said Maury. "He always buys a new girl when he has trouble. And speaking of trouble, what have you done to poor Crom Davies that he should condescend to be seen in your nasty presence?"

"Phah! Crom, he come over from St. Joseph to beg for specie. Pay anything for specie—but I don't want 'is bank paper. Everybody's got money, but it's only that bank paper.

'Tain't none of it hard. Feller with a li'l hard money kin buy the hull damn Territory."

"Then I'll hang onto my gold."

Esteban, the Cuban hunchback who had charge of the *Salvador* whenever Finch was away, came from Whisky George to see him.

"Dem black fella," Esteban reported, "dey come along fine. *Muy bueno. Salvador,* she all ready. You go out again soon, mebbe?"

"I haven't decided yet," Maury told him.

"Weather, she good now. Fresh 'n' clear. No squalls. We make fast trip now, no trouble, bring back plenty black fella, make up for loss, make plenty *dinero.*"

There was much wisdom in what Esteban said. They should take advantage of the weather. One good trip would make up for their losses. If they waited too long the crew would disperse, and there would be more delays while they rounded up new hands. And suddenly the season of heat and squalls would be upon them. And fever. A summer trip could be bad enough without the fever, and you never could tell about that. He had had one experience with fever, and that was enough. They ought to make their next trip within the week.

But still he hesitated.

Esteban said, "I got li'l gold I save; I buy a share. An' Bruin, 'e got plenty gold; 'e say 'e buy ten, mebbe twenty share. 'E say tell you go see Slatter, get Slatter handle t'ings instead o' Two-Jack. Dat Slatter, 'e wanna see you anyway."

"That's an idea." Maury considered Slatter a moment and asked, "Finch isn't back yet?"

"No see Finch."

"Well, hold the boys together till Finch gets back. In the meantime I'll have a talk with Slatter."

The more he thought about Slatter, the more important it became that he go to St. Joseph. He would not have to stay there long. After taking care of his business he could spend a day or two with Carey mending his social roads and then come right back.

The next morning, scorning the daily stage as usual, he stood waiting impatiently on the hotel veranda while Cricket went to the livery stable.

It was not, however, a very prepossessing outfit that his Negro finally showed up with. The horse lacked spirit, and the wheels creaked. "Is this the best you could do?" he grumbled.

"Didn't have no better, suh."

Cricket did not meet his eye but stared fixedly ahead as they rode through town. Maury waited, knowing that Cricket was up to something. The Negro was a black, spidery little man with the body of a boy of twelve; he wore gray pantaloons and a boy's blue jacket, the brass buttons of which he kept shining like doubloons. But Cricket's face was old and astute, and his mind was like a woman's: It bided its time and then tacked obliquely so that the objective was never obvious.

"Marse Maury," he said presently, "you ain't no po' buckra."

"No."

"You's folks."

"You know what I am."

He had never made any pretense with Cricket. He had owned this profane and ugly but doggishly faithful little man only a few years, having bought him from Bruin, yet he felt an attachment for him that he had never felt for his first servant who had grown up with him. The family had sold poor stupid Jack when bankruptcy threatened.

The Negro said, "Sho, but you's folks. You had ought to have yo' own equipage when you calls on folks. Yassuh. Yo' own equipage."

Living as he had, he had never felt the need of a carriage of his own. It would have been a nuisance. Besides, there was no convenient place to keep one.

"You's got a house," Cricket reminded him. "Hit's got a fine stable."

"What's the matter with you? You know I wouldn't put the Gradys out."

"Y' all don't have to. Dey's a-leavin' next week. Gwine back to Columbus."

That was news. Then he peered sharply at Cricket. "So you think we ought to move into my place, eh?"

"Hit do seem lak a man, when he's folks, 'd wanna live in 'is own house. Sho is a pretty house. Got stable, quarters. Keep fine hoss 'n' carriage in stable, nigger in quarters. Man, he got 'im a good nigger what kin take care o' things, e'en do de cookin'. Goddamn good cook. But what dat man do now? Do he live lak folks? Do he ride lak folks?"

They were approaching the small square on the farther side of town. At one corner was a gristmill powered by a team of mules plodding in a circle about the stones. Beyond the mill stretched the stockade where most of the region's horse trading was done. Facing the stockade was a long shed where wagons and carriages were displayed for sale. Cricket drew up beside a handsome new chaise with brass lamps and trimming. He looked at the chaise and said nothing, but his silence was eloquent.

"You black bastard," growled Maury. "You planned this."

"Sho."

"You must think I intend to do a lot of running around."

"Ain't no tellin' 'bout you."

It was afternoon before the journey was resumed. They rode in the chaise now, and Cricket drove a fast sorrel mare.

"Us got to move into de house now," the Negro said. "Us jest got to. Can't keep nothin' fine as dis in dat ole livery stable."

"Why are you so anxious for me to move into the house?"

The answer came with some reluctance. Cricket wanted a wife. He wanted the Garvers' little brown girl Celeste, but he had no private quarters of his own where they could live, and there was not room for them both at the Garver place. The cottage on the bay would solve everything.

"How does Celeste feel about it?" Maury asked.

Cricket looked unhappy. "She cries," he answered simply.

Maury felt a tinge of guilt. "Well, we'll work out something. When we get back I'll speak to Dr. Garver."

The road followed the curving coast, westward and then north, winding tortuously for thirty miles through the almost unbroken belt of pines that lay between the sea and the swamps. Ahead and to the right the pines rose huge and dark, their straight virgin ranks nearly shutting out the sky. The interminable bay lay close on his left, but he saw it only in small, glittering patches through the palm jungles and scrub hiding the beach. In the heat of the afternoon the locusts awoke with a high, thin shrilling. The country seemed incredibly, oppressively lonesome.

Once, reaching a bleak open stretch of dead and broken trees, the Negro shuddered with an old memory. "Goddamn sea," he said. "Look what it done." And he repeated a tale that he always told when they came to this spot. The stark telling of it never changed; too terrible and mighty a thing had happened here for the need of embellishment. In this remoteness the sea had risen once to claim the land; few living knew of it or cared, since it had affected only a few. But the violence of it remained in the Negro's mind, and the shadow of it could be felt here in the land.

"Happen right along hyar. I gwine on fo'teen. Dat trader man own me. Dat sonobitch. We sailing 'long coast, him an' me an' 'is Creek woman. De wind hit us, drive de boat in through de trees yonder. . . ." The trees were going down, breaking off, falling into the water. There was water everywhere. The boat was driven half a mile inland before it hit something and went to pieces. A trader, an Indian woman, a

Negro boy—three frightened souls wading, swimming, trying to find land. "Warn't no land. Jes' water. An' de trees too big to climb. Nothin' to do but keep a-goin'. Night comin'. Water still risin'. His Creek woman she leads us to a runty pine. . . ." They climbed the pine, but the Creek woman was big and the trader, whose name was Price, was afraid the tree would not hold them all. "He kick 'er in de face an' she fall out an' drown. I keep out'n 'is way an' hang on all night, hopin' he'll fall out an' drown too. He don't. Goddamn bastard."

Price, Maury remembered, had lived for ten more years until Mace Bruin caught him stealing and put a bullet in his head. He heard Cricket say, "Goddamn sea, hit gonna come back an' take all dis land. White man an' black un, what dey amount to when de sea rise up?"

They passed the final finger of the southern bay and turned north across the base of a great hook of dunes and pineland enclosing a large new bay to the west. They saw the bay presently, a long brightness beyond the flat level land, and soon they drove along the edge of it. In the late afternoon sun it was an opalescent jewel, glittering green in the shallows, richly blue in the depths. The tide was out, and along the shoals and palm islets at this lower end were countless herons and little white egrets. A few miles beyond was the main anchorage where many vessels lay, and toward it from the shore stretched a great pier so long that it seemed to cut the bay in half. It was lined with ships whose reaching spars and yards made a delicate lace against the sky. St. Joseph itself was hidden by the ubiquitous pines.

The Negro stirred, weary of sitting, and studied a carriage winding toward them through the trees. They had passed few people this afternoon.

"Dat's Marse Two-Jack," he mumbled finally.

The approaching carriage slowed, then turned half out of the road and stopped. As they came up beside it Two-Jack held up his hand, and Cricket pulled the mare to a halt.

"Well?" the gambler said peremptorily.

Maury raised an eyebrow. "Well what?"

"You know what," the other snapped. "I give you seven days. I want it by next Friday morning. All of it."

Maury looked lazily at Two-Jack. "How about cutting the deck for it? Double or nothing."

The gambler's face became a mask, cold-eyed and expressionless. He did not speak for long seconds. Finally his tongue flicked over the edges of his thin precise lips. "No. I do not play with you until I see your cash. I want my money, and I want it by next Friday."

"Why then?"

"Never mind why. Just you have it by then."

"And suppose I don't have it by then?"

"You heard what I said. Next Friday."

There was a flat demand in the tone and a threat. Maury sat up in sudden anger. "Now look here, Jules. I've already told you how I feel about that matter. I don't want trouble with you. But if you insist on trouble, let's have it now and get it over with."

"You are being foolish. Trouble can wait, but money cannot. I advise you to think it over." Two-Jack turned away and jerked his head at his Negro. The carriage moved on.

Maury swore. Then he glared at the silent Cricket and bit out, "What the hell are you waiting for? Get along with you! Take me to Mr. Carey's house."

Chapter Eight

S T. JOSEPH, Maury had always thought, in spite of its great pier and its row of wooden warehouses flanking the railroad, had the bright but unfinished look of a watering place that has expanded too quickly and still needs time for growing up. Cotton may have built it—and certainly all the cotton in the country seemed to be flowing through it now—but the place was really a resort. Gay and sporty. Everybody came here. Everybody in the Territory and beyond. And everybody who was anybody at all owned a cottage here, or a mansion. Houses, big and little, were scattered for nearly two miles along the beach. Back in the pines the town had been laid out on a grand scale; but if there were gaps, and in many places only one building to a block, it was due—as any Saint would hasten to point out—not to any touch of atrophy but to the wise planning of the city fathers. St. Joseph had a future.

The Saints blandly ignored their city's growing reputation for wickedness. Oh, one ran into a bit of vice at the race track and over at Josie Bangs's place on the old bayou landing, and unquestionably there were some very gay ladies at the hotels. But, except for an occasional shooting, it was a pleasant sort of wickedness, really an asset. It attracted moneyed people as virtue would never have done. What irritated every Saint was the term "St. Joseph Bubble" that one saw frequently in the pages of the Territorial papers. It was an evil catch phrase, and it was spreading. Not that it could do any real harm, of course. All this was a solid growth, and no bubble about it. Look at the banks, the shipping, the railroad. Ah, the railroad! One of the first to be built in the world and, if one had an ear for undercurrents, destined soon to be the world's greatest.

It was no longer Rodman Carey's town. Pure whimsey, probably, more than any feeling of outrage or desire for gain, had caused him to lead the rebellion and found St. Joseph. He had seen the opportunity, picked the site and made the initial moves. And, having had his fun, he was content to let Saxon and Crom Davies and the other pioneering Saints carry on against the rival forces on the other bay. If his mercurial spirit moved him, he would still stick a finger in an occasional pie, but he refused to be wedded to commerce or, as he put it, to any of the folly of daily endeavor.

Carey, as one who recognizes that his tenure of life might be brief, looked with tolerant amusement on everything, including all forms of wickedness and, in spite of his afflictions, made it a point to miss nothing that might give him pleasure. An arthritic, emaciated to a shadow, he hobbled about painfully on his wasted limbs, never complaining, always cheerful and full of chatter, his blue eyes ever as bright and beady and full of mischief as a mockingbird's. A bachelor, he lived in a sprawling beach cottage beyond the Saxon place, with five Negroes to see to his comfort and wait on the visitors who trooped in and out at all hours.

This evening, for a wonder, he was alone, and he greeted Maury with something more than his usual enthusiasm. "Speak of the devil," he began. "So help me, I was just writing you another letter. But first get settled and have a drink and give me an accounting. How's our Sinner from Sodom?"

"Thirsty and curious—and damn glad to see you. And our Saint of Gomorrah?"

"The same. Faith, it's good to see the face of an honest rascal again. One that I can talk to. If I mention Bacon in this den of thieves they think I'm speaking of side meat. Ah—I've heard your name often lately."

"Really?"

"Indeed, yes." Carey, leaning on his cane, his slippered feet scraping slowly across the carpet, led the way through the cypress-paneled study to the veranda facing the sea. Billy, his butler, brought glasses and assorted bottles and a small bowl of ice.

Maury eyed the ice. "You do yourself proud, but I'll stick to my rum. Straight. My name has been mentioned a bit lately?"

"Aye. That was one reason I was writing you again—to urge you to come and stay longer than your accustomed fortnight. I was afraid you might ignore my first letter, since it was a trifle premature—all things considered."

Carey, mixing gin and bitters, cocked his pert bald head and eyed him slyly. He looked a little like Voltaire. "I thought, in view of several things," he added, "that a long visit might be propitious at this time."

"But Rod, I can stay but a few days. Honestly——"

"Nonsense. Of course you can stay. You've got to. For one thing, the Saxons are giving a ball next week."

"Christ!"

"Oh, but this is to be a very different sort of ball. It's to honor my godchild Kitty."

"H'm."

"That alters the situation?"

"Lord, yes! I——" Maury, suddenly confused, hastily gulped his rum and then reached for the decanter. "I mean . . . well, it ought to be quite a ball, in spite of the Saxons."

Carey laughed. "I thought you would feel that way. So

of course you are staying—for if you are here on the scene you
are bound to be invited." He set his glass aside and peered out
at the bay where the sun, in the beginning of death, was red-
dening the sky.

"When I first saw her," he mused, "I could hardly believe
my eyes. It's been so many years since I was in Salem. And
Kitty was such a little girl then." He shook his head. "I've always called her Kitty, but it hardly seems to fit her now. I'll
have to call her Catherine."

"I'm surprised you never told me anything much about her,
Rod."

"But, by my faith, there wasn't much to tell. I mean, I had
no idea she would be as she is now. She's so much like her
mother it staggers me. Whenever I look at her I feel twenty
years younger. Damme, I could hop up and dance a rigadoon!
If I'm not careful I'll make a fool of myself at the ball."

Maury smiled. "You actually do look better than when I saw
you last. How're those knees?"

"Wonderful! I could walk a mile tonight. I really could.
In fact we'll walk over and see Kitty later, if you'd care to."

"I'm not sure how I'd be received."

"Oh, come now! After what you did for them? But I'll admit you . . . well . . . you impressed Aaron rather darkishly.
Which is just another reason why you ought to be around
awhile. Sometimes I wonder why I went to such pains to get
the old dried herring to come down here—unless it was to see
the shock of St. Joseph on him. It'll be a shock. Gad, when I
think of the panegyrics I wrote Kitty for his benefit! Of course,
it's just the place for Kitty. She was stifling up there in Salem.
Down here it'll probably be the other way round. Aaron's still
perturbed about your having niggers aboard that morning. Of
course I came nobly to your defense. . . ."

"What'd you tell 'im?"

"More panegyrics. Spoke rapturously of your fine plantation up the river." He grinned maliciously. "That plantation

must be fairly seething with niggers by this time. I'd like to see the place."

"I'll be delighted to show it to you."

"Nonsense. Kitty herself couldn't drag me up into those damn swamps. You know, m'lad, you amaze me. If you were anyone else you'd never get by with what you do. Frankly I don't know why you go in for it—unless it's the awful French-Irish mixture in you that has to have excitement. But you're not quite that kind of a rascal. You and your damn charm. . . ."

Carey stood up unexpectedly like a jack-in-the-box, not even wincing, and peered down at the beach. "Hi!" he shouted. "Come on up and watch the sunset!"

Five figures, straggling in silhouette along the shell walk at the edge of the pines, stopped, turned, then came in through the gate and crossed the stretch of lawn to the veranda. They were Patty Saxon, her father and the two Delafields and— Maury's brows came together as he recognized the redheaded and meticulously groomed man with Catherine—the politician Hugh Bishop.

Patty ran up the steps, saying, "We can't stay. Supper's about ready. We were just walking as far as the governor's house with Mr. Bishop." She was a short plump girl with freckles, not unattractive but so much like her father that one saw all of his unpleasant characteristics echoed in her. They both had blunt noses and bodies that were too sturdy and skins that always turned red in the sun and never tanned. Maury waited for her to squeal and simper when she saw him. She did. "Oh, Mr. St. John! What a surprise! You've been ignoring us poor Saints ever since Christmas!"

"Your servant," he said, bowing and taking her proffered hand. "I pray you can forgive me. If only I had a little less business in New Orleans, I'd spend a lot more time in St. Joseph."

"New Orleans?" Bishop drawled pointedly. "Wouldn't it be a little more correct, mebbe, if you said Cuba?"

There was a moment of silence. Then Patty giggled nervously and Maury looked over his shoulder at Bishop. "I said New Orleans, Hugh. If you're getting a bit weak in geography, among other things, I'll be glad to give you a lesson." Then he bowed to Catherine and felt a sudden tingling go through him as he took her warm firm hand. She was stunning in a simple white cotton dress, and he was seethingly aware that the blunt-featured Bishop could not take his eyes from her.

Then he found himself receiving a cool handshake from Saxon while he listened to Aaron's perfunctory thanks for the courtesy of his rooms. Presently Hugh Bishop, who was expected at a meeting, gave his apologies and left.

They watched Bishop stride purposefully away. Saxon, a square ponderous man with little purple veins mottling his red face, said approvingly, "You got to hand it to that feller. He sure is a comer."

"He seems . . . er . . . quite substantial," remarked Aaron.

"He's that, sir. Made a lot o' money for himself. An' right good family, too. He'll be taking Call's place as governor before long."

"If his pistol hand doesn't fail," Rodman Carey put in dryly.

Saxon bristled. "Now look, Rod. I know Hugh's had a few duels, an' there's been some talk. Personally I don't approve o' duelin'. But there are times when a feller has to fight. If he don't he's no gentleman. Hugh's becoming pretty important in the Territory, an' there's a dirty crowd tryin' to stop 'im. But they won't. Nosirree! He's too good a man for 'em."

Maury glanced at Carey and caught the other's droll look. Most of Bishop's duels, apparently, were calculated affairs by which he managed to shame or eliminate opposition. "Politics," said Carey, and wrinkled his sharp nose. "Sit down, folks, and enjoy the view. You see, Aaron, Why I insisted that you have a big veranda on your house? Over at Clifford's place you can't see a thing. But look at that!"

This was a famous view in a region already renowned for

its miracles of evening color. The sun, framed by Carey's towering pines, was now dying in a stupendous agony beyond four miles of ultramarine. Saxon watched it a moment, unmoved, and then said, "Gad, there goes that fool Ledbetter again! You hear 'im?"

From somewhere over on the edge of town, haunting in the evening stillness, the voice of the gaunt savant of St. Joseph was beginning to throb again after a ten-day silence. Distance made the words indistinguishable, but seemed to increase their quality of dread.

Catherine clenched her hands. "It's sort of terrible and fascinating," she said to Maury. "I've never heard anything quite like it."

"You should see him," he told her. "He looks like something out of the Old Testament—Joshua perhaps."

"Aw, she wouldn't want to see him," said Patty. "He's crazy. He's just a horrible old crazy man."

Saxon grumbled, "I thought we'd be rid o' the feller when the storm tore up his tent. Confound 'im, he's a nuisance! Every nigger in town'll be sneakin' out there tonight to moan an' carry on, an' tomorrow they won't be worth killin'. I'm goin' to run that rascal out o' town if it's the last thing I do!"

"You have to fight fire with fire," Carey told him slyly. "What you should do, Clifford, is start a movement for a church."

"Do you mean to tell me," Aaron rasped almost in horror, "that there isn't a proper church in St. Joseph?"

"Oh, there's a tiny Catholic one, with Father O'Leary officiating."

They were interrupted by the ringing of a dinner bell over at the Saxon place.

"Supper's ready," said Saxon. "Guess we'll have to get back."

Carey offered his arm to Patty and they straggled slowly out to the shell walk, Aaron and Clifford in the lead and Carey moving stiffly behind, using his cane and sliding his feet along carefully like a wooden man but chattering gaily and offering to race the giggling Patty to her gate.

"Poor Uncle Rod," said Catherine softly. "Do you suppose he'll ever get any better?"

"Not a chance," Maury told her. "He's up and down with the weather, getting a little worse every year. But he won't let it interfere with getting around. When he's unable even to make it to his carriage he makes that big nigger Jube carry him. But he's unusually well this evening. You seem to have a good effect upon him."

They dropped gradually behind the others. Finally, with a sidelong glance, Catherine said archly, "Why don't you pay more attention to Patty? She seems rather silly about you."

"She's silly about Bishop. He's been courting her for months. I wouldn't dream of offending him by making too big a fuss over her."

"No? Didn't I hear you offer to give him a lesson in geography a while ago? Just how did you mean that?"

"Hugh can interpret it any way he likes." He shrugged. "After all, I was born in New Orleans, and I do have occasional business there."

She smiled. "But you also have occasional business in Cuba."

"Maybe."

"Of course you do. I've heard a little about you." She glanced at him mischievously, then smiled again and said seriously, "Why don't you tell me more about yourself? I . . . I don't feel the way Father does about what you do. I'm really very much interested. For one thing, I can't understand why you would bring slaves to a place like this. Wouldn't it be safer and a lot less troublesome to land them on the Atlantic Coast— or maybe somewhere down on the Florida Peninsula? It seems such a long trip all the way across the Gulf from Cuba to West Florida."

"It isn't the distance," he told her. "But the Atlantic Coast is more exposed, and the nearest market is St. Augustine—and that's hundreds of miles from the new plantation lands where Negroes are needed. All the new plantations are straight up the river from here. When they want field hands it's much quicker and easier to come down here and buy them. As for landing them down on the Peninsula . . . well, there's nothing there. Just wilderness. Even our dear Mr. Bishop has to come here for his Negroes."

"H'm. I take it you don't approve of Mr. Bishop."

"Do you?"

"I'm beginning to find him very interesting."

He became grimly silent.

"But only for his reputation. I should like to see him in a duel."

"You're a bloodthirsty wench," he muttered.

"Oh, I'm quite aware of it," she agreed amicably. "And you are a heathen and a worshiper of idols. Do you give burned offerings to that fearful little stone monster in your place?"

"No, but I should. He is a wise counselor. How goes the moving?"

She sighed. "We've everything off the ship, including Tawny, but the house is a mess. It's hardly habitable. The Saxons want us to stay with them till everything is straightened out, but . . . well, I'm moving in tomorrow anyway."

He grinned and caught her eye knowingly.

"I'm shameless," she added, lowering her voice, "but I can't stand them a day longer. They're so stuffy and dull. I shouldn't talk that way, of course, because they *are* being so kind about everything—especially the servants. I had no idea . . ."

"Servants?"

"I mean, you just can't hire them down here. You either have to buy them or rent them—and you know how Father is. The Saxons lent us three of their Negroes, and Cousin Etta's been keeping them busy. But I intend to have some of my own. At least a maid—even if I have to buy her with my own money."

He chuckled. "And you a Yankee!"

"Oh, bother! My mother was a Creole—and I'm not living in Salem now."

He looked at her sharply in the twilight. "So you're part Creole! I should have known. Well, if you'll allow me, maybe I can help out in this servant matter."

"That's nice of you, but I'd rather you didn't—at least not right away. I told Uncle Rod the same thing. I know how to handle Father, and it's one of those problems I'll have to settle in my own way."

"Anyway, if you're moving in tomorrow, you could use a few extra hands. You won't object if I come around in the morning with my nigger?"

"You might risk it," she answered, smiling.

"And later, at the proper time, would you accept a Creole's gift to a Creole?"

"What would that be?"

"Say you'll accept it, and you'll find out."

She laughed softly. "Very well. I'll accept it—at the proper time."

He walked thoughtfully back with Carey and found their supper waiting. Carey, full of local gossip, entertained him gaily through most of the meal, but finally in a more serious tone remarked, "You were rather reckless with Bishop."

"He was reckless with me."

"But really, m'lad, that's dangerous ground. I'd hate to see you——"

"He doesn't want trouble with me. Nothing to gain by it."

"That depends on how he looks at it. Unfortunately he's the best shot in the Territory."

"You mean he's been very lucky. But luck's an inconstant wench. Actually I've nothing against the man except his confounded arrogance and the fact that he tries to be so damn traditional when he has no real traditions of his own to back him up. And he has nothing against me except that he can't forgive me for winning a few dollars off him at cards. I don't know why Call puts up with the bastard—though I suppose a governor can't always choose his supporters. I'm surprised, frankly, to see that ass Saxon making such a fuss over him."

"There's more to that than you realize."

"Yeah?"

"For one thing Patty has rather lost her head over him. And of course it would suit Clifford to have a son-in-law in the governor's seat or in Washington. But more than that, there's the railroad."

"What's that got to do with it?"

In Carey's sly smile and beady eyes there was the look of a hen about to lay an egg. "You've heard, no doubt, that we may extend the railroad again?"

"Oh, I've heard some whispers, but I know it's all nonsense."

"It's quite true."

"Eh? What's this? Are you crazy?" Maury stared across the table. "Why, it's already been extended as far as it will go. Twenty-eight miles long, and one of the seven wonders of the world—or so they tell me. Maybe it is at that. Twenty-odd miles of trestle through the swamp. At least it's a national curiosity—and it would be quite long enough if it were on dry land. Where could you possibly extend it any farther? And why?"

"We're going to swing it north," said Carey softly. "To a little place called Atlanta."

Maury frowned. "I've heard of it. Where is it?"

" 'Way up in Georgia."

"Huh? *Georgia!*" Maury gazed at Carey in amazement.

"Surprised? But we're not ready to announce it yet, so keep it to yourself. Now this Atlanta is right in the heart of the new cotton country. The place is beginning to grow already. Do you see what a railroad there would do? It would open up all the lower South, especially if we have branch tracks running east and west. Planters wouldn't have to haul their cotton a hundred miles or so to a river and risk losing part of it to thieves and all the hazards of river travel. It would put an end to all that. Aye, it will be the death of river traffic. And poor Sodom at the river's mouth? Alas, I fear it will be the death of that too. But St. Joseph?"

Suddenly Carey thrust his plate aside and leaned forward, his eyes glittering with more excitement than Maury had ever seen in them. "My God, man, do you see what will happen here? Why, all the cotton in the world will come down to us! This place will expand like nothing on earth! We'll be bigger than New Orleans before you know it!"

It was all Carey's idea, Maury saw. This childless, crippled, whimsical Voltaire who cared nothing for power or wealth or the other things that men strove for, lived only for his brain children—or because of them. Otherwise, Maury realized suddenly, he might have given up the ghost long ago. But each new scheme was an elixir that gave him new life. Carey had conceived St. Joseph, as well as the amazing railroad that ran high on stilts through the swamp; and from his mind had sprung the great pier stretching far over the bay, probably the largest pier in existence. And Carey had had more than a finger in the St. Joseph Convention that had united the Floridas into an entity which was soon to be admitted as a state. Carey dreamed, planned and fired others—and then withdrew. He was no businessman. He was a playwright who created drama that he might watch for his own amusement.

And now here was Carey with a great new drama whose potentialities quite dimmed all the others. This vast extension of the railroad would affect not only St. Joseph, but nearly all of the South.

"But how would it be built? Who would pay for it?"

"Clifford Saxon," said Carey, "may be an ass in some respects, but he's a clever businessman. He's putting a stack of money into this. So is Crom Davies. So is Aaron, the old codfish. By the way, do you own any stock in the present railroad?"

"I've got a few shares, Rod. But I've always thought they were worthless—the stuff has never paid me a copper."

"Of course not. The thing was never intended to earn money as a railroad. It was built for the shippers—its sole purpose being to get the cotton in here. Anyway, Crom's bank will try to buy your shares shortly—they're trying to buy up all the old stock. But you'd better hang on to what you've got. It'll be worth a lot of money soon."

"H'm! Wish I had more of it." He sat back and considered Carey. "Come on, Rod: there's more behind this than you've told me. It's going to take a million or more—maybe several million—to build such a long railroad. And neither Saxon nor Davies is going to toss a lot of cash into it unless he sees a way to line his pockets at the same time."

"Certainly not. They're not altruists. The cash we're raising now is just a working pool. We'll buy up all the old stock we can—before anyone realizes what's happened—and then issue new stock for it. About fifty shares of the new for one of the old. The rest of the money will be used to get things started and make a showing. Then, when we're all ready, we'll offer stock to the public. For every share that's sold, we'll give ourselves a share. There are more details, but that's Clifford's business. The main thing is that the public will pay for the railroad—not us. We'll get our money back very quickly. With interest."

"My sacred stars! I wish I could get in on the thing."

"Well," said Carey, "if you're that interested in a bit of lucre, I suppose you could—though it would have to be in my name, for this is strictly a company affair. Frankly I find all this financial legerdemain a little boring, but if it takes that to make the world more interesting, then so be it. Anyway, to get the thing going, I'm putting up twenty thousand myself. I could easily say I'm putting up a few more thousand. How much do you want to toss into the pot?"

"Er . . . how about five thousand?"

"Good enough."

"How soon do you want it?"

"Immediately. The iron's in the fire."

Maury wrote out a check. For a moment before he signed his name he had the familiar and uncomfortable feeling of again straying from the course of reason, then he shrugged and plunged.

Carey watched him with mischief in his eyes. "And now, m'lad," he said, "to return to our friend Bishop . . ."

"Eh? I'd forgotten all about the bastard."

"Oh, but we mustn't forget him. I trust that you'll not offend him too deeply so that he'll feel constrained to call you out on the field of honor—because he's in the thing too. And we'll need him. He may be a bastard, but he's getting us a right of way up through Georgia, and government support in the bargain."

Chapter Nine

HE ENTIRELY forgot about Slatter. Catherine so occupied him that it was Tuesday before he even remembered the man and realized how the days were flying, and it was Wednesday afternoon before he could force himself away and ride out to see him.

Jug Slatter's place lay out beyond the race track behind St. Joseph, on the continuation of the coastal road that here turned inland toward Marianna. It was a collection of unpainted wooden structures set back in the pines and surrounded by a high stockade of peeled cypress saplings, all of which gave it the appearance of a fort. The more imposing building in front, in which Slatter lived in a sort of lackadaisical mixture of squalor and splendor, formed a corner of the stockade and was graced by a sprawling veranda with columns of palmetto logs. Over the door, the only entrance to the place save a large locked gate facing the road, was a sign reading SLATTER'S EMPORIUM. Jug, however, was denied the dignity of the latter word and his establishment was known to everyone as Slatter's jail. The large barnlike building in the rear, pierced with rows of little barred windows, could house, if necessary, as many as two hundred blacks: usually work gangs for rent or field hands awaiting sale to the new plantations up in the clay country inland. The valuable slaves—the trained house servants, occasional "fancy girls" and Jug's three concubines—were quartered in a long wing leading back from the front building. The greater portion of the front building was given over to a gaudily furnished auction room where extravagant mahogany and crystal clashed with pine and cheap straw matting. Though isolated, a great deal of money changed hands at Slatter's place, for the auction room was the only spot within a hundred miles where transactions of all sorts could be carried on privately.

It was siesta hour when Maury arrived and there was no sign of life save three small, naked pickaninnies staring frog-eyed at him through the palings of the stockade. He tossed them a few half-cent pieces and watched grinning while they scrambled shrieking for them in the sand; then he strode across the veranda and tapped lightly on the door. When he heard no response, he opened the door and went quietly inside.

Slatter, looking like a reclining Buddha, lay asleep on the couch in the corner of the auction room. He was a huge, sloppy man with many chins, fiery-faced and as bald as an egg. Deelie, his favorite, a plump mulatto woman, dozed in a chair beside him with a fly sweep in her hand.

Maury laughed, and Deelie awoke suddenly, blinking.

"Lawsy!" She sat up, shook her head, then smiled and turned and tickled Jug on the summit of his great pink belly where it showed above his unbuttoned shirt. "Wake up, honey, you ole lazybones. Hyar Cap'n Maury come ter see yuh!"

Slatter swore, but rolled his head like a turtle and cocked an eye open. He was instantly wide-awake.

"Such felicity," said Maury. "Run along, Deelie, and get the old goat a drink so we can talk business."

Deelie left and Slatter swung to his feet with an effusive show of hospitality. Deelie returned with glasses and a stone bottle containing whisky. She filled the glasses, set the bottle on the

table by the couch and retired. Maury made only a pretense
of drinking, but Slatter tossed off half a glass, shuddered, sat
down and finished the rest in a gulp. He lived on whisky and
its only apparent effect on him was to maintain his corpulence
and his fiery glow.

"Br-r-r-r!" he spluttered. "Goddamn stuff. Hate to offer it
to visitors, to a gentleman, Maury. But it's all rotten these
days. All of it. H'm. Well, well! It's good to see you again."

They discussed cotton and the price of field hands, then fell
to commiserating over the losses on the *Salvador*. Finally Slatter said, "I been a-wantin' to see you on a li'l matter. Two-
Jack, he tole you, didn't he?"

"See me?" Maury raised an eyebrow. "Why, no. Had no
idea." It was never wise to give Jug too much of a hand. "I'm
visiting Carey and thought while I was over here . . . By the
way, Two-Jack and I are no longer associated. He was a bit
disappointed over the last trip, so I told him he could do his
crying alone."

"That so? Well, I declare. He come over to see me last
week, but he never tole me nothin'. Never let on a thing. I
knowed somethin' was wrong because he was tryin' to buy himself a new girl."

"I take it he didn't buy."

"He tried to, but I'm holdin' what I got."

"What for?"

"That's why I wanted to see you. But first lemme ask you—
you gonna handle things by yo'self from now on?"

"I don't know, Jug. I might try something else. There are
easier ways of making money."

Slatter peered at him blandly. "Mebbe so. Depends how
much hell a feller has in 'im. Anyway, don't forget me. I'm
right here in bizness, day an' night. I won't go partners—too
risky for a po' man. But I got plenty room here an' mighty
good connections all over. I could do better by you than Two-
Jack ever done."

"I don't doubt that. Very well, if I go out again, it's a deal. Now, what I'm interested in at the moment: Have you a young house girl I can have cheap?"

"Why, sure." Slatter beamed, but he was instantly wary. "I got three, four mighty good girls, only they ain't so cheap. Niggers is goin' up all the time."

"I want a nice young girl, about fourteen."

"There's Miss Jill Hamilton's Lissa—you know 'er. They sent 'er over to me t'other day after the ole lady died. Couldn't do no better'n her."

Maury pretended to consider Lissa, although he had had her in mind ever since learning from Cricket that she had been brought over here to be sold. She was a quiet, well-mannered girl, carefully trained and a perfect maid for any lady.

"Well, I don't know," he said. "She's pretty frail. I wouldn't pay more than two hundred for her."

"Two hundred! Now, Maury, lissen. That girl, she's worth three-fifty if she's worth a York shilling. Done been offered three hundred for 'er already. But I'll git 'er price if I have to sell 'er for a fancy girl. By God, that's an idea. I might put 'er up Friday night. Maury, there's goin' to be a big doin's around here Friday night. That's why I wanted to see you."

"Really?" Maury opened his wallet and began toying with a handful of gold pieces. He counted them leisurely and set the stack upon the table. "There's two hundred in hard money, Jug. That's the equivalent of nearly four hundred in this damn paper stuff that's floating around."

Slatter eyed the stack, fascinated in spite of himself. The local paper issues were probably good enough—but gold was gold. And it was scarce.

"What the hell do you want with Lissa?"

"Gift for a friend."

"Oh." Slatter saw the light, or thought he did. "You gonna plumb spoil that pretty Cuban." He reached over and began fingering the gold, loving it. Then a faraway look came into

his eyes and he leaned back, seeming to have forgotten both
Lissa and the gold.

"Maury, ain't nobody tole you about Friday?"

"No."

"Christ, man, everybody's buzzin' with it. Leastways, everybody that counts."

"Yes?"

"Friday night, Maury, I'm gonna have me an auction. Fancy
girls! Maury, I done bought me up the prettiest batch o' fancy
girls you ever seen! There ain't nothin' like 'em no place, not
e'en N' Awleans. Beautiful, man, jest beautiful! An' all well-
bred an' mannered an' genteel. Nary one over twenty, an' all
light-complected. There's a couple you'd swear was pure white.
Yessirree! An' they got accomplishments, Maury. Judy, she
sings pretty as a lark, an' dances; an' Phoebe——"

At these typical extravagances Maury suddenly broke into
a chuckle, and Slatter stopped, looking hurt.

"Lissen, Maury, I ain't foolin'. Wait'll you see them gals."

"I'm not in the market. Except possibly for Lissa."

"We'll come to Lissa in a minute. Lemme tell you about
them gals. They're extra special. I already been offered ten
thousand for the five, an' no questions asked. That feller Gad-
dis from Tallahassee. But, hell, I could git more'n that in Mobile. Only, there's plenty money here. Plenty money."

"And you're going to auction them off Friday night?"

"It's all set. I done passed the word around. It's goin' to be
mighty private—jest the right gentlemen comin'. A few dealers
from up the country, some o' the big planters an' all our local
sportin' gentlemen."

Maury shook his head. "It doesn't sound right."

"How d'ya mean?"

"Oh, you just don't do things that way, Jug. That is, if these
girls are all that you say they are. If they are really nice fancy
girls with background, you just can't sell 'em off the block like
common blacks. Good Lord, man——"

"Sure, sure, I know what you mean. Most times when a man wants him a fancy girl, a prime first-rate one, he goes to a dealer, private, an' he's took to a li'l sittin' room full o' soft cushions an' stuff, an' there's the girl all dressed to fashion an' lookin' demurelike an' mebbe doin' some needle point or playin' the dulcimer. High-toned. Sure, sure. I know all about it. But this ain't Chawlston or N' Awleans."

Slatter fished a ten-inch stogie from a box under the couch, lighted it and filled his lungs, then laid the stogie aside while he fortified himself with another drink. Finally he clamped the stogie in his mouth, crossed his fat hands on his great belly and leaned back against the wall, his little porcine eyes twinkling with cunning between their folds of flesh.

"This town's different, Maury. This here's a speculation town. On the surface it's growed up, an' folks is already tryin' to act like they was born here. But underneath it's sporty new an' rip-rarin'. Takes time to make a town—same as a family. Aside from the gamblin', near every dollar that's turned here is turned on the auction block. Cotton, ships, timber, salt mullet or niggers—it's all the same. You live or die by the auction block."

He rolled the stogie pleasurably across his mouth. "Now I done had a li'l private showin'—by special invitation to a few top gentlemen like Mister Munn an' Mister Rankin an' Mister Montague an' such. Jest somethin' to whet 'em up, see? But all mighty genteel an' proper. Only I wouldn't quote no prices or take no bids. On this here deal I'm goin' a step farther."

He leaned forward, flourishing the stogie. "Maury, Friday night, come nine o'clock, I'm gonna have the goddamnedest fancy-girl auction you ever seen! I'm a-goin' to have all them fine gentlemen a-frothin' in their seats, a-fightin' each other to hand out the money. It's gonna be somethin'! You watch!"

Maury smiled. "I guess it will be quite a show."

Slatter scooped up the stack of gold pieces. "Do a li'l job for me, mister, an' Lissa's yourn."

"How do you mean?"

"Well, y'see, Maury, operatin' a place like this, I gotta be careful. Supposin' a gentleman like Mister Montague, he buys him one o' my wenches, an' in due time he ups an' finds he's got the French disease or somethin' else he don't like. See what I mean? Some o' them gentlemen could plumb ruin me. So I gotta guarantee 'em. Absolute guarantee. An' they gotta be healthy in every other way, too. You know that."

"Didn't you buy 'em with a guarantee in the first place?"

"Oh, their records is all clear—but you can't put no faith in some doctors. They'll sign anything. Specially them Spanish fellers."

"Eh? You don't mean to tell me these girls are all *imported*!"

Slatter smiled. "Sure. That's it."

"You're taking a hell of a chance. It doesn't matter with field hands—they're badly needed. And since they're black, nobody cares. But fancy girls . . ."

"Haw! The law ain't gonna bother as long as the gentlemen are satisfied. You kin do anything down here."

"I hope you're right about it."

"Sure I'm right. Only, I gotta be careful. See? That's where you come in. As for the rest of it, I ain't worried. The gentlemen don't care if they're imported—that's an added sellin' point. They want somethin' different. An', man, these are plenty different! They're all mixed bloods, an' they know English. They got faces like angels, but they'd tease the bark off'n a log. O' course they ain't at their best right now—I ain't got 'em prettied up, an' there's a couple sort of ailin'."

"I don't like it, Jug. Dammit——"

"Aw, come on. 'Tain't no skin off'n your nose. You want Lissa, don't you?"

"Oh, I'll have a look at your girls—but I won't go on record as the attending physician."

"For a blackbirder," said Slatter, "you got some funny ideas." He rubbed the gold pieces sensuously between his fat palms, then reluctantly slid them into a pocket. "I'll fix you up a bill o' sale for Lissa. Where d'you want me to send 'er?"

"Dress her up neat as a pin, tie a big blue ribbon around her waist and pack her off to the Delafields'. To Miss Catherine, compliments of Mr. St. John."

"H'm. So the wind's changed. Well, let's git upstairs."

Slatter waddled to the door behind the raised dais at the end of the room, unlocked it and locked it behind them when they were in the narrow hall on the other side. Maury followed him up the dark stairway to a small but gaily furnished parlor over-looking the compound. With its spinet, wide couch, bright carpet and mantelpiece with carved gilt mirror above, it was the most comfortable room in the establishment and Jug ob-viously had had it furnished under capable direction as a back-ground for his better merchandise.

Slatter disappeared. Maury waited, disinterested, all too well acquainted with the other's weakness for buying damaged wares, very cheaply of course, and then doing a little refurbish-ing and selling them for prime goods.

Slatter returned presently with a tall octoroon, bold-eyed and hipped like a houri. She wore only a red silk shawl. "See, Maury," said the old Buddha, grinning. "I know how to pick 'em, boy! This is Lupe. Lupe, gal, this is the good doctor man —an' don't make eyes at 'im. He's not here to buy you. Save it for Mr. Munn."

"*Si, amo.*" The octoroon stared at Maury with avid inter-est.

Jug said, "Goddamit, girl, where's yo' manners? An' speak English!"

She made a sullen curtsy. "*Si*—yes-s, mahster-r."

Slatter said, going out, "Call me when you want the next one." And he added slyly, "But don't take no liberties with my li'l virgins."

"This one," Maury growled, "has long forgotten that idyllic state."

He was mildly disgusted. "Take off that shawl," he ordered. "Now turn around. Very well. Now lie down over there."

"*Que quiere usted?*" she giggled. "*Que busca usted?*"

"Lesions," he growled. "That's what I'm looking for. What in the hell did you think, you devil's kitty?"

He gave her only a cursory examination and then motioned toward the door. "*Levantese—salga!* Get out!"

She snatched up her shawl and scampered out.

Slatter thrust his head through the door, smirking. "How'd you like 'er, huh? You sure didn't spend much time with 'er."

"Didn't have to. You'd better not sell her around here."

"Eh? Why not?"

"She's diseased."

"Fer Christ's sake!"

"And don't ask me to treat her. Let Doc Ormond do it. Fancy girls, hell! You'll find a dozen like her over at Josie Bangs's place."

"Aw, now, lissen, Maury—she *looked* all right, you gotta admit that. How was I to know?" Jug stood scratching his belly while he muttered obscenities. He looked like a disappointed pig.

"Well, bring on the rest—but don't sell Lupe around here. Not even to Josie. She'll raise bloody hell."

The next two girls rather vindicated Slatter. They were three-quarters white and had obviously been raised as fancy girls from birth, for they were quiet and mannered. In their eyes he could see that faintly sad look of wisdom which was beginning to replace innocence. Poor things, he thought, they've been sheltered till now and trained in the graces and the arts, all for the purpose of bringing the highest possible price at a private sale. Why does creation—and procreation—have to be so damn unjust?

He felt suddenly depressed and wished he had not come to see Jug today.

Slatter paddled in with the fourth girl, a pale slip of an

eighteen-year-old. She was a pretty thing, although her eyes were red from crying. He noticed her too-full breasts and guessed what was wrong even before he questioned her. Then he was furious.

"Hey, Jug!" he barked. "This kid's had a baby recently. "Where is it?"

"How the hell should I know?" grumbled the Buddha, waddling back. "She didn't have it when I got 'er."

"Where'd you get her?"

"From the same feller who brung the rest—McSwade o' Roatan. He sneaked 'em in with a load o' coffee an' copra while you was away. They're all island wenches from down in the Caribbees."

So that was it. He had forgotten about McSwade. He had a moment's vision of a huge red-bearded man with a roaring whisky-hoarse laugh. McSwade would sell his grandmother if he could get a dollar for her. And the girls—he should have known they were from the islands; they all had lovely bodies and their teeth were perfect.

Slatter, with elaborate compassion, waddled over and plucked the wrapper from the girl's shoulders. "Tsk! Tsk! Who'da thought it? McSwade didn't say nothin' about a brat."

"By heaven, she's had one—and you know it. Not many months ago. She's grieving for it."

The Buddha shrugged. "Mebbe McSwade throwed it away. Who cares? Nobody wants a brat."

"Dammit, she wants it! You can't take a child from its mother!"

Slatter made a dirty noise with his lips. "Who says you can't? I've done it. Near every dealer's done it. What the hell? I can't stay in business an' run a nursery."

Maury started for the door.

"Hey!" Slatter bleated. "We ain't through."

"I'm through."

"Naw you ain't. There's one more."

"I said I'm through."

"Damme, you got the craziest temper I ever seen. Now lissen, Maury, don't go runnin' off like this. Honest, I can't help it about the brat. There's another wench out yonder, an' you gotta see 'er. She's ailin'."

"What's wrong with her?"

"I dunno. She can't talk."

"Well, bring her in."

"Er . . . I'm havin' some trouble with 'er. She won't come in. I don't like to use no whip on my girls, but on this un I reckon——"

"Don't bother. Show me where she is."

Slatter led him down the angle of the hall and pushed open the door at the end. It was a tiny bare room with a spindly table and chair in the center, a pine commode on one side and a cot facing the single barred window. The window was outrageously curtained with the remains of one of Slatter's cheap shawls. The ragged light coming through slanted down in a barred patch on the occupant of the cot.

She was huddled at the head of the cot with her back to the wall, staring at him like a frightened kitten with immense dark tragic eyes. One little smooth ivory hand was at her throat and the other was clutching the edge of the tattered yellow blanket which she had pulled up to hide her body.

At the first sight of her he stiffened in sudden shock, for it was like seeing Adrienne again. It may have been the lighting and the girl's posture, or perhaps it was her eyes. Whatever it was, it sent the years thundering back and he forgot the room and Slatter behind him, and for a moment he was reliving the night at home when he had seen Adrienne last. He was the elder and she had always come to him with her troubles, even as a little girl. But that last time, when she'd needed him most, he hadn't been able to help.

Slatter was saying, "What the hell's the matter?"

He closed his eyes and opened them again. The girl on the

cot had not moved. She still made him think of his sister
Adrienne. Her eyes were larger and darker and her lips were
fuller, and in spite of her fear there was a rebellious defiance in
her that had never been a part of Adrienne. And yet, in indefinable ways, she was exquisitely like Adrienne.

"She's white," he found himself saying.

"She ain't white," the Buddha snapped back instantly. "I
reckon I know color when I buy it."

"She's white," he repeated unreasonably. "You can't put
her on the block." The very thought was an outrage.

"Now lissen here, I didn't ask you to come up to argue about
it. I got a legal bill o' sale for her—made out in the islands,
sure—but I mean there ain't no question about what she is.
She's a girl o' color, bastud o' one o' the planters an' a favorite
yeller wench an' wouldn'ta been sold 'cept'n the old sonofabitch died with the plague, an' McSwade bought 'er. Name's
Zeda, age seventeen—an' don't tell me she's white. You orta
know goddamn well I wouldn't peddle a white girl."

"I don't know what you'd do, sometimes."

"Well, you heard me. You gonna find out what's ailin' her,
or have I got to git it out o' her with a whip?"

Maury had a sudden impulse to kill Jug, to choke the life
out of him and heave his gross body down the stairway, but
he thrust his hands into his pockets and jerked his chin toward
the door. "Don't be a damn fool. Just get the hell out of here
while I talk to her."

Slatter scowled and left, grumbling.

Maury closed the door. He turned and smiled sympathetic-
ally and said, *"No tenga usted miedo,"* and went over and sat
down on the chair, facing the cot.

Some of the fear left her eyes, but as she made no move he
repeated the statement in French and then in English—"Please
don't be afraid." A little ghost of a smile flickered across her
face, and he asked, "Do you understand English?"

Suddenly she nodded, and all the tension went out of her.

"Can you speak at all?" he asked. "What seems to be wrong?"

She shook her head, then touched her throat.

"H'm . . . let me have a look at it."

She submitted gravely to the examination. The result was puzzling, for her throat seemed perfectly normal and there was no mark or bruise on her head or neck. Medical science knew so little of these things. This was one of those cases of loss of speech, but it was not the more common type, for the girl herself was alert and intelligent. He tried questioning her and she answered as best she could with a nod or a shake of her head or with little motions of her hands. As nearly as he could learn, she had lost her voice sometime during the past month— the result of some accident or experience.

He sat looking at her, frowning, thinking vividly of Adrienne and feeling a sudden compassion for this strange lost child who was so much like her. For she was a child; she might be seventeen and she was beginning to have a woman's development, but it was just the budding of the bloom to come. There was something very fresh and piquant and naïve about her that McSwade and Slatter hadn't touched. She had beautiful hands. They were very smooth and straight, and every motion she made with them was amazingly expressive. They were in movement now, as if writing—she was asking for pencil and paper.

It had not even occurred to him that she might be able to write. He fished around in his coat pocket and brought forth a small notebook and a carbon pencil. She seized them eagerly.

For a minute she labored painfully to construct certain letters, then her shoulders drooped and she looked up at him helplessly. In a flash she brightened and her pencil began to move rapidly. He watched her curiously, noticing for the first time her long dark curling lashes and the soft modeling of her eyes and nose. Her face, tilted, was broad across the cheeks, then it narrowed and swept down in a clean line to a very determined little chin. He studied the ridges of her cheekbones and the play of light across her skin. It had an ivory smoothness but there was a glow of gold under it as if the skin were transparent and underlaid with color. Only the Latins—and some of the Guatemalan women—had skin like that. There was good blood in her—Castilian with a trace of Indian. Her hair, very soft and fine, was so deep a shade of brown that it seemed black, and there was such a weight of it that it made all the rest of her seem fragile. Perhaps it was this seeming fragility that reminded him of Adrienne, as well as the expressiveness of her hands.

He looked down at her hands again and was startled to see that she was drawing. She was doing it swiftly, with little short sure lines that spoke more eloquently than any number of words. Picture-writing. She had drawn a boat, a small island sloop; it was lee rail down in a squall and there were five figures in it. In the second sketch the boat had overturned and there were five heads in the water. In the third the boat had vanished and a lone swimming figure remained; night had come, for overhead were stars and a moon.

She glanced up, pointed to the swimming figure and then to herself and went on sketching. It was easy to follow her quick sequence of pictures. There was the morning sun rising, the swimmer still alone. She looked up again and touched her throat; the accident and the night's exposure had done for her voice.

A schooner appeared, hove to, and the pencil showed the lone figure being drawn over the side. Standing in a group apart from the crew were four figures wearing skirts—the four other girls McSwade had brought up from the islands. She ended the series with a recognizable cartoon of McSwade. She stared at this last a moment, then her lips compressed, and in a little fit of fury she jabbed the pencil down upon McSwade's likeness and scratched it out.

The door opened abruptly and Slatter came in. "You gonna spend the rest o' the day lookin' at 'er?" he growled.

Maury stood up. "I've been finding out about her," he said

grimly. "You're not going to put her on the block. McSwade had no right to sell her to you. In fact he had no right to her whatever! Look here—here's how he got her!"

He thrust the notebook at Slatter and began to explain.

For a while afterward Slatter stood squinting at the drawings. Finally he grunted and handed the notebook back. "Goddammit, I can't help it. Mebbe McSwade didn't come by 'er legal. Who knows? It's her word agin' mine. But anyhow it don't make no difference. She's a girl o' color."

"She's white, and that makes a hell of a lot of difference!"

Slatter's face turned a deeper red. "Don't argue with me about color! Christ's sake, it don't take but a drop o' the blood to make a nigger, an' I tell you she's a nigger!"

"Jug, there's not the least trace of anything Negroid in her. There's a trace of Indian—it might be Mayan—but hardly enough of that to call her a mestizo. Whatever it is, it's good ——"

"Indian or nigger, it's all the same an' I ain't gonna split hairs over it. She's a fancy girl an' I got money tied up in 'er an' I ain't a-goin' to lose it."

"You don't even know whether she's a slave! McSwade ——"

"I don't give a damn how McSwade come by 'er. She's a slave now, an' that's that."

"The law will have something to say about whether she's a slave or not! And I'll testify in any court in the land that she's white!"

Slatter's little eyes narrowed. "Now looka here, Maury," he began slowly. "You're all the time havin' fits about something. It don't pay. You ain't a-goin' to testify in no court about nobody. Y'hear me? You start something like that, an' first thing you know there'll be a heap o' skeletons come jumpin' out the closet an' fallin' all over you—an' then where'll you be?"

Maury said nothing. On that point he was unable to argue.

Following Slatter into the hall, he glanced back once and saw the girl sitting as he had seen her first, her hand at her throat, her dark eyes wide and mutely pleading. She might have been Adrienne on the night his father had announced her betrothal to Henri Guidry.

Slatter was saying, "I don't know what the hell's come over you, Maury; but we been pretty good friends an' there ain't no use in us lockin' horns on a fool thing like this. You know I can't jest up an' turn 'er loose. I wish I could sell you the wench, but, goddammit, I can't even do that without causin' trouble. There's a couple important gentlemen tried hard to buy 'er, an' to keep from offendin' either one I swore I'd hold 'er an' put 'er up Friday. I got a heap o' money tied up in 'er. McSwade, he drove a hard bargain, an' I——"

"You don't understand. I don't want to buy her. I couldn't anyway. And even if I could, and did, I wouldn't know what to do with her except make her free—and Lord knows what would happen to her alone, with an affliction like that. It might last indefinitely. She needs help. She——"

"There now, y'see? You been hollerin' about her bein' white an' shouldn't be sold—but you gotta admit she'd be a heap better off with some good gentleman who'll give 'er a li'l house off someplace an' pertect 'er. You think I ain't got feelings, but I have, an' I aim to do the right thing by 'er. There's plenty good gentlemen who'd take fine care o' Zeda an' like 'er for bein' as she is. Feller gits mighty tired o' some bitch that's all the time a-talkin' back. Christ's sake, you ain't got no idea what I gotta put up with here, what with Deelie an' Brownie May an' all them——"

"Oh, for God's sake shut up! I want a drink."

Chapter Ten

ONCE OUTSIDE and riding back with Cricket he tried to tell himself that it did not matter, that he had merely been swayed by an accident of physical resemblance and that he had better forget the whole thing. In the vast and senseless scheme of things was the disposition of one lost girl of any more importance than the lives of forty-five black men who smothered beneath a battened hatch? And after all there was the question of Zeda's whiteness. Sometimes it was impossible to tell about such a thing. In Mobile and New Orleans there were any number of women of color who looked white. Their mothers and grandmothers and great-grandmothers had bred only with white men and there had been no mixture of color for generations—and yet the invisible taint of it was there, a line they could never cross. It was too bad, but
. . .

Besides, what could he do about it? What could he possibly do about it without destroying himself? Except, of course, to buy her—and he could hardly afford to do that. Even if he had the money and did buy her, what then? What could he do with her? Someone would have to look after her. And in his posi-

128

tion he could hardly do it without the story getting out and the way to Catherine being forever barred to him.

No, there was nothing he could do except forget about it.

"But she's white," he told himself aloud. "By God, she's as white as I am!"

"Suh?" said Cricket.

"Nothing," he growled, and realized they were in town now and passing one of the hotels. It was the Byron House. "Stop here," he ordered. "I need a drink."

He went into the taproom and ordered five fingers of rum, tossed down half of it, then stood sipping the rest while he scowled at the sharp bronze image of himself in the mirror. It was a great baroque mirror, a copy of the one in the taproom of the Mansion House. His reflection seemed a little sinister, almost saturnine. He turned away from it.

Of course she was white. He'd known that the moment he looked at her. There was no use trying to deny it to himself. But why had he known it? What was it about her? After all what were the qualities of whiteness?

Spirit? Pride? Intelligence? Some inner purity and beauty? All those perhaps, when applied to Zeda, but when you analyzed them there was not one that held to the laws of man and pigment. Tulita, for instance, became a Negro. And Jug Slatter became something much less than one.

He set his glass down and spat out the ancient epithet that signifies man's disgust for the ways of man.

"Is something troubling you, Mr. St. John?"

He glanced up and saw Hugh Bishop, cool and immaculate in pale blue, regarding him over a whisky a few paces away. It was the first time he had seen Hugh since the evening of his arrival in St. Joseph.

His flecked eyes traveled deliberately over Bishop, and all his inner confusion and sudden loathing for the institutions of his race were turned, at that moment, into a cold anger and hatred for the individual before him.

"I was deliberating, Mr. Bishop, on the qualities that distinguish a white person from a black one. I find that the only possible claim that some men can have for the honor of being called white is the doubtful one of pigmentation."

Hugh stared at him, and then his lips pressed tight against his teeth. "Just what are you driving at, mister?"

"I am stating a profound truth. If you are too dull to follow me you do not have to trouble yourself to listen."

Hugh Bishop set his glass down slowly. "Mr. St. John, I don't like your attitude. I didn't like it the other evening, and I don't like it now."

"Personally, Mr. Bishop, it's a matter of complete indifference to me what you don't like. I don't give a continental."

He watched Hugh pick up his glass, and for a moment he thought he was going to receive the contents of it in his face. If that happened he would have to fight the man. And that, he suddenly found, would be a pleasure. He had been detesting Hugh Bishop a little more with each meeting; it would be a great pleasure to kill him. And, the other's reputation notwithstanding, he knew himself well enough to know that he could do it, and would.

He looked steadily at Hugh Bishop and told him these things with his eyes.

Hugh stood motionless, regarding him, the glass poised in his hand. Then, very slowly, he replaced the glass and without another word turned and walked stiffly out.

The taproom, miraculously, was empty save for the mulatto behind the bar, and he was busy cleaning at the other end, his back turned. There had been no one to notice them. But for this, perhaps, Hugh would have taken the other course. Maury sighed, finished his drink and left. He felt no better. Nothing had been solved. Everything was still the same.

When he arrived back for supper he found Carey full of chatter and apologetic over not inviting guests.

"Truth is, m'lad, that the people I could invite would bore us," Carey explained. "And propriety forbids my having those we would prefer. Now we would both enjoy Kitty—but in order to have her we would have to have Aaron also—and he is insufferable. But that's the way it is. At best life is a compromise between what we want and what we can get. Faith, if you were not here tonight I would undoubtedly be calling on Josie Bangs. Not so much to indulge in an orgy of the flesh, but just for the variety of company. To say the least, the people you meet there are interesting."

Carey stopped for breath, then said, "I perceive you're in a foul mood this evening. Is it a sluggish liver or merely the general state of things?"

"The . . . the general state of things, I guess."

"Man," said Carey, "has been suffering under the general state of things since the day of the first recorded thought. But he comes to learn that there is neither good nor bad and that, in a large sense, nothing ever changes. He lives, is driven to procreation, suffers according to his nature and reluctantly dies. His reluctance to die is a curious thing. Even when life is intolerable, something drives him on and on and on. Perhaps sex is the touchstone of it all. But I'm boring you? Perhaps you'd rather hear about the railroad. It progresses. I spent the day with engineers——"

"To hell with the railroad!"

"Pardon me for digressing. I forget that you are not interested in the onward flow of our civilization. I'll return to sex which, no doubt, is the basis of your present indisposition. Thank God, I'm fifty and have reached the age of reason! But young men—gad, they are bundles of sex, and if it doesn't drive them to an early marriage so that their lives are eventually ruined by boredom, responsibility and adherence to convention, they waste themselves in dueling, fornication and other mad excesses."

Carey, with a shrimp poised halfway to his mouth, suddenly

returned his fork to his plate and leaned back. "But the foregoing hardly applies to you, Maury. I do you an injustice. You waste yourself, but in odd ways. H'm. You know, I've often wondered why anyone of your ability and intelligence should engage in your questionable activities. But now I understand it."

"Yes?"

"You are a romanticist."

"I thought all romanticists were poets."

"Perhaps they are at heart. They must either express or seek. You are driven to seeking, so you follow the sea. Personally I loathe it—except to contemplate it from the safety of my veranda. But for you, no doubt, it has a siren call; you see beauty and witchery in every phase of it—and it's always more interesting on the horizon. Naturally your every instinct rebels at trade, and you have little patience with established law. That's the romanticist. Therefore, in your seeking you are forced to cross the line. And since only a hard-bitten realist can succeed in that sort of thing, you are bound to fail."

"I've already failed. Rather horribly."

"H'm. It's too bad you didn't pick a more appropriate period. Fifty or a hundred years ago you could have been a gentleman pirate, with letters of marque and the esteem of your compatriots. But today . . ." Carey shook his head. "Still, down here, there's a certain aura attached to any venture beyond the law. This is still a freebooter's country, and no one really knows about you. I wonder, though, if you know what you seek."

Maury toyed with his shrimp and remembered suddenly that this was Wednesday.

"But what," Carey asked, "does the romanticist always seek? He seeks romance, of course. And what is romance? It is love, my friend. And what is love? Ah, and now we come to the whole crux of the matter, for we are back again where we began. Love, basically, is sex. Only it is a refinement of it.

Love is a word that man has given for a craving that he does not understand. Man is alone and incomplete and afraid. He seeks completion, fulfillment, escape from his aloneness. He seeks, in a small measure, to become immortal, so that he can leave his aloneness and fear behind him. I know, for I have always been horribly alone."

Carey toyed with his wineglass. "Only twice in my life have I partially escaped from it. Once with a wine merchant's daughter in Rome. I was quite young then and it all seemed highly romantic. We lived happily together for a year—until her husband came home from the wars. The second was purely a platonic relationship in which I worshiped from afar. It was after my return to America." He sighed, and his voice changed subtly. "Lucia was amazingly like Kitty, except that she was frozen. I . . . I never really understood her. She was a Daubigny, formerly a very illustrious family in Mobile. I've never been able to understand why Lucia ever married a man like Aaron."

"You . . . you're speaking of Catherine's mother?"

"Yes. She was a remarkably beautiful woman. Whenever I look at Catherine it's like seeing Lucia alive—I mean like seeing Lucia as she should have been when she was alive. I don't mean to say that Kitty's happy now; in fact I don't believe she's ever been really happy, for no female could be, living with Aaron. And she was always an odd sort of child. But certainly she has plenty, and Aaron dotes on her. Anyway she has a vitality and love of life that Lucia never had. Poor Lucia. I think sometimes she hated life. For years I used to contrive every possible excuse to see her. She fascinated me in a way that is hard to explain. Perhaps I wasn't really in love with her as a woman. Just some quality in her . . ."

"I can understand that. Some women are that way." And he thought: *This is Wednesday night. I have only tomorrow and the next day. Forty-eight hours.*

Carey emptied his wineglass and scowled into it. "Now you

can see what a shock it gave me when I saw Kitty again after so many years. It gives me a warm glow just to look at her— and yet I feel a little lost, as if life had dealt me a scurvy trick. There are moments when I'm actually jealous of you and wish I were twenty years younger. Ah me!" He shook his head and then glanced up pertly. "But you should be the jealous one."

"Eh? How's that?"

"Patty Saxon. Poor silly Patty. Well, you know how she feels about Bishop. Hugh's never committed himself, of course, but in his boots he could do a lot worse than marry a Saxon, and I've been expecting an announcement almost any day. But I doubt if it will come now. Hugh's ignoring her completely."

"You don't have to remind me of it," Maury ground out.

"H'm . . . Well, he's certainly not ignoring Kitty. He sent her imported French bonbons and a music box this afternoon. That's a lot more than he ever gave Patty. Frankly, Maury, I'm afraid the fellow's becoming infatuated. You'd better watch your step."

"The bastard had better watch his own step. And I'm going him one better: I'm sending Catherine a maid."

"Well, now!" Carey grinned. "I say, that's grand. She'll love a maid. Aaron will object, naturally, and Maude Saxon will have a lot of pointed remarks to make about the proprieties —but Kitty'll get around 'em both. Er . . . I take it you were out at Slatter's this afternoon."

"Yes, I was."

"I heard, very confidentially, that the old pig is going to auction a few prize bits of flesh Friday night. Did you by any chance have a look at his wenches?"

"I saw them." Maury stared down at his shrimp, barely touched, and wondered if he should tell Carey the whole thing. But what good would that do? Carey would probably listen with indignation at first and then insist on going out and seeing Zeda. If he took action, almost anything could happen. None of it would be good. On the other hand Carey, on reflection, might take the philosophical view and expound lengthily on the wisdom of not interfering with established evil. One could never tell about Carey the sophisticate.

Suddenly he thrust his chair aside and stood up. "Rod, please excuse me. I've been an awful lout all evening, but there's something on my mind and it has to be taken care of. I . . . I may be gone a couple days."

"I say, old fellow——" Carey got up, peering at him with affectionate concern——"I hope it isn't anything serious. Can I possibly be of any help?"

"Thanks, Rod, but I'm afraid not. I . . . I'll tell you about it later. I have to get back to Apalachicola."

"I hate to see you start out like this. That road isn't safe after dark. There've been several robberies in the past few weeks."

"No one's going to stop me—unless he shoots first. I always carry pistols, and I keep 'em primed."

The ride back was without incident except rain. The first squall struck when they were halfway along the coast, and from there on they ran into intermittent squalls that finally drowned out the lanterns. It was midnight and pouring steadily when they reached the Mansion House.

He got out at the taproom entrance, after telling Cricket to come back when the mare was put away, and went in and had a rum. On the way upstairs he stopped awhile and studied the games in progress. The cotton men had settled down for a long session, playing slowly and betting heavily. It was always like this on a rainy night. Two-Jack was not around.

He went thoughtfully to his rooms and stripped off his damp garments. He laid out dry clothing, hesitated, then pulled on a dressing robe and began pacing the study. It was a good night for cards. He had come back here to play, and particularly to play on familiar territory. But suddenly he was afraid. The Mansion House seemed aloof and unfriendly, and even his rooms had become impersonal.

Only Kul seemed alive. Maury stopped and frowned at him a moment and then turned away, repelled by the idol's look of sardonic amusement in the candlelight.

"Will I win?" he asked and mentally answered his own question.

At cards a man who is afraid never wins.

"But I need money. Unless I play I'll have to sell my stock in the railroad or mortgage my houses."

The banks will not give you gold, St. John.

No, of course not. If it was merely money that he needed, he could undoubtedly raise it on his word alone; but of course it would be in notes issued by the Territorial banks. Hard money was something else. And it was gold he ought to have.

He went over to the great ebony bed and peered up at the canopy. Cemented in the hollowed top of each huge post were thirty doubloons, totaling about a thousand dollars in gold. They had been in the bed when he found it—put there, he had always supposed, for good luck—and for the sake of luck he had let them remain.

A hundred and twenty pieces of Spanish gold. They would go a long way, but he would have to have more than that. Much more.

There was a light tapping on the hall door, and then Cricket came in and stood fumbling with his dripping oilskins.

"Us gwine up the river, Marse Maury?"

"Yes, I guess so. I guess I'll have to."

The Negro's eyes went to the window and he listened a moment to the wild turbulence outside, then his glance went hopefully to the study couch. On occasion he had been allowed to sleep here when they were going to Whisky George. It saved time and trouble when they had to rise in the small hours to catch the packet.

Maury said, "Get your blanket out of the closet and turn in. And for God's sake don't let me oversleep!"

It was still raining when they got up four hours later, and the wind was gusty out of the southeast. They dressed and sloshed wearily down to the landing, unlocked the boat shed where the bateau was stored and started to drag the bateau out and load it on the packet. Then Maury realized the landing was deserted and the packet nearly dark.

He took the lantern from Cricket and went up the gangplank. In the saloon he found the second mate and the assistant engineer idling out the watch over a checkerboard and bottle.

"No, we ain't sailin' this mornin'," the second mate answered to his question. "Caught a sonofabitchin' deadhead in the wheel an' busted three blades. Can't fix it till the wind hauls. Ye hear that sea runnin'?"

A heavy swell was rolling in from the bay and smashing against the stern. With every blow the vessel groaned and the paneling in the saloon creaked furiously. Maury cursed and went slowly ashore.

Why did things have to be this way? Was some damnable force trying to prevent him from doing what he intended to do?

"But it won't stop me," he muttered. "I'm going, by God! . . ."

In the lee of the boat shed he looked down at the bateau, then out at the wildness of the graying harbor. He heard Cricket say, "Marse Maury, us can't make it. You know us can't make it. Not today."

They could never do it in a bateau, certainly. At least not from here. Only a larger craft could get them across the harbor and upstream to quiet water. But anything larger than a bateau would be useless in the swamps.

"We can try it from Beadie's landing," he said. "But we'll have to hurry."

They went back to the hotel and into the kitchen and ate a quick breakfast standing while a lunch was being packed; then they went on to the livery stable and routed out the sleepy hostler. It was daylight when they drove forth on the St. Joseph Road.

A mile out of town they turned north on a wagon track that ended, eventually, on a wide bayou some distance west of the main river. Here a space had been cleared out of the tangle for a small cabin and shed and a rough stockade built around it to keep out bears. Cordwood for the occasional river boats using the bayou was stacked between the trees along the bank.

Maury opened the stockade gate and went up and pounded on the cabin door. A sleepy drunken voiced cursed him dispassionately but, finally roused, granted the use of the shed and one of the boats. Cricket unhitched the mare and put her in the shed, then helped clean out the only serviceable bateau, which, it soon developed, leaked badly. It was still raining steadily when they set out down the bayou.

They were on the water route that stretched, behind them, as far as Josie Bangs's place at the back door of St. Joseph. Ahead, Whisky George was no more distant than it had been from town, and they had the advantage of quiet water—but much time had been lost, and the swift river current would be against them part of the way. It was problematical whether they would enjoy Bruin's hospitality tonight or spend it in the darkness of this unfinished world, lost somewhere in the tangles.

They alternately bailed and paddled, flipping out the water with quick movements of their paddle blades, then driving in deep with long slow thrusts, going steadily through the morning and well into the afternoon. Tiring, they stopped and divided their sodden lunch and rested a few minutes while they ate. The rain dripped unceasingly through the swamp's dark vaulted roof. They went on. The Negro began chanting in a low weary monotone. A chant of words without meaning that yet evoked meaning in the consciousness and stirred it with the ancient awes and fears of man in his littleness with Nature. This might have been the Congo.

Darkness tagged them and crept around them in the shadows. And finally its black hand closed upon them like a solid thing.

They stopped paddling, beaten.

Then clearly, not far away, they heard the baying of one of Bruin's hounds.

It was only now that Maury felt the sudden clutch of doubt. What insane and unreasoning hope had ever possessed him to come here? This whole trip was folly, a waste of time. He could see the cold unwinking eye of Mace fixed on him with its saurian stare—unhuman, impersonal and as uncaring as the river. Where lived the man who had ever presumed to ask such a favor of Mace Bruin as he had come here to ask?

The hound announced their approach as they slid up to the landing, and a voice challenged them in the darkness. Finally a lantern glowed on the high veranda and Bruin drawled, "Send yo' nigger out back an' come on up. You et yet?"

The doubt lessened in the familiarity of Bruin's presence and the warmth of his food. And the eye no longer seemed so malevolent or even cold or questioning. It struck Maury all at once that Bruin, in spite of his self-sufficiency, was in some respects a lonely man and genuinely glad to see him.

So, at last, the words came easily to his tongue. "Mace, I need help. I want to borrow five thousand dollars—in gold."

Chapter Eleven

THE GARISH ormolu clock in the stair well of the Mansion House showed a few minutes of five. Maury noted it wearily as he entered. There was plenty of time, providing he wasted none of it. He craved a drink, but that would have to wait. Supper would also have to wait. He was not hungry anyway. Only tired. Tired to his soul.

He climbed stiffly to his rooms and shed his grimy clothing, shaved, permitted himself the luxury of five minutes in a tepid bath and finally pulled on fresh linen and broadcloth. He felt better now and more able to face the world. He found his watch, wound it and set it by the study clock, then took his knife and pistols from his soiled trousers. He frowned a moment at the firearms, knowing that the charges must be damp and that he ought to reload. But that could be done later. He thrust the pistols into his belt and instantly forgot them when he noticed, for the first time, the notes that had been pushed under the door in his absence.

One note was from the hotel. It politely requested payment. The other, terse and demanding, was from Two-Jack. Swearing softly, he crumpled both notes into the wastebasket and glanced again at the clock. The hands seemed to have jumped forward by many minutes. Alarmed, he fumbled hurriedly through the liquor cabinet and found a silver flask, which he slipped into his coat pocket, and caught up the small, heavy deerskin bag which he had placed on the study table. As he went out he almost forgot, in his weariness, to lock the door behind him.

Outside in the waiting chaise he shook the somnolent Cricket awake. "We've got just three hours," he said. "Keep the mare stepping if it kills her."

He sank back with a sigh and took a long pull from the flask, savoring the heavy rum and gradually relaxing as he felt its revitalizing warmth spread through him. He closed his eyes and thought of Mace Bruin.

Mace, he suddenly realized, had taken the request almost as a compliment. Only one question had been asked. "Ye aimin' to settle up debts with it? Two-Jack's, mebbe?"

"No, I'll pay the bastard when I'm ready—and it won't be in hard money. This is for something more important than debts. I'll not need it for long. A few weeks, maybe. I've quite a bit coming in. The only trouble will be to pay you back in gold, but I'll do it somehow."

"H'm."

Bruin had fingered his mandarin's beard a moment and got up to light another taper. "Wait here fer a spell."

He had waited a long time, wondering if the old man was really as rich as rumor held him to be and mildly curious about the hiding place of his money. One thing was certain: A great deal of gold had come to Bruin's hands, and very little of it had ever passed out.

After what may have been an hour Bruin had come back in through the storehouse door and silently handed him the deerskin bag that now lay on the seat beside him. Repaying Mace would have its difficulties, but he ought to be able to manage it from the proceeds of the railroad venture. Beyond that point his mind refused to probe.

He reached for his watch and felt the bulge of one of the pistols in his belt. He took out both, removed the cap from one and after considerable trouble managed to free the ball and tap out the charge. It was damp as he had suspected. He pulled his kit from under the seat and took from it a flat box containing a powder flask, patching and extra caps and balls. He carefully cleaned and reloaded both weapons and thrust them back into his belt. Finally he had another drink, then gave the rest of the rum to Cricket.

The rain had stopped hours ago, but every low place was a pond and the evening vibrated with myriads of frog voices, peeping, shrieking, jingling, croaking, rattling like castanets; great frogs and little frogs, a dozen different kinds of frogs, their orgiastic voices swinging in a wild free orchestration, flinging their spring madness upon the quaking air like insane little elves.

He fell asleep at last to the mad rhythm of them, and when he awoke it was night, the moon was out and they were entering St. Joseph.

The Emporium loomed gray and secretive in the pines, and only a vague yellow escape of candle glow issued from its heavily shuttered front windows. A half-dozen saddle horses lined the hitching rail in front, most of them easily identifiable in the moonlight as belonging to certain of the younger local men of means. Maury got out, and the Negro drove on round the corner of the stockade to an open spot discreetly hidden from the road that was filled with gigs and carriages.

The weight of the bag made it feel conspicuously large in his hand. As he crossed the veranda he shifted it to his coat pocket, but it made his coat sag uncomfortably, so he rolled it into a tight ball and held it close against his side. He tried the door impatiently, then rapped sharply and stood listening to the low indistinct murmur of voices coming through the windows. He was late.

Then the door was unlocked and Deelie was hurriedly urging him inside, then locking the door after him.

"We's jes' startin'," she said and opened the farther door for him.

He stepped into the rear of the crowded auction room and stood there a moment unnoticed while he looked around. Finally he slid into one of the empty chairs in the last row.

The place was close and reeked of tobacco smoke and Slatter's cheap whisky. A few candles sputtered in pewter sconces along the walls. The main illumination came from the large French candelabra that glowed richly on either side of the dais at the front of the room. Behind the dais hung a huge curtain of dark-red velvet that covered the door to the back hall, and to the right of it was a small pine stand holding a pitcher, a goblet and a gavel. The master of ceremonies was evidently busy behind the curtain, for it trembled and occasionally bulged as a large form pressed against it.

Maury closed his eyes, leaned back in his chair and opened his coat. The closeness and the smells made him a little ill, and his head was beginning to throb. No wonder, he thought: He hadn't eaten since dawn. He rubbed his eyes slowly and then sat up and dismally surveyed the room. He hated being here tonight, and now he found himself loathing the place and the men who filled it. He recognized a few, but there were many strangers. In among the factors and shipping men were a number of florid upcountry planters, a sprinkling of merchants and hotel owners, several gamblers who looked like respectable bankers and two bankers who had the pale and sinister look of gamblers. Deelie moved decorously among them, replenishing whisky glasses from a stone jug. A thin stooped man in the row just in front of him got up and slid back to the empty chair beside him, and he found himself star-

ing at the glistening bald head and bright vulpine face of Rodman Carey.

Carey's grin was that of a small boy anticipating some be-
hind-the-barn wickedness. "A noble gathering of Territorial
stud," he commented and clucked his tongue. "But imagine
seeing you here! You shock me, Maury. What will the Delafields say?"

Maury looked at him wearily, and Carey in quick concern
added, "I say, old fellow, are you all right? You don't seem a
bit well. You had no trouble while you were away?"

"No trouble. I'm just tired to hell."

He was not surprised to find Carey here. Carey never missed
anything that promised good entertainment.

Deelie came over and poured whisky for them. For an instant her decorum vanished. She smiled teasingly at Carey and
whispered, "Marse Rodman, if'n I thought you'd bid me in I
declare I'd have dat ole man o' mine put me on de block tonight. Sho, an' wouldn't you like to have a nice, plump brown
woman?"

"You'd be perfect for me, Deelie. Perfect. Shall I speak to
Jug?"

"Nawsuh, I's changed my mind. You's lecherous. Dat's
what you is. Lecherous. All bald-headed mens is lecherous."
She waddled away, chuckling.

Maury smiled. "You evil old man," he said to Carey.

"It's the country, Maury. It eats into one like a subtle
poison, loosening all moral fibers. We Northerners are particularly susceptible; we are conquered and destroyed before
we know it. Now I came tonight merely to bid and enjoy a
vicarious thrill. But I may buy. Who knows?"

"A hundred dollars says you won't. You never have, and
you never will."

"By my faith, I'll just take you up on that, m'lad. Who can
tell what I may do when I don't know my own mind? Why,
one of Slatter's virgins may be the very medicine I need for my

stupid ills. However, those who will actually buy are easy enough to pick. Just look around. The young bloods, most of them, will run short of cash—but there's Flavy Munn yonder. Another hundred says he'll buy."

"I won't cover you."

"Well, take that hominy-fed gentleman from Marianna—a hundred and fifty says he'll buy."

"I won't cover that one, either."

"What's happened to your sporting blood? We can't agree on everything. Two hundred says the next man I pick will buy. Are you on?"

"Two hundred it is, then. Pick your man."

"Very well. My money's on Two-Jack."

"Eh? Where is he?"

"Across the room, beyond the couch."

Maury followed Carey's eyes and saw Two-Jack sitting alone and immobile, chair tilted against a jutting of the wall, thumbs hooked in his waistcoat. The gambler's eyes were fixed on the dais.

Maury fell silent. His depression increased. He tried to take a swallow of Slatter's whisky and felt his stomach turn against it; he spat it back into the glass and thrust the glass under his chair.

The heavy red curtain behind the dais trembled, a hand lifted the edge of it, and the room was suddenly quiet. Slatter appeared.

The sloppy Buddha had vanished; this was a new Slatter magnificently attired in white, with an elaborate green and yellow waistcoat making a posy garden of his belly. Inwardly beaming, he was trying to be all smooth dignity on the surface, a connoisseur of rare gems which he had consented to exhibit to a select few and place on the block. He spoke unctuously, his voice studiedly soft and confidential. He reminded his audience that the occasion was exceptional, that each enjoyed a singular privilege in being present. To begin with, he said, there would be a short review so that each gentleman could decide on his choice. He gave a slight bow, reached behind the curtain and with the air of a courtier drew forth and presented his first offering, a girl named Judy.

She was one of the octoroons, but Maury did not recognize her at once. Careful grooming and Deelie's skill as a dressmaker had utterly transformed her. She wore a simple pale-blue gown, and her black curly hair had been carefully arranged in a becoming chignon. She stood motionless in the candlelight, eyes modestly downcast, a pliant virginal statue of submissive beauty. Against the deep red of the hanging the effect was startling. There was a quick murmur of whispering, and a charged stillness held the room.

While the spell was still on them, Slatter took her hand and led her off. Waiting only long enough for the sudden murmur of approval to die away, he reappeared and with the same courtly air presented his second offering. This girl, paler and more willowy than the first, wore white. Again there were the charged reaction and a heightened tightness in the room. Slatter was whetting them.

It was clever showmanship. Even Carey was impressed. "I say," he whispered. "The old pig has outdone himself. I was expecting a few cheap hussies, but these are lovely. I've never seen better anywhere. So help me, Maury, I think you'll lose your bet tonight!"

Maury said nothing. He wiped his clammy hands on his handkerchief and sat gripping his chair arms while the third girl was led on and off. Then he stiffened and stared at the fourth— the bold Lupe he had cautioned Slatter about. Jug's cupidity had triumphed: She was being offered anyway.

Her reception left him a little nauseated. You could sell anything as candy if you wrapped it right. And Lupe's voluptuousness had been gowned with an immodest simplicity that starkly brought out every full curve. She was suddenly the touchstone of desire. The tempo of the room changed instantly.

The Marianna man, in a voice hoarse with whisky cried,

"Come on, Slatter, let's git a-goin'! Twelve hundred dollars for the wench!"

Slatter, about to lead her off, turned at this psychological moment and left her standing alone on the dais with her jet eyes glittering with excitement and stepped down and snatched up his gavel. At the same time Flavy Munn said, "Fifteen hundred."

"Fifteen hundred," cried Slatter, and brought his gavel down with a crash on the pine stand. "Fifteen hundred dollahs I'm bid for Lupe! The finest bit o' flesh in the Floridas. Look at her, gentlemen! Look at her! Make it sixteen . . . ah, sixteen it is! Make it seventeen . . . ah, seventeen. Show 'em your ankles, girl! They'll never find the like o' you on Royal Street! Gentlemen, gentlemen, 'tis not a cook ye're bidding for this evening—though the lass can cook, an' sing a bit too! Eighteen hundred . . . nineteen . . . nineteen-fifty . . ."

"Two thousand," said Rodman Carey.

"Two thousand," Slatter echoed. Maury leaned over and whispered once in Carey's ear; Carey frowned and remained silent. But Flavy Munn raised a finger and the bidding went on.

"Twenty-five hundred!" cried the Marianna man a little angrily.

"Twenty-six," said Munn.

"Three thousand, by Christ!"

"Thirty-one hundred."

The bidding crept higher.

"Thirty-five fifty," said Flavy Munn at last, and the Marianna man was silent.

"Going for thirty-five fifty!" cried Slatter. "Going . . . going—— Who'll make it thirty-six? Going . . . going—— Your last chance, gentlemen! Going——" And suddenly he brought his gavel down with a resounding whack that made the goblet dance across the stand. "Sold to the lucky gentleman for thirty-five hundred and fifty dollahs!"

Maury peered across the smoky room to the back of Flavy

Munn's swollen, ulcerous neck, then shrugged and looked away. There seemed to be an odd sort of justice in the sale.

When his eyes sought the dais again, Lupe was gone and Slatter was in front of the curtain calling for names.

"Who'll it be, gentlemen? Name yo' choice!"

"Judy! Put up Judy!"

"Aye, Judy!"

"Phoebe!"

"Zeda!"

Who had called for Zeda? A coldness crept through him.

He watched Slatter go behind the curtain and reappear with the girl Judy who wore the blue gown. She seemed frightened now and lost. She stood in the center of the dais with her hands clasped tightly, her eyes closed as if in prayer. Her look of virginal helplessness, which he realized suddenly was genuine, produced a more powerful reaction in the room than Lupe's flagrant sensuality. The bidding, when it got under way, was eager and high. He shut his eyes and tried to close his mind to it. He wanted to get up and leave, and once in a stirring anger he wanted to rise and curse the room. They were pigs. Damn filthy greedy pigs. Carey was a pig too.

" . . . Thirty-seven hundred! Thirty-eight-fifty! Ah . . . forty-one! Make it forty-two. . . ."

He stirred and peered up at the girl again. Her eyes were open now, and like Lupe's they were glittering with excitement.

He spat and with sour unconcern watched her go to a cotton man for forty-three hundred dollars.

Deelie came by to replenish the whisky glasses. "For God's sake," he growled at her, "I can't drink this rotten stump water. Can't you bring me some rum?"

"De world got you down, Marse Maury?"

"The world," he said acrimoniously, "would smell to heaven if there were any heaven, and we in it would be roasting in hell if there were any hell. I see no hope for any of us, black or white, and no reason in anything."

"Sho, 'n' I didn't ask ter be bawn neither—but I's hyar an' I makes out." She waddled away and returned presently with a goblet of rum which he accepted thankfully.

Another girl was on the dais now and Slatter had shed his coat. He looked at Slatter's red streaming face and then at the girl and wondered if she was the one who had had the baby. Not that it made any difference, really. What was another baby? There were too many babies and the race was not getting any better. And this girl was like the others, frightened at first and now excited. Hell, they all loved it. And why not— with a room full of white men debasing themselves and yapping for their favors like a pack of hounds? Every girl who went on the block became, for a little while, superior to every man who cried his bid.

And what did it matter? Whether you courted your woman or bought her or took her by force, and whether she was black or white or red, it was all the same to Nature. Cold, imponderable Nature, by every possible device, urged you to mate. It made you physically uncomfortable if you did not mate. It gave you vanity and made you preen and crow like any barnyard cock to attract a woman and so make your mating easier. And it drove women to every mad extreme so that the seed of man, any man, might be implanted within her. All so that the festering race of man would be perpetuated and go on and on. Blindly on. For what? Was it merely to blight the earth and furnish a passing amusement for a chuckling god? Or was there a pattern to it all that his own feeble brain could not perceive?

He slowly sipped his rum and decided he had been a fool for ever coming here in the first place. A dumb sentimental soft-livered fool.

He realized all at once that Two-Jack was not bidding. The man had not raised a finger all evening.

Why wasn't Two-Jack bidding?

He felt himself going cold again, then came the little wave

of nausea and the clutching inside while he waited for Slatter
to produce the fourth girl. When she finally appeared he went
limp for a moment for her face was meaningless to him; she
was just another of the original four that McSwade had acquired. He looked away and tried to endure the ensuing minutes by finishing his rum. The girl sold for nearly five thousand dollars, something of a record even in Territorial notes.

And now abruptly the room was very still.

"Zeda!" someone cried. "Bring on Zeda!"

"Yea, Zeda!"

He chilled and saw Two-Jack sitting up, gripping his chair.
Slatter vanished behind the curtain.

Slatter was gone a long time. Suddenly the curtain trembled
violently and he watched the perspiring master of ceremonies
reappear scowling, dragging the reluctant Zeda behind him. Her
hair was in disarray and over her revealing white gown she had
gathered an old gray shawl which she refused to relinquish
though Slatter tried forcibly to remove it before going to the
stand. She flung him a look of contempt and loathing and then
stared frantically about the room, searching.

The candlelight played strange tricks with her face. Maury
half rose, for all at once it was Adrienne on the dais. He sank
down again, but in that instance she had seen him, for now he
could feel her eyes on him; she regained her composure and
stood perfectly still, her eyes never leaving him. He heard
Carey say, "B'God, there's a spirited little vixen for you! And
she'd pass for white."

"She *is* white," he said under his breath, and half rose again
as Two-Jack opened the bidding by holding up four fingers.

"Four thousand!" cried Slatter and had only time to em-
phasize the record opener with his gavel before a cotton factor
raised the bid.

"Forty-one hundred."

"Forty-two" came quietly from Flavy Munn.

"Forty-three!" snapped Two-Jack.

"Forty-five!" Maury called and saw Two-Jack whip about in his chair and stare at him in sudden incredulity. Then instantly the face hardened into its cold Napoleonic mask and only the eyes threatened. The eyes drew a line and pronounced sentence and stated in an icy silence that the sentence would be carried out if the line were crossed.

But the factor raised the bid, and now Two-Jack turned and raised it again.

"Forty-eight," countered the factor.

"Forty-nine," said Two-Jack quickly.

The factor hesitated, then topped it with the highest bid of the evening: "Forty-nine fifty."

"Five thousand," said Maury.

Heads turned. Maury was conscious only of Two-Jack.

Two-Jack, without taking his eyes from him, said chillingly, "I make it six thousand even. Ah-yah, do you wish to raise that?"

"I'm bidding in gold, Jules. Are you matching me in gold?"

Rodman Carey whistled softly between his teeth. A murmur went through the smoky room and Slatter bulged against the stand with a round-eyed porcine stare.

Suddenly Slatter's gavel began to pound. "The gentleman bids in gold!" he bleated. "Five thousand in gold for the gem of the evening! Who will raise it in gold?"

Then Slatter stopped, for no one was paying any attention to him. Two-Jack had risen. His hand was reaching into his waistcoat, and the chairs between him and the rear of the room were being evacuated rapidly. Only Carey remained quietly in his seat.

Slatter cried, "Hey, fer the love o' Christ——"

Maury said, "Put your hand down, Jules," and stood stiffly waiting, still clutching the deerskin bag while he watched Two-Jack's arm.

"You do not pay your bets," said Two-Jack, biting out each word in a cold fury. "You are a thief, and tonight you would rob me again. You bid against me with money that should be mine. You are a dog and the son of a dog. Ah-yah, and your mother was a dog."

"You jackleg son of a tavern wench, you cheat at cards and I don't owe you a copper. I'll give you ten seconds to apologize for your insults and then get out of here, or, by the living God, you'll have to be carried out! Mr. Munn, will you kindly count to ten?"

Afterward he asked himself why he had ever called on Flavy for this dubious honor. Mainly, perhaps, it was because he had no wish to involve Rodman Carey in such a business; and, of all those remaining, Flavy would be the least excited and the most amused.

"One . . ." he heard Flavy say in his hoarse wheeze, "two . . . three . . . four . . ."

Then, watching Two-Jack's arm, he saw the faint twitching of the shoulder betraying a movement of the hand still hidden under the coat. Instantly and with a practiced deftness his own hand went to his belt and came forth with the pistol cocked. He saw the jerk of Two-Jack's arm, the derringer gleaming in the candlelight. He was poised, waiting for this, and now he took a quick sideward step away from Carey and pressed the trigger.

The room shook with sound and he lurched, feeling the tug of both of Two-Jack's bullets upon the deerskin bag he had unconsciously brought up and held against his side, and the burn of one glancing bullet as it plowed through his arm. He stared across the room, but powder smoke for a moment obscured Two-Jack's face so that he missed the sudden look of bewilderment on it. He knew, though, as he had known when he pressed the trigger, that the luck of Jules Tujaques had finally run out.

He had forgotten Zeda, nor did he look at her now as he turned blackly away and sat down beside Carey.

Chapter Twelve

I

AARON, WHEN Lissa was presented to him that Friday afternoon, was unable at the moment to voice any of his obvious objections. For Lissa, with her neat white apron and cap and beribboned pigtails, was undeniably appealing. And when she curtsied shyly and he heard himself addressed as "Mahster" for the first time, his convictions were suddenly overshadowed by the personal factor. Her timidity touched him. He peered down at her paternally and a little curiously and, with pardonable lack of foresight, inquired about her people. She looked up at him with her great round eyes swimming. "Ah's got nobody, 'ceptin' you an' mah new mistis," she answered dolefully. "Mah ole mistis, she's daid. She was sho good to me." Her chin quivered and she looked down quickly to hide her sudden tears. Aaron was moved.

It was only after supper, when Cousin Etta was busy in the kitchen with Lissa and the rented cook, that he felt able to speak his mind. And now the entire problem came to a head.

He had walked down to the beach with Catherine and they were watching a brig, which he had at first thought was one of his own, trying to beat up into the bay. There were two brigs in his small fleet, and both were due in from Liverpool. They were a bit late, in fact, but he was not yet worried about them. The matter of Lissa seemed far more important. It concerned something basic, like a crack in the foundation of his being.

"I cannot allow you to keep the girl," he finally announced with a firmness he did not wholly feel. "It is not so much because of that fellow St. John. It is simply the principle of the thing."

"Of course, darling," she answered, verbally swaying with the wind but clinging secretly to her ground. "We both feel the same way."

She glanced curiously down the beach in the direction of Carey's cottage, barely discernible in the shadows beyond the Saxon place, and wondered what had happened to Maury. She had not seen him for two days. He had said nothing about going away, and yet without so much as a note or a word of explanation he had vanished. But he had sent her Lissa. She glowed at the thought.

"Just because we are living down here," Aaron was saying, "is no reason why we should condone certain things. In the first place it's an improper gift. Highly improper. In the second place I'll not have another slave in the house."

"It's a rather large house," she said wryly, "for Cousin Etta and me to manage practically by ourselves. Unless," she added airily, "you want to help with the cleaning."

"Oh, come now," he reproached. "I don't care how many servants you hire. Within reason, of course."

"But, darling, you forget. You just don't *hire* them down here. You either buy them or rent them. We've been forced to rent a cook—from that man Slatter. I don't like it a bit, but——"

"Slatter? Who's he?"

"Oh, surely you know about him. He's the agent for most of the labor here. Uncle Rod said he's the one who's handling all the labor for your warehouse."

"I don't know anything about Slatter. I've contracted with a builder about the warehouse and have nothing whatever to do with the labor."

"Well, he had charge of Lissa. He's a perfectly awful person. I detest him." She sighed. "It's sort of terrible to have to rent servants from him. They're still slaves—owned by someone else. Just like your rented labor at the warehouse."

They went slowly back to the gate and he opened it for her, frowning, feeling like a man whose opponent at checkers has him hemmed in a corner. They stopped within the gate, looking up at the house with its long galleries. Those galleries, he told himself, made the place too ornate—entirely too ornate. Like a pretentious woman. And he thought wistfully of the quiet dignity of Chestnut Street.

She sensed his reaction and hated him for it. She had escaped Chestnut Street, but there seemed to be no escaping this living symbol of it. Why did she have to have a parent whose every instinct and conviction was at odds with her own? Even here, in this beautiful new home that she loved and where she ought to be happy, he somehow managed to bleach the color out of everything. Why did it have to be this way? God forgive her, but he had lived his life. Why couldn't he die?

But because her hatred of him was as yet only a static thing, she felt a certain guilt as well as a pity for him; and, putting her arm about him with a sudden show of affection, she urged him on to the steps and sat down beside him and began rubbing her hand gently over the back of his neck. It always soothed him, and he visibly relaxed now.

"Really," she said, "the only decent thing we can do is to buy our servants outright, but not keep them as slaves. I mean, we could free them but they could keep on working for us, and we could pay them wages. And we could apply their wages against what they cost us, so it would be as if they were working off a debt. I understand other people have handled the matter that way—people who think as we do."

"H'm . . . yes," he admitted grudgingly. "I suppose we could do that."

"As for Lissa," she hastened to add, "I've been thinking. It's a problem. We just can't send her back, darling."

"Eh? Why can't we send her back?"

"Don't you see? We'd be sending her to that disgusting place again—Slatter's jail, they call it. Goodness knows what would happen to her. She has no one in the world but us. She's been thrown on our hands, and now we're responsible." She hesitated a moment, then said, "When you look at it right you can see that . . . that Mr. St. John was really doing a very nice thing when he gave Lissa to me, for now we can give her a good home and, at the proper time, her freedom too."

"H'm." He turned slowly and suddenly demanded, "Catherine, are you interested in that fellow?"

She was ready for him and laughed instantly. "What an idea!"

"Well," he grumbled, "he's been showing you so much attention."

"No more than Mr. Bishop has."

"Well, I can't say that I care for Bishop either, although of the two he's greatly to be preferred."

"I find him rather crude," she said indifferently and thought again of Lissa, knowing that she had won her way. She had very little feeling of responsibility toward Lissa, and the mere matter of having a personal maid to see to her comfort was minor beside the fact that Lissa was her slave. She owned Lissa, body and soul. The knowledge of such possession gave her an odd thrill. Why shouldn't a person have slaves, many slaves? And do with them exactly as one wished? The old Romans, how lucky they were!

She glanced again in the direction of Carey's house and saw, in the twilight, the figure of a man approaching along the shell walk at the edge of the pines. She caught her breath, watching hopefully. Maury? But the figure was too heavy, the stride too long and slow. It was Hugh Bishop.

Disappointed, she got up and went into the music room and began to play. But she would see Maury tomorrow night. He would be at the ball.

II

"Are you sure you'll be all right now?" Rodman Carey asked. "You don't think I'd better send for Dr. Ormond?"

"Devil take Ormond! All he knows is bloodletting, and I've bled enough."

Maury settled back gratefully on the couch in Carey's library. He had insisted on dressing the wound himself. Fortunately the ball had not had to be probed; it had gone through the upper arm and lodged just under the skin, and he had removed it easily with the lancet. At Slatter's place he had bound the wound temporarily with a handkerchief until the hastily summoned coroner's jury had finished their business. But on the way home with Carey it had begun to bleed badly and he had had a little trouble stopping it. He felt very weak now, and physically exhausted, but he was not sleepy. It was nearly two in the morning.

Cricket mopped off the edge of the table and picked up the torn strips of cloth and the bloody basin and went out. Big Jube came in from the kitchen and blinked a question, and Carey said, "Could you eat something? How about some coffee?"

"Please. I haven't had a bite since dawn."

"My word!"

Big Jube padded back into the kitchen and Carey shuffled after him. They returned presently with the Negro carrying a tray which he set on the table by the couch. He poured cof-

fee and drew up a chair for his master and blinked another
question.

Carey said, "That's fine, Jube. You can go on to bed now."

There were rolls and corn bread left from supper, butter
and jam, cold cuts from a roast of venison and a berry pie.
They ate for a while in a sort of evasive silence.

Finally Carey asked idly, "You've read Bartram, of course?"

"Uh-huh."

"It was his descriptions of what he saw in the Floridas,"
said Carey, "that lured me down here in the first place. I was
particularly fascinated by what he wrote about Wakulla
Spring. Couldn't wait till I'd seen it. It's not far out of Tallahassee. But you've been there?"

Maury nodded, darkly silent.

"Ah, what a witchy place! And I'm sure Coleridge read
what Bartram wrote about it and was inspired too. I think
Bartram's description, mixed with a bit of opium, is where
Coleridge got his 'Kubla Khan.' Remember?

> *"Where Alph, the sacred river, ran*
> *Through caverns measureless to man . . .*

"And then:

> *"A savage place! as holy and enchanted*
> *As e'er beneath a waning moon was haunted*
> *By woman wailing for her demon-lover! . . .*

"Faith, m'lad, that's Wakulla. I'm sure it is."

Maury said nothing. He was thinking of the coroner's jury.
There had been no trouble, no question of their verdict from
the beginning. It was just a matter of form, a little ritual of
civilization; a man had been killed, and it had to be officially
determined whether or not the killing of him was justifiable.
No one present wanted the matter publicized. But of course

the story would get out. It would be all over the coast in a few hours.

Carey sighed. "I'm sorry, m'lad. There's no use feeling down about it."

"I can't help it. I don't like having killed a man."

"Faith, it happens all the time down here. What's another killing more or less? Besides, you acquitted yourself very well. I was surprised. It was a beautiful shot. You got him right between the eyes. And you waited until he'd pulled his derringer. He might have killed you."

"No, he didn't have much chance, really. If I hadn't been a little slow tonight he'd never even have nicked me. The trouble was that I wanted to kill him. I've seldom wanted to kill a man so badly. But I had to have a good excuse. I had to wait till he'd drawn. You just don't shoot a man because he calls you names."

"Well, it's certainly done. It seems to be accepted as a legitimate excuse. It's uncouth, but—— Oh, hell, I'm talking nonsense." He stopped and shook his head, his little bright birdlike eyes suddenly grave. "Frankly, Maury, I'm flabbergasted by the whole thing. You realize what this means, don't you?"

"I've been thinking about it."

Again they were silent.

At last Carey said, "Had you merely purchased a fancy girl at a private auction, the matter could have been kept a secret, more or less. A few whispers, perhaps, but no great damage. Most of us here do things that cause a bit of whispering, but it's like your blackbirding. When a gentleman does it, the only real crime is exposure. I think the French have an expression for it. Anyway, your purchase was attended by violence. You shot a man. Had you shot him in public because he insulted you, it would have been quite a different matter. You could have taken your place with other gentlemen of our vicious and hypocritical society who have successfully defended their honor against a person who was . . . er . . . not quite worthy of all the honors of a challenge. Possibly you would have been raised a notch in our social esteem. Anyway you would have appeared only a bit more dangerously fascinating, and no doors would have been closed to you."

Carey paused and removed his shoes and stiffly stretched his feet upon a stool, then fished a long, thin cheroot from a tobacco jar. He lighted the cheroot from a taper and leaned back and blew smoke at the paneled ceiling.

"I'm merely summing up things as they are. A killing cries itself from the housetops. There is no possibility of hushing it up. Soon everyone will know that a certain gentleman of Sodom, in a flagrant brawl over a fancy girl—purchased incidentally at a breath-taking price—has up and killed one of our most notorious gamblers. Oh, the gossips will love it; they'll wag their tongues loose. No one will love you the less for it. But the fact remains that, in the upper social circles, you have cut your own throat from ear to ear."

Maury lay thinking of Catherine, saying nothing.

"In other words," Carey went on, "I'm trying to tell you that you should not go to the Saxons' ball tomorrow night. Or were you thinking of going anyway?"

"I was considering it. Not to go is to admit my perfidy and knuckle under to convention. To go is to flout convention and risk being ordered from the premises."

"And Saxon would do it—with pleasure. And despite the fact that he keeps a yellow woman over on the edge of town and rides out to see her two evenings a week."

"Really?"

"Yes, regularly. Tuesdays and Fridays. Everybody knows about it. Not that I personally blame him. He's a healthy man. I detest only his regularity. He lowers sex to the level of a bowel movement."

"Meanwhile adhering strictly to convention. Damn convention! It's only a shield for people who can't be honest with themselves."

"Oh," said Carey, "it's more than that—a beaten track for the timid, a refuge for the small in mind. Anyway you can't go to the Saxons'. Nor to the Delafields'. For the time being you're beyond the pale. You see that."

"I suppose so. Perhaps I'd better go back home. My presence here would only make things awkward for you."

"Nonsense. I'm a bachelor of means and a pillar in the community, and my position is unassailable. So the best thing you could possibly do is to remain here with me. Anyway life wouldn't be half so interesting if you left. And in a few weeks the thing will blow over, St. Joseph being what it is."

Carey flicked ashes into his cup. When he turned, his eyes were very bright and quizzical. "Maury, what in the devil ever possessed you to bid in that girl tonight?"

"I told you she was white."

"Oh, come now! She couldn't possibly be! Slatter has better sense than that."

"You don't know Slatter as I do."

"But great God, if you believed her to be white, why didn't you let me know? We could have done something about it!"

"I thought it all over, Rod. From every side. Carefully. I couldn't risk a fight with Slatter. There'd have been all manner of trouble. Slatter wouldn't sell her to me—he was determined to put her on the block. I couldn't stop him without hell breaking loose. So I decided that the simplest, most logical thing to do was to bid her in."

"Logic, my word! Logic is of the head. You do your thinking with your heart. Anyway you didn't bid her in just because you thought her white. Why, you could have passed the word along to me and a few others, and some arrangement could have been made and the whole matter handled very quietly. But no, you had to do it all yourself. There must have been another reason. But forgive me. I don't mean to pry."

"That's quite all right. She . . . she reminded me of someone, a relative quite dear to me. And . . . well, maybe I did bungle it all. But I . . . I had to do something. You see, she has an affliction."

"Eh?"

"She was in an accident that paralyzed her vocal cords."

"Good Lord!" Carey sat up. "I'm damned! What do you intend to do with her?"

"I don't know."

Carey stared at him and then slowly eased himself back into his chair. "You idiot," he said finally. "You haven't a grain of sense in your head. Don't you see? All we have to do is explain matters, let people know that you bid in the girl for charitable reasons, to emancipate her, help her——"

"Twaddle! Who would believe that?"

"Well, frankly, I don't know. Your reputation is rather against you. If you were older and a different sort of person, legitimately established and with a family . . . Do you know of anyone who would be willing to take Zeda in? Some lady of standing, or at least someone quite respectable?"

"Only May Garver. And she isn't considered quite respectable. Anyhow she hasn't the room. Furthermore, the way I feel now, I don't give a continental what anyone thinks—except . . . well, except one person."

Carey studied him a moment. "If you'll permit me to ask, just how do you feel about that person."

"You know how I feel."

"It's really serious, eh?"

"Yes, I guess so. But I'm afraid this will finish it."

"I wouldn't say that. If she has half the character I think she has, she'll listen to an explanation and adopt a very broadminded view of the matter."

"And what good would that do?"

"That depends on you, Maury." Carey scratched the tip of his chin with a frail forefinger. "And, naturally, how she happens to feel about you. I'm not blind; I've seen how things have been going. I know she's deeply interested in you. But you both have a stumbling block in Aaron. After this affair at Slatter's he'll never allow you in the house. He'll never in the world sanction a marriage."

Carey stopped and peered at him sharply and then looked down at his cheroot. It had gone out. He crushed it in a copper bowl and took another from the jar and lighted it.

"Maury," he went on slowly, "I think a great deal of Kitty. I want her to be happy. But it isn't in the cards for any young woman in her position to find happiness with a man engaged in your activities. I'm not criticizing or trying to preach reform. I merely state a fact. I'm not opposed to slave running. But the day of it is past. It is against the law, and daily becomes more dangerous. To be caught at it is to be hanged. You are a young man and have all of life ahead of you. To be happy in our modern society one has to make certain concessions and live generally within the law. Forgive me if I sound paternal, but I'm thinking of Kitty and I want to set matters straight. She's an unusual girl. She has a mind of her own. And if she thinks enough of a person she'll walk out on Aaron and tell convention to go hang. Which, really, is what any woman worth her salt would do, if she loved a man and he happened to be the right man."

Carey paused and frowned at his cheroot. "So, as I say, it depends on you."

"Well, Rod, I don't know what I'm going to do, but I'm through with niggers. I've run my last load. I made up my mind to that some time ago. I've already seen the writing on the wall, and I'm done with it."

"Do you really mean that?"

"I certainly do."

"Have you any plans?"

"None whatever. In fact I'm in debt, and I'm a little worried. Of course I have that plantation up the river. It's a pretty wild piece of land, but it could be developed . . ."

"Well, before long you'll have some money from the railroad. A nice bit of it. That should be enough to start you off. And tomorrow I'll put in a word for you with Kitty and explain things."

"Honestly, will you?"

"Of course, now that I know how you feel. I had to know, because I wasn't going to have her jumping out of the frying pan into the fire. Naturally you'll have to pay your court and take your chances—and since you won't be able to see her openly, things are bound to be a little difficult at first. And you'll have to make some fitting arrangement about that girl Zeda."

Slowly, stiffly, Carey got to his feet and shuffled over to the mantel. He reached for one of the lighted tapers, hesitated, then turned, smiling. "I say, I believe I owe you a bit. Let's see: a hundred that I would buy, and two hundred that our recently deceased friend would too. I really shouldn't pay you the last on a technicality, but I won't hedge." He chuckled and took a roll of banknotes from his pocket, counted off the correct amount and placed the money on the table. "There. Now you'd better turn in, m'lad, and give sleep a chance with her knitting."

Maury watched him pick up his taper and shuffle off to bed. For a while afterward he lay motionless, held by the inertia of comfort and fatigue. Once the remaining taper sputtered and flared higher and for a moment seemed ringed with a golden halo. It made him think suddenly of the sun on Catherine's hair that morning at sea. His mind revolved slowly around the thought of marriage with her, then swung off abruptly on the tangent of Zeda and his debts.

What could he do with Zeda? At the moment he wanted never to see her again, but he couldn't leave her at Slatter's. Something had to be arranged. He considered the people he knew, trying to decide which of them, conceivably, might take Zeda in and properly look after her. Always he returned to

the Garvers. But their only spare bed was in the room that
Juan used for an office.

He frowned and thrust himself painfully upright and remembered his bill at the hotel. It dawned on him that the Mansion House was a very expensive place to live and that he could
no longer afford it. Why not move out and store all his things
in the captain's cottage? And, until he could think of something better, why not send Zeda temporarily to the cottage and
have May Garver keep an eye on her?

He got to his feet, reeled and clutched the table; then he
took the remaining taper and went unsteadily to his bedroom.

It was late the following afternoon, when he was trying to
write a note to the Garvers, that he decided quite suddenly
to ride over and see them. There was no use delaying. Better to
settle everything now and put it all behind him.

May, nursing the baby, met him at the door that night.

She called to Juan, "It's that awful man they're talking about.
Shall we let him in, Juan?" And in the next breath she added,
"O Holy God, he's in a mood! Juan, you'd better bring some
rum."

He entered wearily and sat down on a corner of the littered
sofa. "So even Sodom is rocked by the news of my perfidy, eh?"

"Lordy me!" she said, smirking, and then Juan came in from
the back room, barefooted and looking like a monk in his long
gray dressing robe and held out a glass of rum. "Fortify yourself, my friend, and tell us about it. That is, if you want to."
Then he peered down with sudden concern at the arm in a
sling. "Did he break a bone?"

"Oh, no. It's all right." Gratefully Maury sipped the liquor.
"What are they saying about me here?"

May said, "The obvious, of course. What could you expect
them to say?" She stood holding the nursing baby, oblivious of
it. "Is she really such a beauty, Maury? The story is that she's

the most beautiful octoroon ever seen at a private auction. But it seems so ... so ..." She frowned. "I mean, I'm still trying to adjust myself to your sudden change of interest."

"She's not an octoroon," he said. "And I haven't had any change of interest." He looked darkly at his rum, then briefly, between sips of it, he told them about Zeda.

May stared at him. "I'm confounded," she said at last. "I'm just confounded."

Juan said, "Loss of speech, eh? That's extremely interesting. I've seldom encountered a case of it. I'd like to study her and——"

"So help me!" May burst out. "You want to study her! She's just an interesting medical case! Does it occur to you, you oaf, that she's also a very lonely and frightened girl who's had a hell of an experience? What she needs is a woman to look out after her. Maury, you can just go back and get her and bring her here. We'll find room for her."

It was the sort of reaction he had expected from May, though he had hardly hoped for it on the mere summary of facts.

"You're a jewel," he said. "But let's be practical. Let's start off with Cricket and Celeste. I suppose you know about them."

"O Jesus, yes! Celeste has been mooning around, and I've had a talk with her. But I don't see how we——"

"Well, there's my cottage. The Gradys have left, so I'm giving up my rooms at the hotel and storing everything in the cottage. There are good quarters in the carriage house, so that'll take care of Cricket and Celeste. And for the time being Zeda can have the cottage. It's only a minute's walk down the alley from here, so——"

"But what about you?"

"Carey wants me to stay in St. Joseph with him awhile."

"It all sounds very nice," said May. "Very nice."

"Well, what the devil's wrong with it?"

The baby muttered and she shook it and said tenderly, "You damn little brat, you've had enough. You're fat as a pig now."

She carried it into the bedroom and tucked it into its basket. Then she poured herself a goblet of rum from the demijohn and came back and sat down.

Juan grumbled, "That's not water."

"No, thank God!" Then she said, "Maury, I hate to think how all this is going to affect your . . . er . . . plans in St. Joseph. But the thing is, you won't be there forever."

"No, but we'll know soon enough what to do about the girl. She must have a home somewhere, or relatives. And when we find out where to send her——"

"That's just what I'm getting at. Maybe she hasn't anyone. And maybe she wouldn't want to go back where she came from."

He shrugged. "That's up to her."

"Oh, no, my friend, it's not that simple. You say she's white. But no matter what she really is, you bought her as a slave. Even if you freed her there'd still be the problem of her status. How could you legally——"

She stopped and shook her head. "Oh, hell, we can worry about that later. The main thing is now. I hate to think of her penned up at that wretch Slatter's. I wish you'd brought her along. She could at least stay here tonight."

"I did bring her," he said, smiling for the first time. "She's out there waiting in the chaise."

III

The tiny Negro and the two big ones who had brought in the furniture were gone now, and he was gone too. His going left an emptiness, and she wanted to cry because he had said so little and had left so quickly. Even last evening on the long ride through the pines he had hardly looked at her or said a word. Did he wish he'd never seen her? Did he hate her? Did he think, after all, that she was no better than the others? Or was it because she'd cost him so much, so terribly much?

If only she had been able to speak just one little thought, to let him know in even the smallest way how she felt inside! But this was the worst, to have so many thoughts, such a rush of things beating to be spoken, and to have them shut away and sealed and to be choking with the misery of them. O God, was she being punished? Was it because she had run away from Eduardo? But where was the wrong in that? And besides, hadn't she been punished enough without this?

Her hand went to her throat again, clutching it as if to tear away the impounding thing that held her silent. And then suddenly her shoulders shook and the tears came.

She did not notice May Garver, who was watching covertly from the hall while pretending to sort through the pile of rugs and bric-a-brac in the final load. But suddenly May was holding her.

"There now, honey," May said. "It's all behind you. There's nothing to worry about. Let's forget the house and make us a pot of coffee. You like coffee, don't you?"

She nodded quickly and wiped her tears on the sleeve of the gaudy dress that Slatter had given her to ride away in. It was her only dress, and its raw colors reminded her of Slatter's cheap shawls. Unconsciously her nose wrinkled in distaste.

May fingered the dress and said, "You hate it, don't you? Well, I reckon I understand. But if you want to give it to Celeste she'll love you to death, and tomorrow we'll go down and get some new things after we've done the marketing. Can you sew?"

She nodded eagerly as they went into the kitchen. Naturally she could sew! She loved it. And she could embroider and weave too—only not nearly so well as her mother. But of course no one on the island could, for her mother had been a mainland woman and a great artist and had brought all the old crafts to Bonacca. She wished she could tell May about her mother.

She had a sudden warm feeling of kinship with this big homely, mannish woman. At first she had been a little awed by

May, for the women at home would never have dreamed of being so outspoken, especially around their men. And in the clutter and smells of May's disorganized household were none of the intangibles she had been craving after the trials of the past weeks. But now she was deeply grateful that she had someone like May for a friend.

She lighted the charcoal in the kitchen brazier while May filled the pot and put in coffee that had been brought over with the cookies and a few other things in a basket. Then they got out the cups, arranged the table and sat down, waiting for the coffee to boil.

"You won't exactly be here alone," said May. "Now Celeste will be moving into the quarters out back, but until Cricket comes she might just as well sleep here in the house. She could have a cot in that little corner room yonder. And until you sort of get used to things we want you to come over and have your meals with us."

May stopped and looked at her oddly. "I can't get over your knowing English. You don't look a bit English. I mean, it would seem more natural if you knew Spanish, or French maybe. Aren't you from somewhere down in the islands?"

She smiled and tried to form Bonacca with her lips. And why shouldn't she know English? Wasn't that what everyone spoke at home, even those with Spanish blood? Of course she knew Spanish too; but English had been spoken there—oh, for ages— ever since the time of the great pirate who was one of her ancestors.

"And your name," said May. "Is . . . is it really Zeda?"

She found a scrap of paper and a quill and tried to write her name. Many times her lips formed it—Zeda Rosamunda Constancia Montalba Morgan—but her fingers were able to produce only the four symbols by which everyone knew her. It was the only part of her name she had ever seen written, for at home there had been little need for such matters, and neither Eduardo nor her father had believed that learning was good for females. And the beast McSwade, who had known her people all his life, had sold her only as Zeda, thinking it a great joke that a Morgan should be thus reduced to the status of the Africans in whom her family dealt.

May frowned at the paper. "Maybe, if you tried real hard, you could write the name of your island."

If only she knew the symbols that stood for sounds! But no one had ever taught her those mysteries. She sat thinking of the island and remembering the time—it had been in those good days before the coming of the great wind—when she had sailed all around it with her father. She had even sailed around Roatán, the larger island where McSwade lived, and once she had been as far away as Belize on the mainland. She closed her eyes, seeing the shape of Bonacca with its great pine-covered hills and its high ocher cliffs at either end, and close about it the little emerald cays where nearly everyone lived. Suddenly she looked at the ink and then dipped her quill into it. What need had she for symbols when she could draw?

Swiftly she outlined all the islands and even the cays, and then she was sketching the view of the high hills at sea and the little harbor and finally her father's house among the palms. She had not meant to draw the house, but there it was. She blinked down at it, remembering, and abruptly she turned away and covered her eyes. For the house was no more, and the wind that had destroyed it had also taken her father and her mother.

"You poor darling!" said May. "So that's your home. I know just how you feel. It's hell to be homesick. But never mind. As soon as we can find out a few things and get word to your people, we'll see that you're on the first ship back."

She chilled at this thought, and May, studying her intently, said, "What's the matter, honey? Don't you want to go home? Don't you want to see your folks again?"

She shook her head fiercely and crumpled the drawings. There was no one left but her cousin, Eduardo, and she would never go back to him.

It wasn't that she hated Eduardo. After the great wind she

had gone to live in his house, and he hadn't been unkind. Very firm, of course, inflexibly firm, for Eduardo made rules which everyone must obey or be punished. And in Eduardo's house, far more than in her father's, women must keep their place. But everyone thought her very lucky. For it was Eduardo's announced intention, when she reached seventeen, to elevate and honor her by making her his wife. Many women had aspired, and three before her had enjoyed that privilege before passing on to greater rewards. Now the house swarmed with their children, some of them older than herself.

Perhaps, if Eduardo had been younger and thinner and not quite so inflexible, she could have accepted the prospect of sharing his bed. But as the date of sharing it drew near she had found it far easier to slip away on one of the mainland sloops and to take her chances in a totally unknown and frightening world.

She was glad when they finished coffee and May finally left to see about the baby. For she wanted, for a little while, to be alone. The future, while it did not hold the terrors of the recent past, seemed nevertheless formidable, and she could not bear to think of it until she had managed to make herself at peace with the present.

She went slowly through the cottage, touching the silver and the brasses and the bric-a-brac piled on the chairs and chests. In the hall she stooped and spread out a long runner and almost cried because of its close resemblance to one that her mother had woven. Many things here reminded her of her father and mother: the carved chests and the candlesticks and even the great bed. She felt a sudden love and responsibility for the cottage and thought, I must put everything in order and take good care of it for him.

Then she saw the books. There had been few in her father's house and none at all in Eduardo's. But here they jammed a big secretary and were stacked high around it on the floor. Dozens of books. Scores and scores of books. Fascinated, she dropped to the floor and began going through them, hungry with a great yearning. So much knowledge! And she knew so little! *Please God,* she prayed, *let me learn!*

It was now that she looked up and saw for the first time, across the room, enthroned, the leering stone visage of Kul. She knew immediately what it was, for she had seen such things before. But for a moment its ugliness frightened her, and she gasped and crossed herself. Then she thought: It is evil. Why does he have it here? He is good and kind and there is no evil in him. Why does he have a thing of evil in his home?

And instinctively, because the reason for it was as elemental and as simple as her own childish faith, she perceived what neither Maury himself nor anyone—save perhaps Rodman Carey—had ever realized: that Kul was only a symbol of a lack of faith. She crossed herself again and studied it, no longer afraid of it, and yet somehow afraid of the significance of its presence. All at once she wanted to destroy it and get it forever out of the cottage, for some small deep pagan strain in her seemed to insist that its presence here could bring only ill.

But she could not destroy it. She had no right to touch it. She wished suddenly that she knew more of things religious, like the poor old padre who used to come sometimes and pray for the poor black souls in the barracoons. But after her mother died she had never had a chance to talk to him. Often she had made little prayers—but how could she properly gain His ear on matters of consequence? And what should she say? She thought: I must ask that he be protected from evil, for I am afraid that something I do not understand may happen to him. I could not bear that. And I must ask to be able to help him and to repay him somehow for what he did. And would it be wrong if I asked for speech? For surely, if I could speak again, I would not be so useless.

Suddenly she closed her eyes and pressed her hands tightly together. And with her mind straining so that her plea would be carried across the great void, she began: *Please, dear God ...*

Chapter Thirteen

ALL THROUGH the last week in April the wind ground monotonously out of the southeast, a warm heavy sticky wind that frayed nerves and destroyed sleep and flowed with a ceaseless ominous rushing through the pines. Finally it rained torrents.

With May the weather cleared and heat lay in the land long after the sun was sheathed; and there came one of those very still hot evenings when everything seems held in suspense, waiting, and all sounds carry a great distance. And now across the town and almost from one end of the beach road to the other, the voice of the gaunt savant of St. Joseph could be heard clearly again. It rose and fell from his tent in the pines, shouting sometimes, then imploring in a monotone and falling to a hoarse and trembling ardent whisper—and all at once mounting to a shriek, charged with fire, and beating with a feverish and fanatical heat against the quiet. A latter-day John the Baptist wailing in the wilderness, crying a warning. The night seemed to throb with a heavy heartbeat as over it the voice flung forth: *"Repent! Repent! Repent! Gomorrah is doomed,*

173

and the hour is nigh! The gate of hell is open, and the flame
shall rise from the pit and burn Gomorrah!"

Many a Negro, oppressed with bondage and harkening to
the Congo call of that voice, broke curfew and stole through
the pines to crouch enchanted in the tent, swaying and moaning. And from the fringes of the town came the lesser whites,
to forget their lowness in the scheme of things while they huddled in an exalted safety through the spiritual tempest.

Over in his small bare room Father O'Leary, St. Joseph's
only ordained and recognized agent of God, listened uncomfortably while he fought a battle with his conscience. Finally
he crossed himself, knowing it would be unethical to register a
complaint, and put cotton in his ears. In his cottage on the
beach Rodman Carey, untroubled by conscience and ignoring
his cares, listened a bit wistfully. Man, he thought, is a peren-
nial child, born afraid, and he created God in his own image to
give him comfort in his fear. But many of us have no comfort.
For our reason destroys God, and we must walk alone in the
dark.

Farther up the beach Clifford Saxon, jolted to his marrow by
an afternoon of terrible enlightenment at the bank with Crom
Davies and certain of the stockholders, stopped his heavy pacing and shook his fist in the direction of the voice. It seemed
almost as if the voice knew of the bank's insolvency, and was
crying a warning of it to all St. Joseph. He cursed the voice
savagely and went on with his pacing. Give us time, he prayed.
All we need is time. The money from the railroad will cover it
and settle everything. But we must have time, and we've got to
keep Carey and Delafield from knowing. . . .

A hundred yards away, sleepless in the newness of his room
in this land that he could not like, Aaron listened while a name-
less something crept through the netting of his bed and lay cold
beside him, whispering with the dead tongue of Lucia: "Why
did you put so much into the railroad? That was a mistake.
Your very coming here was a mistake. You should have stayed

in the North." And the words drumming through the pines seemed to repeat: *"You should have stayed in the North . . . stayed in the North. . . ."*

In her corner room across the hall Catherine lay motionless, troubled yet curious. That disquieting voice seemed an inextricable part of the night and the land, one with the night sounds of other nights, and the threat of it was the threat of the land. She sat up presently, digging her fingers restlessly into the sheet. The intangible threat sharpened her desire for life and her thoughts circled with undefined longings. I am here, she told herself—here where I wanted to come—but nothing is the way it should be. Nothing. Am I to go on and on like this, until I am empty like Cousin Etta?

Something small came through the window and fell with a soft little rasp upon the rug. With a quick intake of breath she parted the mosquito netting and saw a pine cone lying near the foot of the bed. Suddenly sharply attentive she got up and slipped to the side of the window and peered out.

A shadow detached itself from the larger pine near the house. A hand beckoned. In the mottled light and shadow of the moonlit yard she could not see the owner of the hand clearly but she instantly recognized the quick restless movement, the impatient jerk of the dark head.

She drew away from the window and stood very still, her breath coming a little faster. Not once had Maury been out of her thoughts since the day of the ball. She had walked over to the market with Aaron that morning to find all St. Joseph talking of the shooting at Slatter's. Her sick shock and incredulity had given way to fury by the time she reached home. A cheap brawl over a colored wench! He had ignored her for a slave—a fancy girl! She had writhed at the thought; and going up to her room in a rage she had encountered Lissa and, suddenly hating the small maid, she had turned some of her fury upon her. Hurting Lissa had helped immeasurably.

Then Rodman Carey had come over early that afternoon

and explained the whole affair. He had removed the sting, if not the poison.

Even now some of the poison of it remained.

She went back to the bed and sat down with her hands clenched in her lap. In all this time she had refused to see Maury, and it was only a few days ago that she had relented enough to begin answering his notes. They had been flowing to her in a steady stream via Cricket and Lissa—long notes some of them, beautiful and impassioned, not a bit like the stiff formal letters Hugh Bishop had been writing her from Tallahassee. Hugh's letters she burned with a shrug, but these others she read avidly although she made her replies to them brief and cold.

Damn that girl! she thought. Oh, damn her, damn her!

A second pine cone struck the rug and rolled almost to her feet. She looked at it a moment and then snatched it up. A small folded bit of paper was coiled around it and wedged in the burs. She drew it out quickly and unfolded it and carried it to the square of moonlight near the window. He had scrawled, "Please come down."

Her first impulse was to fly to him; she had punished him enough. Then she tore the paper into tiny pieces. I mustn't see him, she told herself furiously. It simply isn't done. And after all that has happened . . . Anyhow what would he think of me?

But in the next breath she was slipping out of her gown and hastily wriggling into a petticoat and a dress. After all this wasn't Salem. And she had to see him. She had to.

She tied her hair back with a ribbon, caught up her slippers and tiptoed into the hall.

Aaron's voice stopped her at the head of the stairs. "Is that you, Catherine?"

"Yes, Father. I couldn't sleep. I think I'll go out and walk on the beach. It's so stuffy inside."

"What's this?" His voice was irritable. "You can't go parading around at all hours alone."

"Oh, don't be silly, dear. Nothing's going to come out of the sea and grab me."

He stood taut and motionless behind the pine, watching her window, hoping she would appear again and, when she did not appear, softly cursing her and wondering why he himself had to be cursed by the attraction she held for him. Finally, reluctantly, he turned away.

Something rustled near the fence and he stopped abruptly, aware that his light linen shirt and trousers made him conspicuous in the moonlight. But it was only Tawny, her cat. He stooped and held out his hand, whispering to it. The big cat laid back its ears and hissed and then slid away into the palmettos.

"Damn devil," he muttered. "You were friendly enough once. What's come over you?"

The haunting voice of the savant had momentarily stopped, and now in the stillness he thought he heard footsteps. He edged back, flipped over the picket fence into the shadow of the palmettos and stared across the yard. His heart seemed to stop and turn over, then it began beating furiously. He saw Catherine come down from the veranda and without turning her head move with an easy grace out through the gate. She was wearing pale gray and she looked like an angel with her long thick burnished-yellow hair tumbling over her shoulders and gleaming in the moonlight.

He circled through the pines to the edge of the beach and stopped beside a clump of young trees that hid him from the house. He stood watching her, a tightness in his chest as she walked lightly along the sand and then swung casually up the beach toward him. When she was a few paces away he stepped forward impulsively with her name on his lips, and for an instant he thought she was going to come into his arms, but she stopped just in front of him and her chin came up.

"Well?" she said.

"Thank God you came," he said fervently. "It's been so long. So damn long." His eyes drank her in and he reached for her hand, but she drew it away. "Please," he urged. "Don't be angry."

"I'm not angry. But you've no right to expect me to meet you like this, and you must not come again. You realize that, don't you?"

"Oh, the devil, this isn't Salem!"

"No, but Father's Salem, and that's that. He heard me get up. I told him I was going for a walk along the beach. But it was foolish of me to come."

"Surely you're not afraid of him."

"Certainly not. But I respect him and I have to live with him. If you and I were seen together people would start talking, and of course Father would hear of it. I can't have that."

"But I've got to keep on seeing you somehow."

"You should have thought of that before you bought that girl."

"But I had to buy her! I wrote you all about it. Surely you see why——"

"Because she reminded you of your sister?" She laughed softly, derisively. "I didn't know men went around acquiring fancy girls because they resembled members of the family. But I suppose I shouldn't really blame you. After all, men do buy women down here. It's the custom of the country."

"It's a custom I've never followed," he said angrily. "I did what I felt I had to do that night, and if matters turned out as they did—well, it was something I couldn't help. I hardly expected your father to understand—but I certainly thought you would."

"Oh, I understand well enough. I've never said I blamed you. Father does, of course. He looks on you as a terrible sort of person. He was afraid you might come to the house, and he gave orders to the servants not to admit you." She laughed softly again, but with sudden good humor, and glanced at him slyly with her long eyes. "On the other hand, Mr. Bishop, who has had five duels, is allowed to call whenever he wishes."

"I won't trouble you with my opinion of Mr. Bishop," he snapped. "If you prefer the type, you can have it and I'll go my way."

"I think we've talked long enough," she said tartly. "I'll have to go back into the house now."

He glared at her and then suddenly seized her arms. "Dammit, you can stop playing with me! You're not worried about your father or anything else, and you know it! You've hardly got out here and we haven't settled anything yet."

He stopped, for he had drawn her close, and in her nearness his anger vanished and he was conscious only of his terrible longing for her. His arms went about her. He caressed her hair.

"Catherine . . ."

"Please, Maury . . ." Her hands came up and pressed firmly against his chest. He could feel her strong body tensing like a spring.

"Tell me you care for me . . . just a little."

"I . . . I like you a great deal, or I wouldn't have come down." She shook her head and her hands pressed a little more firmly against him. "But we shouldn't stand here. It's as bright as day, and if someone came along the walk . . ."

"Then let's go somewhere else. I've got to talk to you. There's so much I want to say. . . ."

"But not tonight. I really can't stay out long, with Father knowing."

"Then why couldn't you slip away tomorrow evening? We could take the chaise. No one could see you with the top up."

"I . . . I don't think I can. I—— Oh, Maury, you've made things so impossible by doing what you did."

"Nothing is impossible if two people care enough for each other."

She was silent a moment, her hands still pressed against him. Then her lips curled faintly. "That girl. What did you say you did with her?"

"I turned her over to May Garver."

"And who is May Garver?"

"Dr. Garver's wife, in Apalachicola." He did not add that he had sent Zeda to his cottage and merely asked May to keep a motherly watch over her.

Again they were silent. Suddenly he felt her fingers digging into his shirt.

"Listen!" she whispered.

It was the savant again. The voice was low now, but frenzied and intense and somehow deeply terrible. The words, lost and meaningless in the distance, reached them only as a dread implication, an elemental beating of sound as unsettling as the sure knowledge of disaster.

All at once the tenseness went out of her and she clung to him. "That voice, there's something awful about it. It makes me afraid. I . . . I've never been afraid before."

"Don't pay any attention to him. There's nothing to be afraid of."

"Maybe it's just life. He makes it seem so dreadfully uncertain and short."

"It is that, God knows."

"But it shouldn't be that way."

He caressed her hair again. "How should it be?"

"I don't know. I wish I did know. I . . . I just want to crowd all I can into life before I die. I don't mean just parties and social things. I loathe them, really." She raised her head. "Look at the night! It's so beautiful. It seems to promise so much that we never have. I . . . sometimes I wish I'd been born a savage. Or maybe a deer or a wild thing. Then I could be free and run on the beach. . . ." Her hand, toying with his sleeve, crept up his arm and felt the bandage. "Oh—I'd forgotten you were hurt. Is it all right now?"

"Just about. Catherine, you've got to go riding with me. Tell me you will."

"I'll have to think about it."

"Please! Tomorrow evening?"

"No . . . no, not till Father goes."

"He's going away?"

"To Sodom, as you call it—to see about the ship."

"Soon?"

"In a few days."

"You'll find out when he's going and let me know?"

"I . . . All right. Will you take me to the outer beach, where there's space and only wildness? I want to see the surf again."

"Of course! And I'll pack a lunch, and——"

"But no." She shook her head quickly. "I'd better not."

"Oh, now! Say you will . . . please!"

Her long eyes were studying him with a curious intensity. She did not answer, and his arms tightened around her, hungry and impatient. He tilted her head and kissed her throat and then her lips; for a moment she was soft and yielding, and then he sensed the violence in her as the spring came back into her strong body. Suddenly she tore her mouth away and in the next instant he felt her teeth sink into his shoulder with hot pain that was almost an ecstasy. Then abruptly she broke away, gasping, and turned and ran swiftly toward the house.

It was long after she returned to her bed that the tumult within her quieted and she slept a little. Then she was awake again, but suspended in the unreality of the night, and there was the ghost of a melody in her mind.

It was very bright outside, so bright that she could see the glittering of the water beyond the pines and, farther out, the stealthily moving cloud shadows that turned the bay into a sheet of faintly rippling silk. The night was very still now, and she wondered what had wakened her. Then the sound came again, close and somewhere just beyond the window— a sudden melodious trill of bird song. It stopped and started once more, running up and down an infinite scale and sampling a dozen little measures, and then it launched into a rapturous elysian outpouring that surpassed anything she had ever heard in nature. It was a mockingbird.

For a long time she lay in a dreamy languor, listening, faintly conscious of an aching in her thighs and breasts. The night was heavy with the fragrance of the swamps, a strange and vernal fragrance that had in it all the wildness of the land. She thought of Maury, of his deep eyes that seemed to pierce through her and at times gently unclothe her; and she thought of his long, lean and yet steely hands and the pressure of them upon her back, and wondered what it would be like to feel the full strength of those hands about her. Had the song continued she might have lain there in her languor until dawn. But it stopped abruptly in a frightened cry, and there was a sudden mad fluttering of wings and a threshing in the oleanders.

She was out of the bed and at the window in an instant and saw her cat streaking across the lawn with the still-living bird in its jaws.

She gasped, and her body went cold and then hot, and her eyes widened upon the fascination of this small violence. Her lips curled, and for a second she had a swift envy of Tawny. "Kill it!" she whispered fiercely. "Kill it! Kill it!" In a moment the cat was gone and the bird might never have been, and once more the night was very still save for the quiet music of the water and the far-off jingling of the frogs.

She shuddered and went back to bed, only to be driven up in a minute by the flame that had been kindled in her. She began moving softly about the room like a young panther. Once she stopped and clenched her fingers in her hair and her body tightened as if it were trying to release itself of a burden. O God, she thought, why do I have to be this way? Why? Why?

But perhaps it was only the thing that she felt in the land. There was a strangeness in this land, a something insidious and unsettling and slowly exciting like a low prelude to violence. It was in the faint but mad orchestration of the frogs and in the voices of the water. It was always in the water. On the quiet still nights it had the sadness of a lullaby and the softer sounds of loves and lovers; but behind it was a wildness. There was always a singing in it and a wailing. Always a beauty and a terror.

The aching in her had become a hurt. She stripped off her gown and began rubbing it over her firm body as if to rub away the hurt, but it was only aggravated, and she had a sudden desire to run outside and race madly along the beach and fling herself into the sand. And she agonized that she had not stayed with Maury, for all at once she wanted to throw all of her furious strength against him and feel herself fighting him in an orgy of movement. Without realizing what she was doing she began ripping the gown, twisting it, tearing it, shredding it. It became, suddenly, Lissa's small body she was hurting, and again she could feel the pleasure of giving pain. She tore the gown to little bits.

Suddenly she was exhausted. She gripped the edge of the bed, sweat streaming from her hot body, then fell face down on the sheet, sobbing soundlessly. She felt sick and lost and beaten and frightened.

Chapter Fourteen

I

CRICKET, FOLLOWING a route of his own through the palmettos, reached the gate behind the Delafield stable. He loitered awhile, his small body hidden by the gate; finally, with a wary glance at the house and yard, he slipped through and entered the stable and settled himself cross-legged on a box near the door. In his hands was a nearly finished whip of rawhide, the tip of which he set about plaiting while he waited for Lissa.

His entrance was so unobtrusive that Boolie, the new groom, occupied with scattering straw in a stall, did not see him for several minutes. Presently Boolie, hearing a scraping sound, turned and glared with slow anger at the interloper.

"Hyar you is again," he grumbled. "Ain't I done tole you ter keep shy o' dis place? Ev'ry day you comes sneakin' 'round, foolin' wid yo' whips an' tryin' to make sweet talk wid Lissa. Now you git a-goin' befo' I runs you out." He picked up the stable broom and came over belligerently, but stopped short at

184

the sight of the knife that appeared suddenly in Cricket's hand.

"Don't fiddle wid me," Cricket told him, not moving. "I's little, but I's bad. Ary big-mouthed bastud fiddles wid me, I cuts 'im loose."

"You sho talks big fer a li'l pissant dat wouldn't fetch fawty dollahs on de block."

Cricket spat. "I knows you, Boolie. You got de big head. Dat ole Slatter he try ev'rywhere ter sell you, but nobody what's real folks'd have you. Den 'long come a Yankee man what don't know no better. Haw! You ain't got no cause fer de big head."

"Don't talk ter me. I's 'mancipated. I's free."

"You's *what*?"

"I done tole you. Marse Aaron he say I's free."

"Den how come you's workin'?"

"Nigger gotta pay off de debt. What 'e cost. Nigger gotta eat, too."

"Den you's worse off'n you was. You never had to worry 'bout nothin' befo'."

"I had to worry 'bout *dis*," mumbled Boolie, holding out a wrist that showed a ring of red from the long chafing of a slave bracelet. "I don't worry 'bout it now."

"Sho." Cricket nodded slowly, and with this basis for mutual understanding he put his knife away and once more busied himself with the whip. It was a short, heavy drover's whip of a kind much favored by overseers and, like others he had made in his idle time, it would be sold and the money added to the small savings he had entrusted to his master. Presently he asked, "Whar de carriage? Folks out ridin'?"

"Jes' Marse Aaron. He gwine to Apalach."

"How he treat y' all?"

"He funny man, but he treat us good. Say all us niggers free hyar, soon's we work off de debt."

"Sho nuff! Lissa, she free too?"

"I reckon. How come you so curious 'bout Lissa?"

"She my po' sister's chile," Cricket replied soberly, almost believing the lie. "She all I got."

Boolie, satisfied, finished with the barn and went out to the back lot to grub palmettos. Cricket put the final braiding on the whip and slowly coiled it while he thought of Dr. Garver's Celeste. Celeste was his now and every night she waited for him in the quarters behind the captain's cottage. It had all come about as he had schemed and hoped, but little good it did him with his master spending all his time in St. Joseph. He considered the girl Zeda who occupied the cottage, curious about her status. Then he sighed, hungry for Celeste, and wondered how much longer the nature of things would hold him away from her.

For a while he dozed in the afternoon heat. Then a light step on the walk outside brought him instantly awake and he looked up to see Lissa entering the barn door.

"Lo, sad eyes," he whispered, and fished a folded and sealed bit of paper from his jacket pocket. "Y' all got somethin' to gimme fo' dis?"

Silently she took a similar note from her apron and they exchanged messages. And then she turned from him abruptly and would have darted through the door, but he caught her hand and drew her gently back.

"What ails you, chile?"

She shook her head without looking at him.

"Hyar now, lemme see yo' eyes. Sho. You's been cryin'. How come you been cryin', huh? Dat Boolie man bother you?"

"No," she mumbled, and tried to pull away. He took her upper arm and held her firmly and she winced. "Don't," she pleaded. "Hit's sore."

He drew up her wide sleeve and scowled at the welts and broken skin above the elbow. "Who done dat, baby?"

Her chin quivered and her eyes roved.

"Ain't nothin' to be scairt of, honey. How come you actin' scairt?"

She swallowed. "Cricket, w-what d'you reckon they'd do tuh me if'n I was to run away?"

"You crazy, honey?"

" 'Tain't me what's crazy. But *she* is. My ole mistis never, never . . ." Suddenly she gave a little sob and pulled free of him and ran back along the walk to the house.

Cricket wet his lips and stared after her, his spidery hands twisting around the tightly coiled whip. For a moment he seemed to shrink into himself, then his mouth twitched and he slipped from the barn and went out through the gate. He passed Boolie without noticing him and, glumly reluctant to complete his errand, started off slowly through the palmettos.

It was siesta hour and Carey lay dozing in the hammock on his side porch, a half-finished egg-and-whisky on the table at his elbow. Beyond him Maury paced soundlessly. Reaching the far corner he stopped by the railing and studied the park-like expanse of pines and palmettos behind the house. A herd of the half-wild Spanish cattle that roamed the coast were grazing almost up to the back fence. Presently they would wander past the Saxon place and on through town unless someone got up enough energy to drive them out. He scowled at their long horns and spotted backs, forced himself to count to fifty and then turned and paced to the other end of the railing and studied the shell walk and the beach. The walk was empty and the beach was deserted save for two small children wading in the shallows under the watchful eye of an old Negress. Locusts droned in the pines and all St. Joseph seemed asleep. The only signs of industry were on the long pier more than a half mile away where slow-moving black gangs loaded the waiting ships. A faint stirring of air from the southeast brought the low weary rhythm of their chanting to his ear.

He counted to fifty and turned away and saw Cricket coming up the side path to the carriage shed.

He drew a long breath and waited until Cricket had entered

the shed, then he dropped lightly over the porch railing and went around the side of the house, expecting to meet Cricket by the cistern. Not seeing him, he went on into the shed and found the little man standing by the chaise and staring out moodily at the cattle.

"What's the matter with you?" he demanded. "Didn't you bring me anything?"

"Yassuh. I brung it."

Maury snatched the proffered note, broke the seal, and his eyes devoured the single line of its contents. Suddenly the tightness went out of his face and he smiled. He tossed Cricket a coin and then folded the note carefully and put it in his pocket and started back to the house; but at the corner of the harness room he turned and said casually, "I'll be needing the chaise about sundown. Be sure and put the top up."

"Yassuh. Uh . . . Marse Maury."

"Eh?"

Cricket stood twisting the coiled whip, looking down at the ground.

Maury peered at him searchingly. "What the devil's wrong with you?"

"Uh . . . nothin', suh. I . . . I reckon I better curry de hoss."

Maury frowned at him a moment, then shrugged and went on to the kitchen to supervise the packing of a lunch basket.

II

Oleanders, a great flaming armful of them, filled the Chinese vase on the bedroom mantel. Catherine held her hands under the narrow gray-green leaves and then brushed her face against the thick spicy clusters of red and deep scarlet and coral blossoms. Oleanders affected her oddly and, for some reason she could not quite bring to mind, seemed to have a very special meaning for her. She wondered what it was. It was more than just their color—although this too was important. Out in the yard, among the shrubs that Carey had had brought in by ship from Mobile, were some pale pink ones and many that were white. But these she had ignored. Only the reds attracted her.

She sighed and closed her eyes and took a deep breath as if to breathe in the color. Why did she love red so? At times it was intoxicating, and she felt a stirring of something pagan and savage. She trembled at the thought of it. Red, red, red! The color of dark memories and passion, and the color of violence and blood. She had never been able to wear it, for the color was too intimate and personal, and its significance was too great for any casual display. At moments she wanted to abandon herself to it.

She turned and slipped out of her dressing gown and went to the tall gilt mirror and smiled at the alabastine reflection of herself as if she were greeting a beloved twin. My darling, she thought, you are lovelier than ever. You are like Diana. You could never really give yourself to any man, could you, my dear?

Her laugh bubbled softly and she held out her arms to the reflection, then she went over and parted the mosquito netting of her bed and stretched out drowsily on the cool sheet. Back in Salem she had hardly ever taken a nap in the afternoon, but down here everyone did it. Life was so much easier here, and more casual; and with twice as many servants and far more time on her hands she had quickly fallen into the siesta habit. There was, literally, little else to do but sleep in the afternoon, and it had the practical advantage of leaving one fresh to enjoy the long evenings.

Not, of course, that there seemed to be very much to occupy one here during the summer. The races were already over when she arrived, and only last week the theater had closed until fall. A few summer balls were scheduled, but otherwise there stretched only a lazy succession of informal parties and picnics on the beach. It was the men, really, who had all the fun. She envied them. They hunted and fished and gambled and frolicked with the women at the hotels or went off on long orgies at Josie Bangs's place. It wasn't quite fair. She wondered with a little stab of jealousy if Maury had ever been one of Josie's patrons.

Her mind revolved around the time she had first seen Maury. Something inexplicable had happened to her then. And the affair at Slatter's, by making everything so difficult, had only increased the attraction he held for her. Why was it that any man should be given the power to stir in her such excitement? There were moments when she hated him for it. She longed to be with him, and it made her furious that he should thus have the ascendancy. In some way she would have to triumph over him, just as she had triumphed over her father and Hugh Bishop.

As she thought of Hugh, her mouth curled in amusement. For all his cool arrogance among men and his self-assurance with Patty and other women, he had never so much as dared put his arm around her. He had, in fact, become her slave. And when he returned from Tallahassee she had no doubt that he would very properly, on bended knee, declare his love and request permission to speak to Aaron for her hand. That would be just the way Hugh would do it. His love-making would be as stiff and formal as his letters.

She laughed. And that silly, stupid Patty, she thought, she hates me for it. I don't care. But she can have her Hugh. Heaven knows I don't want him!

Then she stirred restlessly and for an instant allowed herself to be projected to the hour when she would be with Maury after sundown, and then half in fear she retreated and opened her eyes again. Through the mosquito netting she could see the glow of the oleanders on the mantel. The netting robbed them of reality and they became two-dimensional as if she were viewing a picture. Suddenly she realized that her odd feeling for them stemmed from something her mother had said years ago. There had been a picture of them in her mother's room, a water color.

She closed her eyes again, thinking curiously of Lucia.

Lucia had begun to worry about her daughter very early. Catherine was not like other children, at least the other Salem children. She was a tall, straight girl at ten, rather surprisingly developed for her age, with a loathing for parties and a queer habit of disappearing for hours at a time. She was inquisitive and inordinately secretive.

Once Catherine had come to her and asked, "Am I really your child, Mother?"

The question had sent a small swift stab of fright through her. "Why do you ask that?" she said, and instantly sought to remember every little item in the boxes stored in the attic. She had found Catherine in the attic only the day before, devoid of clothing and bedecked with crimson baubles from an ancient costume while she pawed avidly through the boxes. She had long been aware of this pagan manifestation in Catherine, who loved red and had a savage craving for things exotic, and it had dawned on her then that she may have made a mistake in not taking her daughter's social life more seriously. Perhaps Catherine needed that outlet.

"Of course you're my child," she answered.

"Then surely I'm not Father's child. I'm not like him at all."

"How ridiculous!" Yet she was alarmed at Catherine's penetration. In thinking back, she could remember nothing incriminating that Catherine might have found. Before marrying Aaron she had burned nearly everything Charles had given her except the water color of the oleanders. She had been especially careful about the letters; she was sure there was nothing left. Remembering the heartbreak of that burning and the thoroughness of it, she was able to feel reassured now.

Nevertheless, she was relieved when Catherine glanced at the water color and irrelevantly changed the subject.

"What are oleanders like, Mother?"

Oleanders? She looked wistfully at the picture, cherishing

it. It was the only sensual reminder she had permitted herself. Before she realized it she was talking happily, glad to have the other out of her mind. She was in the silence of the old garden again and could see the bright blossoms in the shadows of the gray trailing moss. . . . "They have a spicy scent, delicate and strange. Once you've smelled them you'll never forget. Sometimes I go into the pantry just to sniff the cloves. They remind me of oleanders. It's like being home and seeing it all again. Even the air is different there. . . ."

"Do you ever get homesick, Mother?"

"Homesick? No . . . no. Of course not." She was looking out of the window now, into the gloom of winter elms and snow. She was horribly, dreadfully homesick. It was something she had fought against ever since coming up here as Aaron's bride, little more than a month after her brother had killed Charles. She hated this cold land.

"I was very unhappy at home," she said finally. "Sometimes I would like to see it all again—the flowering things and the moss and the palms and the hot sun on the sand——"

Abruptly she pulled her mind away from this precipice. Her face resumed its customary lines of aloof severity.

But Catherine's eyes were bright, very bright and curious. "Mother, can't we go down there sometime? Can't we?"

"I'm afraid I've given you the wrong impression of it, dear. It . . . it isn't nice country, really. You wouldn't like it. Anyway your life is here. This is your home."

After that she was more careful. She did not want to give the least encouragement to the seed of something that might grow out of bounds. She had loved Charles in spite of his sadism and sensuality, but the languid indolence of his homeland was no place for his daughter. Catherine needed the cold and the straight sharp lines of New England.

Lucia prayed then, as she was to pray later when she lay dying, "Please, God, cleanse her. Do not let her be like Charles."

Chapter Fifteen

THE SPOTTED cattle drifted slowly through the open stretches of the town. At length, having grazed, they moved down to the beach beyond the great pier, grouping there and ruminating in the hot breathless evening. A few flies circled them, but their archenemy, the dog fly, had not yet arrived. It would appear in a few weeks, to torment them and drive them into the sea through the day, so that at this hour they would come stumbling forth hungry. But now they were content, unmindful of the heat lightning that shimmered in the east.

Around on the lower curve of the bay, where the shell walk ended, Maury waited at the edge of the pines. The sun vanished in the cloud continents at sea, and for a while the pines were richly vested in the afterglow. Then they dimmed, and the beach dimmed, and reality was suspended. And so at last when he saw her moving along the water's edge, she was more like a half-imagined figure in a dream. He stood very still. Her body had a fluid grace and her long full-skirted dress seemed to flow over the sand. Finally seeing him, she stopped and looked quickly around and then came on up to him, smiling and a little breathless.

She gave him her hands and, briefly, her lips. "I almost didn't get here," she said. "Are you glad to see me?"

"Terribly. What happened?"

"Hugh Bishop's back. I left Cousin Etta to entertain him while I slipped out through the back hall." She laughed. "I told her to tell Hugh I'd gone over to the Saxons'. He won't dare go over there as long as he thinks I'm there."

"Why not?"

"Don't be silly. He and Patty aren't speaking. And he didn't come all the way down here from Tallahassee just to make up with her."

"You're a devil," he told her. "I don't know why I want to marry you. But you'd better make up your mind to it and leave home before you cause any more trouble."

She made a face at him and pulled away, then suddenly clenched her hands as the distant voice of the savant rose in the stillness. "That awful man," she whispered. "I hope I don't have to hear him tonight."

"You won't," he said. "Not where we're going."

He helped her into the chaise, then untethered the mare and came back and swung in beside her. He was bareheaded and coatless as she had seen him three evenings ago. Had so little time passed? It seemed ages. She huddled back in the seat and studied him, his lean face and the dark bushing hair that curled down over the collar of his open shirt outlined in the twilight. There was a gentleness about him, and yet he seemed capable of anything.

He caught up the reins and turned the chaise around. "I've half a mind," he said, "to go through town and let everyone see us together. That would compromise you, and then——"

"Oh, bother! You won't get anywhere with that."

But she watched him uneasily until they reached the sandy road beyond the beach and he drove, not in the direction of town as she had been half-afraid he might, but on north through the darkening pines.

"Where are we going?"

"To a certain spot on the outer beach."

They rode for a while in silence.

Finally he touched her hand. "Catherine."

"What is it, Maury?"

"I . . . I haven't much to offer you," he said hesitantly. "I seem to have made a pretty bad mess of everything."

She waited, saying nothing.

"But I do have a plantation of sorts that could be developed. And I've a cottage. I'm sure you'd like it. I——"

He stopped and peered at her earnestly like a small boy. "I've never lived in that cottage," he went on. "And now I know why. It's because I built it for a home—and it's not a home when you live in it alone. It takes a special woman to make a home, and a family. When I stop and examine it, I guess I'm like most other men in that respect. It's something basic, I suppose. Anyway I've come to a sort of crossroads. I'm a little sick of the old course. But I can't take up the new one alone. I——" He hesitated, then added, "I'm afraid I've made it sound pretty prosaic, but I wanted you to know how I felt."

She looked away, still silent. She had never thought of him in this light. A man who wanted a home and children. She loathed children. She knew that she could never bring herself to have a child by any man, not even by him.

"Do . . . do you realize what you're asking me?" she said.

He stared at her. "Devil take it," he burst out suddenly, "I'm asking you to run away from that stultifying parent of yours and be my wife! Or doesn't the prospect interest you?"

"Oh, Maury, please——"

"Or does this interest you more?" he retorted as he dropped the reins and seized her tightly and drew her to him. The pressure of his lips kindled a flame in her that left her exultant, but with it went a quick hatred that he should have this power.

"You see," he said, when she had thrust away from him, gasping, "that ought to be reason enough for marrying—but if you won't marry me, then, by God, I'll have you anyway!"

"Humph!" she said, and then asked sweetly, "Did you bring a nice lunch?"

"Yes, you ornery vixen. It's in the basket under the seat. Chicken, ham, rolls, salad, preserves, pie, a bottle of dry sherry and——"

"Oh, that's wonderful!" She clapped her hands and then further pacified him by running her hand through his hair. Finally she peered out curiously.

They had turned off on an almost invisible trail through the scrub and were winding around a low dune, and now suddenly ahead of them appeared the open sea, dimly framed in the near dark between the leaning trunks of a small palm grove. The sea was soft velvet of the deepest purple; there was no surf tonight, but an almost indefinable swell caused a low murmuring along the beach. Where the water curled gently upon the sand it became alive and glittered like fox fire.

He drove on up to the edge of the grove and stopped.

"Where are we?" she asked, spellbound.

"Our destination. I imagined it, and lo! . . . here it is."

"It can't be real. Such places don't exist."

She got out before he could offer his hand and, catching up her skirts, ran down through the little grove to the beach. She stood motionless a moment and then whirled and waltzed a few yards and ran back. "It isn't real," she said breathlessly. "It's just some kind of enchantment of the night. By dawn it will vanish and there will be nothing here."

"There'll be mosquitoes here—or at least they'll be here soon. They'll come in clouds in a few weeks."

He had tied the mare and was pulling the lunch basket and a blanket from under the seat. Something fell from the blanket and she stooped and picked it up. She giggled.

"So you brought along one of Cricket's whips. Did you intend to beat me into submission?"

"I brought it in case there happened to be cattle around. But beating you is an idea. I think that's what you need."

"Then I'd better keep it," she said, dancing away from his reaching hand. She uncoiled it and flicked it tentatively, then followed him gaily through the grove.

At the head of the beach he set the basket down and spread the blanket on the sand between two palms.

"How about a fire?" he asked.

"Not yet. It's so strange and beautiful as it is. Wait till it's real dark. Will there be a moon tonight?"

"It ought to rise in a little while. Hungry yet?"

"Oh, let's explore the beach before we eat. But I'll have some of the wine now."

He found the bottle of wine, uncorked it and filled two glasses. She tossed the whip aside and sat down on the edge of the blanket and took one of the glasses. They drank slowly, suddenly shy and silent, each strongly conscious of the other as they stared out at the black velvet of the sea. Heat lightning shimmered on the horizon, lighting up vast fantastic valleys in the cloud continents. Somewhere in the palms behind them a small owl gave a bubbling cry that was like elfin laughter.

"It's so . . . so unreal," she said at last. "I've never been out like this before, away from everything. The world doesn't exist at all. . . ."

He slid over beside her and drew her head against his shoulder. Her hair was coiled in a heavy chignon; his fingers crept over it, found the combs and deftly drew them out. She gave a little gasp as her hair tumbled down.

"I've always wanted to do that," he said. "You have the most beautiful hair in the world." He ran his hand through it, luxuriating in the soft wealth of it, then bent her head gently back and kissed her throat. He could feel her pulse racing.

Suddenly she twisted away from him and sprang to her feet with a little excited laugh and ran out on the beach. He stared after her a moment, then got up and followed and caught her hand.

She moved quietly beside him for a while, clinging to his hand, and then all at once she stopped and said breathlessly, "I'm going wading! I've just got to get my feet wet. Turn your back and don't look."

In another minute they were children, splashing through the shallows in their bare feet, he with his trousers rolled, she with her long skirts caught up in one hand to her knees and exclaiming, "Oh, it's as warm as milk! And it sparkles!"

"Phosphorus," he said. "But be careful and scrape your feet along. There are stingarees. They won't bother you if you don't step on them."

"Are there sharks?"

"Just sand sharks. They're harmless."

She kept going deeper until the water was above her knees.

"I hate clothes," she said presently. "They seem so silly sometimes. I . . . I'd like to go farther out—get all of me into it. All of me."

"Why not? It's dark enough—and there's no one to see us."

"If I do, you . . . you won't think I'm wanton?"

"Of course not."

"Then . . . then lend me your handkerchief to tie up my hair. I mustn't get it wet. And . . . and stay away from the palms."

"All right."

She took his silk handkerchief and waded back to the beach, groped in the starlight for her slippers, then ran on and vanished in the palm grove. He stood motionless a few seconds, breath stifled by the tautness of his muscles; abruptly he pulled his attention from the grove and strode out across the sand to the palmettos by the dunes.

He undressed quickly and came back and waded to his waist, then plunged in and swam far out. Turning, he saw her entering the water, a pale woman-shape, statuesque and vague in the dark. He swam in slowly. Nearing shore he heard her laugh and saw a great phosphorescent swirl as she threw herself forward and swung both hands in a fiery arc around her.

"If I could only swim," she said, "I'd swim out and out and out. I'd swim all night."

He dived and came up near her, shaking his dark head like an otter and reaching for her hand, but she spun playfully away from him, rolling luxuriously and keeping out of his reach, a Nereid with a body outlined in phosphorescent fire. Then suddenly she stopped with a little cry and pointed and they both stood still, half floating, staring eastward.

The moon, immense and blood-red and almost terrible in its beauty, was rising above the cloud banks.

She stood close to him, wordless, her hand interlocked in his while they watched. The color held her. So red! So terribly red and molten! She could feel her blood pulsing with it, burning. She trembled. She wanted, madly, to hurl herself into a wild abandonment of movement. She turned to him, and the sudden urgent pressure of his lips on hers awoke her to a thundering violence in which submission was intolerable.

She tore away and ran out upon the beach. He followed, abject in his misunderstanding and tempered to quick gentleness. "No!" she gasped wildly in rebellion and darted into the palms; then she whirled upon him with the whip in her hands. "Oh, no! You've no right, none at all. I'm not that easy. I'll teach you. You'll never have me! Never, never, never!" She shrilled this last at him and brought the lash of the whip across his face with all her furious strength.

He recoiled, half blinded.

"For God's sake!" he cried. "What's the matter with you? Put that thing down!"

And then he leaped backward as the whip came at him again like an angry snake. It stung his chest and his thighs, and when he caught at it and tried to jerk it from her, he found her possessed with a force greater than his own, for the lash slithered through his fingers and returned to slash into him maddeningly. He could only retreat from it, protesting, still failing to understand the violence that had been kindled in her.

But now suddenly, as they came out of the shadow of the grove, he glimpsed her in the moonlight, a white clean-limbed Amazon with her hair falling free of the handkerchief and streaming wildly, and her face sharpened until it seemed to belong to a witch.

Her face shocked him, and in abrupt comprehension of her madness he stood rooted for an instant, then lunged toward her and tried to seize her. Only now the lash, wet and loaded with sand, cut like a thing of steel across his eyes. The sand was driven into his eyes, and he lost sight of her in a searing agony of red.

But the whip kept on. He groped for her, crying, "For the love of heaven, Catherine, stop it! Stop it!" And in a fury of pain, "You damn sadistic devil!"

She was merciless, and in his blindness he could neither grasp the whip nor avoid it. He tried to run from it and stumbled and fell. And now the heavy rawhide came down on him in the fullness of her passion, laying open the flesh. He lurched upright and away from it and fell again.

Then suddenly it stopped. He got to his knees and felt his way down to the water. He was vaguely aware of her ragged breathing somewhere behind him, and then he buried his face in the brine.

The demon had gone out of her; the whip hung leadenly and slid from her fingers. Something for years pent up seemed to have burst within her, a culmination that had flooded her with a long-sought bitter and sweet and yet frightening relief. Her hot body glistened with sweat. In her exhaustion she sank to her knees in an attitude of prayer and clutched the sand. At last a chill shook her, and a slow black fear crept in with the chill and began to grow. Fear drove her trembling to her feet. She looked once at Maury, then stepped backward and turned and ran unsteadily away with the sort of horror that a murderer feels after passion is spent. For she knew she had murdered love. She reached the blanket and in trembling haste drew on her clothes and her slippers. In her panic she forgot her stockings, her combs, her tangled hair. She could think only of fleeing this accursed spot, of escaping fear in the locked safety of her room.

She ran through the grove and untied the mare, pulled herself into the chaise and seized the reins. There was a frightening instant when she realized she did not know the way home. But the mare chose its path through the scrub, and presently in the moonlight she made out the trail that wound back to St. Joseph. She refused to think of Maury. She knew only that it would be impossible for her to face him again, ever.

As she reached the beach road leading into town she was surprised and alarmed to see lights in many of the houses. It had seemed far later than this, hours later. But people were still up and about. And the moonlight was very bright now. It was terribly, revealingly bright, almost like daylight. She shrank into a corner of the seat and wondered wildly what she had better do with the chaise. Already she was passing the governor's house. The mare, impatient for its familiar stall and manger, quickened stride and, almost before she realized where she was, it was trying to turn in at the shed in the rear of Rodman Carey's place. She fought the reins and managed to urge it on. Suddenly she perceived her mistake when she saw a carriage approaching. Sure that she would be seen and recognized, she turned off in rising panic into the pines between Carey's house and the Saxons'. When the carriage had gone by she sprang out and ran through the palmettos to the path overlooking the beach.

Now she forced herself to a walk, but, nearing the Saxon house, she stopped, thoroughly unnerved for the first time in her life and almost at the point of hysteria. She thought desperately: Why can't I calm down? Why can't I just calm down and go on past as if nothing were the matter?

The house was set well back from the beach and it had no

veranda where anyone might be watching. No one could possibly see her. And the shell walk was deserted. She clenched her hands and took a step and chilled as she heard her name spoken.

"Miss Catherine? I beg your pardon—but is that you?"

It was Hugh Bishop.

Stunned, she stopped without meaning to and whirled about, then tried to back away into the shadow of a pine. But it was too late. He had come up suddenly from the beach, a tall figure in carefully tailored linen, his wide-brimmed Panama under one arm. She knew instantly when she looked at him that he had noticed her disheveled dress and tangled hair. In all probability he had seen her run from the chaise. The chaise was clearly visible over in the pines and, she realized sickly, easily recognizable.

"I . . . I've been waiting for you," he was saying, his voice a little hoarse and unnatural. "Waiting all evening. I . . . I've been walking up and down the beach, watching for you. I thought you were at the Saxons'."

He stopped and his eyes swung to the chaise and back, then his jaws clicked and he turned on her grimly and caught her arm. "But you were not at the Saxons'," he blurted crudely, suddenly stripped of all pretense. "By God, you were out with him! I know! An' I reckon I know what's happened. By God——!"

She tried to jerk away, but he held her. "That sonofabitch!" he spat out in a shaking voice. "I'll kill 'im! By the living God, I'll kill 'im!"

"You . . . you . . ." she cried hysterically. "You dirty stupid jealous fool!" And she struck at him and broke away and ran.

Home at last and in her room with the door locked, she threw herself shuddering on the bed. Her stomach crawled and her bloodless hands tore at the coverlet.

"O God in heaven," she gasped, "O God in heaven, what have I done? What is going to happen to me now?"

Chapter Sixteen

CAREFULLY, LIKE a man who knows he is drunk and is trying desperately not to show it, Maury let himself in at Carey's door and stood a moment in the hall, listening. The house seemed quiet. Reassured, he groped unsteadily to the table and picked up the taper that had been left burning for him and crept slowly down the hall to his room. He could only guess the time; it was probably early in the morning for the taper had burned down almost to the holder.

In his room he set the taper on the washstand, almost missing the edge of it, felt his way to a chair and sank into it with an agonized sigh. His eyes throbbed and burned, and his back was afire. He pressed his palms over his eyes and leaned forward with his elbows on his knees, rocking slowly with a physical nausea that came from the sickness of his soul. He thought of a bloom he had seen one day on Cozumel; he had reached for it, expecting such beauty to have a rare fragrance. But it had been an unnatural thing, loathsome and poisonous.

"Mother in heaven," he murmured, "why does anything have to be like that?"

His eyes were burning unbearably. He drew himself up and

203

got the taper and managed to locate his kit. Sitting down on the floor he opened the kit and fumbled through it, taking out vials and bottles and holding them close to his eyes in an attempt to read the labels. He replaced all but two square brown bottles that were exactly alike, each containing a powder. Unable to make out his own inscriptions upon them, he touched the tip of his tongue to the stopper of each. The first contained ground cinchona, the other boracic acid. He took the boracic acid to the washstand and shook a little of it into a glass and filled the glass with water. When the powder was dissolved he got a fresh handkerchief from his linen, wadded it into the glass then squeezed it into his eyes. It brought almost instant relief.

He undressed, and his finger tips explored the welts on his body. Those on his back were the worst, and he was amazed even now that she had been able to strike so hard. She had cut into him with the strength of a strong man. His back stung with the brine he had lain in for a long time afterward. Knowing it would heal quicker if left untouched, he gingerly drew on a dressing robe, then eased into the chair again and held the sodden handkerchief over his eyes.

He wanted a drink badly. He hated the torture of rising and getting it, but he had to have it. Presently he forced himself up and, leaving the wadded handkerchief on the chair, went to the washstand and found a fresh taper in the drawer. After lighting it from the sputtering wick of the old one, he crept into the dark hall and through the house to Carey's study. He was unaware that the night had turned black outside and that thunder rumbled over the bay. He found the rum decanter and sloshed some into a glass and drank it in a single gulp, and then filled the glass and was about to drink again when a prolonged flash of heat lightning brightened the room and he caught a dim reflection of himself in the oval mirror over the table. He held the taper high and thrust his face close to the mirror, and with the next flash saw the angry welt running across his cheek to his left eye, which was swollen nearly shut. The other eye was swollen and bloodshot, but he was beginning to see out of it fairly well.

After he set the taper aside, he took another swallow of rum. He felt steadier, but involuntarily cringed at the sound of a scraping step behind him. He had not heard Carey get up.

He turned slowly, keeping the left side of his face averted, and made out Carey's thin hunched form standing just within the study door. There was something odd in the way Carey stood there, with his frail hands clenched at the sides of his old blue dressing robe.

"I've been sitting up, waiting for you," Carey said in a tight voice. "I must have fallen asleep. I didn't hear you come in."

"I got in only a little while ago. I . . . I had a bit of trouble."

"So I've gathered."

"What's the matter, Rod?"

He could not see Carey's eyes, but he could feel them reaching across the room, cold and probing.

"You were out with Catherine tonight?"

Catherine. There was a certain formality in the use of the name. Carey had never called her that before.

"What's wrong, Rod. Why do you ask that?"

"Don't hedge. I know you were with her. Furthermore, I know that she drove home alone. I was on the side porch when your horse and chaise went by. I paid no attention to it until it turned off into the pines and someone got out and ran over to the walk, and the horse started back toward the stable with no one at the reins. Only a person highly agitated or frightened would have driven home that way and abandoned the horse as she did."

Carey stopped a moment and ran the tip of his tongue over thin dry lips. In the yellow light of the taper his face was like a mask of death.

"Soon afterward Hugh Bishop came here and asked to see you."

"Bishop came here to . . . to see me? But why?"

"He didn't say, but I can guess. He'd been waiting for Catherine to come home. I deem it rather likely that he saw her leave the chaise and assumed the same thing that I have."

"For God's sake, Rod, surely you don't think——"

"I know what I think, and I don't care to listen to any of your glib explanations! I've overlooked a great deal in you on the assumption that you were a gentleman. I thought you cared deeply for Catherine, and until tonight I never once questioned this clandestine affair you've been carrying on."

"But Rod——"

"I said that I don't want to hear anything out of you! The condition of your face tells me enough. Furthermore, I know Catherine. She is a lady, and her integrity is beyond question. She must have cared a great deal for you to have consented to go riding with you tonight. I can excuse petty philandering with an easy woman; no man is above that. But only a blackguard would attempt what amounts to a criminal assault on a lady."

Maury could only stare at Carey—shocked, incredulous, utterly dumfounded. This was the last thing he would ever have expected from a man like Carey. How could anyone who had been so close a friend, who had always been so tolerant and broad-minded and understanding, turn on him in such a manner? It seemed entirely out of character. Carey, with his worldly philosophy, his debonair acceptance of life and all its perversities, should at least have withheld judgment and given him the benefit of the doubt. But Carey, without allowing him a word, had instantly condemned him.

He looked miserably across the room and then down at his feet, suddenly realizing what he had not perceived before: that Catherine was Carey's blind spot. The man could not see her as he saw other women. And there was nothing, absolutely nothing, that he could tell Carey.

He heard Carey say, "If I were a fighting man, I'd call you

out. But I'll leave that to Bishop. In the meantime I'll have to ask you to leave."

The words cut deeper than the whip had cut. He looked again at Carey and opened his mouth, trying to say what he knew he could not say, then closed it.

Carey said, "I'm ordering you to leave. I mean now. Get on your clothes and get out of here!"

The moon had vanished when Cricket drove him away, and the storm, that had been gathering for hours, now broke with a sudden rush of wind that tore moaning through the pines. Behind them in the bay, far out, he could hear the low roar of the approaching rain. The roar grew to a mighty drumming. When it was almost upon them the mare broke stride, reared once and bolted.

The rain swept over them in a solid sheet and passed on. Following it came a second wall of rain that beat down with such force that the earth seemed to shake with the thunder of it. Through it the frightened mare plunged on madly with the Negro helpless at the reins. Maury, little caring, clung stiffly to the seat and with his one good eye watched the trees ahead in the flickering lightning. If the mare left the road the careening chaise would be smashed instantly in the pines. He considered the prospect disinterestedly. It did not matter what happened or where they went. Nothing mattered.

They tore through town, past the hotels where tapers still burned in the gaming rooms, and down into the street of brothels and cheap taverns near the race track. They flew by Slatter's jail and splashed through a shallow creek. Beyond was a fork in the road. The right fork led only to Josie Bangs's place, but on the left the road wound northward through a hundred miles of wilderness to the plantation lands around Marianna. It was a dangerous road, no longer traveled except under escort, and for a moment he was tempted to seize the reins and aid fate by turning into it. But before he could do anything the mare veered off to the right.

He sighed. It made little difference. At least he could get rum at Josie's. He decided that rum was what he wanted. A great deal of rum.

The rain ceased abruptly and the mare slowed and finally stood still with heaving sides. The Negro sat cursing, then drew back on the reins to turn around.

"Go on," Maury ordered. "Go on to Miss Josie's."

The main building housing the establishment of Josie Bangs had originally been a tavern for rivermen. The railroad had formerly come here, before its extension and change of route, and the place had been notorious for its many vicious brawls and frequent murders. But with the building of the amazing trestle that carried the rails on over the swamps to the main river channel, the tavern's clientele had changed. Then Josie had come to refurbish the long wooden structure under the oaks and convert it into a sumptuous bordello that had few equals anywhere east of New Orleans. What the building lacked in architecture was more than compensated by Josie's furnishings and her lavish and at times indiscriminate use of the color rose. Even the big jalousie doors opening from the veranda had not escaped, and greeted one with the bright glow of dawn.

These doors were closed and barred on the inside when Maury arrived, but he could hear voices and soft laughter coming from the end of the hall and little gay tinkling measures from a mandolin. He rattled the doors and pounded on them. Finally he heard steps and turned and made out a short heavy man waddling across the veranda like a rolling whisky barrel.

"Hello, Cisco."

The man gave him a quick searching glance in the ruby light of the ship's lantern overhead. "Oh, hit's you, Mr. St. John. I'll tell Hannah to let you in."

"Having a little trouble?"

Cisco shrugged and glanced down at the dim bayou where, vaguely, a small paddle-wheeler could be made out at the landing. Cisco's job was to keep out undesirables. Josie herself usually handled altercations within.

"Them freight boats," murmured Cisco. "They still put in here sometimes. Ye know what some o' them are like." He spoke to someone through the doors, then opened one of them as the bar on the other side was lifted.

Maury entered, and a big Negress closed the door and replaced the bar. She curtsied politely and, when he asked for Josie, she led him across the hall to a small Louis XV reception room where guests, if they did not wish to mingle with the patrons in the adjoining salon, could discreetly make their choice and then vanish upstairs. Here a large matronly woman of fifty, reserved and prim in a very plain black dress and severe coiffure, was seated stiffly on a chaise longue, having a whisky while she thumbed through the latest copy of *Godey's*. Josie had ransacked New Orleans for crystal, variegated marble, ottomans, great gilt mirrors and a wealth of heavily carved and rose-upholstered furniture. In the passionate warmth of all this rococo elegance she seemed startlingly out of place. One would have taken her for the headmistress of a seminary.

Seeing Maury she rose instantly, her square composed face suddenly alight. "Well! This is indeed a pleasure!"

"Hello, Josie."

He touched her hand, attempted what he thought was a smile, then turned uncertainly and sank on a sofa. At any other time her cultured voice and deceiving primness would have amused and diverted him. They were old friends who understood each other, but tonight even her extraordinary personality had no effect on his blackness.

"All I want," he mumbled, "is some rum—plenty of it—and a room to drink it in."

She studied him thoughtfully a moment and suddenly sat

down beside him and took his hand. "What's the matter,
honey? Are you in trouble?"

"No. I . . . I'm just a little low."

She touched his forehead. "You look like hell, but you
haven't any fever. Go in yonder while I hunt up a gloom
chaser."

He took one of the candles from the table and entered the
luxurious bedchamber on the left. The place was a lavish
repetition of Josie's flair for rose. He closed his eyes against
it and waited. She returned presently with a goblet and a large
decanter of rum. "If you want anything, just pull the tassel
by the door. And it's all on the house. You don't know it, but
you did me quite a favor recently."

"How's that?"

"Oh, I'll tell you sometime." She hesitated at the door. "I
know a person who can cheer you up. She's new here and
she's a perfect darling. . . ."

"No," he growled.

"Oh, don't be silly. When a man's in your state he needs . . .
er . . . something special in the way of diversion."

"Go on," he muttered. "Leave me alone."

She went out and closed the door softly behind her. He
eased himself on the sofa at the foot of the bed, removed his
shoes and proceeded methodically to get drunk.

Somewhere back in the building he could hear the idle strum-
ming of the mandolin. Occasionally someone came down the
stairway into the hall and was let outside, and presently a saddle horse or a carriage would move slowly away in the night.
Once a coach loaded with young revelers stopped in the
compound, and for a little while the place was awake with
discordant singing, laughter and unsteady footsteps in the upper
halls. At last quiet came. He tried to look at his watch but
could not make out the dial in the candlelight. He seemed to be
holding two watches, and each had a woman's face. He wondered why he had come here.

"I'm drunk," he said profoundly, and heard a giggle near his shoulder.

He fumbled with the watch, trying to put it away, and turned slowly to stare at the girl sitting beside him. He had not seen her enter. She was just there, wearing nothing, it seemed, but her long lustrous yellow hair, so that she appeared to be all soft yellow gold as if she had suddenly materialized from the candlelight. He hardly noticed her face; he could see only her hair.

"I'm Buttercup," he heard her say. "Josie, she said you was awful nice an' feelin' bad, an' mebbe I could make you feel better."

"Buttercup," he said hoarsely. "That's not your name. I've seen you before . . . your hair——" He gaped at it in a sort of fascinated horror and revulsion.

"I never seen you before, an' my name is too Buttercup. Leastways that's my nickname. Ask Miss Josie."

"You've got Catherine's hair. . . ."

"My name ain't Catherine! An' there ain't no other girl. . . . Aw, honey, you's just drunk an' all mixed up. Here, lemme help you off with your clothes an' put you to bed. Don't you wanna go to bed, huh?" She reached out and began unbuttoning his shirt, and one hand crept around his shoulders.

He recoiled in quick pain and nausea and lurched away.

Outside abruptly there was a pistol shot, a sudden rush of feet across the veranda and loud cursing that was drowned by the impact of heavy bodies against the jalousie doors. Wood splintered and the doors crashed inward, filling the hall with a confusion of men's voices, wild, drunken and profane. The girl sprang up like a frightened cat and darted across the room, but whirled and came back screaming as the door burst open and a huge booted and bearded figure sprang inside.

The man yelled and lunged after her. "Come back 'ere, ye li'l yeller-haired kitty!" He caught her as she was going under the bed and was dragging her out when two other figures tumbled cursing through the door and fell sprawling. Behind them came Josie. She carried a cocked pistol in one hand and in the other a heavy shillelagh which she laid about her vigorously. Her culture had vanished.

"You stinkin' river scum!" she shrilled. "You goddamn wallowing hogs! You dirty sons o' yellow-bellied rats! I'll teach you to come breaking into my place an' laying hands on my girls! They're not for the likes o' you! Get out o' here! Get your filthy hides out o' here while you can still crawl!"

Doors banged upstairs, girls screamed, and fighting went on in the hall. The two men on the floor wobbled to their feet, but the bearded man laughed and tore open his shirt and drunkenly pounded his broad hairy chest with both fists. "I'm the ole bull 'gator o' the swamps!" he yelled. "I'm hand-forged o' black iron an' brass-studded, an' nothin' kin touch me! I'm a-gonna rip ye apart, Josie!"

He made a flying leap toward her, and she shot him. He fell, cursing horribly, managed to get up, then staggered back against Maury and collapsed.

Maury, with elaborate distaste, thrust him aside and mumbled, "Lemme 'lone, All I want is peace 'n' quiet. Can't a man have peace 'n' quiet while 'e drinks?"

He sloshed more rum into his goblet, swallowed part of it and, with the decanter in one hand and the goblet in the other, got up and surveyed the room, searching for the door. He made out the door but it seemed to move deliriously back and forth and part of the time it was blocked with a phantasmagoric mass of screaming, roaring, foully cursing figures, some of them nude, some half-clad, others in muddy boots and buckskins, all weaving in and out of the darkness of the adjoining room and only partially glimpsed like demoniac imaginings in the glow of the single candle that still burned near the sofa.

"Nightmare," he muttered. "All life's a nightmare. I'm goin' 'way . . . find quiet . . . peace. . . ."

He closed his eyes, thinking the nightmare would vanish,

and started for the door. The cries, roars, stampings, crashes and cursing continued. He collided with the wall, turned, groped, found open space and went through it. Something knocked the goblet from his hand but he went on. Then a heavy blow stunned him and he fell. Bare feet stumbled over him, boots kicked him and the world seemed to fall on him. He rolled over and began to crawl, still clinging to the decanter. Reaching a corner he sat up and raised the decanter to his lips and drank deeply, then with a great effort managed to get to his feet. He opened his eyes and saw a pale square of light. He groped toward it, stumbled over the broken jalousie doors and tottered out across the veranda into the dawn.

"Peace . . . quiet . . ." he mumbled, and moved through the shadowy oaks and down to the landing, reaching for the new brightness of morning. Something blocked his way, but he groped around it, past stanchions, barrels and piled cordwood, tripping over ropes, until suddenly the red sun, sliding in molten heat above the swamp, burned in his face and he felt the warmth of it cutting through him. It was quiet here and warm and peaceful. He sank down, tried once to raise the decanter to his lips, failed and let it slide from his fingers. His head rolled on his chest. Suddenly he collapsed.

Pain stalked him, crept stealthily around him and pounced like a panther upon him, then tore through his head as if a broken bottle were being twisted in his brain. Pain retreated, came again and gnawed him in a hundred places and awoke a slumbering cat in his belly that clawed to get out. He retched. The deck beneath him shook with a steady rumbling.

A voice said, "Ye want 'is pants too? Them's good pants."

"They ain't good no more. Christ, look at 'em!"

"They's better goddamn pants than ary ones you ever had around you."

"I done tole ye I don't want 'em. If'n ye thinks they's so goddamn good, why the hell don't you take 'em?"

"I got me a good pair o' pants."

A new and stronger voice cut in with a string of obscenities and ordered, "Belay the arguing an' roll the bastard over the side. I'm tired lookin' at 'im."

Pain tore through him again as someone seized his arm and dragged him across the deck. He flopped over on his face.

There was an exclamation. "Look at 'is back! I never seen that when I took 'is shirt off."

"Somebody sure laid it to 'im. Who coulda put a whip to a fancy dude like him?"

"Mebbe he's part nigger an' tried to pass hisself off as white. Grab 'is leg! Heave ho!"

The shock of cold fresh water brought him to a horrid wakefulness. He clawed upward, fighting to reach the surface. He gained it, choking, and managed to fill his lungs with air; then he caught a brief glimpse of a very small and dirty stern-wheeler sliding around a bend. Then he went down again.

He was longer coming up this time, for his first frenzy of movement had taken all his strength. Something brushed against him and he caught at it feebly and clung to it, with his face just above the surface. His head hammered with a blinding pain. It was minutes before the confusing patterns of light and dark assembled themselves into recognizable form, and he saw that he was clinging to a mass of vines and moss trailing from an overhanging limb.

He seemed to be in a bayou or one of the river channels. Directly behind him, instead of a bank, there was only a tight matted growth of vines and twisting roots and gnarled trunks, rising in such a close tangle from the water that a snake would have had difficulty wriggling through it. The opposite bank, seventy or eighty yards away, was hidden in black shadow under the tumbled vegetation.

He pondered his predicament, his mind groping with questions. It was very difficult to hold his thoughts together; while he pursued answers, the questions themselves would slide away and he would have to begin all over again, slowly, wrestling with the simplest points of logic like a small child trying to pyramid a handful of blocks. He could not see the sun, but after much study of the shadows he established the time: It was late in the afternoon. Direction was now apparent: He was on the north side of the watercourse, and probably somewhere on the route between Josie's place and the main river, somewhere in the several hundred square miles of morass that bordered the coast. To get out of it he would have to begin by swimming the watercourse. It hardly seemed worth the bother. It wasn't important that he live. Nothing was important.

His hand slipped from the supporting vines and moss, and he drifted free in the slow placid current.

He had no memory, later, of reaching the other side of the bayou, and of crawling slowly through muck, water, vines and debris. He crawled through tangles of tupelo, thickets of bay and titi into the dry pinelands. He awoke once as if from a long sleep, not refreshed but with his mind free and at peace, his body nonexistent while he gazed upward at the stars. And there came to him a moment of strange clarity when he looked on himself inquiringly and with sudden awe.

Why am I here? he asked. Why am I here in this place of shadows, in this lost corner on an infinitesimal and trifling speck of dust that is whirling through unknown space in so many different directions at once, slavishly following some remote pattern that is beyond comprehension? Why am I here, and what placed me here? And who and what is this that is myself? Not the head or the body of me or that part of me that knows pains and hungers. That is only the machine, the house that I live in. But who and what am *I*, the *unknown* who orders the machine and dwells within the house? No man knows me, and no woman. I am not even allowed to know myself. I am hidden here alone behind two windows, looking out when

I will, seeing, but never seen. Am I, too, like this particle to which I cling, only a slave to some remote and incomprehensible pattern?

When he awoke again it was day and he was shaking with a deathly chill, yet the day was burning and the locusts in the pines were shrilling their song of heat. The two Negroes who found him were out hunting wild cattle; they did not recognize him, but they knew where to take him when he mumbled his name, for they knew his manservant.

When perception returned to him he was in his great carved bed, and Adrienne seemed to be bending over him.

Chapter Seventeen

I

ALWAYS IN that first week at home she was Adrienne, and
when he called her by that name she would appear
instantly, as silently as a wraith, to tend his needs. She
never failed him, and yet wraithlike she never answered
when he spoke. Once he called to her pettishly, demanding a
reply to some trifling question that seemed important, and
suddenly he saw her standing at the foot of the bed, her small
hands clenched and her lips quivering to form speech that
would not come, and tears glistened in her eyes. And now
Adrienne vanished and she became the girl he had bought at
Slatter's.

"You're Zeda," he mumbled. "Zeda. But you're so like
Adrienne. I've been confused."

She stood there looking at him with her lower lip caught
between her teeth, and he said, "You're wondering about
Adrienne. She was my sister. I . . . I treated her very badly."

Her eyes widened on him for an instant, then she looked

217

down and turned away. He watched her curiously as she moved about the darkened room, hastily picking up scattered scraps of cloth and folding them into a workbasket. Evidently she had been cutting out a dress. Finally she adjusted the shutters against the sun, came back and sat down near the head of the bed and began fanning him slowly with a large palm-leaf fan. She was thinner than when he had seen her last, and her dark shadowed eyes were enormous, but they were no longer haunted. She was wearing a neat white cotton dress and her hair was in two thick black braids down her back. She seemed very child-like and fragile and yet intensely and determinedly capable.

He wondered how she had ever contrived here alone. At the thought he had a sudden feeling of guilt for, ever since leaving her here weeks ago, he had mentally turned his back on her and had not even inquired about her welfare, although he had never quite succeeded in denying her to his consciousness.

For a while he lay motionless, comfortably aware of the great bed enclosing him, and his eyes traced the carving on the posts as one would examine the features of an old and beloved friend. Then his glance went slowly round the room again, touching familiar objects. A feeling of deep peace came over him. This, the quiet and the seclusion of his own cottage, was what he had long wanted. It gave him the illusion of protection and escape, as if the world beyond these walls and beyond the tight growth of the yard and the bordering picket fence did not exist.

Then suddenly he thought of Catherine. It was as if a cold hand had clutched his belly. She couldn't help it, he tried to tell himself, and knew that she couldn't help it, that the taint was in her and that she was born with it, and that she was only a victim to be pitied. But the rationalization did no good. He could feel no pity. "Damn her!" he muttered. "Damn her!"

His hands shook. A malarial chill crept through him, racking him with a deadly coldness. He clawed at the bedcovering for warmth. Abruptly he was lost again in the blackness of his own inadequacies, his hates and his failures. Had he been able he would have risen and fled.

Juan Garver stopped in to see him daily, and as he improved May began bringing him delicacies to tempt his appetite. He nibbled them disinterestedly or left them on his tray untouched.

"Holy God!" May said to him at last. "You've got to eat! You're only a skeleton! Juan, can't you give him something to make him eat?"

"I could, but it wouldn't keep the French and Irish in him from being at odds over something. He'll eat when he gets good and ready. He shouldn't eat too much now anyway."

"I'm damn sick and tired of lying here," Maury grumbled. "I've got to get out of here. I've got to do something. If I don't get away from here soon . . ."

"You've got to take it easy," Juan cautioned, regarding him soberly. "You've had a devil of a siege. I was really worried about you for a while. You had every symptom of yellow jack: congestion in the eyes, nausea, swollen face, delirium and a raging fever. But it was just a bad case of ague, with complications. I wish you could remember what happened to you before those Negroes found you."

May said, "I couldn't get anything from Cricket, but I'll lay two bits the rake was out at Josie's place the night of the big fight. Did they catch you with your pants down, Maury?"

"Your indelicacy," Juan said complacently, "is revolting. Have you no shame, woman?"

"I was out at Josie's," Maury admitted sourly. "But I didn't happen to be wenching. I was just getting drunk."

May rolled her eyes. "Oh, come now! There isn't a wench alive could keep her hands off you."

"Shut up!" Juan ordered her. "I'm trying to find out what happened. He was found twenty miles from Josie's, beaten, robbed and left to die. I'd like to catch those damn wretches. There's been altogether too much crime. I'd like to——"

"Forget it," said Maury. "It doesn't matter. You're always

crusading, Juan, trying to right wrongs and make the human race over. Damnation, you've dosed enough gullets to know that a human is only another animal, and that there's nothing you can do about his nature except to geld him or kill him. And he's hardly worth the bother. He's——"

"Inherently, my friend, man has some noble qualities. Man ——"

"Bah! Inherently he's the greediest——"

"God help me!" May interrupted, rising. "I'm all gaîl at the human race. I think I'll go out and find me a throat to cut. Should I use a bistoury, Maury, or just a plain butcher knife?"

"Aw, dammit, sit down! Don't mind me. I lie here all day. . . ." He sighed and his eyes unconsciously sought the hall door where Zeda, if he so much as whispered her name, would suddenly appear.

May went to the door and glanced down the hall and came back. "Your nurse," she said, "is in the kitchen shelling peas for your supper. She's such a shy little thing. She always goes back there to work when we come. At other times she practically lives in the hall. Her cot's just outside the door."

"Oh! I . . . I didn't realize."

"You ungrateful whelp, you don't realize how lucky you are to have her." May sat down and wiped her sleeve across her dark beetling brows and her long upper lip that showed more than a trace of a mustache. "Lordy, it's hot! I'm afraid there's going to be a lot of fever this season. Juan has a dozen cases already. As I was saying about Zeda——"

"I haven't had a chance to thank you for keeping an eye on her."

"Fiddlesticks. After a day or two to get used to things she didn't need any looking after. She's unusually intelligent. And she's made practically all her own clothes. She sews beautifully. I was surprised. She's been well-raised, Maury. I just can't understand how she ever fell into that pig Slatter's hands. I'll swear she's white—a mixture, of course—French, Spanish and something. But I mean there's no Negro in her. She's as white as I am. Don't you think so, Juan?"

"Indubitably, my dove, but that's hardly a recommendation. There are times when I look at you that I entertain the gravest doubts——"

"You cockroach!" she bellowed. She lunged for him, cursing boisterously, pulled him down on the floor and sat on him. "You whelp," she said.

"You're no lady," he panted. "I don't know why I married you. You're not even beautiful."

"Oh, but I am in my way. I have my points."

"Alas, you have, and they're resting heavily upon me."

"Humph, I thought you liked big women."

"Ah, but I do, except when they're pressing the life out of me. Anyway, I've a call to make down the street."

She tweaked his nose and got up. "Run along, pet, and make your call. I'll stay here and gossip awhile."

Juan left. Then May, at the sound of a quick metallic clinking from the back porch, went to the corner window and peered out. "That's her," she said. "She's calling that little nigger of yours to run an errand. You ought to see the way she bosses him around without saying a word. She calls him by tapping on a bottle, and when she wants him to go marketing she draws every little thing she wants on a piece of paper and makes him name it aloud so there won't be any mistake. I think Cricket's jealous. She's hardly let him do a thing for you except empty the slops."

She came over and started to fold the rumpled coverlet at the foot of the bed, then stopped. "No, I'd better leave that for her. She's furious at me now for bringing over puddings she thinks she can make better herself. By the way, Maury, did you ever find out where she came from?"

"I haven't had a chance to question her much."

"Well, I tried, but it's no use. What in the world are you going to do with her?"

"I don't know."

May studied the coverlet. "Aren't you afraid that having her here might complicate matters in St. Joseph?"

"I'm through with St. Joseph. I hope I never see the damn place again."

She peered at him soberly a moment, then sat down on the coverlet and leaned against the bedpost. "I've been afraid of that. I'm sorry, honey. I'm awful sorry."

"Don't feel sorry," he growled. "It doesn't matter."

"I hate to see you turn sour again."

"I'm not sour."

"Yes, you are. You're just like you were when you first came here, only worse. You were in a pretty bad state then. I was hoping she'd be a sort of . . . well, a beacon for a better course. You know what I mean."

"That's one beacon I can't steer by. I'll follow my own damn course from now on."

"Maury, you can't start those Cuban trips again."

"Why the hell can't I?"

"You just can't. It's dangerous."

He shrugged. "What of it? Anyhow, I'm in debt. I've got to do something."

"But not that. They're out to get you if you ever try it again. I know. I've been talking to people and listening. There's another patrol vessel down here. The *Gunderson*—a steam brig. She's put in here several times. And the captains of both vessels, m'lad, have been seeing a lot of that Maxie Pond down at the customs office."

"Well, they should. That's their business."

"Maybe you'll be more interested when I tell you that Maxie has been seeing a lot of your old friend Tulita."

"The bastard always wanted her. He can have her."

"Don't be a fool! They'll see you hanged!"

"Yeah? How? What can that greedy Tulita do? She doesn't know anything."

"She knows about Bruin, and how you deal with him, and about your plantation up the river and how you send Negroes up there at times when Slatter doesn't get 'em. She also knows who your crew members are. I'm sure she knows all those things and more, because I know 'em myself just from being around you. You're not very discreet at times. I'm just trying to talk some sense into you, because you don't know what's going on. If you'd ever read the papers you'd realize the government's out to put an end to this slave running. They mean business. If a vessel gets away from them at sea, they're all set to follow things up ashore. There was a case of that near Savannah a short time ago. The vessel got through and made a landing at night—but they were ready for 'em and caught 'em red-handed at the barracoon."

"That's interesting. It ought to raise the price of blacks."

"Maury, you fool, that'll be happening here next! There's been a lot of whispering lately about Bruin."

"There's always been whispering about Bruin. And there's always been talk of the Franklin Guards being ordered up there to burn 'im out. They'd better not try it."

May stared at him. "Hasn't anything I've said made any impression on your thick head?"

"The thick head rings a bit, but that's just the ground cinchona Juan's been pouring into me."

"Maury, don't you care what you do, or what happens to you?"

His shoulders twitched faintly in an indication of a shrug. His eyes were sunken and there was a grimness about him that she had never seen before. It made him look, she thought, more saturnine than ever. Almost sinister. She realized quite suddenly that he had in him far darker capacities than she had ever suspected of him. How could anything she could say ever deter him in the slightest from going to sea again? He was such an odd and unstable man, with great weaknesses; and yet in some ways he was very strong. Yes, and dangerous.

"Tell me," he said, ignoring her question: "How did Josie come out in that free-for-all? Was she hurt?"

"Not Josie. They nearly wrecked her place, I hear, but she killed one of them and broke a lot of heads. There's a woman for you!" She stood up, then looked down at him, frowning. "Maury, for God's sake, if you won't listen to reason, at least hold off for a while and let them think you're through with it. If you'd wait till fall——"

He laughed thinly. "Why, May, I'm surprised at you. Think of all the poor blacks down in Cuba, overworked and underfed, dying of the lash and praying to be sold in America! Can't you see that I'm a man consecrated to a noble mission? How terrible to delay! How utterly unfeeling——"

"Oh, hell!" she said, starting for the door. "You make me sick."

II

Esteban, the gray little hunchback, came many times to see him and was sent on many errands: to Bruin, to the plantation up the river and at last to Slatter who promised to arrange certain matters with the Georgia planters that had formerly been handled by Two-Jack. Finally Esteban returned to Whisky George to look after the *Salvador*.

Maury followed him as soon as he was strong enough, but another fortnight passed before the schooner could be fully readied and manned.

Early one morning, scrubbed and painted and holystoned, and with her sails freshly limed so that she wore an air of gleaming respectability, she came down with the tide into the upper bay. Ignoring the inconspicuous route around the far eastern tip of the island, she ran brazenly through the main anchorage and out at West Pass, all in plain sight of the town and certain startled gentlemen in the Customs House. Outside, with the keeper of St. George light watching her curiously through his glass, she came lightly about and settled down for a long easy jog across the Gulf. It was a beautiful June morning.

This departure, however bold, was far from auspicious. It did not have Bruin's blessing, nor was Finch aboard. No one had seen Finch since the last trip, and of the former crew members there remained only Bruin's boy and Esteban. Bruin had made up the deficiency by selecting the five most experienced of his mulatto progeny and ordering them aboard, but this was as far as he would go.

"I don't like the looks o' things," Bruin told him. "Ye shoulda made this trip two months ago. If'n ye'd done it then, I'da played along. Hit's too late now. I don't want no part of it."

"What's the matter, Mace?"

"Ye got twice as many eyes as I got. Ye blind in 'em both?"

"You mean you really think they'll send the Guards up here to raid you?"

"I hain't a-thinkin'. I'm jest a-feelin', an' I feel trouble. I don't mind trouble with man, but I don't aim to have it with the guv'mint. I got the Seminole on one side o' me an' the guv'mint on t'other. If'n I war younger, an' ary one come a-pressin' me, I'd fight. But I'm too old, an' I done seen too much. I don't aim to handle no more blacks fer a spell."

"That's going to make things a bit difficult."

"You don't have to make no trip now. You kin wait."

Maury shook his head irritably. "I'm not going to wait around here all summer because of a lot of damn talk. The weather's good now and I could make a killing. I need money. If I don't make it, how d'you expect me to pay you back?"

"I hain't a-pressin' ye fer nothin'. An' I hain't a-tryin' to hold ye ashore if'n ye're bound to go. But I hain't a-puttin' no money in it. An' ye hain't a-landin' no niggers here till I give the word."

Maury found himself staring into Bruin's malignant eye. It

chilled him and he looked away. Esteban had told him that Bruin had become difficult, but he had supposed that it was merely because Esteban did not understand the old man.

"I've been counting on your buying a few shares, Mace."

Bruin shrugged. "I'll buy in at the right time, but this hain't it. Ye hain't fit enough to make no trip now. An' ye can't count on the weather. Hit's been good too long. Ye'll be gittin' down there in the fever season an' comin' back in the squalls an' heat. Ary thing go wrong, an' ye'll lose t'hull damn load to flux an' fever. I'd ruther them Franklin Guards come a-botherin' me than to have somebody bringin' me the fever. Howsomever—" Bruin stopped and studied him thoughtfully— "if'n ye're bound to go, an' ye come through with a healthy load, ye kin run up in the fork east o' here an' into that li'l slough. Bat, he knows the place. Ye'll be safe there. An' I'll have my boys unload ye an' paddle 'em either to Slatter or to that place o' yourn upstream. That's all I'll promise."

Maury sighed. "I reckon that's fair enough, Mace. But it takes cash to buy Negroes."

"Ye got cash enough, now that Two-Jack hain't around to grab hit." Bruin chuckled. "You done yo'self a good turn there."

"How's that?"

"Slatter finally sold them fourteen fellers from the last trip. Some not lookin' so good, they only brung a mite over five thousand. But takin' out his share an' mine, there's better'n four thousand left. I reckon hit's yourn. An' hit's all in hard Georgy money, which makes up fer the low price. With what you an' Esteban already got, ye'll have enough fer a middlin' load. Ye shouldn't try to handle too many anyhow this time o' the year."

Maury had not counted on the sale of those fourteen. Even so, the amount seemed far under his needs. Four thousand. Esteban's savings, pooled with his own, would swell it to nearly seven thousand. In gold and silver, of course, the sum was considerable, with a purchasing power more than double its equivalent in Territorial notes. But no Cuban dealer would look at a note, and seven thousand in hard money wouldn't buy many good blacks. At least not in Cuba.

Of his own money he had only the hundred and twenty good-luck pieces taken from his bed. Removing them had been like robbing a friend, and he had hesitated a long time before deciding to do it. Silly, of course, to feel that way about it. But after getting the pieces out he'd had the empty sensation of having crossed a sort of Rubicon and of feeling that nothing would ever again be the same. And to top it he'd looked up to find Zeda standing in the door, watching, and there'd been an odd expression on her face as if she'd caught him in a sacrilege. Her lips were moving and her hand was making that familiar gesture at her throat. Of course she must have known about everything, for very little could have escaped that quick mind of hers with Esteban around so much.

"What's the matter?" he had asked. "Don't you approve of what I'm doing?" And then he had added sourly, "Of course not. You wouldn't sanction grand larceny. Oh, it's my money —but I swore once I'd never use it. It belongs in the bed. But hidden there it ceases to be money. It becomes only a quality, and therefore intangible. Do you understand?" She had nodded, and he had said, "I used to think once that one could retain intangible things. But you can't. You've got to be realistic. This is all that counts. It's very real, and I need it." And he had clutched a handful of the coins and let them fall one by one, clinking upon the coverlet. But when he had turned to look at Zeda again, she was gone.

One hundred and twenty pieces of Spanish gold. Come what may, he swore that he would get full value from them.

On their course, with St. George light dwindling astern, it suddenly occurred to him that it might be worth the risk of by-passing Cuba entirely. Why not go farther south for his

blacks? Why not buy them direct from the syndicate in the
Bay Islands? The syndicate—a group of British and Spanish
merchants—had been importing wild Negroes from the Río de
Oro for a generation. They were the best blacks anywhere, for
the syndicate went to some pains to restore them to health after
the rigors of the Atlantic crossing, then trained them carefully
in plantation work before offering them for sale. Down in the
islands, on Roatán and Bonacca, you could sometimes pick
them up for as low as a hundred dollars a head. But in Cuba
you paid two hundred dollars and up—mostly up—for Bay
Island Negroes. Get them safely into the Floridas and the
price jumped to eight hundred.

Oh, you could buy cheaper field hands in Cuba. You could
shop around and pick 'em up for a song. But they were half
dead. The fool Spanish drove them eighteen hours a day,
barely fed them and refused to sell them until they were worked
out. Even the toughest Yorubas became only festering bundles
of skin and bones after a few seasons in the cane fields.

Seven thousand dollars. In Cuba it would buy, at the very
most, thirty-five prime Bay Island blacks. And those thirty-
five would bring as much in Georgia as a hundred Cuban hands.
But down in the Islands the money would really count. Distance doubled the risk—but with a little luck it would more
than double the profit.

The second day out he spoke of the matter to Esteban.

The hunchback was a little hairy gnome of a man, with such
a thick bushing mass of gray hair and beard that it made his
head seem too large for his body. His hair was beginning to
turn white, and with his hump forcing his head low between
his shoulders, he had the look of being aged, so that his nimble-
ness always came as a surprise. His eyes, almost lost in their
sockets, had the warm blueness of the Gulf, and his voice was
soft.

Esteban listened thoughtfully, nodding, then smiled and put
his fingers to his lips and blew a kiss southward. "Ah, Bonacca,

beautiful Bonacca!" he murmured in Spanish. "I would like to see it again. If we had Finch . . ."

"We haven't got Finch. But our crew is good."

"Let us see how good they are, my captain. Let us see how quickly they can set the forecourse and tops'l."

"Very well."

Esteban shouted orders in his broken English, and the Bruin boy herded his mulatto half brothers to their stations. Before the topsail could be unfurled and clewed down, the big yard carrying the course—the huge lower square sail—had to be sweated up. As in most small schooners of her type, this yard was not fixed permanently to the mast. Instead, it lay on deck with the canvas neatly furled and ready, and was swung aloft by a halyard. Finch had always been able to have it up and set in a trice. But now when it was nearly up the yard became cockbilled, and the course fouled aback, so that the sudden thrust of the wind on the forward side of it was like a brake. It stopped the vessel in her tracks.

The thing was cleared and lowered with much cursing and difficulty. Maury went forward in a fury.

"Dumb bastards! I ought to break every one of your damn heads! Suppose that had happened with the Revenue Marine after us! You, Bat, what's the matter with you? Why didn't you watch those braces? Can't you remember anything Finch taught you?"

"Hit was the wind done it," growled Bat. "Hit come on a gust. Hit coulda fouled up with Finch too. He warn't so smart."

"You know a lot about 'im, don't you?"

"I don't know nothin' about 'im."

"You were the last person to see him. What happened to him?"

"All I know is he lit out fer the Tuskenegge's country. I tole 'im he oughta keep shy o' the Tuskenegge, but he went anyway."

"Oh, he did, eh? And you didn't have any trouble with him either, did you?"

"No," Bat answered, sleepy-eyed.

"You lying sonofabitch, you'll show respect when you speak to me!" He snatched a wooden pin from the fife rail and struck the surly neolithic youth over the ear. Bat sat down heavily on his rump, a bit dazed but far from out. There had been little strength in the blow. Maury kicked him. "On your feet!" he ordered. "Get that course an' tops'l drawing! And watch your damn manners—or you'll never see Whisky George again."

The sails set and order restored, Maury went aft. His anger suddenly evaporated. He felt drained and ill and disgusted with himself. He longed for his bunk and knew that he ought to go below, but stubbornly he forced himself to remain by the taffrail. How stupid to lose one's temper! he thought. What's the matter with me? I've got to keep a hitch on myself. And I've got to be more careful. I haven't got my strength back yet. If only Finch could be here . . .

He considered Finch, suddenly missing him more keenly than ever. Finch was mate, bosun and crew all rolled into one, and he could handle almost any situation with a minimum of trouble. Furthermore, he knew every reef and bar and inlet from the upper coast to Cuba, and no one understood better those little variables of tide and wind that, in a chase, might mean the difference between safety and disaster. This was his first trip in years without Finch.

Esteban brought coffee. Maury sat down gratefully on the after house to drink it with him.

"*Que va, mi capitan,*" began Esteban. "*No puedo remediarlo.*" He spread his hands and went on in his soft Spanish, "Things are as they are. Most humbly I crave your forgiveness if I am at fault, but I wanted you to see."

"Your demonstration was most enlightening. I do not blame

you. But you must keep after those rascals until they can handle every line in the dark."

"But of course, my captain. I can make them perfect, but it would not make up for Finch. Even if there were two of me, and I were twice the man that I am not, it would still fail to make up for Finch. Without him, we may have much trouble if we go so far as Bonacca."

"You are not afraid, Esteban?"

"I am fifty-five, my captain, and God did not give me the power to enjoy women. My only love is the blue water, and my only wish is to die upon it. How, then, can I be afraid? We will do whatever you think best. But if we would repair our fortunes, we must consider that *Salvador* is very shoal. She was not built to carry living cargo for so long a run. And we would be entering the Caribbean at the season when the great storms begin."

There were times when Esteban made him think of Carey. One was brilliant and the other quiet; but each had his affliction, and each had escaped the warping effect of it by finding a philosophy.

"Very well," he said. "What do you suggest?"

"We should try Cárdenas and Matanzas again," Esteban said. "In Matanzas the last time we loaded some very good black men."

"We were just lucky. We caught that Swede when he was selling out. This time we'll have to go farther up the coast and buy from either Batabano or the German. We'll never get a bargain from the German. Batabano is fair enough, but his blacks are never any good. You know that."

"Who can foretell the changes that come in a day? Let us try the German first. If he is difficult, we will go on to Cárdenas."

They passed Cape Romano and the Ten Thousand Islands, and late of an afternoon they slid down through the bright sea gardens and entered Big Spanish Key Channel, which shoal vessels take to cut through the Florida Keys and reach the break in the reefs. With evening they approached the tip of little Bahía Honda, on the edge of the Gulf Stream thirty-five sea miles easterly from Key West. The wind was on their larboard bow, and rising, and there were squalls on the horizon. They anchored in the lee of the island and sat watching the sky, hoping the wind would haul to the west. With the wind hard against the swift current of the Gulf Stream, the crossing to Cuba would be rough and wet.

And then, as the sun dipped low, two sloops appeared from one of the lagoons around the inner curve of the island.

Maury studied them through the glass. They could be wreckers out of Key West or, as likely, a pair of Cuban *fili-busteros* looking for an easy kill. Even some of the wreckers were not averse to a bit of piracy, and he swore at the Revenue Marine for ignoring such matters while they spent their efforts trying to suppress the slave trade.

The sloops bore down upon him without changing course, and he ordered the brass swivel gun brought up and mounted on its small platform aft. He loaded it while Esteban passed out rifles. But with the appearance of a third sloop he grumpily told Esteban to weigh anchor and make sail. They raced over the five miles of sunken reefs for the deep water, and made it easily as night closed down and left them alone upon the pounding rush of the Gulf Stream.

It was the most uncomfortable crossing in his experience.

Late in the morning following they approached the high blue headlands of Cuba. A few miles east of the Bahía de Matanzas they slipped through the narrow reef into a bight and entered the small channel that led to Guido Meyer's barracoons. Wearily now they broke out the sweeps and pulled slowly up into the tiny anchorage rimmed with mango trees and thick clumps of bananas. It was quiet in here, and the air was heavy with the sickly-sweet and fetid smells of blossoms and decayed fruit and gurry and Negroes. Up the slope, faintly, Maury could hear the familiar clink of chain upon leg irons and a low chanting.

Ahead a flight of steps led up from the water's edge to a stone abutment from which protruded the muzzles of four rusty carronades. To the right of it were two vessels tied up to a wooden bulkhead. One was Guido Meyer's sloop. The other was a schooner. She was a topsail vessel somewhat larger than the *Salvador,* but dirty and ill-kept and, despite the efforts of the cleaning gang busy in her hold, still smelling strongly of her recent cargo. He instantly recognized her as a Bay Islander from Roatán.

A big man with a wiry red beard stood up in the companionway as they came abreast. He had tattooed serpents coiled around his arms, and they seemed to writhe as he scratched his bare hairy chest. He stared at them and chuckled, exposing a row of broken and rotten teeth. "Blarst me!" he said in the cockney accent of the Islands, his voice deep and whisky-hoarse. "So ye're still in the business, heh? 'Ow's that bloody old Bruin?"

Maury looked at him drearily. At last he shrugged and said, "Hello, McSwade."

Chapter Eighteen

HE TURNED away from the man, suddenly angry and
unsettled by his presence, and ordered the *Salvador*
tied up at the far end of the bulkhead near the steps.

The buzzard! he thought. The damn buzzard!

What was McSwade doing here? It was evident, of course,
that he had come in with a load. But was he working with the
German now? Guido Meyer had his own contacts with Bonacca, long established and approved by the syndicate. And
McSwade had never been on the approved list. Gordon Mc-
Swade, in fact, had never been known to handle good Negroes,
except a few stolen ones. And Meyer was particular. Not so
much about the detail of stolen goods, but certainly about
quality. Say what you would of the German, at least his Negroes had always been the best. Why, then, was he dealing
with McSwade?

Meyer's overseer, a lean dark rawboned man named Gomez,
came down through the row of lime trees beyond the abutment.
He wore sandals, pantaloons of old sailcloth and a wide-brimmed straw hat. Over his bare brown shoulders was coiled his
badge of office, a short heavy whip with a long flexible handle

weighted at the butt. Following at his heels, as noisy and curious as monkeys, were a half-dozen ragged urchins ranging in color from dark olive to café au lait. At the abutment he turned suddenly upon them and uncoiled his whip. *"Basta! Abate!* Don Guido comes back soon and he will have your hides. You will not live to see the *fiesta."* The chattering stopped instantly and the children scattered as if some dread imprecation had been pronounced.

Gomez came on down the stone steps to the bulkhead. His greeting was perfunctory and polite, and his attitude was that of a minion whose every thought was apparently gauged to suit the discriminations of an exacting lord.

He trusted that they had had a safe passage. And would they kindly shift the vessel well away from the steps, please? The steps were private, and Don Guido must have easy access to them when he returned. Yes, Don Guido was out fishing along the reef. He was due to return at any moment. But one must not expect an early interview. Perhaps after Don Guido's siesta. Perhaps not until tomorrow.

Maury looked wearily at the overseer and reflected that it was his own fault for coming here. He had nearly forgotten what Meyer was like.

"You might tell me," he said, "what you have in the way of prime field hands."

"Don Guido has ample from which to choose," said Gomez loftily.

"You are exceedingly informative," Maury told him with some acerbity. "Very well, if I must wait, you will send hands to fill my water butts."

"I will be glad to oblige you, Captain. Is there anything else you need? Rice, perhaps, or biscuit?"

"Only the water." He jerked his head toward the empty casks lashed on deck. He was tired from the crossing and had not intended to bother with the water now, but he had given the order out of pique, merely to put Gomez in his place.

Gomez counted the casks and made an entry in a notebook. Later a charge for the water would be listed with whatever other items were acquired here. One got nothing gratis from Meyer. Gomez left, and presently a mulatto assistant appeared, driving four Negroes who carried, litter-fashion, a small water barrel lashed to poles.

McSwade came slowly around the bulkhead. He stood chewing a long cheroot.

" 'Ow many blacks ye want?" he asked finally.

Maury shrugged. "Depends on the price."

"H'm. What ye feel like payin' per 'ead?"

"As little as possible. What's it to you?"

"I might be interested."

For a while the two regarded each other across the ground of imposed neutrality. Coldly, distastefully and yet with some curiosity. Then McSwade removed his cheroot and spat.

"Been over in the Caribbees lately, St. John?"

"Why do you ask?"

"Jest bein' sociable. Ye might try bein' the same."

"Maybe I don't feel sociable."

"Ye'd better be if ye aim to buy blacks 'ere."

"What have you got to do with it?"

"Plenty. The only good blacks 'ere are mine. Brung 'em in last night."

"Very interesting. Where'd you get 'em?"

"That's my business."

"Well! And you mean to say you turned 'em over to Meyer on consignment?"

"That's right."

Maury looked at him sharply. Were Negroes so scarce that Meyer had turned to dealing with the fellow? What could have happened?

"Why did you turn 'em over to Meyer?" he asked. "Why didn't you take 'em on to the Floridas?"

"Wanted to, but I got chased. Didn't ye see that blarsted brig standin' off the point when ye come in?"

"She was miles away. I didn't pay much attention to her."

"Ye should 'ave. She's a bloody fast gunboat. Britisher. They're gittin' thicker'n flying fish. They've bottled things up in the Caribbees. Mine's the first load that's made it through since April."

So that was it. No wonder Meyer had welcomed the man. And if blacks were scarce here, blacks were going to be high.

McSwade asked, " 'Ow's things down Floridy way?"

The Floridas, and all points northward, lay down the slope of the horizon to Island men. This view held even as far north as Key West.

Maury said, "The Revenue Marine is getting active. I'd advise you to keep out of the Gulf."

"Yeah?" McSwade showed his broken teeth.

"Especially if you try running any more fancy girls."

"What're ye drivin' at?"

"You picked up a white girl at sea and palmed her off on Slatter for one of color."

"That's a damn lie. I never done no such a thing."

"Don't call me a liar unless you've got a little more sea room. I know what you did. You picked up a white girl adrift somewhere. Where'd you pick her up?"

McSwade's mouth curled with blasphemy, but before it could fully explode from him he was interrupted by the sound of a bosun's pipe from the mulatto who was looking after the water casks. At the first notes the four Negroes in his charge instantly stopped what they were doing and leaped to the bulkhead and ran to the steps leading up from the water, two standing at attention on either side of it. McSwade, who had little respect for anyone or anything, condescended to a show of deference by stepping back and remaining silent.

Meyer was returning. Don Guido Meyer, sitting comfortably in the shade of an umbrella, was in a shallop being pulled up the lagoon by two sturdy black oarsmen. A third Negro stood behind him at the helm, with head raised to see over the top of the umbrella. The shallop came in smartly to the steps with oars tossed, and the waiting Negroes seized the gunwales and steadied the craft while their master, with all the ponderous dignity of an admiral, stepped ashore.

Had Meyer been a more portly and pompous figure, this arrival would have seemed ridiculous. But he was a huge man with great arms and thick legs and a bristling mustache that swept out fiercely from his red face, and his face was as square and hard as if he were one of the lords of Prussia. He was, in fact, a violent and overbearing man, Spartan in his habits—he lived very frugally in his stone cottage up the slope—and ruling his stronghold with such a heavy hand that every creature on the place seemed in mortal fear of him. If he had a virtue it was cleanliness, and even the white linens in which he had been fishing all morning were spotless.

On the steps he stopped and glared about him, the thumbs of his big hands hooked in his cummerbund. Suddenly he bellowed at the Negroes and sent them hurrying up the slope with fish and gear, then imperiously he told McSwade that his schooner still smelled and to get it cleaner or take it away—to which McSwade, for a wonder, merely nodded and held his peace. Finally he looked contemptuously at the *Salvador*.

"Vot you vant?" he demanded of Maury.

"The same thing I've always wanted," Maury told him. "What have you got?"

"More than you haff the money to pay for," Meyer said, and turned away and started up the steps. Indifferently he added over his shoulder, "I vill send for you when I feel like business."

Maury opened his mouth to hurl an acid retort at the broad back going up through the row of lime trees, but thought better of it and went wearily below. Devil take the German! Better to get some sleep. But suddenly he was shaking with anger.

Esteban came down the companion ladder, poured drinks for them both and murmured that there was a *fiesta* over in the village that night and the crew wanted liberty. "Ev'body go," said Esteban. " 'Cept me. I no wanna go. You go, 'ave big time. Do you mucha good. I stay, look after *Salvador*."

"No," said Maury. "Nobody goes ashore. Tell the boys to get some sleep; then we're pulling out of here."

Esteban finished his drink. He said in Spanish, "I am sorry, my captain, that I urged you to come here. The German is worse than ever, now that he has a monopoly. Such insolence robs one of personal dignity. However, if we left here, where would we go?"

"To Cárdenas. Batabano may have something."

"If there were blacks to be had, that brute of a German would not deal with that *filibustero* McSwade."

"True. But I'm not going to wait around here indefinitely on Meyer's pleasure and be eaten up by his mosquitoes. If he doesn't do something by sundown, we're leaving."

At sundown they were making ready for the run around to Cárdenas when a boy came down the steps and announced that the barracoons could now be visited.

Maury followed him up through the lime trees. The boy was one of the urchins who had appeared earlier with Gomez, but now he wore clean canvas trousers and sandals and a gaudy shirt. He was on his best behavior, though occasionally he skipped happily and laughed and snapped his fingers. Where was he going? Why, to the *fiesta*, of course. Everyone was going to the *fiesta*. Except Don Guido, who had a stone where his heart should be, and no music in him.

The boy, as he said this, suddenly put his hand to his mouth and looked fearfully at Maury. "You will forget my words, *señor capitan*? If Don Guido heard them I would not see the *fiesta*, and my rump would be sorely blistered."

"Your words are already forgotten," Maury assured him.

The barracoons lay in an open area beyond Meyer's stone cottage. They were surrounded by a high stockade, with a single gate that opened into a large courtyard. Around the courtyard were smaller enclosures, in each of which was a tabby jail where the Negroes were secured at night. Twice daily the pens were opened, and the Negroes were marched into the courtyard and past the cooking shed where a kitchen crew prepared big kettles of rice mixed with bits of fish.

The feeding was nearly over now, and Don Guido and McSwade were standing under a silk-cotton tree by the cooking shed, watching the last two coffles of McSwade's blacks being marched past the kettles. There were ten men in each coffle, naked and still wearing the leg irons connected to a long chain by which they had been fastened aboard McSwade's schooner. They moved slowly, silently, every man clasping a drinking gourd, a tin plate and spoon in one hand and holding the connecting chain off the ground with the other; but on approaching the water barrel and kettles, tended by old crones, they were forced to drop the chain and use both hands to fill gourd and plate. Gomez, dressed now in clean linen and wearing a bright scarlet sash, stood by with his whip, flicking it rhythmically to speed up the dragging chain.

The blacks paid scant attention to the whip. They were big men, most of them six feet and over, narrow-eyed and dark-lipped and with the long rangy bodies of north Africans. Prime blacks. They ought to fetch top prices anywhere.

How had McSwade ever come by men like these?

Maury went over to the side of the courtyard where one coffle, having finished eating, stood by an open pen waiting to be put away for the night. Beyond the cooking shed he could hear laughter and snatches of chanting from some of the more seasoned slaves, but these shackled men were melancholy and silent. He examined them quickly and looked at their teeth and felt their hard muscles and looked at their hands. Their hands were well calloused.

"Do you know what cotton is?" he asked one of them.

"Yassuh, massa."

"What do you do with cotton?"

"Plant 'em, massa. Hoe 'em, pick 'em."

Plant 'em, hoe 'em, pick 'em. The stock English phrases taught them by the syndicate's overseers down at Bonacca.

"Have you ever had fever—dock, I mean?"

"Nawsuh, massa. No dock."

He asked the question idly out of medical curiosity, always on the watch for one of those victims who had had yellow fever and recovered. Odd about Negroes. Some tribes seemed entirely immune to the dreadful thing, while others would die from it like flies. Men as hardy-looking as these were probably immune.

He knew he would be lucky if he could buy two strings of them. At the very least, conditions being what they were, Meyer could get three hundred dollars a head for them from the local planters. He would undoubtedly ask much more and then come down a little. Maury decided that, if he had to, he would pay as much as three hundred and fifty a head. Certainly he could more than double his money through Slatter.

By twilight the last black was quartered and the doors to the tabby jails locked. A few smudge fires were lighted to drive away the swarms of mosquitoes that appeared suddenly at dusk, and the big outer gate was barred and locked. Gomez, like a captain of the guard performing a nightly ritual, presented the keys to Meyer, bowed and stood stiffly at attention until the big German dismissed him with a curt wave of the hand. The children, the helpers and the little group of waiting women quickly melted down the lane that led to the village.

McSwade this evening had made some concession to the amenities by wearing a shirt, an almost clean one. It clung stickily to his broad chest. He listened a moment to the distant beat of the marimbas, then said, "I'd like to go in an' 'ave meself a bit o' fun, but it's too bloody 'ot. 'Ow many o' my niggers ye want, St. John?"

"How much do you want a head?"

McSwade scratched his beard and looked slyly at Meyer. The German grunted and said, "Come into my office."

They went around the slope to the rear of the cottage nestling among the lime trees. The cottage had been built upon the masonry remains of an earlier structure, and the office had at one time been part of the wine cellar. It was now Meyer's place of business, where he kept everything from kegs of rice and biscuit to irons and records. Meyer unlocked the great iron-studded outer door, and they entered and stood waiting in the dark interior while he unlocked an inner door opening into the house proper. He shouted irascibly into the hall beyond, and a buxom woman of color hastened to bring candles. She set them on a big desk under one of the barred windows and hurriedly left, closing the door behind her.

Meyer opened a cabinet on the wall and hung the barracoon keys upon a peg inside. After closing the cabinet, he sat down at the desk, took a cigar from a pottery jar and lighted it from a candle. McSwade, without invitation, availed himself of a cigar and settled into the remaining chair. Maury stood leaning against the bales of cheap blankets and pantaloons which were issued to every group of slaves Meyer sold.

"Vell," said the German. "All business is cash. No Yankee paper. No drafts. You got cash?"

"I always have cash," Maury told him. "The question is not the quality of my money, but the price of those field hands."

"How many you vant?"

"I might not want any. They look all right, but I wouldn't put one aboard until I'd had the chance to examine him carefully in daylight."

"Bah! You quibble. The price is five hundred a head."

"That's preposterous."

"You vant me to giff them to you?" Meyer roared. "Or are you such a *dummkopf* that you do not know the value of a field hand? You take up my time. You vant to get off cheap, you buy females and children. I haff plenty. But field hands! You think ve grow them like turnips? Hah!" He stopped and gave a vast rumbling snort of disdain. "Everybody vants field hands.

Five, ten, maybe two strings. For the man who saves me troubles and buys in quantity, I maybe discount a little. Otherwise it is five hundred a head."

McSwade blew a cloud of smoke toward the blackened mahogany ceiling beams. He said lazily to the German, "Let 'im 'ave the load—that's twelve strings, St. John—for fifty thousand."

"That's mighty generous of you," Maury bit out. "But for stolen Negroes I find it a bit high."

"Who th' 'ell says I stole 'em?"

"I didn't say you stole 'em—but if you insist on it I'll say it. Those are syndicate niggers, an' you know it. If you didn't steal 'em, let's see your bill of sale from the syndicate!"

McSwade sprang up, swearing hoarsely, but the German slapped the desk with his huge palm and bellowed him to silence. "Sit down! Ve split hairs. Who cares how you got the niggers? They are here now, and the Yankee quibbles. Phah!" He looked at Maury and said sarcastically, "Who are you to quibble? You haff no money or you vould not vaste my time quibbling at five hundred for niggers that vill fetch twelve hundred in Georgia."

"If they'll fetch that much, McSwade had better try the Gulf run himself. As for me, my connections won't pay me more than eight hundred—and I'm damn sure not going to take the risk with blacks that cost me five hundred. You won't find anyone that will. My top offer is three hundred and fifty a head."

He strode to the door and opened it. "You can think it over while I get something to eat." He went out and kicked the door shut behind him and groped through the darkness of the patio and down through the lime trees.

Five hundred a head! Fifty thousand for the lot! Did they take him for a fool? Stolen Negroes! They had the gall to demand nearly double what such Negroes had always brought. Even the price he'd offered was too much.

He was in a cold fury by the time he reached the schooner.

Esteban sat bundled in a scrap of canvas aft, fanning away the mosquitoes with a palm leaf while he smoked. The Bruin boy and the others were forward under a mosquito bar draped over the gaff, dozing or playing cards in the light of a lantern suspended overhead.

"Those buzzards want five hundred a head for some blacks stolen from the syndicate," he told Esteban. "I offered 'em three-fifty."

"I would rather steal them myself than to pay them such money," said Esteban. He studied his cigarillo and shook his head. "We have so little money. I hardly know what to do. Perhaps, after you have eaten, you will be able to view the matter with more clarity."

Maury lifted the flap of netting covering the companionway and slid below. He tried to eat the ham and squash Esteban had set out for him, but he was not hungry. Aye, it would be much better to steal the blacks themselves than to toss away their money—especially those good-luck pieces—and allow that insufferable pair to profit so enormously.

Suddenly he stared blankly at the bulkhead. Why not steal them? Why not just go up and raid the place? Confound those rascals! What a pleasure it would be to take their Negroes! *Go on and try it!* he told himself. *They can't stop you! They can't do a thing! Those Negroes are yours for the taking!*

The thought ate into him, burning. His hands shook a little and his breath came faster. Abruptly he went over to the companion ladder and thrust his head and shoulders above the netting. He stood there peering out into the soft black dark where the fireflies glowed like tiny shooting stars among the lime trees. The only light to be seen was the vague yellow glow, high up among the trees, coming from one of the windows of Meyer's office. There was not a soul about. Above the headland he could hear the rushing of the night wind, and with it, faintly, came the music from the village.

His heart pounded furiously. Nearly everyone had gone to the *fiesta*. All of McSwade's men had gone and all of Meyer's helpers, except possibly the woman in the cottage and an old retainer or two on the other side of the stables. There was no watchman on duty. Why should there be a watchman? The blacks were safely locked away for the night, the stockade gate was locked and barred and the keys were hanging in their accustomed place in Meyer's office. This nightly locking in of the blacks was more ritual than precaution, for where would they go if they did escape? And who would feed them? As for anyone raiding the place, who would think of it? Impossible!

But at the moment it was possible.

He clutched the cabin slide and listened to the wind. He could hardly feel it here in the protection of the lagoon, but out beyond the headlands it was booming. Until well after midnight it should be roaring out of the east at twenty knots or better. One could not always trust the trade wind on this coast, for often it died at sundown or hauled around. But now it was in his favor. Everything, in fact, was in his favor.

In an instant he had visualized every step that had to be taken. The whole thing appeared so ridiculously simple and easy that he checked himself and searched for details that he might have overlooked. But no, there was nothing to it. He had but to act quickly, and the Negroes were his. And didn't he have as much right to them as anyone?

A few months ago he would have put these thoughts aside by telling himself that he was not a thief. He had never stolen, and in his mind he had always been able to clothe his dealings with a certain semblance of respectability. He broke a law, yes, but it was a law devised by men who had come to envy the slave wealth of the plantations. Who were they to forbid a man to bring Negroes into a land that sorely needed them and gave them far better treatment than was the lot of slaves in any other land? Devil take the righteous busybodies!

But now he found himself viewing his activities with a cold realism. He no longer occupied the same notch in his personal esteem; he was what he was, and no bones about it. And both McSwade and the German, if given the chance, would think nothing of doing to him what he planned to do to them. Besides, he had a score to settle with McSwade.

He did not try to analyze why the affair of Zeda had caused him to feel as he did about McSwade. He had always loathed the man. Now he hated him.

For perhaps a minute longer he stood in the companionway, oblivious of the whining insects while he studied the lagoon, the abutment and the vague steps leading up to the darkness of the lime trees. At last, when he called Esteban below, he was outwardly calm with the assurance of one whose course is clear and who knows exactly what he intends to do.

He explained it to Esteban. Then he sat watching the little hunchback intently, waiting for him to speak. But Esteban sat with his eyes averted, saying nothing.

He was suddenly irritated that Esteban should act like this. "Come, come!" he burst out impatiently. "We haven't got all night! If you don't like it, say so."

Esteban looked at him reproachfully. "I did not dream that my idle words could sprout such roots," he answered mildly. "I do not criticize. It is simply that I am surprised that you would propose doing such a thing."

"What's the matter with you? Why shouldn't we take them? We have as much right to them as those rascals."

"Perhaps so. It is not that such a theft would greatly trouble my conscience. But something about it causes me a great uneasiness. I cannot explain it. I would feel much better if we went elsewhere and bought our blacks."

"Nonsense! Damned if I'll pass up a chance like this! In an hour we can have the whole bunch aboard and be on our way." Suddenly he was burning with it, charged and alive with a vast energy. He reached over and shook Esteban as if to waken him. "Think of it! They'll bring a hundred thousand at the very least! And most of it clear profit! Lord God, man, do you realize that?"

Esteban nodded. Then the gnomelike head tilted up, and the deep eyes brightened in the lantern light. Esteban's eyes began to gleam. He clutched the table. "Let us go over the plan again, my captain. Carefully."

"First, let's consider our boys. We'll have to depend on them. And what about Bat?"

"He has the nature of a brigand. In such an enterprise he will be much more willing than in a matter of honest routine. They have never had much money. Offer them all a bonus, and they will break their necks for you."

"Very well. We'll leave four of the boys—Will, Brassy, Sawyer and Snipe—here in Bat's charge. We'll take that little Pode with us. He's smart, and he's quick. Now, we'll go up to the office, and as soon as those left here see us wave our lantern from the top of the slope, they will rip off the hatch covers and set out lanterns. Two lanterns in the hold, two on deck, two up on the abutment. Then they will turn the vessel around and bring it closer to the steps. Is that clear?"

"Yes, my captain."

"Now, I will go first up the slope, carrying a lantern. You and Pode will follow about ten yards behind. Very quietly. You remember the German's office from last year?"

Esteban nodded.

"I will ask Meyer to let me in. The moment he does so, you and Pode are to come quickly with your pistols ready. Next, the barracoons. Remember how they are laid out?"

"But yes."

"The keys to the barracoons are hanging in the wall cabinet beside Meyer's desk. I'll take charge of them—but I'll explain about them now in case we have trouble. There are just two keys. The big one unlocks the outer gate. The other unlocks all the jails. McSwade's blacks are jailed in the two pens to the left as you enter the courtyard. They are still chained, ten men to a string. You and Pode will lead them out of the first jail, and Bat and one of his boys will meet you on the slope and bring them down here to be put below. We'll clean out the first jail before we open the second."

"You will lead the last ones to the vessel?"

"No, you and Pode will have to do it. Toward the last I will have to keep watch by the gate. It is likely that someone will get to the village and give the alarm. But it will take them a half hour to get there, and by the time they return with help we should be nearly through."

Esteban tapped his short fingers upon the table. "Suppose McSwade and the German are not in the office?"

"It makes no difference. They will be in the house somewhere. I'll go across the patio to the main door, and we will follow the same plan."

"But those carronades on the abutment. They look very formidable. If anything goes wrong, and they are manned before we can get out of the lagoon——"

"Forget them! The tampions have rotted out and the barrels are rusty inside. We'd be at sea before anyone could possibly get them loaded."

Esteban tapped the table again. "We must take lines to tie up McSwade and the German. Is anyone else in the house?"

"There was a woman. Possibly she went to the *fiesta*. But we will have to watch for her."

Esteban was silent a moment. He frowned and tugged at his beard. Then he nodded. "The thing seems very easy. I can find no fault. But we will have to work quickly or we will be caught in a hornet's nest." He shrugged. "We take that chance. Now let us tell the others and be on our way."

It had seemed ridiculously easy while talking it over with Esteban, but now, as he went up through the lime trees with the lantern, he began to see flaws and have his doubts. He had been taking too much for granted. What if McSwade had left the office? And what if some of McSwade's men returned early and saw them entering the barracoons? And then there was the possibility of other domestics than the woman or male helpers whose presence he did not know about.

Behind him, faintly, he could hear the careful footsteps of Esteban and the mulatto boy, Pode. He checked an inclination to glance back at them and forced himself to keep moving steadily. There was always the chance that someone might be about, and he held the lantern carefully in front of him so there would be no telltale gleam upon the two pistols thrust into his belt at the back of his trousers.

Halfway up the slope the light in Meyer's office vanished, and he stopped, sharply uneasy while he listened. Esteban and Pode must have stopped also, for he could hear no movement from them.

Suddenly there came to him the deep hoarse twang of Mc-Swade's voice. It was muffled, and he could not tell where the man was. He reached swiftly behind him and touched the butt of one pistol with his right hand and took a cautious step forward. Abruptly the office light appeared again. He realized that the dense growth of some shrub must have hidden it, and that McSwade and Meyer were still in the office.

Purposefully now he swung on up to the corner of the patio, crossed it and rapped lightly on the office door.

"Don Guido?" he called.

"Vell?" Meyer rumbled. "You come to do business, or you come to quibble again? The price is still five hundred."

"I've been thinking matters over. Possibly we can come to terms."

Was the door unlocked and would Meyer tell him to enter, or would Meyer have to get up and let him in? He had not thought of this small detail. But it was important now.

He heard McSwade chuckle; then there came the rasp of Meyer's chair upon the stone floor. The key turned in the lock. The door opened a foot and Meyer's bulk filled the opening.

"So?" said Meyer. "Vot sort of terms?"

He looked at Meyer and hesitated a moment; then he stooped casually and set his lantern upon the patio flagging. When he straightened he held a cocked pistol in either hand. Abruptly his foot shot out and kicked the door open.

"These are my terms!" he snapped. "Up with your hands! Both of you!"

Chapter Nineteen

IT WAS, in truth, ridiculously easy. It came off exactly as he had planned it. There was no trouble at all. Afterward, many times afterward, he was to lie abed thinking of the utter ease of it with a sort of horror, wondering if the blame for this precipitant act should be laid to an inherent evil within himself, or to some malign force without.

But now, as it was happening, the whole thing was suddenly a lark; and his victims, livid and choking with fury and sputtering blasphemies until Esteban had trussed them together and stuffed rags into their mouths, were merely a pair of outraged buffoons in an impromptu comedy. Even Meyer's woman, speedily caught and dragged into the office to be bound, was too frightened to cry out and became only a foolish player pretending fear in silly pantomime. Maury was laughing as he snatched the keys from the cabinet. He rattled them with sophomoric glee over the bulging eyes of the two on the floor, then ran outside, picked up the lantern and began waving it to the boys watching on the schooner. Pode lighted the extra lanterns in the office and followed with one of them, grinning. Only Esteban was grave. Thoughtfully he locked the inner door

250

of the office and extinguished the candles on the desk. Taking the remaining lantern, he went outside, locked the outer door and stood a moment listening before hurrying to the barracoons.

But there was no trouble. And it was only a matter of minutes before the first jail was opened and the strings of Negroes were moving down the slope. They were orderly and for the most part silent, the men in each coffle walking at a slight crouch in order to lift the impeding chain with one hand, and of necessity keeping step. In the light of the lanterns their naked black bodies had the look of demons, and they seemed to move down the slope in a kind of slow limping dance. There was no excitement save the little waves of murmuring from the women in the other pens and the crying of a child.

The second jail was nearly empty when Maury realized that the music in the village had stopped. He knew what it meant but he shrugged lightly when Esteban, hurrying to the gate, called his attention to the fact. Someone, perhaps an old retainer down below the stables, had seen them and given an alarm. He had expected it. But it made little difference now. Presently Gomez, with whatever assistance could be quickly mustered, would come pounding up the lane. Only, by that time, the Negroes would be aboard and the *Salvador* would be on her way.

When at last he did hear the clatter of approaching horses, there were still three strings of Negroes to be loaded. Yet he delayed long enough to drive one string aboard before jumping to the lines, casting off and ordering all the hands to give way with the sweeps. There was some confusion until they were in the clear and moving, with lights out, down through the blackness of the lagoon; but behind them there was greater confusion, with a sudden eruption of voices and wild shouting up and down the slope. He looked back and saw, by the light of the lanterns left burning on the abutment, a vague huddle of Negroes on the steps and men leaping past them and running along the bulkhead. But in a moment the scene was curtained by the rank growth along the curving channel. Then they were out of the trees and feeling the first tug of the night wind. Instantly the sweeps were boated and the boys scrambled to the halyards. Up went the canvas into the starry night. The schooner heeled, came suddenly to life and raced through the reef opening and out over the dark sea.

The thing was done. And they'd managed it without firing a shot. What a night's work!

The mulattoes leaped and yelled like schoolboys; and Esteban, forgetting his gravity, yelled with them and pounded his captain upon the back. Maury laughed and ordered rum for all hands. A hundred prime blacks! He wished, mainly to confound McSwade, that he had been able to take them all. But a hundred made a load, and they'd fetch a fortune. Holy Mother, what a haul!

Then, as he went about the task of getting order in the hold and the vessel snugged down for the night's run, the excitement went out of him. Suddenly he felt old and tired and unable to savor even the wine of accomplishment. This thing he had done seemed a sorry piece of business. He thought of Zeda, who had stood silently censoring in the door that day. How would she take it when he told her about McSwade?

He would make light of it. He would say, *I've evened your score with him. I raided him and took a hundred niggers from him; I left him locked up and tied to the German with a dirty rag in his mouth. You should have seen him! He was in such a fit his eyes were popping from his head. I thought he'd burst a blood vessel.*

Perhaps, if he told it just right, he could make her feel the humor of it. She might even laugh. And surely, if he could ever make her laugh, he could make her speak again. Would her voice be anything like Adrienne's?

But thinking of Zeda did not lift his depression. He wished he could turn the hours back, and even the days.

His hands were shaking. Ice was creeping through his blood and eating into his marrow. What was the matter with him? Stupid, it was the ague again. That damnable ague.

He went below and turned up the cabin light and groped through his store of pharmaceuticals for the medicine he knew he should have been taking daily, but had forgotten. Oh, what a fool he was! Didn't he know that it took months to cure malaria? Finally he crept into his bunk, shaking with the abysmal chill that would be followed swiftly by the inevitable fever.

Hardly had he drawn the blanket about him when Esteban shouted down the companionway. There was a vessel on their weather beam. She was bearing down upon them like the wind. A schooner? No, no, she was not McSwade's schooner. She seemed to be a brig, and she had been lying there in the lee of the Hicacos peninsula. A plague upon her, but she must be the gunboat that had chased McSwade.

There was no help for it. They were in for a night of running, and he had to face it. He swung out of the bunk and, with the blanket over his shoulders, crawled bleakly back on deck.

It was the beginning of a dreadful flow of days in which he was to lose all reckoning of time.

They shook the brig at last, but at dawn they were miles off their course, rolling and plunging in the axis of the Gulf Stream. The incident had upset all his calculations. By noon, instead of fetching in to the quiet waters of the reefs, they were still making heavy weather of it. An attempt was made to light the charcoal in the sandbox on deck, and put the big rice pot on to boil. But squalls drowned out the fire, and rain followed them through the afternoon. The blacks had to be content with a little biscuit, and it was impossible to remove the gratings and bring them on deck so they could relieve themselves.

With evening the rain slacked off, and they slid at last

through the long break in the reefs below Sombrero. Ahead
lay their old channel at the tip of Bahía Honda, with its promise of days of easy sailing up along the coast. They were tired,
and in the night's dodging the *Salvador* had split her mainsail
and suffered some damage to her larboard shrouds, all of which
had been impossible to repair. But now these matters could be
taken care of at their leisure, and the blacks looked after.

They ran in past the island, keeping a sharp lookout at first
for the wrecking craft that had troubled them coming down.
But the way seemed clear. They proceeded leisurely now, getting the vessel shipshape and lighting the fire under the rice
pot. Esteban was having the gratings removed when the yellow boy Pode suddenly gave a shrill cry and pointed over the
larboard bow.

"Oh, Lawdy, dar she is again! Hit's de gunboat!"

Even Maury, hearing this, had his moment of shock. Coming
round the point of the piny key ahead, swiftly in the twilight,
was an armed brig. She had been lying in wait behind the key,
where the tangle of pines masked her spars. It seemed from the
look of her that she was the same vessel that had chased them
last night. But by what unholy means had she managed to
cross the Stream and get in here ahead of them? Then reason
told him that she was a different brig. She must be a Revenue
Marine craft—and a very shoal one at that or she would not
have risked being so far up in the channel.

Had the brig waited a minute longer, she would have caught
them very neatly in a trap. As it was they had just time enough
to change course and run out across the flats, with the brig
following barely out of gunshot. To have come about and
risked the open sea again with weakened rigging and a torn
mainsail was out of the question. But the flats offered sanctu-
ary—providing the *Salvador* drew less water than the brig.

Again he missed Finch keenly. There were shallow channels
out here, and Finch could have brought them safely into one
before dark. But less than a mile over the mud they ran

aground. Behind them the brig anchored on the outer edge of the main channel and put out a boat.

There was no rest for anyone that night. The boys worked for hours kedging from the flats while he stood by the swivel gun, keeping the brig's boat out of rifle range by an occasional shot across her bow. Finally they were free and becalmed. They were too exhausted to man the sweeps, yet the sweeps had to be manned. One string of blacks was hauled on deck, the end links of the connecting chain struck off, and the chain withdrawn from the shackle rings. The Negroes had had no experience rowing, but in the shoal water they were able to use the long sweeps as poles. The brig's boat followed doggedly on the chance that the *Salvador* would again be grounded and this time find herself helpless with a falling tide. With the approach of dawn, however, the water deepened, and a faint breeze bellied her sails. Reluctantly the brig's boat gave up the chase.

Morning brought heat and sudden squalls followed by greater heat. They drifted northward over the sea gardens, poling sometimes through the brilliant shallows or tacking carefully when the fitful breezes came, fearful of running aground or striking one of the innumerable coral heads. Once that day, in the far distance between the little mangrove islets, they made out the topsails of the brig as she moved cautiously through the long reach of Big Spanish Key Channel. Unquestionably she meant to follow them.

And follow them she did, with stunsails, staysails and every available scrap of canvas bent on to catch the fickle airs.

It became a drifting match. They moved slowly northward along the mangrove coast, the brig usually hull down on the horizon except when an occasional squall gave one vessel or the other an advantage. Once, for an entire day, the brig was not sighted at all. But the next morning she appeared again, a few miles to leeward on their quarter. Without a weather change there seemed to be no possibility of shaking her. And the weather did not change.

Still they drifted, and the white sun cut down upon them unmercifully, sapping strength and will and making a reeking furnace of the hold. As many blacks as possible were kept on deck, the strings changing places hourly; and now they were taught to man the sweeps. The *Salvador* became a galley. Other Negroes were unchained and set to sluicing down the bilges with sea water and ejecting it through the pumps. But the stench remained.

A Negro died. His companions dragged him out of the hold one dawn and laid him on deck. The man had been dead for hours. There was no mark on his body, and in the rigor of death the face was only a black mask that gave no clue to any illness.

Perhaps, Maury reasoned, death had been due to some constitutional ailment that had escaped notice. It was very hard, sometimes, to tell about Negroes. One had to expect an occasional death. And in this heat . . .

But the matter troubled him. Long after the body had been disposed of over the side, he sat in the shadow of the limp mainsail and tried to study the Negroes on deck. It had become very difficult for him to keep his thoughts together. He had managed to hold down his ague with large doses of cinchona, but he was so weakened now that the lightest task seemed to present insurmountable difficulties. As a result he had neglected his razor, and put from him everything but the vessel's routine and the business of somehow dropping the brig over the horizon. Now, as he tried to grapple with this new problem, his mind seemed to play tricks upon him.

Did he only imagine it, or was there an odd and somehow dangerous lassitude among all the blacks? Those fellows at the sweeps—they were like somnambulists. And those groups sitting around the hatch—didn't they ever move except to turn their eyes? And what was that humming?

The men at the sweeps had started it. Just a low grunt at first, just something to keep time. He'd hardly noticed it. But the slow rhythm of it had turned into a low melancholy humming. It was like a dirge. Were they lamenting the dead man? Or had they worked themselves into a sort of fearful trance?

It was suddenly maddening. Wasn't it enough to be plagued by this ordeal of damnable heat and stench and stillness without having to be driven out of his mind by a tuneless sound?

He sprang up, trembling. "Stop it!" he cried. "Silence!"

They did not even turn their heads to look at him. The humming continued.

He stared at them. Suddenly he no longer saw them as human beings: men, far from home, lost, afraid, still appalled by the vastness of a world they did not understand. They were black demons sent here to torment him. He cursed and lurched over to the companionway and got the whip hanging just inside.

Esteban, coming aft, gently took his arm. "Please, my captain. It is the heat and something in the air. Always, when it is like this, there is a great storm somewhere. We will be lucky if it misses us." Esteban sighed and studied the distant brig drifting on the horizon. He added, "The boy Pode is not feeling well. Perhaps you had better give him some of your medicine."

"What's the matter with Pode?"

"He has an ache in the stomach."

"Bah!"

But he went forward to look at Pode, who was lying on the forecastle head.

"What seems to be wrong with you, boy?"

"I hurts all over," Pode mumbled. "Jes' ache an' ache. In my belly an' my bones. An' seem lak my eyes 'bout to bust."

"Eh?" He stooped and looked closely at the yellow boy. "How long have you felt bad?"

"Two-three days. Didn't think nothin' of it. Hit's been so hot, an' ain't nobody been feelin' good."

He touched Pode's forehead. It was burning. Then he examined the boy's eyes and his tongue. Finally he stood up slowly and clutched the capstan and stared off over the brilliant green water with its patches of blue and purple. Away out there beyond the brig the water was the very essence of the richest blue, and miles away on the seaward horizon was a line of squalls from which a single waterspout dangled like a tiny black cable. So much wind over yonder, he thought, and none of it here. Why couldn't they have a little of it here? Maybe it would blow away this dreadful miasma that seemed to be enveloping the vessel and everyone aboard. He watched the waterspout until it vanished, trying to keep his mind on it and away from Pode and hoping the clutching in his stomach would go away so that he could think rationally.

That congestion in Pode's eyes and the tongue that was like an oyster and the aches and the swollen face. Ague? Dandy fever? Any of a half-dozen different kinds of acute inflammation? O God, that it were any of those!

He turned abruptly and glared at the two-score blacks sitting like crows on the spar deck. The hypnotic rhythm of their humming seemed to have put them into a kind of trance; but now they were swaying to the beat of it and the sound was louder. Did they know? Of course they knew, the poor doomed devils! Hadn't one of them died of it?

He went slowly aft and looked at Esteban.

Esteban whispered, "What is wrong, my captain?"

"Pode's got yellow jack."

Pode died that night. Quickly they carried his hot body to the side and delivered it to the sea. The forecastle and the deck where the boy had lain were sprinkled with lime, and at daybreak the remaining lime was mixed with sea water and used to sluice down the hold. From his precious store of cinchona Maury doled out careful doses for himself and the remaining members of the crew. There was not enough for the blacks, but he gave all of them cathartics, followed later by swallows of a vile broth composed of pennyroyal and sassafras mixed with turpentine and balsam of Peru. Not that he had any great faith in such a brew, but the ingredients were among those commonly prescribed for yellow fever and he happened to have them on board.

Despite all these precautions the pestilence rode with them. One of Pode's brothers, Sawyer, was suddenly stricken, and soon afterward nearly a dozen blacks were down with it. Many others showed the undeniable early symptoms. To make it worse, it was discovered that their water supply was dangerously low.

What should they do? They had to have water. Ordinarily there would have been enough, even for such a large load. But ordinarily they would have been long at home by now, instead of just above the mouth of the Suwannee.

Should they watch their chance tonight, run into an inlet and row up as far as possible and establish a sick camp until the scourge had worn itself out? The idea was Esteban's— but Esteban did not know the coast. Such a thing, Maury told him, could not be done—at least not late in June. The coast was a morass, and without protection the sand flies and mosquitoes would drive men mad. They were better off aboard.

"But we must slip in somewhere and get water!" Esteban cried. "The sick ones beg for it! Another day and the butts will be empty!"

"Another day," his captain reminded him sardonically, "and the two of us may be past caring about such matters." He gripped the taffrail and glared at the brig, which at the moment was barely two miles astern. "Don't think she doesn't know our water is running low. They're bound to know it by this time —her skipper would be a fool if he didn't. They're just hoping we'll run in somewhere so they can bottle us up. I'm not ready for that. Not yet."

"I think they would leave us quickly if they found out what is wrong with us."

"I wouldn't bet on that. There's no telling what the Revenue

Marine may do. We've come this far. All we need now is a wind."

"Then pray it comes soon," Esteban reminded him, "or it will do us no good. Unless you can teach black men to handle lines."

Maury's weary fumbling mind had touched upon that thought, but had not held it long enough for examination. In fact, he was not yet able to perceive the full horror of their situation, nor did he now feel any great desperation. Both, for the time being, were too far beyond his comprehension. It was enough that he should have to grapple with logic. And of necessity this concerned only matters of the moment. This death in the vessel might take both Esteban and himself; if it did, then nothing would matter. Why concern himself with it now? Pode was gone, and it was doubtful about Sawyer. A pity, yes, but there still were the others. And not too many of the blacks were ill. He hated their melancholy humming—but better that than panic. Men resigned would never cause trouble. And they had water for a day. Tomorrow night, if he were forced to it, he would do something about the water. But that was tomorrow's worry. All they really needed was a wind.

Aye, a wind! Give them a wind! Give them a good strong wind and he would put the helm over and make a straight run of it across the Gulf to St. George. What mattered it if they had water only for a day? They could make the run in a day—and leave this whole foul coast with its pestilential vapors forever behind.

For surely, he told himself, it must be the coast that had somehow poisoned them. Every indication, every study he had made of it, had pointed to the probability that the pestilence was bred of heat and decay. Why, then, wouldn't the fresh clean air far out at sea put an end to it? Of course! It would cleanse the vessel, cleanse everyone!

A wind! A wind! A clean cold fresh wind!

Almost deliriously he began to imagine how clean and cold

that wind would be when it came. But throughout the remainder of that glaring white day they drifted, with the Negroes at the sweeps putting so little effort into their task that the vessel left hardly a stirring in her wake. And two miles astern the brig, aided by an occasional cat's-paw of a breeze, drifted with them and almost kept pace. Both vessels were borne slowly northward by the inshore current that brushes the coast. Once the lieutenant in command of the brig, watching through his glass, might have seen a splash by the side of the schooner, but he could have had no way of knowing that it was caused by a mulatto boy crazed with fever. Sawyer, raving, had leaped over the rail; he sank quickly out of sight and did not reappear.

With twilight the wind came. Not clean and cold, but fetid from the hot steamy land and sticky with its burden of moisture from the far caldron of the Atlantic. It came faintly at first, building up slowly and becoming stronger and stronger, so that by moonrise it was grinding steadily out of the southeast.

The *Salvador* flew before it, running like a frightened thing. And her fear was not of the following brig, but of what rode with them.

He would not have believed that Negroes could die so quickly. He had known of plague spots where the blacks had apparently thrived, while every white among them had sickened and died. Maybe he had diagnosed the thing wrong. Maybe this was bubonic, or perhaps typhus. But no, it couldn't be. For there was that vomit, that terrible black vomit. Sawyer had escaped it, but Pode had had it. And now these others. *Vomito negro.* You ached and you chilled and you burned up and then you vomited black and suddenly you died. If you were lucky you just burned a bit and died quickly, or went out of your head like Sawyer. Yellow jack. If you were white and got it, you turned as yellow as gold, so that after you died you looked like a golden image. Hah! How would he and Esteban look when they got it? Forget it, fool! Don't think of it. Watch the vessel. Keep order. Try to separate the sick from the well. Place the sick forward and get rid of the dead. What's happened to Bat? Why isn't he helping? He's not sick. Just frightened. Panicky. Confounded animal!

Better get the pistols; keep them handy. There'll be trouble with Bat. There may be trouble with a lot of them. They aren't humming any more.

What day was this? Where were they? Where was Esteban? "Esteban?" he called.

"Yes, my captain." Esteban appeared beside him, crawling. "Are you all right, my captain?"

"Yes, yes, of course I'm all right." He touched Esteban's forehead. It was cold. Icy. "How do you feel, Esteban?"

"Tired. Tired. We have only Bat left and Brassy. The one is no good, the other little better. And I am only half a man. We are nearing St. George, my captain. What are we going to do?"

What are we going to do?

For an instant he saw it all with terrible clarity, and he was appalled by what had happened and what he had done. Almost he wished he had given up to the brig, or remained on the other coast and sought a doubtful refuge up in one of the rivers. But that was behind him. Perhaps, after all, this was best. Only, where could they go? With the way things were he might have to beach the vessel. But if it could be managed, why not land on one of the islands? Slip in to the lee of one of them. Not St. George. Too open, too exposed to the city across the bay. And there was no water on St. George. But St. Vincent? That was better. Plenty of cover on St. Vincent—and water. No one would see them there.

"We'll hope for luck after dark," he said, "and try to make it in to St. Vincent. We can build a shelter there and look after those that are left."

He fumbled for Esteban's hand. "I have been a fool, my

friend. If I had listened to you back at the German's, none of this would have happened."

"If there is fault, my captain, we share it equally. Truly, there is a great evil here, but whether it is all on our shoulders, I cannot tell. I am too simple a man to understand such things."

Why was Esteban's voice so weak? Lord God, don't let him be stricken! But no, Esteban was just tired. They were both exhausted. And the cinchona was all gone and his ague was returning. The fever was beginning to affect his mind. There were moments like this when he could see things in their proper relation, but all in a breath a seeming madness would come over the sea and the vessel; everything would be horribly distorted and he would have to struggle to separate fact from hallucination. He was no longer sure of anything, and he kept a lashing on the wheel so that he needed only to check the compass while the vessel, for the most part, sailed herself.

He dreaded the coming of night. But suddenly it was night, and it had been night a long while, though he had no memory of its coming. And there was land close on their starboard beam, for he could glimpse the black line of it whenever the moon came out feebly from the flung clouds. What was it? He had missed the light on St. George. Was this St. Vincent, or had he overshot it still farther and was this the long peninsula off St. Joseph?

He looked astern and tried to pierce the blackness beyond the gleam of phosphorus in their wake. He saw no distant light, but there was something astern. As he studied it the night assumed terrifying form, and he imagined he saw a great vessel sweeping out of the dark and growing tall in the path of the moon.

He shook Esteban and cried out. Esteban struggled up beside him and clutched his arm and gasped, *"Ah Madre!* They hound us still!"

Was it really the brig again, overtaking them at last and

grown huge in the distorted night? Or were he and Esteban dead men, sailing a dead ship doomed to be pursued by a phantom through all eternity? Later he was to doubt that he had seen anything, or at the most only a harmless packet; but now in the rushing night it was *something*, if only winged retribution. It clung to their wake, coming no closer but always following, dim in the night and vanishing when the feeble moon vanished, but ever reappearing.

It was still behind them when he made out the break in the ragged coast ahead and knew that he had missed the islands entirely and that they were hard upon St. Joseph Point.

He was in a frenzy. If he were pursued by a phantom, he could never escape it. But if it were a brig he would have a chance, for no brig can point as high as a schooner, and it could never follow around St. Joseph Point and up into the very eye of the wind.

He became very cunning now. He eased the helm up, and the *Salvador* veered to seaward as if she would avoid St. Joseph entirely. Did his pursuer veer also? He could not tell. He cursed it and waited until the black dark came again, and quickly he put the helm hard down. The schooner came shudderingly around and heeled sharply with the wind abeam and raced for where he judged the point should be. He bawled out for the hands to trim sheets, forgetting that the last of the yellow boys lay helpless on the spar deck and that Bat cowered in the forecastle. Fortunately the sheets needed little trimming, having long ago been hauled well aft, so that, as they slid over the shallows and rounded up into the bay, the schooner footed easily, untended.

When the moon came out again he looked astern, but saw nothing following them. Nothing at all.

He began to laugh wildly.

Esteban struggled to sit up. "My captain," he mumbled. "Where are we? What are those lights?" He raised a trembling hand toward the lights winking into view across the bay.

"It is St. Joseph!" Maury cried. "We've won, Esteban! We tricked 'em! It's all over but the landing. We'll land on the beach south of town and run our niggers straight up to Slatter's. Right under their very noses! Ha! What do you think of that?"

For it seemed to him now that he really had won and that the long ordeal was only an imagined thing, one with all the other hallucinations and distortions of the night. So he could not at first understand when Esteban crawled to him, protesting, begging him to come about, to beach the vessel, to do anything but enter the bay.

"My captain, please listen to me!" Esteban begged. "We must not go anywhere near St. Joseph! We no longer carry slaves—we carry plague and death! Much better if we could sink the vessel and let the living go down with the dead. We are all contaminated. We must not spread this thing. . . ."

He looked stupidly at Esteban lying gasping and spent beside him and reached down and touched his forehead and found it burning. *We must not spread this thing.* And suddenly it all came back to him, horribly. He knew now that Esteban had been stricken. He groaned and looked at the twinkling lights across the bay, and at the moment was able to feel only a violent hatred for St. Joseph and everyone in it. He had no friends there. Even Carey had turned against him. But for that golden-haired devil of a Salem woman, this trouble might never have been.

Then slowly, as the *Salvador* quartered across the bay, his anger began to cool. He sat inert, not knowing what to do and lacking the will to put the wheel over. The schooner slid past the ships at anchor and past the great pier. Far up the bay she nosed shoreward and grated upon a sand bar. She lay motionless on the bar, her sails slatting in the rising wind.

There was a sudden stirring of life aboard her. The Bruin boy crept from his hiding place in the forecastle, dropped over the side and splashed through the shallows toward the dark wall of pines. A black man crawled from the hatch and went to the rail, and others crouching along the bulwarks gathered about him and stared uncertainly into the unknown where the Bruin boy had gone. One of them spoke, a high rapid stream of monosyllables, and in an instant all of them were over the side and gone.

We must not spread this thing.

Maury held his hands to his head, but it did not stop the pounding of Esteban's words across his brain. The words were beginning to beat upon him like blows. Beside him Esteban moved feebly.

"My captain, did . . . did I hear men leaving the vessel?"

"Yes, Esteban. They are gone. All who were . . . able to go."

"But that must not be! We must bring them back!" Esteban's voice was rising. He struggled to his knees. "My captain, before God, we must go after them!"

"What can we do? They are gone. How can we bring them back?"

Suddenly Esteban was crawling to the companionway, gasping, straining, in a frenzy to get below. He tumbled down the ladder into the cabin. Maury, fearful, crawled after him, and by the vague light of the cabin lamp saw Esteban pawing through the locker where their money was hidden. "We will buy them back!" Esteban cried shrilly, his voice high and mad with fever. "They will come back for gold! Yes, yes! If our souls would enter heaven we must get them back!" He thrust forth one of the small leather bags. "Take it, my captain!" he screamed. "Hurry! Hurry! There is still time! Offer them the gold and bring them back—and I will be getting the vessel ready!"

Maury went back on deck and over the side, and the night seemed to thunder with the urgency of what he had to do. As he splashed shoreward clutching the bag, he saw nothing illogical in his mission; it was very sharp and clear in his mind, and terribly necessary. But in his weakness he stumbled and abruptly fell prone in the shallows. With the sudden shock of it reality returned.

He sat up and stared at the bag; shaking his head, he mumblingly cursed himself for being lost in such stupidity. Esteban was ill and needed him. He must return to the vessel and take care of Esteban.

He struggled to his feet and tried to retrace his steps. In the darkness he could not see the schooner. He called out, but Esteban did not answer. Then a flicker of lightning showed the *Salvador* drifting back into the deep water. He went churning across the bar, stumbling and falling and sick with apprehension, knowing even before his knees finally buckled under and he fell exhausted that it would be impossible to reach her.

He heard a low, flat explosion and saw, at the same instant, a flash of red and white flame from the *Salvador's* cabin. It shot upward as high as the main truck, and the mainsail and the tarred rigging aft were suddenly enveloped in flame. Now yellow fire gushed from the cabin, and the wind whipped it along the decks until the vessel was a mass of fire.

It was impossible to do anything except watch her, choking and agonized in his futility. Oh, Esteban! he cried inside of him. Was this what you meant when you spoke of getting the vessel ready? A tin of oil and the last of the gunpowder and the cabin lamp to make of her a funeral pyre? Poor fever-mad Esteban! Can you hear me now wherever you are? Listen to me, Esteban! The fault is mine, all mine. Can you forgive me?

Chapter Twenty

I

THE BURNING of the *Salvador* attracted very little attention. It happened about two o'clock in the morning, an hour when those who might have been inquisitive enough to investigate, whether among the righteous or the wicked, were either safely in their beds or deeply engrossed for the night. The few souls who did notice it stood watching the distant flame with the impersonal curiosity of strangers viewing some remote phenomenon. It did not concern them. The fire was well beyond the main anchorage and close in to the timber in the upper reaches of the bay. Since it could hardly be a vessel, it was therefore not important. The watchman on the great pier was of the opinion that the blaze came from some barrels of pitch that had been barged out from a turpentine camp. Before the glare of it could attract more discerning interest, a squall blanketed the area with torrents of rain, and the sinking hulk was swept far out into the bay where, mercifully, it was sepulchered forever in the deep water.

After sunup a fisherman, poling over the flats in his skiff, came upon the charred body of a Negro. There was only this, and a blackened water butt awash upon a sand bar. They told nothing. The next day a Negro was found ill in the palmettos at the southern edge of town. He was nude and wore a shackle on his left ankle, and it was at first presumed that he had escaped from Slatter's jail. Slatter, in fact, was forced to take him in since the city had charged him with the duty of jailing all captured escaped slaves until their owners could be located. But the Negro died before any information could be gleaned from him. Dr. Ormond, on a routine call, attributed the death to ague and a touch of lung fever, no doubt contracted from exposure to poisonous swamp vapors.

Of the remainder of the *Salvador's* Negroes who managed to reach shore, only two ever came to the direct attention of the St. Joseph authorities, and each of these was dead when found. There were occasional rumors, however, of live Negroes being seen along the edges of the swamps. It occurred to Rodman Carey, who in due course heard all these reports and rumors, that there was undoubtedly a connection between the Negroes and the unexplained fire on the bay. At another time his enthusiasm for any odd circumstance would have sent him questing for an explanation. But he was not well these days, and too many matters were preying on his mind.

He had valued Maury's friendship, and his renouncement of it had badly upset him. And Catherine's subsequent behavior, to which were added bits of gossip picked up from his cook and houseboy, had further disturbed him. He was by no means willing to admit that he had erred or been hasty in his judgment; for, when youth is past, one clings most tenaciously to any illusion that recaptures it. Catherine was Lucia reborn. He saw Lucia in her every gesture. But his was too penetrating an intelligence to allow facts to gather mental dust; and, while he might refuse conscious assembly of them, his inner mind was unhappily busy with them. These deep disturbances did his frail body no good. For weeks, when he was sorely needed abroad to help launch the railroad venture, he was pain-fully confined to his cottage.

The Saxons, and particularly Patty, were in to see him almost daily, and occasionally Aaron came to give him a dutiful but dampening half hour. Catherine came twice. Her visits were brief, almost perfunctory, and each time she left hurriedly. He suspected that she came mainly on Aaron's insistence, for he had learned that she hardly ever left the house these days.

By the time he was able to be up a bit, the railroad venture had suddenly become a matter of grave concern. The stock was not selling. And men who had earlier pledged support were now retrenching, preferring, they said, to wait and see how the wind would blow. This sudden reluctance on the part of in-vestors might be only an echo of the depression that had gripped the North, but he was afraid that the cause was more local. There were doubters and jealous dissenters everywhere in the Territory, and both the Tallahassee and the Pensacola papers were blatantly of the opinion that the "St. Joseph Bubble" was about to burst, and that the "ridiculous opium dream" of the new railroad was only a red herring intended to divert the public and delay the inevitable crash. Gleefully the Apalachi-cola paper enlarged on this view and intimated that the new railroad was a fraudulent scheme devised by rascals whose only intention was to give the public cow a final milking. The pres-ent line of track, it pointed out, had never paid investors so much as a worthless paper dime on a St. Joseph bank. Even now, it added, far more cotton was being shipped out of Apa-lachicola than St. Joseph, and at lower cost.

Unfortunately, these last three statements were true. But they were infuriatingly misleading. Of course the present rail-road had never paid cash dividends! The rub, Carey knew, was that they'd been forced to build it with private money when it was really a public thing—the very life line of St. Joseph. What did it matter if it had to be operated at a loss? Without it the city could not exist! But not a penny extra did it cost the shippers. The loss came out of local pockets, as it should. Were not those pockets bulging with trade made possible by the railroad? And if there wasn't quite so much trade as in Apalachicola, wasn't it because they needed a greater railroad to bring in more cotton?

Ordinarily Carey would have fought criticism with wit, and would have taken great relish in leading an attack on his enemies. But now he was moved first to wrath and then to an uneasy probing. " 'Ridiculous opium dream!' " he spat out, crumpling the Territorial papers in one of his rare moments of anger. "The jealous fools! Is St. Joseph itself an opium dream?"

But he could not place all the blame on the Territorial papers. The real fault lay here at home. It was the local people who had the money. Why weren't they supporting the new railroad and buying more stock? They had supported everything so far: the first railroad, the dredging of the swamp channel and finally the great pier. Their profits had been huge. Were they such idiots that they failed now to see the value of further support?

Or was something else wrong?

Of course, there was the local money. No one wanted the paper issues, more the pity, and everyone was willing to pay a premium for gold or silver. Didn't they have confidence in Davies' bank, and in Saxon? Was it possible that the bank was in some financial difficulty through issuing too much paper, and were Davies and Saxon trying to cover up by raising cash through the new railroad scheme?

Horrible thought! He tried to put it from him, but it persisted. Suddenly he wished that his abhorrence for the details of finance had not prevented him from inquiring very deeply into the bank's affairs. After all, he was one of the directors. About time he checked up on a thing or two. Better have a talk with someone tonight. Saxon first.

He started to call his big Negro Jube to come and carry him

over to the Saxon house, but decided against it. He would walk.
It was only a little distance. He would pretend he was out for
his health and had merely stopped in a moment to rest his legs.
Catch Saxon off guard.

Slowly, painfully, he arose and took his cane and shuffled
out of the cottage.

It was not until he was nearly in front of Clifford Saxon's
gate that he remembered this was a Tuesday, and that Saxon,
under the usual pretense of civic duties, would be across town
visiting his yellow woman.

Carey stopped and leaned against the fence. The short futile walk had taken his strength and he wanted to sit down,
but at the moment he was unwilling to exchange mosquitoes
for Maude Saxon's pompous absurdities. Frowning and preoccupied, he retreated to Saxon's pier and sought refuge from
the insects out at the end of it.

In his preoccupation he discovered too late that he would
not be alone here. Patty Saxon was huddled on the bench.

"Forgive me," he apologized. "I didn't mean to intrude, my
dear. I . . . I merely wanted to rest these reluctant bones a
bit."

"P-please sit down," she said in a small voice, and with a
sigh he sank gratefully beside her.

He rather liked Patty. She was a good little thing, and her
silly chatter seldom annoyed him—though he hoped he would
not have to listen to too much of it tonight. But after a full
minute of silence from her he peered at her curiously. He had
never thought her very attractive, mainly because she looked
so much like Clifford; but the starlight softened her rubicund
sturdiness and she seemed quite pretty, if unhappy. He was
suddenly aware that she had been crying.

As usual at the sight of tears he melted and forgot his own
cares.

"I say, my dear, are you all right?"

"I reckon so," she murmured, sniffing faintly.

He stroked her pale-brown hair a moment. "If you were all

right," he said lightly, "you wouldn't be out here wasting your lovely tears on Neptune. The old scoundrel doesn't deserve it. Come now, give Uncle Rod a smile!"

"Please," she said almost reproachfully.

He peered at her again sharply. He had been too concerned with other matters to notice it before, but he realized now that she had changed a lot in the past few weeks. The simper was gone, and so was the idle chatter. She had matured. And the process had not made her any happier.

"Perhaps," he said gently, "I can help a bit if something is troubling you. Unless you'd rather be alone. Sometimes we are much better off alone when we are trying to see into ourselves."

"Oh, no," she answered quickly. "I'm glad you came. I . . . I haven't anyone to talk to. I . . . I feel so awful."

He touched her hair again. "What's wrong, my dear?"

"You ought to know what's wrong."

"Eh?" Had she learned about Clifford and his yellow woman, or was this just the aftermath of her infatuation for Hugh Bishop?

"If it's Hugh," he said, "the beggar isn't worth it. Or don't you know that?"

"I can't help how I feel," she said. "I know he's not perfect, and I know he's twelve years older'n me. But it . . . it doesn't make any difference. I know I'm not so wonderful either. I'm not even pretty."

"I think you're very pretty. I've always——"

"You're just saying that. I . . . I used to think I was once— before I saw *her*." She raised her head and looked bitterly down the beach at the Delafield house. "I'm not even very smart. But I never would have treated her like she's treated me." She stopped and bit her lip. "Now you'll be angry with me. You think Catherine's wonderful."

He stared at her. "I say now, what's Kitty done to you?"

"She's acted like a witch, that's what! She's acted like a witch with everybody. She met Hugh when she was staying at our house an' she knew how I felt about 'im 'cause . . . well, 'cause I was fool enough to tell her. So what'd she do? She took him away from me and made him crazy about her and turned him against me. She never did want 'im, and now she's stopped seeing 'im. She did the same thing to Maury St. John. An' that's not all. She's started trouble between Hugh and Maury, and you know what's going to happen if they ever meet again!"

All this poured out of her in a rush, and in the next breath she was sobbing.

Carey shook her and managed to get her quiet. "Now listen to me, my dear. There's a lot you don't understand. And where'd you get this business about Hugh and Maury?"

Patty sniffed. "You can't hide things from the Negroes. They know what's going on. And there's been a lot going on. I understand more than you think I do."

"I'm afraid that what you've heard has given you the wrong view of everything. I think we'd better straighten this out. Just what have you heard, my dear?"

She looked at him with eyes full of misery. "I guess I'm not much of a lady, carrying on like this. I'm sorry. I couldn't help it. I . . . I just felt so bad. And there's no use in talking about it. It wouldn't change anything. I think I'd better go."

"Please, my dear. For Catherine's sake as well as yours ——"

"Catherine's sake!" she cried, springing up. "I'm sick of her! I hate her! You think she's so wonderful, but she's not. It was because of her that you drove Maury out of your house that night. Yes, I heard all about it! I got it from my Selah who got it from your stable boy, so I know it's true. I'm not very smart, maybe, but I'm sure that whatever happened wasn't Maury's fault. I don't care what folks say about 'im, he's good inside—but she's not! She's a devil and she doesn't care about anybody but herself. And you wouldn't think so much of her either if you knew about that little maid of hers running away!"

"What's all this? Wait a minute! Patty——"

But she was hurrying away along the narrow pier, sniffling faintly, her shoulders hunched. She did not stop or look back.

Long after big Jube had helped him to bed, Carey lay sleepless in the hot night. It was true about Catherine's Lissa. The girl really had run away. Big Jube knew about it, although he was reluctant to discuss details. Carey did not press the issue. He knew enough. He did not even want to think about it.

Far back in the pines he could hear the voice of the savant rising feverishly in the heat. He closed his eyes and listened to it, tried to let it fill his mind to the exclusion of all thought and so turn the impassioned augury into a kind of anodyne. *"Repent! Repent! Repent! Gomorrah is doomed! The hour is nigh!"* There they were again: the same urgent crying, the same wildly beating phrases that he had heard so often. And yet no matter how many times he heard them, there was always in them that odd quality of dread. What madness drove the man to don his long robes and cry out thus, night after night? Who was he? Whence did he come?

"The gate of hell is open! The flame shall rise from the pit. . . ."

Shut up, you fool! What do you know of heaven or hell? Life itself has too little of one and too much of the other. Why should you plague us with your damnable cry of doom?

Carey thought of the bank.

Suddenly he clawed at the bed and sat up, clammy with sweat. For in a moment of vision he had seen the swift inevitable pattern of dissolution if anything was wrong at the bank. The bank was the king post of the city. If it tottered, the railroad couldn't save it now. The railroad would go, and everything else would go, even the three lesser banks that existed on sufferance and lived on the overflow. The factors, the shippers, the business houses—all these would have to close their doors. The cotton tide, that had so greatly flooded, would abruptly ebb; and the wealth it had brought—the wealth that seemed so solidly based in the land and in all the works of the land—would ebb with it and be nothing because the land would be nothing. Who, indeed, would want it? And those who had come here and thrived on the land, on this flatness of pine and sand, would be forced to leave. *Ah, doom! The hour is nigh!* Shut up, you fool! Shut up! And the hotels and the taprooms and the gambling houses and the ordinaries and the places of pleasure—Oh, Josie, Josie, with your lush rose rooms!—all would have to close. And who would ever come again to St. Joseph when the heart of it was dead and all of its works were crumbling?

"Almighty God!" he whispered. "It *is* a bubble! Why didn't I ever see it before?"

II

Three slim does came down in the dawn and tripped lightly along the narrow beach; soft-eyed and curious and delicately feminine, they stopped and stared at Maury. He lay motionless and watched them, his head resting against the trunk of a fallen palm. He felt a sudden peace, as if he and the does and the sea and the bannered sky were isolated in a moment of blessed tranquillity apart from all other moments, and yesterday had never been. He tried to perpetuate the moment by holding his eyes open, but weakness closed them. When he did get them open the deer had vanished like smoke, and he faced the torment of his second day of heat and hunger and blood-sucking flies and memories.

He thought of home. Never had the desire to return to it been so strong in him. But it was unthinkable that he go there now. Not for long could he escape the contagion that had taken Esteban and the yellow boys and so many of the blacks. He had lived with it for too many days; he had breathed too much of the poison of it; it was in his flesh and his blood. In an hour, two hours, by another dawn at the latest, the thing would seize upon him, and after an interval he would go to join Esteban. Possibly he could manage to reach home before the fever came —but it would come, and Zeda would be exposed to it. Zeda and Juan and May and everyone he knew. He could not add that to the burden already on his soul.

He stirred and sat up, slapping weakly at the flies that came suddenly with the sun. Mosquitoes at night and the hellish dog flies by day. They had the appearance of houseflies, but they drove the wild cattle into the water with their bite that was like a hot coal drawn over the flesh. This was their season, and they were beginning to come in swarms. He looked out at the little islets scattered through the upper quarter of the bay. They seemed so cool and remote. No flies there, and no troubling humans who might happen by. Only a few palms and the stretch of the horizon and peace.

Very slowly he got to his feet and went down the beach to an abandoned turpentine camp where yesterday he had come upon a barrel brimming with rain water and a broken skiff partially buried in the sand. He located a rusty tin and with great effort managed to scoop the sand from the skiff and get it to float. It leaked badly, but it would take him where he wanted to go. He found a large bottle and, after cleaning the tin, filled both of them with rain water from the barrel and placed them in the skiff. In the collapsed wreckage of the shed he found a pole and a scrap of canvas almost large enough to cover him.

By the time the skiff was ready he was almost too exhausted to continue. He slumped down to rest, wondering what weighed so leadenly in the bag tied to his belt. Then he remembered it was one of the moneybags Esteban had urged him to take. Small as it was, the thing was a burden; money was useless to him now and he might have thrown it away but for the trouble of having to untie the damp cords that bound it to him. He could have cut it free with his sheath knife, but in his debility it did not occur to him that he still had a knife until after he had poled out to the tiny islet of his choice.

Here he thrust the pole into the sand and secured the skiff to it with the frayed painter; and now, mildly surprised that hunger should be gnawing at him so persistently, he waded out to an oyster bar. Sitting in the shallows, he methodically began opening oysters with his sheath knife and gulped them greedily. At last, far from satisfied but too weary to continue, he carried his containers of water ashore, then stretched out in the shade of the islet's half-dozen stunted palms. He was almost instantly asleep.

He awoke in the dark, shaking with a chill. After the first paroxysm, which was followed swiftly by fever, he thought his hour had come. But as the fever began to subside toward dawn and he had no other symptoms, he realized it was only one of the intermittent attacks of ague which had been coming every other day. After sunup he crept out to the oyster bar and ate his fill, then returned to the palms and slept again. That afternoon he awoke refreshed. He could not understand it. Surely the contagion should have taken him by now. Why was he being spared?

Still he waited, uncertain. Daily he crept to the oyster bar. The chills and fever came again, but left him no worse than before. He began to loathe the sight of shellfish and to have a great craving for fresh vegetables. One morning he awoke knowing that, by some miracle, death had passed him by and that he need no longer shun the company of others.

He poled back to the mainland and, without stopping to rest, forced his trembling legs to carry him through the pines to the coastal road. The driver of the Apalachicola stage, who had never been too particular about his fares, took one look at him and whipped up his horses. Soon afterward he was likewise avoided by a gentleman in a passing carriage. But later that day a Negro with a mule team stopped and gave him a ride.

The Negro was old and had known trouble, and in this ragged bearded white man with the sunken eyes and uncertain step he saw only another mortal who had been through trial.

Chapter Twenty—one

I

DR. JUAN Garver stepped from his dilapidated carriage and paused a moment in the shade of the oaks by Maury's gate while he mopped his face with a sodden handkerchief. The heat this summer was a dreadful thing. He had never seen anything like it. He glanced to the east where the thunderheads were boiling skyward from the kettles of the swamps and piling into great mountains of steaming vapor. Presently the water front would get another drenching of warm rain, and afterward the air would be hot and heavy enough to cut with a knife. He sighed and visioned a bottle of cold ale. But there was nothing cold in town, nor anything cool. There was no ice to be had for love or money. Even the drinking water from the best cisterns was tepid, and more than likely to have wiggle-tails in it.

He dropped the reins over the hitching post, opened the gate and went wearily up the brick walk to the veranda. Lean as he was, his shirt was sopping from the slight exertion by the time he reached the top of the steps. He sank into his favorite rocker near Maury's hammock, loosened his collar and began fanning himself with his wide straw hat. "Gad," he muttered. "What we need is a hurricane. At least it would clear the atmosphere and get rid of these devilish vapors. Everyone has chills and fever. Five more cases of it." He sighed. "Well, how's our patient?"

The daily question, after nearly a week, had become only a salutation. The patient was mending, at least physically. Whatever else troubled him was beyond Juan's province. He could do no more. On the other hand he had discovered that there was much the patient could do for him. The few doctors in town were mainly quacks whose leeches and jalap powders were poor weapons against the season's onslaught of ills, and the ills were many. Juan was always busy now. His treasured cold machine, still uncompleted, gathered dust while his rounds became longer and his little porch more crowded. He had no illusions about his ability; he was, perhaps, a better surgeon than a medical practitioner, but in both he was wise enough to know his limitations. So he had fallen into the habit of dropping in on Maury between calls, to let the weariness drain out of him while he discussed certain of his cases. He always left enlightened, yet it disturbed him to realize that anyone whose training and perception were so definitely superior to his own should have so wasted himself.

Today Juan was more depressed than usual. "We've lost a neighbor," he said finally. "Mrs. Galt was in a coma all last night. She died this morning." He shook his head and missed the sudden tightening in Maury's face.

Maury asked, "Did you have a chance to give her some of that pure quinine instead of the cinchona?"

"Yes, and I'm sorry I tried it on her. You can't tell about these new products. Maybe the stuff is adulterated, or has something missing."

"Your quinine is all right. You tested it on me. It's far better than the cinchona. Anyway, Mrs. Galt's fever wasn't the typical paroxysmal variety. It was continual, and there was a heart complication. Tell me, did she have many aches and epigastric pains at first and . . . and was there much jaundice later?"

"Jaundice? Epigastric pains? Yes, somewhat, but not to any marked degree." Juan frowned. "You've asked the same questions about a dozen patients. Why? Are you afraid of some sort of an epidemic?"

"I . . . I merely wanted to make sure," Maury told him. "I'm certain that Mrs. Galt had pernicious malaria. That's wicked, but it isn't to be feared like . . . say, yellow jack."

Juan sat up. "Wait a minute. I've never been able to see any real difference between yellow jack and pernicious malaria, as you call it. This pernicious variety has no relationship to ordinary malaria—or ague or chills and fever, as it's called. It's a killer. It's just like yellow jack. Both have flushing, nausea, jaundice and continual high fever, and both are the result of breathing noxious swamp vapors. Of course, some cases are more pronounced than others—and so they're given the more evil name. But I think it's the same disease. We have a little of it here every year, but fortunately it's never reached that point of violence where we've had to worry about it. And it's much safer, my friend, to call it malaria. The name yellow jack has a bad effect on people."

Maury closed his eyes. When he opened them he did not look at Juan. He said drearily, "I'm sorry, Juan, but I'll have to differ. Heat and swamp vapors may cause malaria. No one really knows. But I do know for a certainty that it has nothing to do with yellow jack. This thing called yellow jack is a terrible contagion. It is absolutely distinct from and far worse than the most deadly form of malaria. It's transmitted from one human to another in some way, and if one case appears, you'll see it rage like a forest fire. You can stop malaria—any type of malaria—with cinchona or quinine. You could have cured Mrs. Galt if she hadn't had a heart ailment. But you might just as well throw your cinchona and quinine away as give it to a yellow-fever victim. The thing's as deadly as the plague. It ought to be called the yellow plague."

Juan peered at him curiously, a little incredulously. "You . . . you've had experience with it . . . recently?"

Maury closed his eyes again. He wanted to shout at Juan and shake him and cry: Yes, by the living God, I've had too much to do with it! The cross is getting too heavy for me. You don't know what it's like to be driven up in the night with the thought of it, and have it dog you till dawn with no way to escape it. . . .

But he only nodded and said, "I . . . I've seen what it can do. Let's forget about it." And he added, very casually as if it did not concern him, as if the worry of it were not a cancer eating at his vitals, "How're things in St. Joseph? Any better than they are here?"

"Oh, yes," Juan assured him. "Much better, I understand. But of course they should be. That's one of the healthiest spots in the Territory."

Long after Juan had gone he gnawed at this small bone of assurance. It had been more than two weeks since the thing had happened. Surely, by this time, wouldn't all the danger be past? Certainly those blacks who had managed to reach shore would avoid people. They would hide in the swamps. Those who lived would, in time, probably be taken in by the Seminole. He could discount them entirely.

But what of Bat Bruin?

Still, maybe Bat had escaped it. If he himself by some miracle had escaped it, why not Bat also? It seemed unlikely that the contagion had appeared at Whisky George, or there would have been some news of it. Bruin would have got word to him.

As soon as he felt like making the trip he knew he ought to go and see the old man and pay his respects and regrets, if not his debts—not that Mace would give more than a passing damn over the loss of a few of his progeny, but an explanation was due. Only, what could he say to Bruin? The old man would have even less use for him now, unless he could repay the money he had borrowed. And how could he ever manage that?

He cursed and slid from the hammock and began pacing the veranda. How stupid of him! If he had all the wealth in the Territory, it would not matter now. The only thing that mattered was what had happened. A man could repay borrowed money in time, but there were some debts that no amount of gold could ever settle. How could he bring Esteban back? How could he turn back the days and change what he'd done?

He did not notice Zeda watching him from the shadow of the hall. His mind was beating again in the maddening circle of his recriminations.

Why, he asked himself, did any of it have to happen as it did? Why had he ever stooped to such a thing as the stealing of McSwade's Negroes? Fool even to go to Cuba! Fool! Fool! A hundred times a fool! And he'd walked right into some devilish trap of fate and taken, not healthy blacks, but infected ones!

Of course they'd been infected when he got them. He was sure of it now. There'd been that odd lassitude about them almost from the beginning. What nonsense to suppose that swamp vapors had anything to do with yellow jack! What drivel! Why, if that were true then both Bruin and he would have been dead years ago, as well as every Indian and settler in the Territory. Those Negroes had been doomed from the start.

It was an important thing to know, although the fact didn't absolve him from what had happened. It didn't change the nightmare of the voyage or the memory of the *Salvador's* burning. The fault was his. There was a wrongness in him somewhere. A weakness, a rot. Much better if he had died with Esteban!

Suddenly he saw Zeda standing in the doorway. He stopped

his pacing and looked at her with a quick lightening of spirit
as if he were a lost man viewing a light in the dark. She always
affected him this way. He remembered the night he had come
home, and the way she had rushed to the door with her lips
forming a silent cry of joy. It was the only reason he'd wanted
so badly to get back, to have her greet him with that look of
thankfulness and relief and wonder in her face, to see that
instant concern over his being and know that he was vastly important to her. He had never been made to feel really important
and necessary to anyone except possibly Adrienne.

He wondered how long she had been watching him. Then he
saw she had been studying, for in her hand was a child's primer
and her pad and pencil. In her eyes was a question.

"What is it, kitten?" he asked. "Need some help with your
spelling?"

She shook her head and came over and touched his forehead with the tip of her slim forefinger. Her great eyes widened
on him sorrowfully.

"You want to know what's troubling me?" he said. He
frowned and turned away and went back to the hammock and
slumped down. She followed and took a chair and sat making
practice letters on her pad while she studied him from under
her long lashes.

"I wish telling you would help," he muttered. "But it
wouldn't. It would just make you think as little of me as I
think of myself."

She shook her head quickly. Her lips seemed to form the
words: "Please. You must. It always helps."

Whatever her words, the thought was plain. Well, perhaps
confession was good for the soul. She was so much like Adrienne, and yet she was wise in so many little ways where
Adrienne had never been wise. Maybe he should tell her.
Maybe it would help. She was far older inside than her naïve
and piquant outer self would indicate. Like him, she was no
stranger to trouble. She would understand.

He decided to tell her.

"I went to Cuba," he said. "Instead of buying niggers, I stole them. I took them from McSwade. He'd just come in with a load he'd stolen down in the Islands. I thought it was a great joke on McSwade to take his blacks, and at the same time sort of even your score with him. But after I took them everything went wrong. A . . . a contagion broke out on board. Nearly everyone died. Even . . . even Esteban died. The schooner was burned."

He stopped and looked at her and saw her eyes wide on him, her small hands clenched in her lap. He looked away and said, "The contagion was yellow jack. I brought the schooner, with the dying and the dead, into St. Joseph Bay. That was a terrible thing to do."

He stood up and walked down to the end of the veranda and back, then told her of Esteban and the vessel's burning and of the days he had spent on the island. "The thing that happened was . . . bad enough," he said. "But it's knowing what may happen that plagues me. The danger isn't over yet. It . . . it can break out somewhere at any time. Whenever Juan tells me of another fever case I'm afraid it may be the wrong kind of fever. The . . . the damn uncertainty of it! If I could do something . . ."

He sat down on the edge of the hammock with his face in his hands, wondering what he could do. Watching him, Zeda sat motionless a moment, with her lower lip clenched between her teeth. Suddenly she sprang up, dropping her book and pad of paper and ran to him and put her arms about him. She held him as a mother might hold a small boy frightened by a dream.

He had never been so close to her or felt such an awareness of her. He was conscious of something fresh and clean about her that was as much a quality of her whole being as it was a physical thing. She was so unselfish, so instantly ready with her sympathy. He thought, I don't deserve any sympathy. She's the one who needs it. And I haven't done a damn thing

about her. I've been selfish. I've always been selfish. It's made
me so blind. And he thought: Lord knows how I'll manage
here without her, but I've no right to keep her here. It isn't fair
to her.

He stood up slowly and held her out at arm's length as if he
were seeing her for the very first time, thinking how empty this
place would be without her. She was such an odd, quick, lively
little thing, and if she wasn't busy about the house or with her
sewing she would be intent with her pencil or going avidly
through his books. She was like a wren. She was indisputable
mistress of the house, and it always amazed him that she could
manage to say so much with a nod, a tap of her foot or a gesture.

"There isn't anyone like you," he said. "You're just about
the nicest person I know." Then he frowned. "But it's time I
found out more about you. Can you write your full name for
me yet?"

For an instant, at his first words, she brightened and everything about her seemed to glow. Then she shook her head
slightly, bit her lip and looked away.

He said severely, "Sometimes I think you don't want me to
know your name. How can I write to your people and do anything for you if I can't find out anything about you?"

She looked up at him out of the corner of her eyes, then
lowered her head.

"Haven't you got people?"

She did not move.

Suddenly an awful thought came to him. "Have you anyone
with a claim to you—a husband, say, or . . . or a lover?"

Again she looked up at him, almost mischievously. But immediately she shook her head in emphatic denial.

He turned away from her, grumbling, but after a few paces
he whirled and said, "You know Spanish, but you think in
English. You must be from one of the English-speaking islands.
Is it Jamaica?"

She shook her head.

"Grand Cayman?"

Again the negative shake, like a teasing kitten.

"H'm. That doesn't leave much. It's nowhere in the West Indies, because that's out of McSwade's orbit. English. You may be part English, but there's a lot of Spanish in you. That sounds like the Bay Islands. Eh?"

He knew he was nearly right by her little intake of breath. He closed his eyes and thought of the Islands, and abruptly he saw it. "McSwade's from down there," he said. "He's from Roatán. And there's nothing he hates more than the syndicate over on Bonacca. Most of the syndicate people are named Morgan. Two of them are part Spanish, and one of them had a mestizo wife, I believe. I don't remember them well, but it seems like——"

He stopped. She was looking at him tragically with her enormous eyes, and two large tears were running down her cheeks. All at once she turned away from him and ran.

He overtook her in the hall. "Oh, Zeda, please—— I'm so sorry. I didn't understand. I was pretty sure you were a Morgan, but I didn't know they were your father and mother." He had only the briefest recollection of Miguel Morgan and his mestizo wife, but he had heard many times how the two had been lost in a hurricane.

So she was Miguel's daughter. Miguel had been a rather good sort, but he didn't think so much of the rest of the tribe. Knowing what he did of them, it was not hard to guess what Zeda's life had been like.

"You never want to go back to Bonacca, do you?"

She shook her head fiercely and hid her face against his shirt.

He sighed and touched her thick black braids. "Very well. We'll just forget about Bonacca. You'll never have to do anything you don't want to do—that I promise you."

Impulsively she clung to him, then in a flash she drew away at the sound of the back door opening and Cricket's voice coming from the kitchen.

Cricket entered the hall and stood blinking owlishly while he fumbled with the buttons of the white jacket he had put on to wear in the house. "Marse Maury?"

"What is it?" said Maury, resenting the intrusion.

"I . . . I been thinkin'. Miss Zeda, she sho need a maid."

"What are you driving at, Cricket?"

The small manservant glanced uneasily behind him and wet his thin lips. "Marse Maury, you know dat girl Lissa what you got from dat man Slatter? Well, she didn't take too kindly to . . . to them peoples what you gave 'er to. She run off. She jes' had to. Marse Maury, dat Lissa she's a *good* girl."

"Yes," Maury said quietly. "You don't have to tell me that."

He started slowly toward the kitchen with Cricket's implication sifting through his mind and finally taking its place with other knowledge he had tried to put from him. Before he reached the kitchen he knew he would find Lissa there, hungry and badly frightened over the thought of having committed the major sin of the slave, but hoping in her extremity to be granted refuge by the man who had purchased her and given her to the wrong mistress.

At least, he thought, that was one mistake he could quickly rectify.

II

For his own salvation he had to do something, and there was only one thing he could do. The realization that he should be doing it came to him suddenly that evening as he lay thinking about Juan. It was either that or drink, and, knowing he was in no condition for the latter alternative, he had sternly put his rum aside.

He got up and went over to the Garvers and found May in

the office. She was rolling pills on a slab of marble by the light of three candles. Cricket's Celeste was fanning her and slapping the occasional mosquitoes that had crept inside in spite of the cotton nettings over the windows and a smudge fire on either side of the house.

May had been in to see him several times since his return, but this was his first venture beyond his own gate. "So you've turned apothecary," he said, frowning at her handiwork.

"Oh, Lordy, yes. Somebody has to do it. Juan hasn't got time."

"Where is Juan?"

"God knows. He has so many calls he hardly ever gets back before midnight any more. Is there anything I can do for you?"

"No. You and Juan have done enough. Now it's my turn. Tell Juan to stop by for me first thing in the morning. I can at least take over his charity cases while he looks after the rest."

May wrecked a row of perfectly good cathartics. She thrust them aside, pushed her chair back and, wiping the back of her hand over her beetling brows, stared at him. Finally she said, "Celeste, pour me a glass of rum before I have a fainting spell. I think the world's coming to an end."

In the morning Maury ignored Juan's protestations that he was not yet well enough and insisted on accompanying the busy doctor until he was acquainted with those poorer patients who had been taking so much of Juan's attention without contributing to his scanty income. Juan, always conscientious, had never put money above need. Now, with Maury's assumption of part of the burden, Juan's relief was visible.

His kit, with most of his medicines and instruments, had been lost with the schooner. Juan lent him another and he stocked it with pharmaceuticals and what extra surgical equipment he could find among his own things and Juan's. He discovered early that what Juan may have lacked in knowledge was largely compensated for by a genuine regard for his suffering fellow mortals and by something in his approach that seemed to accomplish as much if not more than his pills. Juan always gave something of himself. It was like a mental laying on of hands.

He suddenly found himself envying the regard that others had for Juan. In his own approach he knew that his interest, unlike Juan's, was mainly in the malady. He was brusque, probing, scientific. The patient was merely a patient, one of a large class of unfortunates forced to lie abed or hobble around painfully. If any of them had individuality for him at first, it lay in the disease and the absorbing special course of it.

To stop the jealous mutterings of the leech-and-jalap brethren he produced his certificates from London and Paris and obtained a local license to practice. During that first week he set broken bones, treated infections, amputated a gangrenous foot resulting from a sting ray barb and prescribed endlessly for malaria and minor ills. Once, in Juan's absence, he compounded a salve for Flavy Munn's scrofula, which so relieved that gross assembly of flesh that Flavy was moved to speak glowingly of him to anyone needing medical assistance.

Flavy's reaction amused him, until he realized that he had not looked upon him as a patient but as an old—if not too respected—acquaintance whose suffering in the heat had suddenly become acute. Flavy, for all his grossness, his weaknesses of the flesh, was a very human creature, and Maury soon found himself admiring the man's fortitude and wanted to help him. Essentially, he saw, Flavy was no different from the others. Rich or poor, they were all victims of something. Victims of disease, of poverty, of circumstance. Victims, many of them, of their own natures. Good or bad, most of them could not help themselves. They were all individuals, however, each in his different way a victim of what life or circumstance or inheritance had done for him. And in the worst there was always a little good, often something to be admired.

Maury had always hated people. It stemmed from away back, from his own early failures and those of his family. And, hating people, he had rebelled against them. The individual, he had never valued, save those few who had been necessary to him in his small sphere. In a way he had looked on all people as he had looked on the blacks in whom he had dealt. The Negroes he had transported had been only so many strange, ignorant creatures whom he had considered remotely as a class, just as he had at first considered his patients.

Therein lay his weakness, the rot that had slowly been destroying him. It was a truth that might never have come to him if he had not had Juan for comparison, and had not been forced to see it in his own need.

It was good to work, to be busy all the time. He worked hard and late. There were a number of cases of the deadly malaria, and each he watched with trepidation, fearful that it might be the other thing. But gradually his fears vanished and he put the thought behind him. There could be no danger now. His spirit began to mend with his body, and the nights ceased to be a torment.

It was good, too, when his rounds were finished, to come home. Without Zeda, home would not have been what it was. No matter how late he came in, she was always up waiting for him. When he was not too tired she amused him with little sketches of what had happened during the day, enlivening them with pantomime. Sometimes he helped her with her writing. When he could manage it he brought her small presents: a painted fan, ribbons and a silk bag and copies of periodicals. He began to consider the future and find that it could be pleasant.

Then, in the space of a night, his small new world suddenly crumbled.

He had returned early one evening and was looking forward to a few hours of the first freedom he had felt in a long time when he saw a carriage stop by the gate. Big Jube got out, gathered the frail form of Rodman Carey in his arms, carried him up the walk to the veranda and set him carefully on his feet as one might set a wooden doll that would totter and fall unless placed just right.

For a moment Maury stared at Carey, wordless, wondering what could have brought him here, and thinking he had never seen his old friend looking so ill and old. He could guess the tortures the long ride must have cost the invalid. And Carey, noting the hollows in the other's face, the edging of gray along the dark mane, was amazed that a man could have changed so much in so short a time.

Maury took a step forward. "Rod!" he said. Then he exclaimed, "My God, you've no business being up! You . . . you should be in bed. You come right in the house——"

"No," said Carey quietly. "There's no time, my friend. I . . . I've come to beg your forgiveness—and to request a favor."

Maury took Carey's hand. "Of course, Rod. I . . . I've never really held it against you. Honestly. And I'll do anything I possibly can for you."

"Then get your kit and come back to St. Joseph with me. Right away."

"What's the matter, Rod?"

"Patty Saxon is seriously ill. If something isn't done for her immediately, I fear the worst. That fool Ormond and those other doctors can't do anything for her. But I believe you can——"

"Saxon would never allow me to see her, Rod."

"Yes, he will. I've had it out with him. The idiot isn't so worried as I am, but Maude is beside herself. And they've both heard some accounts of the wonderful cures you've effected over here. To be frank, I'm surprised myself. But that's beside the point. Patty's suffered enough without this happening to her. And I know, if you don't help her . . ." Carey shook his head. "But get your bag. We can talk on the way back."

"Just a moment, Rod. What . . . what seems to be wrong with her?"

"Ague, they say. But she's had a raging fever, and she's been in pain. I . . . I'm afraid it's typhoid." Carey turned to his Negro. "Take me back, Jube. Hurry, Maury. I'll be waiting in the carriage."

Maury went into his study. He opened his kit and peered into it blindly, then put his hand over his stomach as if to press away the sudden clutching inside. It could not be, he told himself. It must not be. Possibly it was typhoid, as Carey thought. More likely it was that deadly malaria. Bad enough, but pray to God it was nothing worse!

He looked up and saw Zeda watching him uneasily. He went over and touched her cheek with his finger tips. "I have to go to St. Joseph, kitten. Guess you'd better pack my carpetbag with a few shirts and things while I write Juan a note. I may be gone a day or two."

He scribbled the note, then went out back and left orders with Cricket to follow him with the chaise in the morning. When he returned to the study, he was suddenly arrested by the leering stone visage of Kul. It was the first time he had more than glanced at the idol in months. Abruptly, without knowing quite why he did it, he went over and picked up the ugly thing and staggered with it to the window, lifted the mosquito netting with his elbow and hurled it outside. Perhaps it was only his imagination, but he felt stronger, as if he had torn from him the final cords that had long held him in some hideous bondage.

When he turned he saw that Zeda was waiting with his carpetbag.

Chapter Twenty-two

I

WHEN THEY drew up by the Saxon gate nearly every room in the house seemed to be lighted and two carriages with dozing drivers were waiting under the pines. It was nearly midnight.

Carey said, "Something's happened. She must be worse. That's Doc Ormond's rig yonder. I'll bet the other belongs to Treadway. I'd better go in with you."

"You'd better go on home," Maury urged. "You ought to be in bed. You're in no condition to be up."

"No, I'm going in with you. Take me in, Jube."

Saxon himself met them at the door and led them into the drawing room. His shirt, soaked through in the heat, clung to the fatty folds of his thick chest and belly. He was chewing a dead cigar while he fanned himself with a palm leaf. He looked tired and irritable. "Thank you for comin'," he mumbled, indicating a sofa and sinking into the chair opposite. "Mighty fine of you both. Er . . . I wouldn't go up just yet,

Maury. Everybody's with her. She got to crying out an' carrying on a while back, sort of out of her mind, an' Maude was too scared to wait any longer. She sent for Ormond. The nigger couldn't find anyone but Treadway at first, but finally they both come. Between 'em they got her quieted. They ought to be through in a minute."

Maury did not sit down. He frowned at Saxon and said uneasily, "With your permission I think I'd better have a look at Patty before Ormond takes it into his head to bleed her. If she's seriously ill with any kind of fever, she shouldn't be bled." He did not add that he considered Ormond an ignorant fool. Old bleed-'em-an'-purge-'em! And Treadway was no better.

"Ormond knows what he's about," replied Saxon, with a stony finality that precluded further argument.

The house was quiet save for little rustlings upstairs. But presently there were soft footfalls on the stairway, then Ormond and Treadway came into the hall and entered the drawing room. Ormond was a large pear-shaped man with pale, drooping whiskers that were stained with snuff at the corners of his mouth. Treadway, who followed obsequiously behind him, was a small, seedy person who seemed a little overwhelmed by the lavish furnishings, which apparently had been assembled by the yardstick of price rather than good taste.

Ormond, beaming assurance, waddled over to Saxon and patted him on the back. "She's all right now, sir. Her fever's gone down and she's sleeping like a kitten. In a day or two she'll be fit as a fiddle. Yessirree!"

Saxon stood up and took his dead cigar from his mouth. "Thank you, Doc. I wasn't worried so bad myself, but Mrs. Saxon . . . well, you know how ladies are."

"Quite, sir. Quite. Mrs. Saxon has been very overwrought. I gave her a sleeping powder. She's retired, and I think you'll find her resting comfortably." His eye fell on Maury for a moment with a dead-fish stare, and he added, "I'd caution against disturbing Miss Patty. Old Selah will be up there to watch her the rest of the night, and I'll drop in and see her again in the morning."

He turned to go, with Treadway following, but stopped as Maury said, "A moment, please. Would you mind telling what kind of fever Patty had?"

"Fever?" said Ormond. He smiled deprecatingly. "Fever is fever, my friend. It is merely a heightening of the humors, an increased pressure. Ague, lung fever, dandy fever or just plain fever—they all arise from the same cause. The body is struggling to throw off an accumulation of imprisoned vapors. It burdens the heart, and the veins become overheated. For such and kindred ills of the flesh we have recourse to the ancient science of phlebotomy."

"You mean to tell me that you bled her?" Maury burst out.

"Now, now," chided Ormond. "Leave us not confuse bleeding with phlebotomy. Any fool can let blood, but in phlebotomy ——"

"I'm not interested in the difference. My concern is for Patty. You had no business bleeding her. If she had a high fever with delirium, and it has suddenly subsided, it's because the disease has reached a crisis. Bleeding at such a time is the worst possible thing you could do!"

Ormond glared at him balefully. "Young man, I think you'd better keep your nose out of such matters as these and leave them to gentlemen who are professionally qualified. You don't know what you're talking about. And I'll remind you further that Miss Patty is sleeping——"

"If she appears to be sleeping," Maury interrupted, "she's probably in a coma. You wouldn't know the difference."

Rodman Carey was sitting up, his eyes suddenly as beady and bright as a bird's. Treadway, who had said nothing, opened his mouth foolishly, then closed it and looked at Ormond. And Ormond, in rising anger, blew through his whiskers while he groped for invectives. But his opponent had turned from him to appeal to Saxon.

"She may be dying," Maury insisted to Saxon. "If she is, those idiots wouldn't know it. They don't even know what's wrong with her. They couldn't be expected to know, since they've never seen the inside of a medical school. If Patty's in a coma there's little that I or anyone can do—but at least I ought to see her and make sure and do whatever is possible for her."

Saxon gaped at him. "All right," he said slowly. "Come on; I'll show you her room."

They went upstairs to Patty's room. Saxon hovered at the door, watching, uneasy, while Maury tiptoed inside.

A single taper burned in a hurricane shade near the small poster bed. By the light of it Patty seemed to be sleeping. As he entered, old Selah her nurse, who sat beside her, raised her eyes in recognition, then shook her head faintly and went on with her fanning. He bent over the bed and touched Patty's forehead with his finger tips and found it clammy. Her pulse was so faint he could hardly feel the fluttery action of it at first. Her skin was saffron.

Selah murmured, "She ain't right. She ain't right a-tall."

Even Selah knew Patty wasn't sleeping. Maury compressed his lips and searched his memory for something he might have seen or heard or read that would be of help now, yet knowing that no one in all the history of medicine had ever discovered anything that would change matters in the slightest.

Selah said, "Her heart's broke. When she was fevered she keep a-sayin' Marse Hugh's name. He never come no mo'."

Maury swallowed and turned away; he stood by the foot of the bed a minute trying to organize his thoughts in the midst of the sudden chaos that seemed to be engulfing him. There were steps he would have to take, things he would have to do. If he chose his course carefully and held to it, perhaps he could avert the worst of it. But it was not going to be easy.

He looked up finally and became aware of Saxon waiting in the hall. He went out and plucked Saxon's sleeve and drew him away from the door.

"It . . . it's very hard for me to tell you this," he began. "But she's in a coma. And she . . . she's got yellow jack."

"No," said Saxon faintly. "No. You must be wrong. She can't have anything like that." He rubbed his hand across his eyes. Abruptly he seized Maury's arm and said hoarsely, "You're lying! She can't have it, I tell you!"

"I'm sorry, but it's true. We've got to face it."

Like a man in a dream Saxon moved to the head of the stairs. He sat down suddenly on the top step and wiped his hand over his eyes again. All at once he stood up and demanded, "Now looka here, Maury. You dead sure you know what you're talkin' about? There ain't no doubt of it?"

"There's no doubt whatever. I . . . I'm too well acquainted with it."

Saxon's heavy jaws clamped shut. By the light of the hall taper he looked piggish and frightened. His fleshy red face was oily with sweat. He licked his lips. "Now listen to me, Maury. Mebbe it ain't so bad, really. But folks are scared of it. You know what happened in New Orleans, an' in other places. It just about wrecked business. We can't afford to have that happen here. Not now. Not with the new railroad startin' up. Things are sort of . . . er . . . unsettled. We can't afford to alarm people by saying there's yellow jack in town. You hear me? We got to keep it quiet."

"I'm afraid that's impossible."

Saxon eyed him intently. "It ain't impossible. I'll give you a thousand dollars to keep your mouth shut. Call it ague, call it anything you wish! You . . . you don't want to ruin things here, do you?"

"Good Lord, this isn't a question of business! It's people's lives! The . . . the thing may spread. We've got to be careful."

"All the more reason for keeping it quiet! I'll make it two thousand, Maury."

"What kind of man are you? Or don't you realize Patty's in there dying?"

He thrust Saxon away from him and went slowly down the stairs.

Ormond and Treadway were still standing in the drawing room. They were whispering together, their backs to Carey. As he entered both men turned, and even the obsequious Treadway managed a sneer. "Well," said Ormond. "Are you satisfied?"

"Sit down," he ordered grimly. "I want to talk to both of you."

By his manner he might have been speaking to a pair of fumbling forecastle hands. They backed away from him and sat down on the lounge.

"In bleeding Patty you've robbed her of her only chance of living. If I had my way about it I'd clap you both in irons. Now listen to me carefully, and don't give me any argument or back talk. Think: How many other cases like Patty's have come to your attention?"

"Wh-what are you driving at?" Ormond managed to bluster.

"Answer me!"

"A . . . a dozen maybe."

"Did all of them have jaundice?"

"Some were niggers. You can't tell about them. But of the whites about five were sort of yellowed."

"Have any of those five recovered?"

"N-not yet. They're mostly those people over by the race track."

"How many of them died?"

Ormond gulped and looked down at his shoes. "Three," he said.

"How about you, Treadway?"

The smaller man mopped his face with a soiled handkerchief. Like Ormond, he had sidled into medicine via the door of the veterinarian. Both men had found it easy to become established in a place like St. Joseph because, of the two other medical men in town, one was a drunkard and the other a wastrel who could never be found when needed.

Treadway said, "It . . . it's kinda hard to tell. Been so much ague goin' around the last couple weeks. Been fixin' 'em up with jalap an' cinchona an' a bit o' phlebotomy once in a while. But there was a couple girls over at one o' the hotels that didn't respond to treatment. They . . . they passed away awful quick. An' they turned yellow as lemons. Sort of scared me at first, till I figgered they had complications like liver complaints an' some other things that girls like them usually have."

"I see."

He saw it all too clearly. And he also realized that these men, ignorant and bungling as they were, might be sorely needed if matters worsened. He glanced at Carey and was reassured by the knowledge that, no matter what course he took, he would have Carey's support.

"The patients you lost all died of the same thing," he went on. "It's a contagion that has started here. You've got to help stop it. I'm going to tell you what you must do, and what you must not do. And you must proceed exactly as I order. Is that clear?"

Ormond, much the elder, glared at him resentfully. "It seems to me, mister, that you're acting mighty highhanded!"

"I am. And if I have the least bit of trouble with either of you, I'll be even more highhanded. I'll run you out of town."

"With my approval," Rodman Carey interrupted. "However, I'll see that the city handles that detail if necessary. You'll do as St. John orders. Proceed, Maury."

He told them quickly how to recognize the disease. Then he laid down his rules. In no circumstances were they to practice bleeding. They were to observe rigid cleanliness. They were to see that the contagion's victims were kept isolated as much as possible, and no one was to come in contact with them except those who took care of them.

He was debating how much more it would be practical to tell them when Treadway interrupted.

"What's the name o' this here thing? Or ain't it got a name?"

"The name is not important," he replied slowly, frowning. After all, he decided, there was some wisdom in Saxon's attitude. If the thing became serious the truth would out. But in the meantime it might cause more harm than good. "We are fighting a disease, not a name. Keep that in mind."

"I swear to God," said Treadway, "but it's startin' to sound like dock. I seen a feller die of dock over in Charles Town oncet. It was terrible. He turned as yellow as them girls I spoke about. Only he vomited up black. I ain't seen nobody do that yet."

Ormond said, "One of my patients—one that died—vomited black." He looked uneasily at Treadway. "I didn't see it but the woman's son told me about it afterward."

They were silent a moment. Suddenly Treadway whispered, "It *is* dock. *It's the real thing!*" He stood up slowly. "Good Goda'mighty!"

Maury thrust him back on the lounge. "Quiet down! I told you we were fighting a disease—not a name. Don't think of it as dock or yellow jack or yellow fever. Just look on it as you would malaria, and remember that it's up to you to help those poor devils among your patients who happen to catch it. Have you got that through your head?"

"I don't want nothin' to do with it! I don't want nothin' at all to do with it!"

He hardly knew whether to argue with the man or to hit him. His inclination was to hit him. Instead he tried an appeal to his pride, and finally, as much by threat as anything, he wrung from him a promise to continue his daily rounds and to follow orders. Ormond, also fearful and reluctant, was forced to the same promise. Maury was relieved, at last, to see both men out of the house; he had little faith in their promises, but possibly they would help a little. At least they would not make matters worse by administering the wrong treatment.

Saxon came down the stairs and paused in the drawing room doorway. He stood there as if he had forgotten where he was or what he had come down for. Presently he turned and entered the study across the hall, and they heard the unsteady clinking of a glass against a decanter.

Maury went up to Patty's room again. He returned in a few minutes, looked dispiritedly at Carey and shook his head.

"It's all over," he said.

II

He did not see Catherine at the funeral the following afternoon, but she saw him. In the crowd she was able to avoid him just in time and, watching her chance, she pleaded faintness to Aaron and managed to slip away unnoticed and hide in the carriage. The sudden and unexpected sight of Maury shocked her almost as much as had the news of Patty's death. She had told herself that she never wanted to see him again, and she knew that she would never be able to face him; but now the abrupt sight of him brought back in a rush all the wildness and torment she had experienced the night she had been with him last. The thought of it left her weak and trembling. No other man, she realized, could ever so awaken her, and for a despairing minute she wished that life could be different and that she could go on seeing him always. But life was not that way. Life was horrible. The day and the hour and the heat and this silent crowd waiting under the pines were horrible. And there was no escaping it. She wished she were back in her room, locked in with her brandy, but even there she knew she would not be able to escape it. Only Patty had escaped it.

She leaned forward and peered out of the carriage and saw the dumpy black-robed figure of Father O'Leary standing with bowed head beside the grave. She fell back and put her hand over her eyes to shut out the searching blinding sunlight and sobbed quietly without knowing why she cried. She thought of Salem, and for a moment the memory of the cool arching elms and the raw winds that whipped in from the Atlantic was lulling and pleasant. Then a locust began to shrill in the tall pines; the sound was a hot thing and again the heat became palpable. She could smell the resin in the trees and hear the slow crunch of feet in the dry sand, and she wanted to scream and tear off the suffocating black dress she wore and escape into the sea.

At last the ordeal was over. Aaron was seated grimly beside her and they were on their way home. He was silent until they neared the house, then he whispered a little hoarsely, "Did you hear what I heard about Patty?"

"I haven't talked to anyone. What did you hear?"

"That it wasn't ague after all. I'd been wondering why the casket was sealed."

"Why?"

"I . . . I hate to think about it. It's a very serious thing. I've had it confidentially from three sources that Patty's death was due to yellow jack."

She gasped involuntarily.

"I'm afraid it's true," he said. "And I heard there's a lot more of it in town. I don't like it, Catherine. I think we would be wise to go away for the time being."

She said nothing. Where could they go? Back to Salem? But that was unthinkable. It wouldn't help to go there. She wished, when night came, that she could find the courage to wade out into the bay until she was beyond her depth and let the tide carry her on out to sea. But she knew she could not do that, for she had already tried it once. At the last minute, when she had felt the bottom slipping away beneath her, she had begun struggling in a frenzy to save herself. She most certainly would have drowned then but for the accident of a sand bar jutting out from the beach. Damnable life! Why was it so precious?

Home at last, she hurried trembling up to her room, locked the door, tore off the hated dress and hurled it into a corner. She slipped out of the rest of her clothing and stood a moment in front of the mirror in a mute and sad and understanding comradeship with the being who peered back at her. Then she opened the closet door, found the bottle of brandy and held it a long time to her lips.

Aaron came up the stairs and knocked at her door. "Catherine, may I see you a little while? I think we'd better discuss this matter of going away."

She looked angrily at the door. "I'm not going away," she said. "Leave me alone."

At the odd sound of her voice he seemed to shrink a trifle more into his skin. Then he shook his head, as he always did at his failure to understand what was making her so difficult these days, and went slowly down the stairs. He had found it useless to question or to argue with her. He was not sure, but he was afraid that she was secretly drinking when she locked herself in this way. And he had come to suspect that she had not really sent Lissa back to Slatter, as she had told him, but that Lissa had run away. He could have inquired, but he was fearful of what inquiry might reveal.

If she had not been the image of Lucia, and if he had not been almost idolatrously worshipful of that image in his own secret mind, he would have seen by now what would have been apparent to any other man but a fool.

III

The news was out. Maury had seen it in every face back in the little cemetery, and he knew it was being discussed in every carriage in the long cortege winding toward town. Even Cricket, who had come earlier in the day with the chaise and was driving him back to Carey's place, had gleaned from the other drivers not only the truth about Patty but the fact that half-a-dozen prominent people in town had been stricken during the night. By now probably twice as many were ill. He wondered if Carey, who had been too battered by his trip to leave the house this afternoon, had heard how quickly the thing was spreading.

The funeral had left him sick at heart. Now, as he tried to consider what was happening, he was aware only of his utter helplessness. What could he do? What could any man do? The most dreaded form of malaria had its specific, but this had nothing. He mopped his face. Perhaps, after all, there was something in the heat that helped to spread it, that made it worse. His tongue felt thick and dry in his mouth, and suddenly he wished he had a drink. He needed a drink. He had never needed a drink so badly.

As he entered town his Damoclean oppression became unbearable. At the first hotel he ordered Cricket to stop, then got out and headed for the taproom.

He was too preoccupied to notice the hired carriage by the steps discharging its passenger from Apalachicola. But the passenger, who had come down from Tallahassee on a political matter, saw him instantly and followed.

Maury ordered rum. The mulatto at the bar filled a glass and set it before him. He reached for it, took a swallow and closed his eyes. Abruptly the glass was knocked from his hand.

He turned and saw Hugh Bishop.

The man's blunt features, sun-bitten until they were as red as his hair, were compressed and cold and vindictive. Maury considered him drearily. For the moment he felt no other emotion than disgust. This seemed a stupid anticlimax after the past twenty-four hours.

"You've picked a most unseemly time for a fight, Hugh."

"There's nothin' unseemly but your presence!" Bishop snapped back at him. "The quicker I rid the Territory of it, the better!"

Maury shook his head. "No, Hugh. You won't do anything now. I should think you'd have a little more consideration for poor Patty. Or didn't she ever mean anything to you?"

Bishop snorted. "What the hell has she got to do with it?"

It was the way the man said it that touched off the spark in him. He closed his eyes a moment, remembering Patty as he had seen her last night and remembering what the old nurse had said. He suddenly realized that Bishop must have just reached town and had not heard the news, but the fact made no difference. The flame had leaped through him, white and searing and ungovernable, and for an instant of fury he had more strength than he had ever possessed. He struck Bishop full in the face, wrecking his nose and sending him tumbling backward across the floor of the taproom with a spurt of blood staining his shirt.

"You need never think of Patty again," Maury told him in a voice that trembled. "She's dead."

He turned then and walked out, entirely oblivious of the group of staring and half-frightened onlookers who had retreated to the far end of the bar.

It was not until he had reached Carey's place that he regained control of himself, and now the depression settled down upon him again, heavier and blacker than before. As he went through the house he thought of Zeda, wishing with all his heart that he could feel free to go back and be with her. To be with her, to have their own little world with his practice and their home, and to be able to spend all the rest of his days there with her—this was everything he desired in life. All the rest was nothing. He had found that out. But even to return, seemed impossible for the time being.

He found Carey in the library, lying wedged on the lounge amid a mass of cushions. Carey's thin face, with the skin drawn tight across the cheekbones, had almost the look of a death's-head. But his eyes were brightly alive and speculative.

Maury sank into a chair and loosened his collar. He had already forgotten about Bishop. He closed his eyes and tried not to think about anything.

After a long while Carey said, "You'd better pour us something to drink, m'lad. I think we both need it."

Maury mixed gin and bitters for Carey and poured a goblet of rum for himself. He sat down again and they drank in silence.

Presently Carey said, "I've been discovering that my philosophy is somewhat inadequate. One should be able to face the inevitable with equanimity—at least at my age. But equanimity is a difficult goal. One must break through so many mental barriers to reach it."

"What do you mean by inevitable, Rod?"

"I haven't the erudition of Bacon or Hobbes to explain myself adequately. But I'm beginning to believe that everything that actually happens is inevitable. It was inevitable, for instance, that a foolish dreamer like me should come to this spot and create this bubble in the pines."

"This . . . *bubble?*"

"Aye, bubble it is . . . or was."

Maury looked at him strangely. "What's happened, Rod?"

"I'll tell you presently. First I must see this damnable plague in its proper relationship. It *is* a plague, isn't it?"

"To be medically exact, no. But for its actual course and effect, yes. I . . . I hate to alarm you, but I'm afraid there's going to be hell here. This fever, this contagion—whatever it is—seems to have come in an unusually violent form. As far as stopping it goes—well, medicine is powerless. There are a lot of new cases today. There'll be many, many more tomorrow." He stopped and looked away and swallowed. "I . . . I'm sorry, Rod."

"It's not your fault, m'lad."

"Yes it is."

"Eh? What on earth do you mean by that?"

Maury eyed him steadily a moment, then peered out of the window in a torment of guilt. "I may as well tell you, Rod. I'd feel better if I did. It'll cost me your friendship, but somehow I feel that you have a right to know. Rod, I . . . I got a bit sour over things and went into the trade again. I brought a load of blacks up from Cuba, and that contagion broke out on the way." Dispassionately, without evasion or palliation, he managed to go on and quietly tell the whole thing. "I was entirely to blame that night," he finished. "Being sick was no excuse. I knew what I was doing. I didn't have to enter the bay or land here. But I did it. So I'm responsible for what's happening now."

Carey said nothing for a long time. He closed his eyes and seemed to be sleeping. Finally he stirred slightly and finished his drink.

At last, softly, he said, "But it *was* inevitable, Maury. Don't you see that?"

"No, I don't."

"You didn't put the disease in those blacks. Something beyond your control did that. And you had no intention of coming here. Again there was something beyond your control. If . . . if something hadn't happened between you and Catherine, you would not even have gone to Cuba. I . . . I don't know what happened between you two . . . but I can roughly guess, in the light of what I have come to know and understand about her."

Carey paused a moment, then asked, "Maury, do you blame her for whatever she did?"

"No. Not now. I . . . I just feel terribly sorry for her. Sadism is rare in a woman. It's something inherited. She couldn't help herself. It's tragic. She's to be pitied, really."

Carey sighed. "I'm glad to hear you say that. I can't help loving her. It hurt deeply at first, not knowing. But when one understands, it makes everything different."

He paused again, then smiled with an odd twisted quirk of his lips. "Maury, can't you see yet how inevitable it was? If I hadn't been quite so blind that night, I wouldn't have ordered you away from here. That was one time when you needed a bit of help. If I'd only realized, and given it, you would never have made the Cuban trip and all this would never have been. So, you see, if anyone is to blame, it is I. It is on my shoulders, not yours."

"You should have been a lawyer," Maury told Carey. "I believe you could have exonerated Judas."

"No. I . . . I'm trying to see things philosophically. I can see what you've been through, and what it's done to you. In the last few weeks I've had to probe pretty deep to find a few answers. It's those mental barriers I mentioned awhile ago. Breaking through them in my search for equanimity. Because the inevitable is ahead of me, and I must face it."

He stopped and smiled oddly again. "So we return to the St. Joseph bubble. It's burst, Maury. Pfft! Like that. It's gone. Men like me have no business creating such dreams, for inevitably we come under the influence of greedy men like Saxon and weak men like Crom Davies at the bank."

"What are you trying to tell me, Rod?"

"One little thing. I'll come to it in a moment. I want to tell you first that the railroad was a beautiful dream, and I've no doubt whatever that someday one will actually be built to Atlanta. But not in my time. For neither Saxon nor Davies actually believed in it. They pretended to believe in it, hoping to save the bank. Did you know the bank was ready to collapse, Maury?"

Maury shook his head.

Carey said, "I didn't either, until a little while ago. I didn't know that Davies was holding on, hoping to raise enough on the railroad to cover it. In spite of everything I think he kept praying until today for a miracle. Well, poor devil, he didn't get a miracle. With Patty dead, with this plague creeping over the town, he saw dissolution. About an hour ago I sent Jube over with a note asking him to come here for a talk. He couldn't come. Big Jube got there just a trifle too late. Davies had just shot himself."

"Good Lord!"

Carey shrugged slightly. "It's over as far as he's concerned. We can dispense with him and forget about him. And while we're about it we can dispense with commerce and everything pertaining to it. I've always loathed it anyhow. It's part of the bubble, and, though no one knows it yet, it's gone." He waved his hand feebly. "We can forget about it entirely. There's only one thing now that we must think about, and that's the only thing of any real importance."

"What is it?"

"Life, Maury—or lives. People. I've seen a bit of what yellow jack can do. You don't have to tell me it's going to be hell here. I know it is. We've got to think, plan. I . . . I'm going to need your help badly."

"Well, you've got it. But I think we're going to need a lift from heaven, too."

Chapter Twenty-three

I

THE EXODUS began quietly. At first there was no apparent rush to leave St. Joseph; rather, it seemed only a normal and seasonal drifting away of those people who had no roots in the town. The coastal stage that next morning was full—though not unusually crowded—of summer visitors returning home. The little open railroad coaches that went rumbling once daily through the swamps to the distant river landing were likewise filled, though not quite to capacity. More vehicles were seen on the coastal road. The livery stables were busier than they had been, and there was a small crowd down at the pier seeking passage on the outgoing vessels. With the exception of the closing of the main bank, business went on as usual. But anxiety was evident everywhere.

In the taprooms, on the verandas of the hotels, on the shady street corners, men collected in little groups to stand talking in low tones while their eyes roved furtively as if on the watch for something as yet invisible. In the afternoon these outdoor groups were forced indoors under the menace of the dog flies that had already driven the cattle into the surf. But in spite of the flies and the heat there was a quickening of activity outside. There were more carriages on the streets and most of these were moving east toward Apalachicola. On the pier and at the shipping offices there was a sudden clamor for space, any sort of space. It was a little frightening to discover that, in the past few hours, all passenger space on every outbound vessel and coasting schooner had been sold.

As yet there was no great excitement, but anxiety grew with rumor. And hourly rumor multiplied the victims. By noon it was whispered that there were nearly fifty cases of yellow jack in the city. By evening this had been increased to a hundred, and it was said that more than a score were dead. Certainly there were some dead, for the wagons of the city's three undertakers were seen going and coming at intervals through the day. The suicide of Davies was discussed, and there was some speculation about the bank. At another time this catastrophe would have shaken the city. But at the moment few could realize that the bank had closed for good, and to those who were beginning to be concerned about leaving the area it seemed a matter of small importance. The only funeral of note that day was for Davies. Out in the pines, however, there were many quiet burials: some Negroes, a number of sailors, three women from a tavern, a young seamstress and her baby and a peddler who had been found dead in a ditch. These had none to mourn them, and their passing went almost unnoticed.

Rodman Carey had sent out messages calling a private meeting of certain members of the city council, together with the local doctors, the sheriff and the town marshal. Of all those whose presence he requested at his house that night—men who ordinarily would have hastened to comply—only four appeared. No doctor came but Maury, although these may have found themselves too busy. Of the remainder it was learned that nearly half either had fever in the family or had been stricken themselves. Some of the others had discovered urgent business out of town. A paralysis seemed to have crept through everything.

The meeting, Maury saw at once, could accomplish very little. It had been called too late, and these four who attended were too demoralized to do much more than add to one another's fears. In the middle of it a frightened housemaid came, begging him to hurry over to the governor's cottage. Mrs. Duval, the wife of the former governor, had been taken ill and her servants had been searching all evening for a doctor. Maury got his kit and left.

He returned hours later. At Carey's tight look of inquiry he shook his head dully, then poured drinks for them both and slumped down to try to think. It seemed too late to bother with plans, too late for anything. He felt trapped.

"If we could have seen a week ago what was going to happen . . ." he said. "If we could have organized then . . ."

Carey lay motionless amid the heap of pillows where he had been all day. "Has it turned so bad?" he whispered. "Already?"

"Yes. Just in the past few hours. It wasn't only Mrs. Duval. It's hit the Raineys next door to her and another family down the beach. I don't remember their name. I did what I could for them, then I came back for another look at Mrs. Duval. In just that short a time . . ." He got up suddenly and began pacing round the room. He stopped before a cabinet. "Aren't there some pistols in here, Rod?"

"Should be. Help yourself."

Maury opened the cabinet and took out an assortment of weapons, examined and loaded each and gave one to Carey. "Better keep that handy. And I'm borrowing this pair of derringers. I lost my pistols with the schooner."

Carey asked, "Has there been any . . . any trouble yet?"

"No. Not exactly. I drove through town on the way back here. The night crowd is cutting up a bit. Everybody's getting drunk. The damn fools. You'd think they were celebrating a holiday."

"That's understandable. It's just the first reaction."

"Well, I didn't like the feel of things. It's hard to put it into words. I'd gone to find an undertaker for Mrs. Duval. The first one refused to go. His place was full of bodies, and there were pine boxes all over the yard. His help had quit, and he swore he wouldn't touch another person that had died of dock. I finally got a man to go and get her, but I had to help him. Imagine, the former governor's wife! And Duval doesn't know it yet. He's still in Tallahassee. I was coming through town afterward, seeing everybody getting drunk . . . I could feel a . . . a disintegration of all those forces that hold a community together."

II

In the morning the coastal stage was jammed. A crowd milled around the string of railroad coaches trying to find seats. They became frightened when it was learned that both engineers had vanished and that no one knew how to operate the engine. There was a rush for the livery stables. A gambler and an excited commercial traveler came to blows over the possession of a gig. The gambler won, with a knife, but there was no outcry as he drove away. No one, suddenly, cared.

Clifford Saxon, wobbling a little on his thick legs, moved uncertainly in the direction of the Davies bank. It seemed imperative that he reach the bank and remove certain items from the vault. At the street corner opposite the bank he stopped and clung to a lamppost, waiting for a funeral procession to go by. It was a long procession. Or was it two funerals? He passed his hand over his eyes and tried to remember who had died. Was it Davies? But no, Davies had been buried yesterday. And before that it was Patty. He trembled. He had not been feeling very well lately. It was so hot. So damn hot. He felt as if he were in a furnace, burning.

The funeral procession went on and Saxon, very slowly, started across the street. In the middle of the street he stopped, for the first time aware of the mob waiting in front of the bank, angrily shaking the bank's door. He turned and tried to re-trace his steps, but his feet would not work. Abruptly, as if a scorching hand had pressed down upon him, he collapsed in the hot sand of the street. Once he struggled futilely to rise, to turn his face away from the molten sun. The effort only made him vomit.

The mob in front of the bank was suddenly only a group of frightened staring men. A teamster, whipping his span of mules down the street, turned his wagon out of the ruts in time to avoid Saxon. The wagon was loaded with household equip-ment and bedding and sniffling children. As he drove past the bank the teamster yelled to the men grouped in front of it: "You'd better get out of this damn pesthole! If you stay here you'll all die!"

Hugh Bishop, coming out of the Byron House, had noticed Saxon crossing the street and had seen him fall. He stood very still at the top of the veranda steps, looking over at Saxon and at the men by the bank and hearing the teamster's words beat-ing through the street. He thought, Why in the hell doesn't someone go and help Saxon? Don't they know who he is?

He started down the steps, then stopped, a little tremor of uncertainty running through him. The men at the bank were dispersing, moving hurriedly away. No one paid any attention to Saxon except to avoid him. The whole town, Bishop sud-denly realized, was in movement. A thin elderly man with rumpled white hair tottered down the steps beside him and clutched his arm. "Mr. Bishop," he wheezed, "have you got a carriage? I've been trying since breakfast to get a carriage, but they've all been taken."

"I haven't got a carriage," Bishop told him. "I don't know where you'd get one now. This damn place is going crazy."

The man's breath whistled through his teeth. "I've got to get a carriage. My wife is ill. This plague will kill her if I don't take her away from here." He stumbled down to the boardwalk, started to run in one direction, changed his mind and ran the other way. After a few paces he stopped abruptly and began to sway. Then he fell. He tried feebly to get up, but could not.

Bishop went down to the walk, stepped carefully over the white-haired man and moved with apparent deliberation toward Saxon. Reaching Saxon he stopped and grasped one of the outstretched arms and pulled him out of the street to the edge of the boardwalk. He did not know whether Saxon was alive or dead, and all at once he did not care. He dropped Saxon's arm as if he had suddenly come in contact with something loathsome and backed away. In that instant he remembered where he could acquire a saddle horse, and he turned and began to run.

At the next street of small shops behind the bank he forced himself to stop. No sense running away, he thought. Acting panicky, just like a nigger. He wasn't any nigger. He cursed and gingerly felt his crushed and swollen nose, then touched the loaded pistol in his pocket. He couldn't leave here until he'd settled a debt, and this time he was going to settle it on sight.

A black beggar with shriveled legs leered up at him maliciously from the shade of an open and strangely deserted vegetable market where peaches from an overturned basket were scattered over the sand. The beggar spat out a peach seed and laughed. "You better hurry, white folks! You better git a-goin'! You stay hyar an' de ole Black Angel gonna point de finger at you!"

Bishop cursed him and struck at him, but the beggar rolled his head, laughing shrilly, and motioned across the street. There, lining the alley beside an undertaker's establishment, was a long row of pine boxes.

"Ain't no niggers in dem boxes," said the beggar. "Dey's all white folkses. You better run, white folks! You better run fast befo' Somethin' points de finger at you!"

Bishop remembered the saddle horse. He moved swiftly away, oblivious of the beggar's laughter. Presently he was running.

III

Maury that morning had scribbled a quick note to Juan and carefully lettered another to Zeda, explaining that he would be delayed here indefinitely. He placed both messages in his kit, intending to post them when he rode in to the local druggist to renew his quickly vanishing supplies. But the Raineys sent for him early, and he had hardly left one sickbed before he found himself drawn to another. It was late in the morning before he managed to break away and start downtown.

He was out of opium and Hoffman's anodyne. Not that either had the slightest effect on the fever, but together they somewhat relieved the stomach pains and lessened the dangerous tendency to vomit. Some patients, of course, didn't have a chance. The thing hit them quickly, violently. But with others it was slower. If he could make these comfortable, manage to keep them alive for a few days, possibly they'd recover. It was too early to tell about anything yet. . . .

He thought of Zeda, wishing he had had time to prepare a longer message. Script, of course, was still beyond her, but she knew her alphabet and it was amazing how much she had managed to decipher from some of his books. He closed his eyes a moment, visualizing her and suddenly wishing he could free himself of this unhallowed mess and go home. Last night Carey had even suggested it. Carey had said, "The thing's got ahead of us. There's nothing in the world that any mortal can do about it now. Unless, of course, we could have soldiers and martial law. But that's out of the question. There are no soldiers to spare. People are just going to have to hang on and make the best of it somehow until the thing runs its course. If you stay here you'll just be run to death—and I mean it literally. It's bound to get you. Anyhow, there are four regular doctors in town—and as many more who spend their summers here. Let them do a little honest work for a change." Carey had been pretty gloomy last night.

But Carey was right. Why should he stay here? He had done what he could. Stupid to get any more involved. He had his own tomorrows to think about, and they had become very precious to him. Let Ormond and Treadway and that old dandy James and whoever else was here ladle out their powders and sign the death certificates and collect their fees. He wanted none of it. It was time he looked at matters realistically.

A crowded carriage cut around him, the driver frantically lashing his horses onward. The fool, he thought. Where the devil does the fellow think he's going? Then he saw that other carriages, and loaded wagons and people on horseback and afoot, were moving through town in the same direction, all hurrying, some even running along the boardwalks or plunging through the open stretches of pines between the scattered buildings as if something invisible and horrible were in close pursuit.

Cricket, driving, had turned down past the bank and the row of hotels. Now suddenly Maury took the reins from him and pulled the mare to a stop. "My God!" he muttered. "What's got into people?" But even as he spoke he saw the limp form of Saxon near the bank and he could feel the dreadful urgency to get away from this place and in wild flight escape the thing that seemed to be striking indiscriminately all about him.

Ahead, in front of the Byron House, a shrilling jam of men and women were trying to buy space on a freight wagon. To avoid them he whirled the chaise around and almost collided with Hugh Bishop on a pony. Bishop, hatless, looked at him almost without recognition and, slashing down on the pony's flanks with a stick, made off through the pines. It was a girl's pony, far too small for so large a man, and he might have been a ridiculous figure with his knees cocked high in the little sidesaddle, except that at the moment nothing was ridiculous. A thin old woman in a nightgown tottered almost mincingly across the street and into the pines, her mouth agape and one gnarled hand clutching a trailing bed sheet. Maury called out to her but his voice seemed only to add to her panic and she began to run haltingly. As he started to drive after her, he saw her collapse. A pair of dance-hall girls and a bearded seaman in pantaloons ran toward him shouting. The seaman hurled the girls aside and tried to crowd into the chaise. Maury kicked him in the chest and heaved him out, but the man spun round and made a flying jump for the mare's bridle. Maury lashed at him with a whip and the mare plunged in sudden fright and bolted.

He sawed at the reins. The mare had the bit in her teeth and was unmanageable. He sat back and let her run. They passed a house where someone, in flight through the kitchen, must have upset a brazier of charcoal. Flame was pouring from the windows and mounting to the roof. He could feel the heat of it beating out into the sun's heat and hear the crackling of it behind him in the morning stillness. The stillness was a hot deadly pall that lay over all the small sounds of movement and of fear. He tried once more to stop the mare, then decided to let her have her way and take him on and forever beyond this place of heat and death and fear and madness where even the ill were trying to escape their beds and crawl away in the pines.

Ahead the coastal road was jammed with vehicles. He managed to jerk the mare aside from the city's flight and turn her north on the Marianna Road. This is insanity, he told himself. Must everything go down like this, in the blind stupidity of panic like a bolting mare?

He stood up and sawed at the reins again and pulled the mare to a walk. She stopped abruptly with her sides heaving and a bloody froth dripping from the bridle. He saw now that he was far out on the edge of town beyond the race track. Even here there was some traffic from the city.

A man with a carpetbag called his name and ran waddling

up to the chaise, breathing heavily. It was Doc Ormond. His linen shirt and trousers were soaked with sweat, and it ran in rivulets down his face and dripped from his chin.

"St. John!" he gasped. "For God's sake, give me a ride! I'm in the devil of a fix! Some rascals stole my carriage!"

"Where do you want to go?"

"My God, I don't care where I go! Anywhere away from here!"

Ormond had tossed his bag aboard and was heaving himself in and thrusting Cricket aside. Maury, considering him, felt a sudden violent revulsion for the man. Seeing Ormond at this moment was like seeing a projection of himself, like coming face to face with a self that might await him in the future and submerge his present self. It was an unbearable vision. But more unbearable was the sudden vision of his past self. In the past he had been nothing—a man without a course, a rebel, a renegade. He had never faced an issue or been true to his profession. He had always run away, or let chance decide what he should have decided with his own will. He had been far worse than Ormond.

His revulsion for Ormond abruptly translated itself into a more violent revulsion for his past self. Must he revert to that past self and again become the renegade doctor he had formerly been? To run away now would be to take the downward path into an oblivion from which he could never salvage his integrity.

Slowly, firmly, he pulled the mare around.

"I'm going back to town," he told Ormond. "That's where both of us belong."

"Hey, wait a minute!" Ormond gasped. "Are you crazy? You can't go back there! The place is a pesthole! It's full of plague! The air's alive with it! Every moment we delay here ——"

"Either come with me or get out," Maury told him flatly.

"Listen to me, St. John! You've seen what's happening—

you know yourself that there won't be a soul alive in St. Joseph in another forty-eight hours. Don't be a damn fool! Every doctor in town has left. Let's get away from here!"

"Then get out and start walking."

Ormond gaped at him like a frightened goat. His right hand darted to his hip pocket and suddenly came up clutching a pistol. He thrust it into Maury's side. "Now, sir, *you* get out and walk! I've no patience with a fool! I've got to have this rig."

Maury sighed. He looked wearily at the pistol and shook his head. "No, Ormond," he said quietly. "I'm armed, and so is Cricket, and you can't handle us both. And this is no time for this sort of thing. I don't want to go back into town any more than you do. There's too much to be done. But it's got to be done—and I'll have to have the chaise. If you don't feel like coming along and helping, there's no law saying you must. But if you've any claim to respectability left, you'll go your way without any more fuss, and I'll just forget about you."

A look almost of shock came over Ormond's face. He swallowed. Slowly he pocketed his pistol. Then he took his bag and got out. He stood there a moment by the side of the road, shamed and uncertain, while he blinked across the race track at the city sprawling through the pines beyond the grandstand. Black smoke from the burning house was boiling almost straight upward into the hot still sky. It was a vaguely terrifying thing, that smoke. A sign of disintegration, of destruction beyond any human power to control. But it was much worse to see, so soon, the many buzzards high in the stillness, slowly wheeling.

Suddenly Ormond turned and began making his way through the woods on a course that would take him well around St. Joseph and out to the distant coastal road.

Maury looked at Cricket. It had just occurred to him that he had no right to expect his servant to remain with him. "If you'd like," he said, "you may go back to Apalachicola. I won't mind, Cricket. In fact, I think you'd better go. It isn't right for you to be away from Celeste, and anyhow Miss Zeda will be needing you. I . . . I want her to be well taken care of."

"Sho," said Cricket. "Sho. But what about you?"

"I'll make out all right. Mr. Carey has plenty of help."

"Sho." Cricket groped for the reins. He looked intently at the mare and shook the reins a little, and the mare began to plod hesitantly back into town. Presently Cricket said, "I ain't seen many cullud folks bein' took with the plague, but I seen a heap of 'em leavin'."

"They're not to be blamed."

"Dey ain't no credit, dem what run off an' left dey white folks. Dey ain't no credit to anybody."

Maury said, "A lot of white people that were no credit to anyone left today."

"Sho. But what I mean, when a nigger leave his folks, hit don't speak too well for his folks. You ain't a-goin' to see Marse Rodman's niggers runnin' off. Dey loves dat man more'n dey fears de Death Angel."

They were silent till they passed the burning house. The sound of it was now the only sound in the emptiness of the streets around the hotels. A few people were in sight, but they lay motionless where they had fallen. It was as if a violent squall had ripped through this area of the city, sweeping it of the touts, tourists, gamblers and speculators and the women of fashion or pleasure, and leaving behind only the litter of their haste and the sick and the dead and, in the scattered houses beyond, those few hundred souls whose roots had gone in too deeply to be shaken loose in a moment. To them St. Joseph was home, and here, stubbornly, they would remain.

The Negro said, "I never had no life till you bought me. If'n I was to go off an' leave you now, I wouldn't be no credit. You gonna need me. So I reckons you better not tell me to go 'way, 'cause I ain't."

Hearing that, he wondered how he had ever been so callow as

to trade in Negroes as if they were merely beasts, without realizing their human dignity and the worth of their souls.

Gratefully he grasped the little man's black spidery hand. Yes, he would need Cricket badly. And he would need all Carey's Negroes and Carey too—if Carey could manage to get about in his carriage and direct a few things. He would need many people to help, if he could get them together. And that was not going to be easy. At such a time as this it was only human to bottle oneself up at home and never stir abroad except for food. He had seen it happen in other places. It would be like that here. There were dead that would have to be buried, very soon. And there would be more dead to come. And there would be stricken ones left all alone in some of the hotel rooms, in cottages and shacks all about the city. White and colored. They were all equal now, and with care many of them could be saved. Medicine might not do it, but nursing would. He would have to gather them together, establish a hospital of sorts. And later, when some of the fear of this place had died, there would be other matters to worry about, for in time the ghouls always came to rob the dead. It happened everywhere.

He wiped his sleeve across his face and peered out through the hot stillness of the pines. His hands shook a little. What had to be done here seemed impossible. Where should he begin? How? By what authority could he act?

He took the two derringers from his pockets and looked at them thoughtfully. There was no law here except in these. To accomplish anything he would have to be the power here and make the law and act by his own authority.

Well, so be it.

He tried not to think of Zeda, for he knew well enough that there was little chance that he would ever see her again. But she was in his mind always.

Chapter Twenty-four

I

ZEDA RAN out to the gate and stood listening in the still evening to the distant *clop-clop* of a horse somewhere over on one of the back streets. Her mind reached toward it, and with a sudden intensity of wishing she tried to draw the sound closer and materialize it into the right horse and vehicle. But it remained only a sound, receding. Finally she opened the gate and went out on the boardwalk and studied the shadows along the bay front. Far down where the boardwalk dipped through a palm tangle she discerned a vague movement. Was it someone coming? Hesitantly, not allowing herself to hope, she moved along the picket fence to the corner, then realized that what she saw was only the stray pony she had noticed last evening on the beach.

She considered it a moment curiously, but forgot it as her gaze drifted out over the red sweep of the bay. All the sky this evening was crimson, and the color of it seemed to have run down and stained the bay to a deeper richness that was somehow more terrible than beautiful. It was as if sea and sky reflected the horror that lay up the coast. She trembled, thinking of the stream of frightened people that had poured through town yesterday and remembering some of the things she had heard.

He had said he would be gone only a day or two, and this was the end of the fourth day. Of course, after what had happened, he would be delayed. It couldn't be helped. He had friends in St. Joseph. Naturally he would stay for a little while to look after them, to do what he could. She had no right to expect him home before the end of the week.

But this rationalization did not help her in the least. The fact remained that he was where he was. St. Joseph was a place of plague and death, and no one from here would go near it. Even the stage had stopped running, so there was no possibility of getting a message from him. Suppose he were ill? How would she ever learn of it? What could she do?

She clenched her small hands and went slowly back to the gate. Here she hesitated, wanting badly to run over to the Garvers' again to see if May had heard any more news. But she had been there three times today.

She glanced up and saw Lissa on the veranda.

"Miss Zeda," Lissa called, "don't y' all want me tuh fix a li'l supper?"

She forced herself to go in and smile at Lissa and help her in the kitchen, for she knew that Lissa would not eat until she herself had made a pretense of doing so.

But she was hardly seated at the dining table when she heard the quick beating of hoofs near the gate, and in an instant she was flying through the house and down the walk.

It was the stray pony again, and someone—in the dusk she could not tell whether it was a white man or a Negro—was trying to catch it. It was most certainly not the pony's owner, for at the sight of her the man ran. For the first time she looked thoughtfully at the pony and realized it was not a local animal or it would have been claimed by now. Someone must have used

it to flee St. Joseph. And it must have been stolen, for whoever
had brought it here had abandoned it instead of placing it in a
livery stable to be cared for. It was still bridled and saddled,
with the reins looped over the pommel. A black pony.

The poor little thing, she thought. It must be hungry and
thirsty. How awful for it to have been treated like this!

It had stopped down by the fence corner and was watching
her. She made a soft sucking sound with her lips and held out
her hand. The pony whinnied. Presently it came up to her and
nuzzled her cheek. Now she could see that it had been badly
used, for its mouth had been cut by the bit and there were
bloody streaks on its flank as if it had been beaten with a stick.
The thought made her furious. She loved horses as she did all
animals, and she could not bear to see them mistreated. While
she petted the pony she peered again at the saddle. It was a
girl's sidesaddle, but on the right where there was no stirrup
a length of rope had been roughly looped to support a man's
foot. The story was clear to her now. She could almost see the
thief who had taken it whipping it madly along the coast, afraid
with every step that the horror he was trying to escape would
catch up with him. She shuddered. Perhaps it had.

She opened the gate, and the pony followed her willingly
across the yard and around the side of the house to the stable.
Lissa, watching from the veranda, darted into the house and
appeared presently with a lantern to light the stable's darkness.
She helped Zeda remove the saddle and bridle. They put oats
and hay in the manger and filled the watering trough.

After returning finally to the house, Zeda sat down again to
her supper. She tried to eat. But her imagination, kindled and
sharpened by the incident of the pony, began to build ever more
vivid scenes from the stories she had heard. Her apprehension
grew. Suddenly she got up, found her pencil and notebook and
hurried out of the rear of the house and down the dim alley to
the Garver place on the other street.

May Garver, recognizing her quick tapping on the back door,
called to her, "Come on in, honey."

She found May and Juan in the office. Instantly, as she entered, she was aware of a tension between them. May, fanning herself nervously, peered at her mutely a moment while Juan, frowning abstractedly, got up to offer her a chair. When she was seated Juan settled down again to a dark contemplation of his desk. Finally May said, "Honey, we've had a little bit of news."

At her quick intake of breath, May shook her head. "It's nothing direct. We've mainly been piecing things together. Juan's come to the conclusion that there are no doctors left in St. Joseph. Except Maury."

Juan said, "I know that fellow Treadway skipped out, because I saw him myself two days ago. He was taking the boat up the river. And I've had it from several sources that both James and Ormond left. They say the other man, Peabody or Pembroke—I can't remember his name, but he's the one that drank so much—is dead." Juan spread his hands. "So, you see how things must be there. I know I'm right. Maury has the whole thing on his shoulders!"

Zeda clutched her throat as she tried involuntarily to force a question from it. She looked at May.

May told her, "We are pretty sure Maury was all right up to yesterday morning because Celeste was asking some of the St. Joseph Negroes about Cricket, and one of them was certain he'd seen Cricket driving his master up to the Montague house where they say nearly the whole family is sick. Lord knows how many are sick over there. So, even if he had some way to send a message to us, he'd hardly have time to write it."

Juan unfolded a note on his desk. It was the one Maury had written the evening he left. "Now listen to this," said Juan, then read: " 'I'm leaving with Rodman Carey to see Patty Saxon, who is seriously ill. I'll return as soon as possible. If anything should happen to delay me, please look after Zeda, for she means more to me than anyone.' "

Gravely Juan refolded the note. He frowned down at the floor. "Odd," he murmured. "He wrote that in a hurry, but he

seemed to have had a premonition that something was going to
happen. Anyway," he added, "I'm sure he's staying with
Carey. They are old friends. And knowing him as I do, it's
obvious that he'll never leave St. Joseph as long as he's needed
there. It's time you both realized that."

Zeda's eyes widened upon him. She got up with her hands
clenched tightly together and moved to the window, her back
to them. May looked at her helplessly, then wiped her beetling
brows and stared worriedly at Juan. Still frowning at the floor,
Juan rose slowly, went to the door and stood there tapping on
the door frame with his big strong fingers.

Suddenly he turned to May. "I've got to go there and help
him," he burst out. "Can't you see that?"

"No," said May. She did not look at him.

"But I've *got* to! It's too much for any man to handle alone!"

"You've got patients here," May reminded him stonily.

"None to worry about, thanks to him. The ague's under
control."

"Suppose the plague breaks out here. It could, you know."

"It hasn't yet. If it does, I'll come back, of course. But right
now I'm needed over there. I've got to go. He gave me a hand
when I needed help. But it's more than that. It's all those
people . . ."

"Oh, Juan, there's nothing you can do to help them!" She
looked at him miserably. "Surely you know that."

"I've got to do what I can," he said quietly.

"Juan—" She stopped a moment and closed her eyes. She
sighed. "Oh, Lord!" she said, "I can't argue with you. But if
you go, then I'm going with you."

"No," he said.

"Why not?"

"There's the baby."

"Zeda and Celeste can take care of him."

Juan shook his head. "The baby needs his mother."

"He also needs his father."

He turned away with his hands clenched behind his back.

"Don't make it any harder for me. You're staying here with the baby. I'm going over there in the morning. It's got to be that way."

May was silent awhile. Suddenly, determinedly, she said, "Now you listen to me, Juan. Let's look at this thing sensibly. There's a great deal you can do without going over there and . . . and throwing yourself away for nothing. What on earth can you do alone but give 'em pills? Those people are going to need nursing more than anything else. And food. With all communication cut off, they're going to run short of supplies before long. Something's going to have to be done about that. And they'll need volunteer nurses. The fact is that no one here really knows the true situation over there. Why don't you go there and see Maury and size things up? Find out what he wants. Then hurry back and tell people here so we can organize and really do something. You'll accomplish fifty times as much that way."

Juan stood considering. "Maybe you're right," he admitted.

"Of course I'm right!"

"Very well. I'll go see him and find out about things and come right back. I won't promise not to return later and help him if he wants me, but I'll follow your plan first. We'd better pack what drugs I have—he'll need 'em. And Zeda, maybe you'd better get some of his clothes together. He'll be needing some clean things."

May said, "You . . . you're leaving tonight?"

"Certainly. It would be criminal to delay another hour. The sooner I get over there and find out . . ."

Zeda, moving to the door, turned suddenly and touched Juan's arm and pointed to herself. She was trying almost desperately to make her lips form the shapes of words.

Juan was slow to comprehend, but May said quietly, "She wants to go with you."

Juan shook his head. "No," he said emphatically. "Absolutely not. It's no place for you. Anyhow, you remember what Maury said in his note. He'd never forgive me if I brought you along."

Had she been able to find speech she would have argued. She would have fought to go, and she would have gone. She knew that for a certainty. But now she was powerless to combat them both. She could only listen while May said, "He's right, honey. I . . . I know exactly how you feel—but it would just complicate matters to have you along. Heaven knows what Juan's going to run into."

So Zeda did not protest. But as she hurried home to pack Maury's clothing her mind was busy. For the time being, until Juan returned, there was little she could do but wait. Life, suddenly, seemed dreadfully short and incomplete and unfair in its abrupt denial of tomorrows, so that any waiting seemed a waste. But possibly she could be of more help if she waited long enough to hear any requests that Maury might send back by Juan.

After Juan had gone she went home again and quietly gathered her own things together and packed them into a small canvas bag. Then she went slowly through the cottage, trying to think of things she had overlooked that might be needed. Needles and thread for mending and her scissors. And what about a weapon? The only firearms were a fowling piece and a rifle, and either one seemed too heavy and bulky to carry far. But in the study was a small boarding cutlass. It was feather-light and as sharp as a razor, and she placed it beside the bag. In her room she stopped before a small crucifix, an ancient thing of beaten silver that Maury had given her. She crossed herself and stood before it awhile, humbly trying to form into a prayer the torment of fears and hopes and doubts that filled her mind. Finally she took the crucifix from the wall and packed it with the other things.

She slept little that night. She was up at dawn, and twice

before anyone was stirring she slipped over to the Garver place to watch for Juan, although reason told her not to expect him before noon.

Juan, however, appeared not long after sunup.

He had not slept, except to doze in the carriage coming back. He had arrived in St. Joseph after midnight and had spent less than an hour there, most of it in search for Maury.

"He wouldn't let me come near him," said Juan. "At first he tried to drive me away. He even pulled a pistol on me and told me to leave before I got contaminated. He said my place is here, that so many people had come through Apalachicola that the plague might break out here, and that I must be on the watch for it and keep those who get it segregated. I told him why I'd come and asked him what he needed, and he sat down on the boardwalk right there in the middle of town where I found him—he wouldn't let me get out of the carriage or touch him or come closer than ten feet—and there with the fires burning all around us we planned——"

"Fires?" said May.

"Yes, fires everywhere—up and down the streets, in every open place, fires all over town. He's got every spare darky in the place dragging in wood to keep 'em burning and tearing off green pine boughs to make 'em smoke. I don't know what good it does, and he's not sure himself. It's possible that the plague's in the air. Anyway, it helps keep the insects away. God, what a spot! You'd never know it. What with the fires and the smoke it looks like a lost corner of hell. And he's running it— with a pair of derringers and Carey and a few local people to help."

Juan rubbed his hands over his eyes and took a sip of the coffee May had poured for him. He went on: "He's taken over the Byron House for a hospital. He had to break down the doors and threaten to kill the manager—the fellow had locked himself up in the place and barred it on the inside and wasn't going to let anyone enter. A lot of people there have done that

—locked themselves up in their homes and won't put a foot
outside unless somebody in the family is stricken. Then they
go crying for Dr. St. John. In the few minutes I talked to him
—and it was after midnight—three people sent for him. With
each call he sent a message back telling the family what to do
and saying he'd get to them as soon as possible. Gad, he's incredible! I don't know how he keeps going. He's had hardly
any sleep since he left here. Everybody depends on him for
everything. He's more than a doctor. Only someone like him
could do what he's doing and make it work. He's laid down his
rules, and believe me they're followed. He's the law there. He's
got the Rainey boys and that young Montague on patrol. I
had some trouble just getting into town to see him—he won't
allow anyone to enter or leave the place—and they wouldn't
let me go any farther than the square where the hotels are or
put foot to ground or touch anything."

Juan stopped. He shook his head. He seemed hardly aware
of the breakfast Celeste had placed before him. Zeda sat watching with her hands clenched tightly in her lap.

May asked, "What does he need? What sort of plan did you
work out?"

"He wants bed sheets and mosquito tents more than anything
else at the moment. And pine boxes. They've had to bury a
lot of the dead together in an open grave out in the pines. I'd
better go over to the Mansion House and see Flavy Munn about
having the things sent over. Maury says to have the teamsters
go as far as that little bridge about a mile out of St. Joseph and
unload the stuff there. He'll have it brought on into the town."

May said, "That's good—if we can get the teamsters to go
that far along the coast."

"They'll go if Munn tells 'em to. There shouldn't be any
danger up to the bridge."

"What about food?" May asked. "And nurses?"

"They've got food for a while. As for nurses—well, that's
up to us. He says he could use a few volunteers. But anyone

who crosses that little bridge has got to go prepared to stay.
There'll not be any turning back. Not till it's all over—and
Lord knows when that'll be. At least not until cold weather."
Juan shook his head again. "God! Those poor devils."

"Poor Maury," said May quietly.

Juan met her eyes significantly, then looked at Zeda. He
said, "Zeda, he'd written you a note but he decided not to send
it because it might carry the plague. I told him you wanted to
ride over with me, and he said in no circumstances were you to
come anywhere near St. Joseph. He wants you to be very careful and stay indoors if we have any trouble over here. And he
. . . he asked me to convey to you his very deepest regard."

Zeda sat motionless, looking intently down at her hands.
Behind her she heard Celeste, who had been hovering in the
doorway, ask, "D-did you see Cricket, Marse Juan?"

"Yes," Juan told her. "He's all right. Don't worry about
him. The colored people don't seem to be affected as much as
the whites."

Zeda rose to go. She tried to make her exit seem natural, to
show no haste. But with the alley gate closed behind her she
ran.

After entering her own yard, she went immediately to the
stable and fed and watered the pony. Then she hurried into
the house and with considerable effort managed to construct a
legible note to May, telling her destination and requesting May
to look after Lissa. She had forgotten breakfast until Lissa
called her. In her anxiety to leave before her plan was discovered she was half-inclined not to bother with breakfast.
Then, reflecting upon the uncertainties ahead, she ate all she
could and afterward went into the kitchen and packed a lunch
to take along.

Mosquito bars and bed linen. It hadn't occurred to her that
such things would be badly needed. She got out what sheets
she could carry, took the mosquito bar from her bed and rolled
them all up in a poncho to be tied to the saddle. Finally, with

bag, poncho and cutlass, she returned to the stable. Lissa, wide-eyed and curious, followed.

She had never used a sidesaddle before, and at first it seemed very awkward. At home, when she'd toured the island with her father, she'd worn pantaloons and ridden like the men. But of course she was older now, and a dress made a difference.

She rode out to the side gate that Lissa held open for her, and only now did she give Lissa the note to May.

Fearfully Lissa asked, "Wh-where you goin', Miss Zeda?"

Zeda pointed to the note and put her finger to her lips, then urged the pony on toward the bay road. At the street corner she glanced back, indelibly fixing in her mind the picket fence, the clumps of oleanders, the gnarled oaks and the cottage with its captain's walk and curved windows looking out over the bay. For more than three months the place had been her home, and in spite of all that had happened to her she had come to be happier there than she had ever been anywhere. She left it now, not reluctantly, but with a pang that brought sudden tears to her eyes.

As she rode on toward St. Joseph she had no expectation of ever seeing the cottage again.

II

Once that morning a rain squall drifted in from the sea. She dismounted and stood with her back against a pine, holding the trembling pony's reins while the thunder rolled overhead and the great raindrops battered the other side of the tree with a sound like buckshot. While she stood there waiting for the squall to pass she began to question herself, wondering if, after all, she were doing the right thing.

But they need help, she told herself. I'm strong and I can work. He'll be angry with me for coming, but he'll need me. I know he'll need me. If he should get sick . . .

She thrust this last thought quickly aside, refusing to dwell on it. But it was a matter she had already faced, and all her decisions stemmed from it. Reason told her that only by the most remote chance could he escape being a victim. He had escaped it once, but in the present circumstances it was too much to expect it to happen again. If he were stricken she was sure she could do more for him than anyone, and if she failed to do enough she prayed that she herself would be taken quickly, for without him life would have no meaning for her.

These were not matters, however, that she could bring herself to accept coldly, for, although she knew the truth of them, she was young and could not help but have hope. At the moment her only fear in going to St. Joseph was that her affliction might make her more of a hindrance than a help. She hated this inability to speak. It seemed so unreasonable, so stupid, so utterly incomprehensible. She did not realize that it was the result of both physical injury and shock, as Maury had come to suspect, and that only time could tell whether or not it would pass. She felt no pity for herself, and daily struggled to break through the barrier that held her thoughts imprisoned. Even now, as she waited under the tree, she was unconsciously rubbing her throat, hoping to find suddenly the speech that seemed always on the tip of her tongue.

The squall passed and the rain turned into a steamy drizzle. She was already soaked to the skin, so she climbed back into the saddle and continued her journey. Presently the drizzle stopped and the blinding sun cut down on the narrow road, and in the tall pines the locusts began to shrill their high piercing song of heat. She took off her limp bonnet and tied it to the saddle, then shook out her braids to let her hair dry. In her occupation with her toilet she did not at once notice the two men who had come up from the beach on her left and now stood watching her curiously from the shadow of the trees ahead.

They were rough-looking and rather brutish young fellows, and in their camp hidden farther back in the pines was a horse and carriage that obviously could not have belonged to them.

Hidden there also were articles that had come from one of the abandoned cottages on the outskirts of St. Joseph. They had been drinking a little, but at the moment, seeing a stranger approaching on a pony, they had only a moronic curiosity and a desire to find out why anyone would be traveling in this direction. Then they saw it was a girl. They became, suddenly, very much aware of the piquant oval of her face and of the fresh roundness of her body where the damp dress clung to her. For a few seconds they could only stand motionless, staring at her as she came closer. Involuntarily one of them sucked in his breath in a low whistle of appreciation.

In an instant Zeda slapped the pony with the reins, trying to urge it on. But the man who had whistled leaped abruptly into the road and caught the bridle.

"Easy, sister," he said, smiling sleepily. "What's the hurry? Why don't you git off an' visit a li'l while?"

Zeda jerked at the reins. The pony reared in fright but the man clung to the bridle. Now his companion stepped into the road. "Hang on, Jack," he said, grinning. "I'll git the gal."

She had almost forgotten the cutlass. Then she saw the handle of it sticking up by the canvas bag on the other side of the saddle. She jerked it from the scabbard. At the flashing arc of it in the sun the second man jumped aside with a yell, barely escaping the swinging blade. But the first hung stubbornly to the bridle, trying to force the pony around and unseat her. She made a thrust at him, and the point laid his face open from ear to mouth. He staggered away, groaning and clasping both hands to his streaming cheek. The frightened pony raced down the road.

It was minutes before she could bring it under control.

She felt a little sick and her hands were still trembling from reaction, though her fear was past. The experience, she realized, was only a sample of what could happen unless she was careful. In St. Joseph almost anything could happen from now on. She must always be on her guard and be prepared.

Warily she finished her toilet and tied back her wildly tumbled hair with a bit of ribbon. Her clothing soon dried, and by the time she had reached the little bridge Juan had spoken of she was composed and ready for whatever lay ahead.

She, too, had some trouble finding Maury. A quarter mile beyond the bridge, where the smoke from the innumerable fires hung low over the road, a man on horseback suddenly appeared. He carried a rifle. "Don't come any farther!" he shouted. "Unless you want to stay here!"

Calmly she rode toward him.

"Hey," he cried. "Wait a minute. Are you a volunteer?"

She nodded quickly and continued toward him.

He looked at her sharply and took off his Panama. "Doggone," he said. "It's not right. You don't belong in this sort o' thing. You don't know what you're gettin' into, lady. It's hell here. It's plain hell. I wish you'd go back."

He was only a boy, she saw, hardly as old as she. She smiled at him faintly, shook her head and rode past. He stared at her and scratched his chin, then called to her: "I reckon you'd better report to Dr. St. John. You might find 'im at the Byron House. And my respects, ma'am. You're the first volunteer from Apalachicola."

She rode on through the smoky pines, wondering where the Byron House was.

Eventually she located it, since it was the only hotel in which there seemed to be any activity. She entered it timidly and stood, tight-lipped, looking at the rows of mattresses that had been dragged down from the upper rooms. Each mattress had its occupant. She glanced along the hall into what had once been a ballroom and saw other rows of mattresses, some covered with mosquito bars. A few people moved quietly among the sick—an elderly woman with a pitcher of water, two old Negresses with slop jars, a mulatto and a white youth carrying a stretcher on which something lay swathed in a sheet. The place stank.

She remained inside only long enough to be sure that Maury was not there; then she retreated to the veranda and clung a minute to the railing, her stomach quivering. Finally the wave of nausea passed and she gained control of herself. She knew she would be all right now. She had seen it; she had smelled it; she knew what it was like. When she came in more direct contact with it she would be able to face it without flinching.

She looked up and saw Maury coming in the chaise.

It stopped by the steps and he got out and came slowly up to the veranda, moving as if he had lead in his shoes. He glanced at her without recognition and might have gone on inside if she had not stepped forward quickly and touched his arm. He stopped and stared at her as if he had been shot. His eyes seemed almost lost in their sockets; he was unshaved and grim and in the heat his soiled shirt clung to him stickily. He looked as if he had not been out of his clothes since she had seen him last.

"My God!" he said hoarsely. "Oh, my Lord God!"

Then suddenly he backed away from her. "Go home!" he ordered. "Now, while you have the chance. Hurry! Don't touch anything—don't come near me! Just go home!"

She shook her head fiercely and followed him and caught his arm. For a little while he was angry, as she had expected him to be. He cursed Juan. "I told him to keep an eye on you!" he fumed. "Didn't he tell you what it was like here?" And when she nodded gravely he charged upon her more directly. "You should have had better sense! Whatever possessed you to come here? Didn't you know that you'd have to stay if you came?" She stood looking up at him intently, her lips struggling to form syllables while he raged on: "Somebody's going to answer to me for this! Who was it brought you here?"

She pointed to the pony tied up at the hitching rail.

He stared at it. He shook his head and swallowed, then said

irrelevantly, "That looks like the pony I saw Hugh Bishop running away on." He swallowed again and began to wilt. "You . . . you rode here alone. You just packed your things and came. And now I can't send you back. It . . . it's too late."

Abruptly all the fight went out of him. He wilted completely. He looked down at her and tried to speak and could not. Suddenly he put his arms about her and held her tightly as if he never wanted to let her go. He had never been so glad to see anyone as he was this determined little silent person whom he'd been afraid he would never see again. But the reality of having her here was frightening. Till now he had been able to approach his task with the assurance that she was safe. But from this hour on he would be in terror every moment she was out of his sight.

Chapter Twenty-five

I

THERE WERE neither hours, nor days, nor nights, for these are divisions of time, and there was no reckoning of time. One toiled and did what had to be done and snatched at sleep or food as best one could and without regard for the hour, and the long glaring days and the hot mosquito-filled nights became only a blending of light and dark that ran on endlessly. There were moments only, scattered brightly or darkly through the flow of time and having no part of time. They stood forth separately as if all the rest did not exist and formed little islands of remembrance that were sharper than reality. A word spoken so at a bedside and the creaking of a wagon; voices rising suddenly, loudly, in the night and a shot; or the color of a dawn that might have been a sunset, cherished only because, burdened with death, one stood watching it awhile and dreamed hungrily of life.

There were faces to be remembered as long as there was memory. The sick had one face, and if it was not waxen it was flushed and delirious, begging feebly for water or mumbling

340

hour after hour without meaning. And the dead had one face, and it was a yellow mask that often in the light of the candles had the richness and the texture of beaten gold. Only the faces of the busy living had individuality. For the living even in repose are four-dimensional, and memory retains them not within the static limitations of definite space, but always in the movement of many planes seen at once.

There was the round and very patient but faintly puzzled face of Father O'Leary. He was in and out of the hospital at all hours and all over town, ubiquitously at every bedside that needed him. Zeda came to love him, as she did Carey. Poor Carey! She saw him only briefly when Big Jube carried him in or out of the house or when he passed in the carriage, made comfortable amid a heap of cushions while he rode about seeing that the fires were kept burning, that the dead were speedily collected and carted away and buried, and investigating any report from Father O'Leary who was usually the first to learn of anyone's trouble or need. And there were the dark faces of Carey's Negroes, glistening in the heat and stoic as they went about their grisly duties. And in the reeking hospital where, until the arrival of Miss Josie, it seemed beyond human endeavor to achieve cleanliness or order, there were the worried, the grave, the resigned and the ever-weary faces of those who came in to help. Too few faces at first, until Miss Josie came with her two big Negresses.

Though she did not know who Miss Josie was at first, Zeda had an instant liking for this straight-backed, composed and matronly woman. Miss Josie appeared soon after her own arrival, established herself in one of the vacant upper rooms and very calmly and efficiently took over the hospital's management. She did an incredible amount of work. Yet through it all she maintained her composure and an air of almost prim detachment, except for an odd look—so like Father O'Leary's—of being faintly puzzled. It was as if this ordeal held a deep meaning that eluded her.

Father O'Leary, coming in one evening drooping with fatigue and seeing Miss Josie at work, stopped and watched her a moment in perplexity. *"Tempora mutantur et nos mutamur in illis,"* he murmured. "I do not understand the ways of God, but I thank Him that you are here, Miss Josie."

She smiled faintly, busy gathering a pile of filthy sheets to be taken out to the washpots. "After all," she said, "why shouldn't I be here? My business is vanished. My girls have all gone. I've locked up my place. I had to do something— and this is just a matter of changing from one establishment to another."

"A longish step, I'd say, from a house of pleasure to one of mercy."

She smiled again, elusively. "It's a step I almost didn't find the courage to take. If it hadn't been for the example of Dr. St. John . . ."

"God bless him," he said fervently.

"If you have God's ear," she told him quietly, "you should be more inclusive in your prayers." And she glanced significantly down the hall into the ward for the colored where Zeda, carrying a tray of medicines and glasses, was following Maury slowly among the sickbeds. "Neither one wants to let the other out of sight," she added in a low voice. "It frightens me when I think what's almost bound to happen. They can hardly both escape it. I wish we could do something for them."

Miss Josie wadded the sheets into a basket and carried it into the back hall, wondering what she could do and having little confidence even in the powers of a remote God that life had tempted her to deny. She wondered, too, if she could ever tell Maury why she felt indebted to him, for it concerned an early mistake she had never mentioned to anyone. The mistake was the gambler Two-Jack, her first lover in whom she had foolishly confided the truth about her family. Her family, an old and respected one from whom she had run away in a moment of pique, had long supposed her dead. In her regard for it she preferred to remain dead, and only constant payments to Two-

Jack had kept him quiet. But toward the last he had become increasingly threatening and demanding, and, in dread lest the odium of herself become associated with her people, she had resolved on murder. The affair at Slatter's had brought her the only peace of mind she had known in years.

After returning to the lobby, Miss Josie saw Father O'Leary talking to what she hoped was another volunteer—a rather tall blonde young woman in green. What a handsome creature, she thought. Isn't she that Delafield girl that Maury used to be interested in? How pale she looks. But no wonder—this place is enough to turn anyone's stomach until you get used to it. God help us all!

Father O'Leary said, "Another angel of mercy for you, Miss Josie. This is Mr. Delafield's daughter, Miss Catherine."

"Bless you," Miss Josie said thankfully. "You're a dear."

Only Maury, entering at that moment and seeing Catherine for the first time in months, could comprehend something of what this appearance had cost her. Even in his weariness he was aware of her pallor and the tightness in her face. Their eyes met and he could feel the entreaty in them, but for seconds he could only stand motionless, trying to pull his thoughts together.

At last he managed to say, "I'm so glad to see you. We need you badly."

"Thank you," she murmured.

It had taken her days to find the courage to leave the house and come here. She had dreaded the ordeal of meeting him more than anything else, but only in coming here and offering herself as others were offering themselves and in doing whatever was possible for her to do, could she find any peace or justification for anything. There was no peace at home. Aaron was not only a ruined man, but he was broken. With the bank's collapse and the sudden ending of everything that had been St. Joseph, he had folded up like his business, crumpled on the inside, and now he sat all day by the window, a silent bag of bones, staring off over the sea at nothing. She hated him more than ever. Cousin Etta, rabbity and lost, she only despised.

But now, as she followed Miss Josie along the dim rows of mattresses, each with its silent or muttering or babbling occupant, she had an almost uncontrollable urge to run out of this place and fly back to the seclusion of her room and never leave it. She had known it would be unpleasant, but she had never dreamed it would be like this. This stench of vomit and excrement that persisted in spite of all the work to control it; this nerve-shattering muttering of the stricken; this horrid contact with death—she was not afraid of the closeness of it, but she, who loved beauty, was revolted by the loathsome and abominable feel of it.

With a power of will that she did not know she possessed, Catherine forced herself to go through the routines of nursing. Her stomach gathered in knots and crawled. Her every instinct rebelled. She felt contaminated, outraged. Once she went outside and leaned for a long time over the veranda railing. Only her pride before a woman like Miss Josie prevented her from fleeing then. She went back in and desperately, as if she would save herself, managed to keep on through that night.

At dawn she turned her back on it and went out into the empty smoky street, shuddering. She walked straight home, taking the shortest course through the pines and underbrush. She stumbled up to her room and literally tore her clothing from her, then flung it into the fireplace and burned it. Carefully, meticulously, she bathed with scented soap, then went over every inch of her body with cologne. Finally she took a fresh bottle of brandy from her closet, opened it and sat back on the bed to drink herself to insensibility.

No power on earth could have forced her into the hospital again.

Miss Josie was afraid. Certainly she was not afraid for herself, for she had lived her life and at this point death had ceased to hold any further terrors for her. She wondered, a little curiously, if she were going to die and what it would be like. But as she conducted a mental examination of herself, she was forced to admit that, aside from an inordinate craving to take a bath and sleep the clock around, her health was as sound as it had been in years. Why, then, was she afraid? Aside from this trial, this business of somehow enduring what everyone was enduring, there seemed to be no logical basis for the way she felt. Perhaps it was only the heat, or something in the air. Or perhaps it was only the effect of that eternal and half-demented voice out in the pines. That ridiculous savant. Her establishment had been too far out of St. Joseph for the fellow's voice to reach it. But here in town, in this stillness, it was all too audible—and rather unsettling. It would start up in the morning, almost with the birds, and continue through the day. Monotonously most of the time so that during the daylight hours it blended with the sound of the locusts and you came to accept it just as you accepted the heat and the mutterings of the sick and the smell of death. But toward evening the voice would rise and the words come pouring forth faster until by night the air was throbbing with them. One would have thought the poor fool would have torn out his throat by now. But of course he was touched. And she couldn't complain. Perhaps he did a little good. The Negroes were always slipping out there to listen awhile and pray. It seemed to keep them going, poor things.

Miss Josie wondered, suddenly, what day it was and what time it was. But she could not, for the life of her, determine whether it was a Sunday or a Thursday. Not that it mattered. The very hour was lost, for no one had so much as thought to wind the clocks. Even the barometer over the office door seemed out of kilter. It was entirely too low. The moving hand pointed far over to the left, toward *Storm*. Which was certainly all wrong, for in spite of the smoke it was evident that the day was clear, and there was not a breath of wind.

As she went about her interminable duties she began to think, a little wistfully, how pleasant it would be to have a bit of wind. It would lift the heat and perhaps drive away this horrid pall of death.

II

In his kingdom on Whisky George, Mace Bruin stood a long time in the doorway of his storehouse while he looked down at the body of his only white son. Bat, whom he had caught in the act of trying to break into his strongbox, had turned on him with a knife. Now Bat lay on the puncheon floor with a bullet in his breast.

"Ye never was no good," Bruin muttered. "But I favored ye. Warn't no call fer ye to steal from me. Ye'da got it all in time. Everything. But ye had to turn on me."

Slowly, a little mechanically, he reloaded his rifle. At last, stooping, he caught Bat by the hair and dragged him out into the compound. With a motion of his thumb and a jerk of his head, he gave a silent order to some of his frightened progeny watching from the stockade. Then he returned to the storehouse, locked it and walked down by the landing and climbed the high flight of steps to his veranda. He placed his rifle against the wall and slumped into his hammock, feeling older and lonelier than he had felt in years. He had never had any use for Bat. The boy had been a bad one, a varmint. He did not regret the killing of him, but now he felt a loss. Bat, though worthless, had satisfied something.

Mace Bruin wondered if he were too old to beget another son, a white one whom he could look on as his own flesh and blood.

He was still pondering his loss an hour later when one of his alert yellow grandchildren climbed the steps and announced that a bateau was coming down the channel from the upper swamp. The child was not sure, but the man in the bateau looked like the former mate of the *Salvador*.

Bruin sat up. He had heard rumors that Finch was alive and living with a *hokte* beyond the big cypress. That Finch should appear again at this moment seemed somehow more than chance.

"Send 'im here when he comes," he ordered.

A little later young Finch, with a rifle under his arm, came wearily around to the landing and climbed to the veranda. A summer in the sunless swamps had left him unusually pale, and his left shoulder drooped slightly from the effects of Bat's bullet. Dangling from a cord around his neck was a small silver gorget given him by the Apalachee girl who had nursed him back to health.

Bruin, studying him with seeming malevolence with his one good eye, instantly noted the gorget and remarked dryly, "Ye been gone a good spell. I see ye warn't lonesome."

"No, suh." Finch's mouth twisted without humor as he studied the evening shadows and noted the height of the tide at the landing. "Bat around?" he asked casually.

"No," said Bruin.

"He off with Cap'n Maury?"

"No, he ain't. What ye want with Bat?"

Finch looked into the old man's unwinking eye, then looked away. "Jest . . . jest aimed to see 'im."

"Aimed to settle with 'im, ye mean. Ye had trouble with 'im, didn't ye?"

"A little."

"Well, ye come too late. I done settled with 'im. He's out back o' the stockade."

Finch peered at him quickly. Behind the stockade, he knew, was Bruin's burying ground. He scowled and set his rifle beside Bruin's, then sat down on the steps and took out a twist of tobacco his girl had prepared for him. For a moment he thought of her quiet capable ways and her satin-smooth body that was so little darker than his own. He had left her reluctantly, planning to return as soon as he had taken care of Bat and perhaps made another trip on the *Salvador*. He was more disappointed than surprised to learn that Bat could no longer be counted in his plans.

He bit off a chew of tobacco and frowned at the landing, uneasily aware of old Bruin's eye fixed upon him. Why, he wondered, does the old devil keep looking at me like that? "The tide's pretty damn high up here," he commented finally.

Bruin grunted. "Hit's gittin' set to storm," he said. "Been buildin' up to it all summer." He shrugged. "Hit'll be a bad un when it comes. Liable to flood the country. But 'twon't hurt us here. The water won't come over these pilin's."

Finch stood up and looked at the patch of red evening sky above the swamp. Storm. He'd been away from the sea so long he hadn't thought about the weather. But he could feel it now. They were in for something, and soon. Suddenly he asked, "Where's the *Salvador?*"

"Burned."

"What?"

Bruin fingered his mandarin's beard. "Maury, he brung up a load from Cuby, an' yeller jack broke out aboard. He come in at St. Joseph with nigh everybody dead but him an' Bat. Dunno jest how it happened, but the vessel was fired. Then yeller jack broke loose in St. Joseph. Near everybody left but the sick uns. Been hell there. Maury, he up an' turned doctor. He's runnin' the place. Leastways he *was* doin' hit. Mebbe he's dead now. Ain't had no recent news."

Finch sat down slowly. "Jesusgod!" he whispered.

Plague in St. Joseph. It was difficult for a minute to imagine his captain running the place, and in the role of doctor. Then he remembered his first meeting with Maury, in New Orleans. He'd been just a fool kid then who'd jumped ship and got to helling around ashore one night, to wake up later in an alley with empty pockets and a broken head and near dead with lung fever. He'd have died for sure if Cap'n Maury, an utter stranger, hadn't found him and taken him to a hotel and personally doctored him for a couple weeks. You could expect anything from such a man.

Finch stood up again. He spat thoughtfully over the steps and considered his Apalachee girl who waited for him in the upper swamp. Then his mind swung to St. Joseph, wondering what it would be like there. Suddenly he turned and reached for his rifle.

"Reckon I better be gittin' under way, suh," he said respectfully to Bruin.

"Ain't no need to hurry," said Bruin, rising, strangely reluctant to have Finch leave. "Ye ain't et yet. Like to have ye stay an' eat with me."

The old devil's lonesome, Finch thought. I'm damned. I never figgered 'im that way. He said, "Thank ye, suh. Kinda like to stay, but time's short. Like to fetch town tonight an' git an early start fer St. Joseph tomorrow."

"Ye ain't got no call to go to that place. Damn plague'll git ye."

Finch shrugged. "Cap'n might need me. Kinda like to help 'im."

"H'm." Slowly Bruin reached forth and put his hand on young Finch's shoulder. "Go ahead, boy. When ye see 'im, tell 'im I'm all fer 'im. An' when ye git done, come on back here. If'n ye'd like, bring that li'l *hokte* along to stay. Hit's a good place here. Ye kin make hit yourn."

III

The tide was unusually high this afternoon. It covered the beach and was up almost to the top of Carey's little pier. Zeda noted it uneasily and touched Maury's arm and pointed to it. He studied it a moment almost abstractedly as Cricket drove them back to the hospital. It was the season, he told her. They always had high tides this time of the year. Possibly there was a storm brewing.

Her hand, as always when questions crowded through her mind, went to her throat and began pressing and kneading it while she fought to break through the wall of incommunicability that held her so far from him. Please God, she prayed, help me. I'm so little use this way. If anything should happen to him . . . And I'm so afraid.

Only a few times in her life had she ever felt so apprehensive. She glanced back along the beach and her fingers dug tightly into her throat. It was September, but there was no lessening of the heat, no feel of autumn in the air. The coast lay brooding under a vacuum stillness, and the bay was a great mirror reflecting the gathering cloud continents that hemmed the horizon. It was as if everything waited for something.

A dozen times today she had caught herself listening—for what, she did not know. There was only that strange old man praying over there in the pines and, occasionally, a crash of glass in one of the barrooms down by the railroad and drunken laughter. There were looters about, and they were getting bolder, but she was not afraid of them. It was something else. She peered covertly at Maury. He was so thin, so tired. Sometimes he would fall asleep beside her in the chaise, and more than once she and Cricket had carried him into the cottage and put him to bed without even waking him. Like a hen with a chick she watched over him, kept him fed, kept him going, did all within her small power to ease the burden he had assumed. But now, with the plague wearing itself out and things becoming a little easier, he was suddenly distant and remote from her. What was wrong? Was he getting ill? Something was worrying him. She could feel the worry in him as if something black and dreadful had taken possession of him.

She closed her eyes and prayed again for speech. Never had she felt in greater need of it.

Nearing the hospital they met Carey, and he stopped beside them, wheel to wheel, to talk for a few minutes. For several days they had hardly seen him except in passing. Seldom were they ever at home and awake at the same time.

Carey seemed uneasy. "I say, m'lad, have you seen Kitty lately?"

Maury shook his head. He had entirely forgotten about Catherine. "She . . . she was helping us recently," he said "I don't know whether she's been back in the last day or two or not."

Carey frowned. "I've been trying to find time to go by her house and see if she and Aaron are all right."

"I'm sure they must be. They'd have sent word if anyone was sick." He said that only to ease Carey's worry. Actually one couldn't be sure about anything yet, even though the worst was past and they were beginning to win. Only yesterday he'd made a routine call on a sick woman across town who was being cared for by her husband and a maid. He had found all three of them dead. Those things happened, and because of it they tried to watch everyone closely.

"I'll drop by and see them," he offered. "Some time this evening. Anything new?"

"Oh, yes," said Carey. "Another volunteer. A lad from Whisky George. Says he used to sail with you. I put him to work helping Munn."

"Remember his name?"

"Finch, I believe. Said he'd had some trouble up in the swamps and had just got back. He brought old Bruin's blessings to you."

So young Finch had returned and had come to help. Somehow he was not surprised. Nothing surprised him any more. Flavy Munn himself had come over recently, saying that merely sending supplies was not enough. Well, you never could tell about people. Who would have believed that an old devil like Munn, who had been St. Joseph's enemy for years, would have done so much and finally come over in person?

Carey said, "Have you had a look at a barometer today?"

"No."

"It's down. 'Way down. I don't like the feel of things." Carey frowned, then he shifted feebly on his cushions, smiled fondly at Zeda and said with a lightness he could not possibly have felt, "Well, carry on, you two. See you later."

Poor Carey! Maury wondered how he ever managed to keep going. And he wondered, too, how much longer he himself could keep going. All day he had felt an inexplicable dread. Was it a knowledge of death, a forewarning? That dismal aching in his back and his thighs—was it just weariness? Or was it the beginning of this other thing? Days ago he had accepted the likelihood of death, but now the implications of it frightened him. What about Zeda? If he died, what would happen to her?

At the hospital he looked hopefully for Finch, then presently forgot him. The matter of the barometer also slipped his mind. As he moved along the rows of mattresses with Zeda following with the tray of medicines, he found it impossible, suddenly, to keep his mind on what he was doing. Finally, reaching the end of the ballroom, he sat down under one of the shuttered windows to collect his thoughts. Zeda put her tray aside and sat by him. She peered up at him a little wistfully, her great eyes shadowed and sad. He took her hand. He could say nothing. He had an overwhelming sense of finality.

At last he murmured, "When I first knew you I used to think of my sister Adrienne. You are a great deal like her. But I don't think of the resemblance any more. You're yourself. You're Zeda Morgan." He stopped and looked down at her, then looked away, troubled. "It's strange," he went on, "how some things are meant to be, and you can't change them or do anything about them. Remember the gold in the big bed at home? I took it away and tried to use it, but I couldn't. It came right back. It was all in that little bag of money Esteban made me take that night."

Again he stopped. He knew what he wanted to say, but he shunned the blunt truth. "Take ourselves. I . . . I love you so very much. But maybe it was meant to be just as it is. Something that can't be changed, that has to be accepted."

He could say no more. But she understood. A tear was running slowly down her cheek. He put his arms about her and held her close.

He thought, I haven't much time. I can feel it coming over me now. When it hits I'll be helpless, and I haven't even made a will. How can I word a will so that she'll be taken care of without trouble?

Suddenly, sickeningly, he realized how it would be if such a will were ever probated. It would come out that Zeda had been purchased as a slave, and at best her status would be that of a former slave unless she could furnish proof to the contrary. It was the sort of thing that could drag through the courts for years, and no matter what the decision, there would be no escaping a certain stigma.

Why hadn't he taken the matter up with a lawyer before this? Maybe Carey could help or Father O'Leary. Only, they were not around, and it might take awhile to find them. Why not Josie? She knew a thing or two.

"I've got to see Josie," he told Zeda. "It's something I forgot, and it's important. I'll be back as soon as I can."

He found Josie and drew her out on the veranda, then told her the whole thing.

"What do you think I'd better do?" he asked.

She walked over to the steps and stood frowning out through the smoky pines toward the sea. Days of fatigue pressed upon her, making her body seem heavier than it was; but she was still straight-backed and composed, her squarish face looking a little more prim because it was thinner. Almost the only sound was the voice of the savant praying with a sort of high feverish monotony in his tent three blocks away in an empty lot.

Josie said absently, "There's a little breeze. See that smoke drifting?"

"Yes," he said. "What can I do about her, Josie?"

"It's very simple, I think."

"I don't see anything simple about it. It's damn complicated. That's just the trouble."

"No, it isn't. Everything in life is simple if you learn to look at it right. Maury."

"Yes, Josie?"

She touched his arm with a firm square hand. "Are . . . are you sure you're catching it?"

"It's coming on me now, the first symptoms." He compressed his lips. "Most people have 'em a day or two ahead, but don't realize what's happening till it hits. I . . . I may have a little while. There's no telling."

Her hand on his arm trembled. He said to her, "I'll be just another case, Josie. Don't be afraid."

She shook her head, then looked away and drew the back of her hand across her eyes. "We're saving a lot of people, honey, and we'll pull you out of it if it's the last thing we ever do. I . . . I'm not afraid that way. I'm just afraid. I've been this way for the past two days. I don't know what it is, but it's in everybody. We're all afraid. Right now, standing here, I feel as if I were facing the end of the world."

The end of the world. He wished she hadn't said it that way. But she was right. There was something in the air. Something impending.

It was the feel of storm.

She said, "Go find Father O'Leary. And bring Carey and anyone else you can find. The more witnesses, the better. Hurry."

"Huh? Witnesses for what?"

She unclasped a thin gold chain from around her neck and took from it something that had been hidden in her bosom. It was a wedding ring. She pressed it into his hand. "It was my grandmother's," she said. "I've been wearing it for luck, but it's time I passed it on. You can give it to Zeda. If she's your wife, there'll never be any question about her status or anything else. Now hurry and get Father O'Leary. He mentioned going by to see Mrs. Saxon and maybe the Delafields. You should find him somewhere out there. Hurry, Maury."

He stood looking at the ring as if hypnotized by it, fascinated by its smallness and wondering if it would fit Zeda's small hand. Suddenly he drew out his handkerchief, knotted it through the ring for safety and thrust it into his pocket.

All at once he kissed Josie on the cheek. "You're an angel," he said, then turned and sped swiftly down the steps.

IV

From the ballroom window Zeda watched him leave. Why was he hurrying so? What was wrong? Before he had left her he had managed to imply the thing she had already begun to suspect. He was getting ill. There was no help for it. Things were to be a certain way. It was something that had to be accepted. But at the moment she was unable to accept it. She wanted to scream and run after him.

Instead she sat very still in the chair, huddled and withdrawn by the window. Slowly her thoughts revolved around the fact of what was going to be. Hadn't she known from the beginning that he couldn't escape it? Wasn't that why she had come here, to help him and to do all she could for him when he did get sick? If this had happened earlier she might not have known what to do when the time came. But she knew now. She knew all about it, every phase and stage of it. Hadn't she been at his elbow for days, helping, watching everything he did? By this time there was not a bottle or a vial in his kit whose contents and use she was not thoroughly acquainted with. And not everyone died. Here, scattered among these rooms, were many victims who were recovering.

Resolutely she put from her mind the uncounted scores that Carey's crew had hauled away through the pines. She allowed herself only one premise: that recovery was possible and that she would somehow bring it about. She determined to fight for it and achieve it even as he, with so much concentrated effort, had managed to achieve it for these few who represented victory.

She picked up the tray and started down the row of mattresses where they had left off. Suddenly she stopped, listening.

What was it she heard? With a swift returning of the fear that had been in her all day she set the tray aside and went to the window. Far down the street she could hear the savant. In the past few minutes his voice had been rising insanely, but now as she listened it ceased abruptly in mid-phrase. It was as if a hand had reached down from the heavens and choked it off. He, too, she thought—then forgot him instantly as she became aware of the other sound that she had actually been hearing for hours. It had been mounting gradually all day, and now it was very loud.

It was the deep and ominous booming of the surf, miles away on the outer beaches.

She ran through the halls and out upon the veranda. Josie and one of the Negro women followed, questioning, but at the moment she hardly noticed them. Twice in her life she had heard this mighty thundering of surf when there was scarcely a stirring of air to ruffle the sea. It had happened the first time while on a visit to Belize, on the mainland. Her father, hearing that thunder on the offshore reefs, had said, "That's hurricane sign. It's driving the seas ahead of it. That means it will strike here—and when it strikes it will bring in a wall of water and flood everything. We've got to get to high ground."

They had piled their belongings upon an oxcart and fled inland. And behind them when the wind came, a mighty storm tide had swept through the low country, smashing boats and buildings and leaving such desolation as she had never seen.

That had been bad enough. But the next time it had happened at Bonacca, at night. She and her father had sailed over from their little cay to go hunting at Eduardo's plantation up in the hills. When they heard the surf her father had raced to

get back to the cay and take her mother off. She never saw
either of them again.

What had happened there could happen here. It was so low
here, so flat. There was no high ground anywhere, not even a
low ridge. As she stood listening to the distant booming she
looked out over the bay and gasped. Even from this point in
the pines she could see that the tide was far higher than it had
been an hour ago. The great pier was almost awash. And now,
all at once, she felt wind and saw the pine tops move as if a
finger had been drawn across them lightly.

Miss Josie said, "What in the world's wrong, honey?"

She tried to say it. Moisture glistened on her face as she
pointed toward the bay and strained for speech.

Where was Maury? Why didn't he come back? She heard
Miss Josie say, "That surf is awfully loud. Do you think we're
going to have a storm?"

She gave Miss Josie a frightened nod of affirmation and
darted into the lobby to find paper and pencil.

Father O'Leary's shabby gig was drawn up at the Delafield
gate. Maury saw it as he rode past the hedge of palmettos by
the Saxon house. At the same time he saw the height of the
tide and heard, louder than he had ever heard it before, the
great booming on the peninsula across the bay. Cricket, driving, heard it also and turned to stare at the thin black line of
the peninsula four miles away. It seemed, suddenly, a very
thin and fragile barrier against the mightiness on the other side
of it.

"Dat's bad," Cricket said. "Somethin's gonna happen."

Maury wiped his hand over his face and shook his head. It
was difficult at this moment for him to grasp cause and effect.
He was becoming a little feverish and his thoughts wanted to
slide away into unreality. Yet he could sense a tightening of
a stark reality about him that was in itself unreal.

Then, as Cricket turned the chaise in by the Delafield gate, he glanced up at the house and saw the dumpy black-robed figure of Father O'Leary come hesitantly out of the door, stop and beckon to him quickly.

He swung from the chaise and almost ran up the walk to the steps. The priest peered at him with that look of faint bewilderment that was as much a part of him as his thin cotton robe and said gravely, "I'm glad you came. There's something wrong here. I can't get much out of Mr. Delafield. He's——" Father O'Leary tapped his brow significantly and shook his head. "Perhaps you'd better have a look upstairs while I see what I can do for the old gentleman."

Maury went inside. He caught a glimpse of Aaron sitting alone in the drawing room, gaunt, wasted and unkempt, just sitting there vacantly, grasping the chair arms with his long bony fingers. He frowned and started swiftly up the stairway, but halfway up he slowed and went on softly to the upper hall.

The door to Catherine's room was closed. He tapped on it and said, "Catherine?"

There was no sound up here save the far thunder of the surf and a gusty stirring of wind in the pines.

The door was locked, and the key was on the inside. He rattled the knob and called again, louder.

Finally he knew that he would have to break in.

He managed to splinter the upper panel of the door with his shoulder, then he got his hand through the corner of it, reached down inside and found the key and turned it.

Slowly, as if he were committing a sacrilege by trespassing here, he eased the door open and stepped into the room. His eyes went to the bed where Catherine lay. He stood motionless.

She might have been a Phidian statue cast in gold. Her long fine body was turned a little, giving an illusion of faint movement; her eyes were half closed, her lips faintly parted as if in an instant she would awaken to golden life. Death had touched her only recently. It had been miraculously kind, for it had left her beautiful.

He stood there for perhaps a minute, thinking of her as he had seen her that first morning, remembering moments when he had been with her and things she had said, trying to reconcile all that she had been and had said and done with what she was now, but finding only, as always, that in imponderable death there can never be any answer.

Then a hand of wind seemed to slap at the house and twist it slightly, and he was reminded that his time was short.

He stepped swiftly to the bed and wrapped the sheets tightly about her. Outside he heard his name called. He turned and left the room and ran down the stairs.

Beyond the gate he saw Flavy Munn's carriage, and Flavy climbing ponderously from it. On the other side of the carriage a towheaded young man in pantaloons, who had just dashed up on horseback, sprang from the saddle, burst through the gate and raced up the walk. It was Finch.

As he took young Finch's hand he wondered what he had ever done to deserve this loyalty, and he felt a deep thankfulness that Finch was here, for never had he felt the need of him more. Finch had always been his voice and his right arm, and he was swift to act where others leaned. Having him now was like being given new strength.

"What a day!" Finch blurted. "Been lookin' all over for ye. Hell of a time to find ye! You all right, suh?"

"No, Finch. I'm not. The plague's in me. I haven't much time, and there's a lot to do. We've got a storm on our hands. . . ."

"Jesusgod!" Finch looked at him strangely, then he swallowed and frowned at Flavy Munn and Father O'Leary who had come up on either side. Suddenly he turned and looked out over the bay. They all looked at the bay. Despite the protection of the peninsula a long ground swell was beginning to surge in from the seas beyond the point. The water was so high now that the swell sloshed along the edge of the pines and gave the land the effect of sinking.

Finch said, "Cap'n Maury, ye seen the barometer?"

"No. What's it say?"

"Well, 'twas twenty-nine twenty an hour ago, an' fallin' fast. An' the tide ain't gone out for two days. Hit's been risin' all that time. I never seen nothin' like that before, an' I been in plenty breezes."

"What do you think about it, Finch?"

"I think there's a devilish big wind a-comin', the biggest hurricane wind ever seen on this coast. Hear that swell a-poundin' out yonder? When the wind comes I think hit's goin' to pile the water right over that spit o' land out yonder. If'n hit does that hit'll come near washin' this whole town away. We ain't got no protection here."

Flavy Munn said, "Maury, I just come from the hospital, and that li'l girl o' yourn, Zeda, seems to believe the same thing. She was drawin' up some pictures tryin' to show Josie how it'd be. She's got Josie all scared. Me, I don't know. I thought I'd better tell you. I found Carey an' told him an' he's gone back to the hospital to wait for us. What d'you think we'd better do?"

Maury studied the sky. He said to Finch, "How long do you think we've got?"

"Not more'n a couple hours. If'n that barometer weren't already so low . . ."

Father O'Leary said, "What about our patients? If it's going to be flooded here, perhaps we'd better move them to the upper rooms."

"No." Maury shook his head. "Any wind that floods this place will tear that hotel building to bits. It wasn't built for wind. We've got to get everybody out of there."

"But where can we take them?"

Finch said, "There ain't hardly a place in town I'd want to

take 'em. The people what built up this town didn't know nothin' about wind. An' they never had a breeze o' wind here to teach 'em. 'Ceptin' some o' these rich places, everything's jest throwed together."

High ground. Where was the nearest high ground and reasonable protection? There was only one such spot that Maury could remember. "There's Josie's old place," he said. "It's high there, and there's plenty of room to shelter a lot of people." He stopped and looked at each of them, trying to assemble his thoughts into a concise pattern and suddenly finding it a struggle to keep anything straight in his mind. He ached and felt hot all over. "We'll have to warn everyone," he said. "And we'll need carriages, wagons, blankets, food, candles . . ."

He frowned at Finch. "Get going on that horse and pass the word on and tell everyone you see to pass it. And order everyone with a wagon to go by the hospital. We're moving out to Josie's place. Flavy, round up your crew and send 'em along to load food and patients. And for God's sake remind everyone to bring whatever provisions they have at home. Tomorrow there'll be nothing to eat except what we take with us."

When they were gone Father O'Leary turned to him inquiringly and nodded toward the house. "What did you find?"

"She . . . she's up there in her room," he said. "I had to break open the door. But we'll have to leave her. Later, when this is over . . . The living come first. What about the old man? Is he alone? They had a housekeeper. . . ."

"I found her in the kitchen. Rather demoralized. Er . . . let me think. Wait a moment."

Father O'Leary trotted back into the house. He returned presently, looking a little worried, and asked, "Do you think the Saxon place will weather it?"

"It might. It's certainly the stoutest house in town."

"Well, Mrs. Saxon is sick. Not fever. Grief, perhaps. I took the liberty of telling them that she's all alone and needs help. which—God forgive me—is not strictly the truth, for she has three servants left. Anyway they are better off over there, feeling they are needed. Later, if we can find time to send for Mrs. Saxon after the patients are moved, we can pick up all three. If not, well—but we'd better hurry back to the hospital."

"Yes. I——" Maury hesitated. "Let me ride back with you. I . . . I want to tell you something. When we get there I'd like to have you perform a marriage ceremony. We should have a few minutes to spare before the wagons come."

"Eh?" The look of puzzlement on Father O'Leary's round and rather studious face changed to stupefaction. "Who, pray tell me, is considering marriage at a time like this?"

"You are looking at the man. The lady is Zeda Morgan— although she has yet to be notified. When I explain the circumstances I think you'll agree that it's the best thing to do."

V

The ceremony required only a few minutes, and it was performed in front of the hospital beside Carey's carriage. During the course of it two wagons arrived and the loading of them proceeded swiftly without interruption. The ring fitted. The question of whether it would or would not fit had, illogically, assumed great importance in Maury's mind; the fact that it did fit seemed a good omen. Miss Josie, for the first time, lost her composure and cried. Father O'Leary, finishing, hurried into the lobby for quill and ink, and in fine but uneven script—uneven because a gust of wind wrenched the building and his hand became unsteady—recorded the event in his prayer book. Those present quickly signed their names under his own, and he thrust the book on Zeda, saying, "Keep it, my dear. And take good care of it—no matter what happens. And . . . and take good care of your husband. God bless you both."

He pressed Maury's hand silently in understanding, then he was gone to look after his scattered flock. A flurry of rain whipped along the street and the pine tops swayed as if raked by the hand of a playful giant. A sense of urgency, a need for haste, was suddenly driving everyone. Carriages came, and more wagons, and with them confusion and a rush to get them loaded. There was Finch shouting above the shuddering of the wind, trying to bring order, and Miss Josie running across the veranda remembering that her place was locked, and over everything was a deepening grayness as if a curtain were being drawn across the world.

But now there were many to help, and the evacuation, which might have taken an hour, was accomplished in a quarter that time.

Maury could not find his kit. It was not in the chaise, and he started back unsteadily, searching through the empty halls with Zeda tugging at him and trying to speak, her eyes black and enormous. "My kit," he said to her, his voice sounding far away and lost in the sudden banging roar of wind that shook the building. "My kit—we've got to have it." Abruptly she darted into the ballroom ahead of him and came back with the kit. He saw her open it and thrust the prayer book inside, then she was tugging at him again and he was trying to keep his balance and follow her outside.

On the veranda he saw Big Jube coming up the steps with Carey in his arms. He stopped and stared at Carey and heard him say, "Put me in that chair yonder, Jube. That big one against the wall. Ah, that's fine. This is just the place. I can see it all."

"Rod!" he cried to Carey. "What are you doing here? Take him away, Jube! Take him out to Miss Josie's."

Big Jube looked at him helplessly, his broad black face a mask of melancholy. His lips moved but no sound came from them.

Carey said, "No . . . no, Maury. This is the end. I stay here. Jube, fetch me the pillows and make me comfortable."

Jube ran out to the carriage, and Carey said, "You must let me have it my own way, m'lad. I haven't long. You should know that." As the Negro came back with the pillows and began tucking them around him, Carey smiled a bit wistfully. "This has always been my show, m'lad. I started it. I lived through it and saw it grow and die. This is the last act." He reached up feebly and took Maury's hand and held it while he waited for a gust of wind to pass. The gusts were coming stronger now; they would strike with a banging roar, then pale away in a long distant rushing of sound and leave a few seconds of stark silence before the slapping hand of the giant moved again.

He smiled once more, seeming almost cheerful. "There's nothing left of me. Only a pair of eyes to see with, and I must see this and go with it. Have you ever thought, m'lad, what mighty men we are? We build so mightily and we have such a mighty pride that we've even created God in our own image. And what are we against Nature? Perhaps we are only her little experiments, and she has moments like this when she gets tired of an experiment and decides to wipe the slate clean. But I digress. Zeda, I wish I could have known you better. Give me a kiss, my dear."

Zeda put her arms tightly about him. Then he was thrusting them both away and ordering, "Go now—all of you! You too, Jube—do as I say. Hurry!"

Maury tried to say what he felt, but his words were lost in the shuddering wind. Big Jube propelled him down the steps, and Cricket and Zeda drew him into the chaise. It was darker, and as Cricket shook the reins and the chaise whirled into the street he wondered for an instant if the darkness were in his own mind or if it were part of this unreality that had overtaken them. He had a glimpse of Big Jube standing motionless for a brief second at the foot of the steps, then shaking his head vigorously in disobedience to the last order given him and starting back up the steps to where his master lay.

The chaise splashed through the rivulets into the Marianna Road. He heard a shout behind them and, looking back, made out Finch pacing them on horseback. Beyond Finch he could see the gray water creeping greedily through the pines and racing in long swells through the open spaces as if eager to overwhelm the land. Farther on, where the pines seemed to be growing out of the sea, there was only a wild nothingness of darkening gray.

Now squalls of rain, solid sheets of straight-driven thundering rain, passed over them, shaking the earth and blotting everything from sight.

He had only one other memory of the great hurricane that tore at the coast that night and changed the face of it and poured a mighty tide in upon the land and destroyed St. Joseph. In the years to come the stray traveler, chancing upon this empty and desolate area of broken pines and seeing only an occasional crumbling foundation or a few twisted houses all but lost in the tangle, would find it hard to believe that once a bright city had stood here and looked hopefully upon the sea.

But he was spared the sight of this destruction. He had only one other memory, for time and memory were to cease for him before the real fury came. They went only as far as the creek beyond Slatter's place, where everything seemed to cease for him and all that he held dear seemed lost. Often afterward when his mind sought to retrace those paths that had carried him into and finally away from St. Joseph, he would find them dim, and only at intervals would they come into focus so that he could see them. But this one and final memory always remained with him, graven in him with a sharp and terrible clarity.

There was that creek beyond Slatter's, and they were approaching it in the rain. They could not see it until they were upon it, then the rain lifted for a moment and he was aware that the road had vanished and that they were plunging into a wide expanse of swirling blackness. The creek had become a river, and in the premature dark he could hardly make out the way of safety on the high ground beyond. The sea was backing up in here swiftly, the water rising with every thrust of wind.

Cricket could only try to force the frightened mare onward. She lost her footing and went down, threshing madly, and the chaise turned over. Cricket passed from his vision and from his mind, as did Finch somewhere behind him. He saw only Zeda vanishing in the swirling water, and he leaped for her and missed her. There was an interval of frenzied groping, of fighting to the surface and shouting and trying to be everywhere at once, of crying Zeda's name over and over and lunging through the flood for every dimly seen object only to have it turn into bobbing driftwood. A ghastly interval of wind and thundering rain that seemed to stretch through years of darkness.

That was part of the memory. There were moments of waking when he seemed to be in one of the beds at Josie's place, and his mind, groping and wondering what hands had brought him here, would come to that first part of the memory and recoil from it, lest the portion be the only reality.

And later, when he awoke to peace in his great bed at home, wondering where the summer had gone and hearing the familiar voices of Cricket and Lissa and seeing Finch and other old friends who had come to call, that part of the memory rushed back upon him and he felt the terror of it again. But the clear thread of it carried him on through the darkness and the swirling water, and he came again to the moment when his strength was fast dwindling with the mounting fever. A squall had swept over him, and for a few seconds there was a lull in the wind. And in the stillness a voice he had never heard before cried faintly near him, *"Mauree! Mauree!"*

By that he found her; and the memory, complete, became in time a remembered miracle. Because of that, her voice always had for him the quality of a miracle whenever she spoke his name.

THE END